Darshan

Amrit Chima

ISBN: 0989786803
ISBN-13: 978-0989786805
Kickstarter Limited Edition 2013
1. Families—Fiction. 2. Interpersonal relations—Fiction. 3.
Community life—Fiction. 4. India—Fiction. 5. Domestic fiction.

Photography and cover design by Kerry Ellis (www.kerry-ellis.com)

For my parents

Contents

Part III
Darshan
The Bay Area, California

Darshan

Toor Family Tree

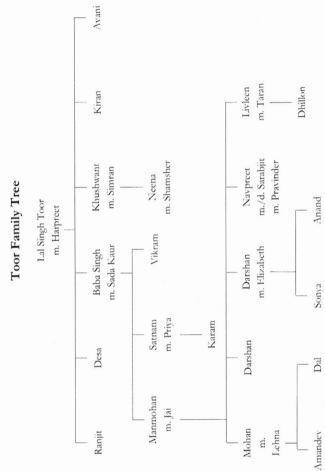

Lal Singh Toor
m. Harpreet

Ranjit

Desa

Baba Singh
m. Sada Kaur

Khushwant
m. Simran

Kiran

Avani

Manmohan
m. Jai

Satnam
m. Priya

Vikram

Neena
m. Shamsher

Karam

Mohan
m.
Lehna

Darshan

Darshan
m. Elizabeth

Navpreet
m./d. Sarabjit
m. Pravinder

Livleen
m. Taran

Amandev

Dal

Sonya

Anand

Dhillon

Prologue
1942–1945

Baba Singh Toor removed his shoes at the door and surveyed his son's living room. Evidence of guests still textured the house: empty cups of chai, half-filled plates of sweets, crumpled sheets on the floor where people had been seated for the *kirtan* honoring the birth of his second grandson. He was sorry he had not made it to the prayer in time. He supposed he could have tried harder. The outer Fiji island where he lived was not so very far away. But the man who chartered the boat was an old friend of his from India, and he had found himself lingering to chat.

Two gifts were in his hands: a metal toy truck painted yellow and a solid gold bracelet, the size of a pocket watch or a compass. Clutching them tightly, feeling a little haggard, he turned to his son. "I cannot believe the year."

Manmohan shut the door behind his father. "You are late," he said.

Baba Singh listlessly noted the kitchen sink, crammed with dirty dishes. "She has missed so much," he murmured. "It has been a very long time." The dusty hay smell of his village in India and the memory of the last time he had seen his wife were suddenly vivid, almost tangible, the memories rushing toward him like a clunky Fijian bus.

"You can go back any time," Manmohan said. "She is waiting for you."

Baba Singh's expression hardened. "I thought so once, but your mother was never waiting for me." He glanced at his daughter-in-law, Jai.

She was seated on the couch swaddling the baby in a gray hospital blanket with a final, snug tuck. She smiled at Baba Singh and leaned back, humming absently. A young boy sat stiffly next to her, as if on guard. Baba Singh regarded him critically. His oldest grandson was a little too plump, still not grown out of his baby fat, his four-year-old face grave. He was a big brother now and appeared to take the job seriously. His name was Mohan, after his father, but he had inherited more than just a name. Manmohan and Mohan were so much alike, both sober and humorless.

Sitting beside the boy, Baba Singh put the truck on the cushion next to his knee. He reached over, firmly pressing some money and the bracelet into Jai's hand. "For the baby."

She accepted, squeezing his hand before letting go. "His name is Darshan," she said. She continued to hum.

He gently touched Darshan's cheek with a solid, thick fingertip, age worn and creased with labor. "It is a very good name," he said, satisfied. "Sight. Visions of God."

Manmohan brought in a chair from the kitchen. "You missed the kirtan," he said, sitting.

"I know." Baba Singh nodded curtly. He turned to Mohan. "You are growing up very fast."

Mohan regarded the yellow truck with a sidelong look of

exaggerated indifference.

Manmohan crossed his legs. "Must have been something very important," he said, "to keep you away."

Baba Singh looked at his son, not speaking for several moments until Manmohan dropped his eyes. "Darshan seems very strong," he said. "You were much smaller when you were born."

"I am sure I was," Manmohan muttered.

"I was big and very, *very* strong," Mohan said, his voice loud, the solemnity in his expression gone, replaced by indignation.

"Of course you were," Manmohan said, beckoning, patting his knees. Mohan clambered off the couch and onto his father's lap.

Baba Singh held his arms out, and Jai passed him the baby. She slouched lower into the cushions, her eyelids heavy. Settling Darshan on his legs, Baba Singh measured the smallness of the infant against his muscular forearms, feeling powerless. He began to sing under his breath in a near whisper. "*Chir jeevan oupajiaa sanjog*, The long-lived one has been born to this destiny…*Vadhhee vael bahu peerree chaalee*, The vine has grown, and shall last for many generations…" He stopped, unable to recall the rest of the words.

Manmohan pointed at the yellow truck. "Is that for Mohan?"

"Yes," Baba Singh said with impatience. "Take it, take it."

Mohan squirmed out of his father's lap, dropped to the floor and reached for the truck. He began to roll it across the linoleum, making the low grumbling sounds of an engine.

Murmuring to the infant, Baba Singh said, "I am here." Darshan woke and stared up at him.

"I hope you are not just saying it," Manmohan said.

Baba Singh stiffened, like he had been hit.

Manmohan was angry now. Too much had been neglected for too many years. "I was a little older than Mohan when you left us."

"I was not gone very long."

"We were not babies anymore when you came back."

"No," Baba Singh said quietly. "Nearly men."

Manmohan shook his head, remembering. "The last thing you told me before leaving was that I was spilling too much water. I was bringing it to Bebe. You told me that I was wasting it."

"I had forgotten about that."

"I never did."

"Your mother needed a full pot," Baba Singh said, gently bouncing the baby on his knees. There were things he would also never forget. He wished it could be different, but maybe they all had something like that, something that stuck, like field burs hooking into their clothes. "It was a challenge. It kept you from spilling more."

Manmohan bit the inside of his cheek, feeling small again.

Baba Singh bent down and touched his long nose to Darshan's. The baby's eyelids fluttered momentarily and Darshan studied his grandfather's looming face with unruffled intensity. Then drowsily he closed his eyes again, falling seamlessly from consciousness back into sleep.

~ ~ ~

At one year of age, before uttering his first word, Darshan took his first steps. Crawling did not come naturally to him. It was almost painful for Manmohan and Jai to watch him struggle across the floor on one knee and one foot in a crawl-limp. The motion was not only awkward, but it was very clear how much Darshan hated the slow pace. This was the only time Manmohan had seen his son's expression, usually lively with laughter, colored red with impatience and frustration.

Walking was better suited to Darshan. It allowed him to more easily map out his environment as he peeked into rooms and drawers and closets, to more quickly traverse the space of the living room, and to carry toy blocks over to the corner where he liked to arrange them in relative neatness. Jai had great difficulty putting him to sleep at night. His legs flailed like motors long after he closed his eyes as he battled his drowsiness. The boy had a need for movement that sometimes seemed more primal than the need for even food and water.

It was not until Darshan reached two years of age and his increased dexterity allowed him to undertake more challenging activities that Manmohan thought he understood why. While polishing one of his police boots before his assigned patrol of their neighborhood in Tamavua, Darshan struggled with the other. Dipping a rag into the black polish, he clumsily imitated his father's circular hand motions across the leather. When Manmohan was in the garden picking cucumbers, Darshan also tugged at the vegetables, holding each one up triumphantly before depositing it on his own small pile. If Manmohan opened a book, Darshan climbed onto his lap and stared patiently at it as though he too should read. He seemed to achieve a profound sense of satisfaction with each turn of the page, like living was a series of tasks requiring immediate completion, even if he did not yet comprehend the reason why those tasks needed to be accomplished. His mind was consumed with action, with always doing.

It was not surprising then that Darshan developed a particularly keen interest in tools. Though his first word was *bebe* for his mother, his second sounded much like the word hammer. The word was not always attributed to an actual hammer but was his term for all tools, even the rag with which Manmohan polished his boots. Darshan often stood beside his father to peer into the toolbox, carefully examining the level, the cable cutters, pliers, and manual crank hand drill. He frequently watched his father use them: a trowel to dig holes in the garden, or the hammer to replace a slat in the fence out back. Each instrument allowed for a more productive means to *do* things. Soon he began to participate, clutching the trowel with Manmohan's help to dig holes for seeds and wrapping a hand over his father's grip on the hammer, staring at the nail as it sank deeper into the wood with each blow.

So it was that when Manmohan happened across a novel set of plastic toy tools in Suva's local general store, he brought them home. They had been quite expensive, rare, and manufactured to appear real. The handles of the hammer, shovel, and screwdrivers were painted a wood-brown grain, their heads as well as the plastic wrench, coated gray to look like carbon steel.

Delighted with his new tools, Darshan used them for every imaginable repair in and around the house. He banged the knobs on the stove with his hammer as well as the corners of linoleum flooring that had started to peel away with age. He tried to tighten bolts under the sink with his wrench while Manmohan fixed a leak, he dug holes for cucumber seeds with his shovel, and where he thought necessary attempted to adjust screws with his screwdriver.

Jai—who had noticed that Darshan was tucking his tools into the waistline of his trousers because they kept falling out of his pockets—tailored a cotton sack in which he could comfortably carry them all. This she soon regretted. Slung over the boy's head and across his shoulders, it was difficult to pry away. Darshan wore it always: during meal times, in bed at night, and often during bath time where it would need to be forcibly removed.

His favorite game was asking Manmohan to arrange bricks one by one into a square in the backyard. Smiling, he would pound each brick with his plastic hammer as though nailing it in. When the structure was done, a piece of wood placed over the top for the roof, he would point at it and say, "Home." The game never became tedious. Manmohan would dismantle the bricks in the evenings, but the next day Darshan would insist they rebuild. He and Jai assumed the boy would eventually tire of it, but their son continued to erect his little houses well into his third year.

Just as Jai concluded that perhaps Darshan might one day become a master architect, he became suddenly and seriously ill. His movements one morning were sluggish, his face the gray color of clouds, his forehead alarmingly hot, his body wracked by shivers.

"Get the doctor," Jai told her husband.

The examination was brief. "His temperature is too high," the doctor said gravely.

Jai rubbed her son's hand as though rolling a snake of dough. "What does that mean?"

The doctor shook his head. "I do not know what else to say. There is nothing I can do. Keep his body cool and wait for the fever to break."

Manmohan and Jai sent word to Baba Singh, who came as soon as he received the message, and they all waited, together. Most days they sat silently in Darshan's room, wishing for some miraculous shift, for some invisible healing hand to revive the boy. Jai bathed him in cold water twice a day and tucked wet towels around his body when she put him in bed, staring at him hopefully, waiting for some tangible sign that his temperature was normalizing. Some days the waiting was too unbearable, the silence too unnerving, and they each sat with Darshan in shifts, taking time away from the sickroom to pray and reassure Mohan.

The fever had been steadily high for over a week when Baba Singh again found himself sitting alone next to Darshan's bed while Manmohan, outside in the backyard, gazed blankly at the setting sun, and Jai slept clinging to Mohan in the other room. He looked at his grandson, the small withered body, the dark rings around the toddler's eyes, the sack of tools hugged to his side, his arm protectively holding it close.

"Home," Darshan said, his voice tired.

"Sleep, Darshan, so you can get well," Baba Singh said, placing a hand over the boy's chest. "It is time to get better. This house is falling apart. There is much to be done."

The wet cloth on Darshan's head dripped cold water down his temples. "I want to build my house," he said, eyelids half shut as he pointed toward the backyard where the Toors had a view of the thick, jungly hills below.

"I understand. I think I see now," Baba Singh said, wiping the tears dampening his thick black beard. He had also built a house once, back in India. He built it so that it would be there for him when he finally had the courage to return home. "I was always able to see things, Darshan. I have had dreams. For a long time I did not know what I was seeing."

Later that night, after Baba Singh had gone to bed, Manmohan settled into the sickroom to read Guru Arjun's *Psalm of Peace* to his sleeping son. Despite his worry, Manmohan smiled faintly at the tools clasped under Darshan's arm. Then he frowned, noticing something in the crook of the boy's other arm just beneath the hem of the blanket. Pulling back the covers, he discovered a coconut.

"Where did this come from?"

His voice was too loud. Everything was wrong, too still. Closing his eyes, beating back his fear, Manmohan already knew.

Placing his ear over Darshan's chest, he felt and heard nothing. His son was no longer breathing.

~ ~ ~

The Toors stood around the funeral pyre on the beach. Jai had bathed and clothed Darshan. She had wanted to strap the cotton sack over her son's shoulders, but Manmohan had grimly refused to let her.

"No," he had told her, not knowing how else to articulate what he was feeling, but knowing he needed evidence of Darshan's existence.

Baba Singh lit the fire. Manmohan was unable to discern any hint of grief in his father's face; it was simply cold and unforgiving. A priest recited the *Kirtan Sohila*, the nighttime prayer, as the body burned away to ash.

The wind carried Darshan out over the Pacific as the priest sang. "*Sunneh sunn miliaa samdarsee pavan roop ho-e jaavehgae*, Meeting with the supreme soul, my soul shall become unbiased and pure like air. *Bahur ham kaahae aavehgae*, Why should I come into the world again?"

In the space between life and death, Darshan was grateful. Humming at first, he willingly moved upward. Then he joined his voice with the priest's and sang with all his might, raising his head to the stars, "*Jot milee sang jot reh-i-aa ghaal-daa*, My light merges with the Supreme light, and my labors are over. *Sookh*

11

sehaj aanand vutthae tit ghar, Peacefully I take abode in the house of bliss. *Aavan jaan rehae janam na tehaa mar*, My comings and goings have ended and there is no more birth or death."

But then he stopped, his voice quieted by something absent.

Darshan peered down at his family, tiny dots on the shore. Jai was sobbing. Mohan was confused, pulling at her. Manmohan had stepped away from the funeral pyre and walked toward the ocean, following the smoke and the ashes. Baba Singh gazed unflinchingly and bleakly into the fire.

Staring hard at his family, it took him a moment, but then it was clear. Touching his side, Darshan understood.

His tools were missing.

Part I
Baba Singh
Punjab, Northern India

Hotel Toor
1910

Baba Singh squatted on the dusty side street of Amarpur town, the unfamiliar smells and sounds reeking of tumult and trade. He ran his hand over the loose clay grit of the earth, which began to thicken under his nails. A sizeable pebble caught beneath his palm. Closing his fist around it, he stood, pushing up on wiry, young legs. Refusing to look at his mother and father, at his siblings as they shifted uncomfortably, he flung the stone at the wall of the wretched, squat building that was to be their new residence. His father glared at him. There would be no sympathy. They had all—the whole family—been forced here.

There had once been a murder, Baba Singh's teacher had told his class back home in the village, born of a woman's blind jealousy and rage. At her hand, her husband had suffered a brutal and painful end, and now she roamed the earth, muttering all the time with madness. The story clung in Baba Singh's mind now, but he willed himself not to be afraid. He was twelve, almost a man. He did not believe in such tales anymore. His teacher had only meant to terrify them into obedience, to point out the harsh realities of the world, that fury and hate were the fall of men, that misbehavior and offense had an awful price. "Remember," the teacher had said with severity. "Do not forget. Do not lose yourselves in weakness. On that day, your lives will end."

Someone should have told it to Mr. Grewal. Maybe then he would have thought twice about being a cheating moneylender, about stealing away people's livelihood. Maybe the Toors would still be back in Harpind. Maybe this day would be like all the other village days. No different. Just the same. That is what Baba Singh wanted. He wanted their money back, their land that had been taken away plot by plot, their animals, the pond where he and his siblings liked to play. He wanted the taste of a red, juicy pomegranate seed popped between his tongue and the roof of his mouth. He wanted the velvety morning sun on the back of his neck, a feeling he had never really noticed while he had it, that mixture of warmth and field dust brushing his skin, telling him he was safe and young and had everything.

If the moral of his teacher's lesson reflected even a small kernel of real justice, the brutal end to the Toors' ancestral village life should have caused Mr. Grewal to go mad, to be pierced with guilt and remorse. But right now the moneylender was in his office on the town's main road, peering at one of his ledgers through his thick spectacles, recording this latest victory and filing it away on his shelves. He had taken so much from so many—and nothing had ever happened to *him*. That was proof that Baba Singh's teacher was wrong, that there was not always payment for a crime, that not *all* men suffered. Only some. Only the weak. It was a merciless lesson to learn at the age of twelve. Baba Singh glanced over at his brothers and sisters, not at Ranjit and Desa who were older, but at the younger ones, Khushwant eight, Kiran six, Avani only four. They looked confused and frightened.

Baba Singh knelt before them. He would make them understand. "There was a murder once—"

Khushwant shook his head. "Stop it, Baba. I know that story. Do not scare them."

"What is he talking about?" Kiran asked apprehensively, her dark hair pulled back into a tight braid.

"I was going to tell it differently," Baba Singh told his brother. "The ending would have been different."

Kiran turned to their mother. "When are we going home?"

Harpreet smiled at her daughter. Many considered Baba Singh's mother beautiful. She was often complimented on her thick, black hair that was frizzy on humid days, softening the angular lines of her face, and sleek and straight on cool days, giving her an air of industriousness. Today she seemed tired, like she might be sick. "Please leave them be, Baba."

"I am only telling the truth. It is better that way. Those goats Kiran likes so much. They aren't hers anymore. We aren't going back. We *are* home."

Avani gripped her hand-painted wooden elephant and leaned into Khushwant.

"What will happen to my goats?" Kiran asked.

"They are not your goats."

"Baba," their father said, his voice sharp; Lal had a tone that sometimes stung. "Enough." He began to fumble for a key tied to his loose-fitting drawstring trousers.

Baba Singh tossed another pebble at the wall, this time with less force. It was a one-story building that had once served as a hotel, the façade dirty and smudged, the color of cornhusk. It was beaten and abused, as though not one person had ever loved it. He did not want to go inside. He was somehow aware

17

that once he did, what little remained of his boyhood would be leeched out of him, like moisture evaporating from picked flowers drying in the sun, their vibrant hues fading to the color of mud. Digesting this new reality was like a too-hot chili sitting painfully in his stomach. But truthfully, though it had only been a day since the Toors packed up their belongings and trekked the several miles of dirt road on a horse tonga to this nearby town, Baba Singh was already changing. He was cross and dejected, like the men of other families he had seen, men who had, like his own father, been shoved off their land and made to lead their wives and children away from the village, sometimes much, much farther away than here.

That is what Ranjit had said. His older brother was seventeen now and had been in the fields for over a year before they were sent to Amarpur. He had overheard the men talking and knew a great deal about everything. Fertile land was more valuable than gold, and moneylenders had come up with a scheme to steal it away. Preying on the difficulties caused by dry seasons, they would offer promises of low interest they never intended to uphold, altering their books, charging double, triple, and often ten times the interest. And the price for nonpayment was high. Ranjit said that was how honest families were cut down and cast out. He told Baba Singh that they might have to go too, maybe move to Africa or Australia. None of them knew exactly where those places were, but they would need to take trains and ships to get there. They would be left with nothing except what the British felt they were worthy enough to have, perhaps merely a train ticket or passage on a ship or some old ruin of a building, dumped in new places to flounder like fish out of water.

Harpreet—their mother had always been an optimist—had said it was a blessing that they were relocated only a few miles away in Amarpur, with which they were at least somewhat familiar. They had come into town two or three times a year to trade their crops and stock up on spices, fabrics, cooking oils, and kerosene for their lamps. They knew people here, and that was something. But it made no difference to Baba Singh. They may as well have been exiled to Africa. Amarpur would never be home. There were too many bicyclists hurrying along Suraj Road, the town's main strip, too much plodding horse-tonga traffic, arrogant Brits sometimes pulling into town in puttering motorcars, and the vegetable pushcart vendor was always shouting in his unpleasantly monotonous voice, "*Aloo, pyaj, tommatter, ghobbi! Aloo, pyaj, tommatter, ghobbi!* Potatoes, onions, tomatoes, cauliflower!"

Their rented horse snorted, and Baba Singh turned to regard the sweat-streaked animal. It was tired and pawed softly at the earth with a hoof before adjusting its weight on weary legs. Baba Singh patted its head and glanced at the load it had carried, the tonga laden with all his family's possessions.

Lal swore under his breath, unable to free the key, his fingers too large for the knot in the string.

Harpreet gently pushed her husband's fingers aside. "Let me help."

"It was almost undone," Lal said, watching her pull at the strings. "I could have gotten it."

A flicker of flame shot through her eyes as she loosened the key. "I know you could have," she replied.

He looked away as she pressed it into his hand. She was not angry, just tired. She never really got angry.

"Thank you," he murmured.

"I don't want to live here," Kiran said, watching Lal unlock the door. She pointed at Avani. "She doesn't either. We want to go back to our goats."

Khushwant jabbed a twig into the dirt. He had just started school in Harpind and had been excited about it. Baba Singh threw another pebble at the wall, and their older sister Desa pursed her lips. She was fourteen and had left someone behind in Harpind. There was supposed to have been a wedding next year.

Ranjit squatted on his haunches to face Kiran. He was tall, with his father's high forehead and his mother's almond-shaped eyes. "Don't you like this place?" he asked her.

She tugged at her braid. "Does it have goats and a pond?"

Ranjit smiled encouragingly. The smile spread carefully across his mouth as though he did not want her to think he did not take her seriously. "Maybe not. But we should at least go inside and find out."

Baba Singh took Avani's hand. "Everything will be okay," he said, looking at his brother for reassurance.

Lal pushed open the door, but quickly stepped back as the rank smell of stale urine escaped in a thick, malodorous gust. Harpreet gagged and they all turned away, covering their mouths and noses as Lal kicked the door the rest of the way open.

Feces were in nearly every corner of the closed-in space, debris scattered across the floors. To the right, Ranjit flung another door open. It led to a small outdoor courtyard where they found a cracked clay oven caked in dried grime and sticky cooking oils. At the end of the hallway, past six small sleeping quarters, the washroom's ceramic basin was cracked. There was another door by the basin, and Baba Singh opened it, discovering the collapsed outhouse.

Harpreet clung to the doorframe of the front entrance, not able to enter. She pulled her *chuni* over her head with her free hand. The thin cotton shawl had fallen down around her shoulders, revealing her hair—frizzy that day—making her appear all the more exhausted. "It just needs to be cleaned," she said, then made a face and clutched her stomach.

"What is it?" Baba Singh asked her in alarm.

"Nothing," she said. "Just a small pain."

Ranjit shook his head. "They told us that it was ready, that we could live here."

"The British do not really care what happens to us," Lal replied, defeated.

Ranjit looked at Kiran with sympathy. She was very distressed. "I am sorry about the goats and pond."

"We should talk to Mr. Grewal," Baba Singh said. "Maybe he—"

"That man is a liar," Lal said, his voice rising. "There is no negotiating with liars."

Sweat dotted Ranjit's forehead just under the rim of his turban. He wiped it with the back of his hand. "Don't worry, Bapu. I will find work."

"We all will," Desa said.

"What did Mr. Grewal do?" Kiran asked.

Lal turned to her, his expression so severe that she took a step back. He seemed to be taking her question into account, determining whether or not he should answer it. Finally, he replied, "He stole our land."

"But isn't land too big to steal?"

Lal frowned, a tinge of red coloring his cheeks. "Not for him."

"Oi!" Khushwant shouted from down the hall. "Stay out of this room here!"

"What is it?" Baba Singh asked, hurrying over with Ranjit to discover a decaying dog corpse in one of the guest rooms at the back of the hotel.

~ ~ ~

That night, after a cheap meal of dhal and yellow maize chapatis from a steaming food stall on Suraj Road, the Toors slept outside on unfurled mats by the hotel's entrance.

Ranjit removed his turban, undid his topknot, and shook out his long, wavy mane of hair. "Khushwant, Baba, come here," he said as he briskly flicked his wrist, twisting his hair back into a bun. He shook out the yards of cloth that was his turban and held up one end.

Khushwant crawled over, and Ranjit handed him the turban. Baba Singh remained on his mat.

"Baba," Ranjit said again, showing Khushwant how to begin wrapping the cloth in tight, layered pleats around his head.

"Later," Baba Singh replied from his mat. Reclining, he could see the stars through holes in the murky patches of clouds. It was so dark and empty. He turned onto his side, wishing for home: the ambling storks cutting through the cluster of golden mud huts, frogs in the reeds, the scent of cattle and sweet chai tea, the distant swish of water flowing down the irrigation canals, the cawing crows in the neem trees.

His favorite time of day had been after school, in the afternoons when he escaped the rear room of the small gurdwara in search of play and fresh air, pardoned from the confining heat of the temple and the crushing, downward gaze of his teacher. He would race to the pond with Khushwant— and also Ranjit before he began working in the fields—to ride a bullock into the water. He straddled the animal's steaming back as it stepped in, his brothers pressed up behind him, their legs tense with the thrill of anticipation for the game that was to follow. Standing on the bullock as it shifted and puffed out through its nostrils to settle itself comfortably in the cool water, one by one, the boys leapt high, balling their knees up tight, spreading their arms like wings, their palms cupped downward like steely trowels, willing their bodies to be heavy with force. The biggest splash-maker would win.

Ranjit was always the champion.

Afterwards, when the large orange sphere of the sun hovered over the horizon of potato and cotton crops, they would dry under the shade of the rosewoods. While Harpreet beat wet clothes on a slab of stone, Khushwant and Baba Singh wrapped their soaked dhotis around their heads, using the loincloths to look like grown men donning turbans. At dusk, just before the sky darkened, Harpreet would disperse with the other women, heading home to prepare the evening meal, and the boys would run to the outskirts of the village to greet Lal as he came in from the fields, taking his farming implements like proud attendants to a soldier.

From his mat, Baba Singh glanced at his father now, a shadowy figure in the darkness. Lal was leaning against the outer wall of the hotel, his forearm across his forehead, his eyes bright with moisture. Avani was there, half asleep against him, her wooden elephant hugged to her chest. Harpreet watched them, rocking Kiran in her lap.

~ ~ ~

His body sore, Baba Singh woke. He had been dreaming but could not remember his dream, only that he had been alone and his family had all gone missing, or some of them. He was not sure anymore. He looked around. They were all there. Except Ranjit. Panic hit him. "Ranjit," he whispered, his dream once again taking shape.

The hotel door was open, and Baba Singh went inside. He should have been relieved to see his brother there but instead felt dread. "I thought you had left."

Ranjit was tugging the leg of the dog corpse with one hand wrapped in the lower portion of his tunic and the other covering his mouth. "Why would I do that?"

Baba Singh shook his head. He did not know. It seemed so unlike Ranjit.

"You should be sleeping," his brother said.

"Where will you take him?"

Ranjit released the leg and gazed down at the creature's patchy hair and the snout that death had frozen into a growl. "To the back to bury it. It should not be here when they wake. I already dug a hole."

Baba Singh nodded. The dread, and his already hazy dream, began to fade entirely. His brother would fix everything. He was brave that way and had always been like that. He once defied their teacher simply over a matter of principle. The bhaiji, who had been lecturing them on the history of the ten Sikh gurus, asked Ranjit to withdraw his statement that the caste system was still relevant to present-day Sikh society despite Guru Amar Das's efforts to eradicate it. A thread of hostility silenced the hot, muggy schoolroom. Even the younger, usually boisterous children quieted.

"We Sikhs do not live by the caste system any longer," the teacher said, his tone belligerent. "We have learned to be higher minded."

"Then why is it that when I decide to marry, my parents want my wife to be a Jat?" Ranjit replied calmly. "Perhaps I might like to marry a non-Jat."

"It is not a point of caste. Why would you *want* to marry

someone not from a line of warriors?"

"I am not a warrior, so what difference would it make?"

"Because a history of warriors in the family is respectable. If you are from a line of warriors, why would you want to be husband to a potter's daughter?"

"You have just proven my point, Bhaiji."

The teacher snatched up a ruler from his desk. "I have done no such thing," he said, grabbing Ranjit by the wrist and sharply whacking the back of his hand. He continued to slap the ruler down with sharp precision. Baba Singh had watched, open-mouthed, but his brother did not once flinch or move away. He absorbed the blow of each stroke as though his hand was made of cork. Only Baba Singh knew, by Ranjit's mocking smile, that every strike had felt like fire.

His brother again grabbed the dog's leg and dragged the animal toward the washroom. "I'll take care of this, Baba." And he was as good as his word.

After breakfast, Desa and Khushwant joined them inside the hotel. Lal went in search of employment, and Harpreet stayed outside with Kiran and Avani. She was feeling too nauseous and weak to help. Khushwant fetched bucketfuls of water from the pump in the center of town, and they used it to clean. Desa scrubbed down the clay stove and unpacked their pots and pans, readying the kitchen. Baba Singh scrubbed away the urine and feces in the six guest quarters, wiping down walls and tiles with old rags. He had never labored so hard. After watching Ranjit bury the dog, he had to. He had to help make it right for all of them.

The sun had set when Harpreet brought in their sleeping mats and laid them out in the lobby. She knew that none of them wanted to spread out in the rooms. They would stay together for now.

Kiran and Avani were already sleeping when Lal came home, his clothes dirty and his armpits sweat stained. "I found work," he said stiffly.

Harpreet sadly appraised his clothing.

"As a farmhand." He would not look at her. He would not look at any of them. "I am tired. Have you all eaten?"

Harpreet nodded.

"I am not hungry," he said.

Baba Singh moved toward his father. "Let me get you some fresh water."

"Whatever is in there is fine," Lal replied, pushing past and walking down the hallway toward the washroom, an opium pipe in his hand.

He had taken his *chappals* off at the door, but still, his feet were coated with mud from the fields, and he left a trail along the freshly cleaned ceramic tiles. Baba Singh stared at the impressions on the floor, the half footprints, like a ghost's, like only a shell of a person had left them, a man who had lost his land to a cheat and now worked another's.

~ ~ ~

There was one widow living in Amarpur in those days, before the coming wars widowed many more. She was middle aged and had no remaining family nearby. Her kin had abandoned her, claiming that her shadow was a particularly malevolent *manhoo*, bringing them bad luck by the elephant load. When residents in town discovered that Ranjit had begun to work for her two mornings a week—sweeping the front of her home and delivering sundries—mutterings of criticism pitched like bats along Suraj Road. One man felt it his civic duty to rap on the Toor door and caution the family against such blind and careless undertakings.

Amarpur had still not fully recovered from the monsoon disaster of last year, the man told them, just before which this very same widow had stepped outside wearing not the white of perpetual mourning, but *blue*, gold bangles tinkling shamelessly on her wrists. He shuddered. And she had the temerity to walk about without her chuni, revealing the indecency of her recently oiled, tumbling hair, making a lewd spectacle of herself with the men folk.

"Everyone knows widows are bound to keep their heads clean shaven, for what man can resist such seductive curls?" he asked them, gratefully sipping tea Harpreet had delivered into his trembling hands. Doubtless the deluge that followed, sweeping away homes and livestock and heirloom family trinkets, was a direct result of her manhoo. The town nearly crucified her after that. "See for yourself," he begged them. "Her house still bears the scars, dents in the wood from many swinging batons." She only survived, the man insisted, because she had opened her second-story window and chopped off her hair in a display of contrition.

"He is exaggerating," Ranjit said after the man left.

Desa stared at her brother in shock. "What if he is right?"

"We have already had our bad luck."

Ranjit also found employment as one of two tailor's apprentices at India Quality Cloth—regrettably located next door to Mr. Grewal's thin-bricked money-lending establishment. The proximity bothered him, but he told Baba Singh that it never hurt to watch the man. Someday, when all the farmers' anger rose high enough and bubbled over like a boiling pot of milky tea, there would be retribution. He was happy to be close enough to watch.

Desa began to work for the administrator of the local two-room schoolhouse, washing his and his wife's laundry, as well as keeping the school's grounds tidy. Khushwant, who still had dreams of attending school, split his time between his duties as the street hawker's assistant—selling cigarettes, tea, biscuits, and sweetmeats to customers along Suraj Road—and peeking through the schoolhouse window at the lesson board so he could practice his writing with a stick in the dirt.

Baba Singh was not as successful. He had found it more difficult to find employment, turned away from a number of places, including the main sundry store and the carpenter's. He had found the courage to enter the astrologer's shop with its shelves packed tightly with massage oils, aphrodisiacs, opium, and animal skulls, only to be sent out. And the telegraph operator would not have him either, shooing him away as though annoyed by a relentlessly buzzing fly so he could concentrate on his many gadgets and instruments.

Gloomily leaving the telegraph office, Baba Singh sat outside on his heels at the base of the staircase to the town's sleepy train-station platform. He missed his cousins, his aunts and uncles, the pond and animals. Hot tears came to his eyes. Hopelessly, he wiped his face on his sleeve, and stood.

He wandered down Suraj Road until he came across the smithy, owned by Yashbir Chand. Peering through the aged, clouded glass, he saw that familiar abundance of metal where the Toors had often come for farming tools. Every corner and free bit of floor was cluttered with metal objects, some worn with age, others glinting with newness: *thali* plates, aluminum tumblers, pots, eating utensils, garden tools, and iron buckets. An anvil and sledgehammer were centered in the middle of the shop, an iron-chimney stove nearby. A desk was off to the side, chisels strewn on its nicked surface. Swinging open the door, he went inside to say hello.

"Yashji?" Baba Singh called out, stumbling over a pile of hinges. Steadying himself, he edged through the narrow corridor of objects toward the blacksmith's apartment at the rear of the shop. Two swords were crossed above the door. The blades flashed in clean, curved lines, the detail work on the hilts intricate. The curtained doorframe itself was nothing spectacular, but the swords above had always given it the impression of majesty, an entrance fit for a palace, beyond which he had always imagined a mattress lined with silk bedding, hand-carved wooden furniture, and decorative metal plates propped on a dresser.

"Yes?" a man said from behind him.

Baba Singh whirled around. An aging, thin Sikh stood in the middle of the aisle. He was very tall and wore a tightly wrapped sky-blue turban, a white, mid-length tunic, a dhoti tied loosely between his legs, and tattered, dusty sandals on his feet. "Hello, Baba," Yashbir said, smiling kindly.

"Sat sri akal, Yashji."

The blacksmith glanced outside. "Where is your father?" His hands were clasped together over his flat abdomen as if in prayer. They were coarse hands. But not like a farmer's. Farmers' hands were made of grit and torn nails. His were like stone, the gray-brown of rock, with white healthy nails cut close to the skin. They were cast, chiseled, like the metal he worked with. "Did he send you alone?"

"He did not send me."

Yashbir frowned. "Did something happen?"

"Everyone is here," Baba Singh said quietly. "We are staying."

"I see," Yashbir replied. "Where did they put you?"

"The hotel."

"Not so smart, the British, but getting smarter. They are

scared of an uprising now. Too many of you. At least they did not leave you to wander into Amritsar to starve."

"Ranjit said they have already done that to many others."

"Yes," the blacksmith murmured. "Any more and they would have a riot on their hands." He pointed at the swords. "Do you like them?"

Baba Singh nodded. "Did you make them?"

"Some time ago."

"Our teacher in Harpind has swords like those crossed over the schoolhouse doors," Baba Singh said. "But they are not as nice." They had always been there, representing an article of Sikh faith, once used to fight against the Moguls for freedom of land and religion.

The old man thoughtfully ran his fingers through his long beard and stepped back toward his desk, indicating that Baba Singh should follow. He sat, looking pensive. "They were once weapons of war, but today they have no purpose. They are merely figurative, representing the power of truth to cut through all that is untrue, meant simply to be hung above doorways. Now we have guns."

He squinted thoughtfully at Baba Singh. "It was a long time ago, but I remember the hotel when it was open. We had so many guests before they laid the train tracks, people who stayed the night. I used to like their stories, to hear where they had come from and where they were going." He crossed his legs, and his sandal hung loosely off his big toe. "Amritsar is only two hours away by train now. People do not stay anymore. Trains and motorcars have made everyone so impatient, but it was nice to have guests who stayed a while, not rushing in and out."

"Yashji," Baba Singh said, looking around. "Where is Raj?"

"He left me," Yashbir said. "Last year. He went to

apprentice with a well-known blacksmith in Amritsar."

Baba Singh was instantly hopeful.

Uncrossing his legs, the old man leaned forward, understanding. He rested his forearms on his thighs, the end of his beard brushing the backs of his hands. "You are a bit small to be my apprentice."

"But I am very strong."

The blacksmith let his eyes roam the length of his shop. "It would be good to have another person around again." He stood. His eyes were soft and wrinkled, like Baba Singh's favorite dog in Harpind. "I am at the temple in the mornings. You can come by tomorrow afternoon and we will see."

Baba Singh smiled, pressing his palms together and bowing. "Thank you, ji."

"You should also visit Dr. Bansal," Yashbir said. "He is always looking for someone to get his office in order. It is disastrous—criminal even—especially for a doctor."

Baba Singh's smile faded.

The blacksmith chuckled. "Give him a chance. He is not so bad."

Dr. Nalin Bansal was a Hindu with neatly combed, short hair that was so heavily oiled trickles of grease stained his shirt collar. He constantly swept his tongue over the chip in his front tooth and flicked his wrists about when he spoke as though he were inelegantly dancing to music. "Yashji sent you, I know," he said cheerfully when Baba Singh visited his office. There was an intense furrow between his bushy eyebrows that made it seem as if he was perpetually confused. The doctor scrutinized Baba Singh, but not critically. His expression was oddly sympathetic. He offered the young boy half of a sweet, round, honey-golden ladoo.

"No thank you," Baba Singh said, shaking his head.

"But you *must* have one."

Baba Singh hesitantly reached for the ladoo and bit off a piece. It crumbled, then melted in his mouth.

The doctor smiled. His office was eerily dim, reminding Baba Singh of the astrologer's shop. Behind the counter and tacked to the cracked wall were two faded certificates, their basis uncertain, next to which hung twigs the doctor said were curative herbs. A shelf was stocked with several vials of mint extract, old cigarette tins containing cures for various ailments, and many bottles, numbered serially. Baba Singh recalled a particularly bad day when the doctor had been in Harpind to check on the children, forcing them all to swallow some of number three. Admittedly it had worked, but the children had always been terrified of Dr. Bansal and the vile taste of his medications, administered with that peculiar, jovial grin.

"There is nothing to be scared of," the doctor said, watching Baba Singh carefully. "You are not little any longer." He pointed at the plate of ladoos. "Another?"

"I wasn't worried," Baba Singh said, flushing.

"Just clearing the air," Dr. Bansal replied, smiling again.

Baba Singh took another bite.

The doctor nodded happily. "We can begin tomorrow while Yashji is at the temple."

The next morning Baba Singh approached the black storefront of Dr. Bansal's office and knocked on the door, rapping on the silver stethoscope painted on the small glass window. The doctor flung the door open in wide-eyed surprise. "So glad you could come," he said, waving the boy inside. He removed his faded, dark blue jacket, sweat stains already circling his armpits, and hung it on a hook by the door. He then headed directly to the back, yelling over his shoulder, "I am about to make chai. Let's have a cup."

Baba Singh heard the doctor rummaging around for earthenware mugs and then the clanking of a tin kettle being placed on the stove. After several minutes of more clanking and rummaging, Dr. Bansal returned with a tray of hot tea and ladoos, which he circumspectly placed on the counter.

"Enjoy," he said, and they ate and sipped their tea, sitting in what Baba Singh felt was awkward silence, although the doctor seemed quite content.

When the business of the day finally commenced, Dr. Bansal asked Baba Singh to fill vials with accurate dosages—which he would check later in the day—as well as dust shelves and the glass counter laden with heaps of unorganized papers and tins, and record in-home patient visits in the patient log. Then the doctor went out into the town to see patients—as he would most mornings—leaving Baba Singh to tidy and organize. Cleaning consumed the rest of that first morning and Baba Singh still had not made much headway. He found trinkets and glass jars full of filmy, dark liquids not unearthed in what seemed like centuries, and dust thick as a wool blanket over everything.

Just before lunch the doctor returned, and under his arm was a brown-paper-wrapped package tied with string. His spirits were especially high as he regarded the mess of his office that Baba Singh had made while trying his best to put it in order.

"Well done," he said with enthusiasm. "A bit of chaos is what we need. It means a new beginning is approaching." He gave the package to Baba Singh. "Please take this to the train station master for the post, and then you can go see Yashji. He is waiting."

Baba Singh stood and slapped the dust off of his clothes, receiving the package gratefully. He was tired of cleaning.

"Hurry," the doctor said, shooing the boy out. "I can hear the train's whistle. It never stays long."

Baba Singh stumbled out of the office and ran down Suraj Road toward the station to catch the weekly train. Panting, he leapt up the stairs and onto the platform, shoving the package into the station master's arms. "From the doctor," he gasped. "For the post."

The station master gave the boy a curious look. "I see he finally found help."

"Yes, ji."

"I will see you next week, then."

"Ji?"

"He sends these every week," the station master said, considering the package for a moment. "To a woman. But he has been here for a long time and none of us has ever seen her."

~ ~ ~

It had been nothing but tedium at Yashbir's that afternoon. Following a morning wading through the doctor's mess, Baba Singh hoped the blacksmith would have some inclination to begin educating his new pupil. But all Yashbir did was ask Baba Singh to hold the sledgehammer in various positions: high, low, straight out to the side. "Give it a good swing," the old man said, patting the anvil and grunting with approval when Baba Singh slammed it down with such a clang the room vibrated with the echo. That was it. After, it had just been more cleaning. And although Yashbir's clutter was not as chaotic as Dr. Bansal's, the job was nonetheless as immense. Baba Singh had barely made any progress when the sky began to darken and he was sent home.

Exhausted, he stopped outside the hotel, and for the second time that day slapped the dust from his clothes. Kicking off his sandals, he went inside. He was surprised when he saw the furniture: two reed chairs and a table, all looking a bit shabby. His mother sat in one of the chairs, staring at a picture of Guru Nanak, his hand raised in angelic benediction. She turned to look at Baba Singh and smiled. "Come, sit with us," she said.

Lal was in the other chair at the far corner of the lobby. His pipe was lit, held casually in his hand, the room full of the tar-smoke smell of opium, much like burnt butter. His feet were unwashed, still covered in soil from the fields.

Ranjit was on the floor with Kiran and Avani. The girls were helping him to construct a charpoy, the wooden bed frame already built. "Hold it tight," he told them as they struggled to keep pressure on one end of the wide strip of heavy cotton he was using to wrap around the frame for the pallet.

"Where did all this come from?" Baba Singh asked.

"The carpenter had scraps and such," Ranjit replied.

"What about our mats?"

Harpreet placed a hand on her stomach, and Baba Singh felt there was something odd about the way she did it, like she was protecting herself. "This place is a hotel—or was—and it needs beds." She rested her head against the back of the chair like she wanted to sleep.

Lal inhaled deeply from his pipe. "It is not a hotel. It is some other man's finished business," he muttered.

"It is such a big place for us," she murmured, glancing at her husband with sympathy. "It is more than we need. We lost everything and now we have something else, something we did not want. I do not understand it."

"I want to go home," Kiran said as Avani released the cotton strip and picked her elephant up from the floor.

None of them replied, and she sulked.

"Where are Desa and Khushwant?" Baba Singh asked.

Ranjit shrugged. "They should be home soon."

Baba Singh watched his family uneasily. They had only been here a few days, but in all that time he had been having the same foreboding dream. He thought of it now, but it was too indistinct, just a sense that the Toors had all vanished, scattered like pollens.

He supposed they had.

Wiping his sweaty palms on his kurta tunic, feeling the granules of dirt from the day's work, he kneeled on the floor, joining Ranjit and his two little sisters.

Dr. Bansal's Ladoos
1911

Baba Singh stared at Dr. Bansal's usual weekly post from across his plate of ladoos. The package sat there on the edge of the counter, just as it always did. Six months of that same brown paper, same string, same exact proportions. Not one bit of difference. His curiosity—constrained by good manners alone—was tormenting and ruthless. It made his fingers tingle, heartlessly prodding him to do the very thing for which he could never forgive himself. Rip away the paper. Tear open the box. Consider the consequences later.

Guilt, however, made his case hopeless, and the mystery around the secret contents continued to intensify, compounded by each passing week and by each new package.

The woman had been the worst of it for Baba Singh. In his daydreams she was a shadowy figure of curvy lines and swishing fabrics, hips swinging bell-like, smiling boldly with invitation. Only a woman like that deserved the privilege of receiving regular weekly gifts. But one look at the doctor—with his oily hair and chipped tooth, his good cheer and many peculiarities—and the possibility of such a woman disintegrated.

"Who do you think she is?" Baba Singh had once asked the train station master.

"The woman? Some say she is so beautiful that she is painful to behold. A man with such fortune should hide her away so as not to fall victim to her loveliness." He shrugged then. "Others say that she is dreadfully ugly, and that is why she is painful to behold."

"And you?"

"I think the doctor loves a woman who will not have him," the station master had replied, gazing thoughtfully out into the empty plain beyond the train tracks. "Men like that have big hearts but never women who can appreciate them."

Baba Singh considered the station master's words now, still eying the package on the counter. He broke off a piece of ladoo and slowly put it in his mouth.

The doctor waved a hand in front of the boy's face, leaning forward over the counter. "Another?" he offered.

Baba Singh pulled his eyes from the parcel and shook his head. "Doctorji?" he asked.

"Hmm?"

"Are you married?"

Laughing, Dr. Bansal wiped his mouth clean. "If I were lucky enough to have a wife, everyone would know about it. She would be the light of my life, a princess for all to see." He nudged the ceramic plate, stacked with sweet, yellow orbs of ladoos across the counter toward Baba Singh. He shook the crumbs off his shirt, the morsels leaving behind freckled spots of oil. Reaching into his pocket he pulled out a square of *paan* and popped it in his mouth, the betel leaves mixed with areca nut and slaked lime paste instantly staining his mouth red.

Relaxed now, he leaned back in his chair, which squeaked with the shift in his weight. "Why do you ask?"

"I just thought there might be someone in Calcutta."

The doctor's expression changed, like he was remembering something. "I left before I had the chance to think about marriage."

Baba Singh finished his tea, swishing the last sip in his mouth, trying not to look at Dr. Bansal. He suddenly lost interest in the package, gripped by a fear that something was changing. His dream still bothered him. Not every night, but enough. He was not certain who was lost or who remained.

"Something wrong, Baba?" the doctor asked.

"Ranjit told me that something big will happen. He thinks it is only a matter of time."

The doctor's face turned grim. "Maybe he is right. The British are recruiting again, for the police and military. I have seen flyers at the market."

"Will you go with them?"

Surprised, Dr. Bansal shook his head. "Not me. But others. Those wages will tempt people to the devil."

"I will never leave," Baba Singh said. "I am going back to Harpind." There were memories there. They made him feel safe.

"It will not be the same as it was," the doctor replied. "You will not be the same. You are already different. This is the reason why your father has not gone back, not even to visit."

"Maybe *he* is different, but I am not. It has not been that long."

"All it takes is a day. I know. It is why I cannot return to Calcutta."

Baba Singh felt himself getting angry. "You could go back if you really wanted to."

"No, Baba."

"You just haven't tried hard enough."

"I have certainly tried," the doctor said. "But once a thing changes, there is no reversing it."

"You don't know that," Baba Singh said, his voice rising in panic.

The doctor stood abruptly. "My nephew was very little when he was hit by a car." He raised his hand to prevent Baba Singh from interrupting. "Some rich man in a hurry drove too fast. He was not watching the road, and he crushed the boy's leg. My family believes I am to blame for what came next. I knew the leg would have to come off, and I performed the surgery." He pressed his finger against a crumb on the counter and lifted it to the plate. "They never forgave me."

Baba Singh held back tears. He took a deep breath. "It is not the same."

"It is exactly the same. It is change," the doctor said, briskly brushing his hands together. He indicated the tray. "I'll take that. Please get started on today's inventory." And he disappeared to the back with the tray of dirty dishes and leftover ladoos, leaving Baba Singh alone with the parcel.

~ ~ ~

The train was already there. Baba Singh could hear it, so foreign and powerful, its engines disturbing the country air. It whistled with reproach, telling him to hurry. But he did not. He moved slowly down Suraj Road, not entirely certain what he was doing until it was too late and the train had already begun speeding away toward Amritsar. He looked down at the package, the Calcutta address written in such a careful hand. Later, when he was old enough, he would never forget that particular package, that carefree handwriting of swirly ink on the paper. He would know a tremendous guilt that he did not feel on that day. On that day, he felt only anger because he had been told that he could never go home.

Nonetheless, he went to the train station. The station master would be expecting him, but Baba Singh already knew what the man would say. "So she will get two next week. She will not miss it. She probably throws them away. Bring it back next time."

Still, despite feeling justified in his anger, Baba Singh had a difficult time concentrating at Yashbir's. The old man was patient, but it was dangerous work. The moment he realized that his apprentice was not entirely focused, he took away the tools. It was not enough that Baba Singh had grown strong after several months working with the sledgehammer, or that he possessed a natural artistic talent. He had to pay attention. If the iron was hot, there were no excuses.

The blacksmith sat at the anvil, adjusted the tongs, raised the heavy sledgehammer with a sinewy arm, and began pounding the hot metal into a sickle. Baba Singh watched miserably. In the beginning Yashbir had once asked him, "Do you see the arc of the hammer? The manner with which you should hold it? This helps with the weight and allows for stronger impact." Stranger to his own body, Baba Singh was now intensely aware of his own arms, still the size of a boy's but now taut with muscles he could feel as he bent his elbows and flexed his fingers. He wanted to rid himself of this new, developing form. Nobody had told him that by swinging a hammer with enough force to mold metal he would also alter his own shape. Until now, nobody had told him that he was changing, that he was already too far changed.

At the end of the day, Yashbir pointed at Dr. Bansal's

package on the desk. He had seen it. He had known all along.

"Do not forget that. It was your job to deliver it."

"Will you tell him?" Baba Singh asked.

Yashbir looked at it sadly. "It will only hurt him. As far as I know, he has never missed a week."

"He told me I could never go home. How does he know?"

The blacksmith turned the coals in the fire, letting them cool. "I know you are upset, and you have a right to be, but not with him. He only meant to do you a kindness. He likes you."

Confused and still angry, Baba Singh made his way home, the parcel heavy in his hand. He did not even want to know anymore what was inside. He did not want to know more about the doctor. He wanted to be done with that strange man, with his strange packages and false wisdom. At the hotel he set it on his bedside table.

The table, too, was different. Adjusting to this new life, Ranjit had been slowly furnishing the rooms with charpoys and bed sheets, end tables and lamps, chests for their belongings. The family had dispersed, had spread out to settle in several of the sleeping quarters, he and Khushwant together, his parents in another room, the girls with Desa, Ranjit on his own. As he joined his family in the lobby, sitting against the wall next to Khushwant, Baba Singh felt burdened by all these new possessions and arrangements. He willed himself to remember Harpind. He did not want to forget what it had been like, and he worried that he was already forgetting.

"How is Yashji?" Harpreet asked him. "Did you thank him for the thali plates and tumblers?"

"Yes, Bebe."

"And Dr. Bansal?"

Baba Singh pulled a vial of mint extract from his pocket.

"He sent this for your stomach pains. He said it would help."

"So much kindness here," she murmured, adjusting in her reed chair. She did not look well.

"We had kindness at home," Baba Singh muttered.

"Has anyone heard from Ajmer?" Desa asked. Their parents had been trying to discourage her, but she still hoped for a wedding.

None of them responded, but Lal, who had been half asleep in his chair, opened his eyes. His opium pipe sent up thin tendrils of smoke.

"What about my goats?" Kiran demanded. "No one ever tells me about them."

"Enough about your goats," Khushwant said. "They were never yours."

"Is it so difficult for you to be nice to each other?" Harpreet asked. She seemed about to launch into a scolding, but instead exhaled with frustration. She flicked her wrist, giving up. "Just be nice."

"Bebeji," Ranjit said, his eyes widening.

"Hmm?" She rested her hand over her abdomen and leaned her head back.

"Bebe," Ranjit said again, staring at the floor.

She leaned her head over the arm of her chair and saw what he was looking at. "I did not even feel that," she said quietly, her face suddenly twisting in pain as she dropped the doctor's vial.

Moisture had soaked her *kameez* pantaloons, and a puddle of water mixed with something deeply red had formed beneath her chair.

~ ~ ~

The mood was hushed in the aftermath. It was over now. The children were still in the lobby, huddled together, helpless. Even Ranjit. Lal had moved more quickly than any of them could have hoped. He got Harpreet to a charpoy in one of the farthest back rooms and then summoned the midwife, who arrived not an hour later from her village. Even then, it had not been enough.

"I thought she was just getting a little fat," Khushwant said miserably.

"Where did the baby come from?" Kiran asked, frightened. Avani sat silently beside her, elephant in hand.

"From God," Desa replied, her face wet with tears.

"Where did the baby go?"

"Back to God. With Bebe."

"Where is God?"

"Bebeji said that he is everywhere."

Kiran's expression turned fierce. "Then we should look for them. We should look everywhere."

Desa pulled her sister close and again began to cry.

Lal had taken the bodies away. He had not spoken much since the night before when the sound of his wife's screams had drained the color from his face. And in the morning, when it was over, he had lifted Harpreet and the baby off the bloodied bed, wrapped them in a clean sheet, and carried them to Harpind, his cloak pulled tightly around him as much for the brisk morning air as for the chill of anguish, his knees bent under the weight of his burden.

Baba Singh had watched his father leave town, unable to follow.

Lal returned the next morning with family. Aunts, uncles, and cousins made the pilgrimage from Harpind to Amarpur, holding aloft the two bodies, now cleansed and purified, arranged on a pyre. In a procession down Suraj Road, wearing the white color of mourning, Lal somberly led the way to the hotel. They set Harpreet and the baby down in the lobby to pray over them. They spread out on the floor like newborn puppies, wailing, blinded by heartache, snuggling against one another for comfort.

When the priests arrived for the prayer, Lal had refused to allow them into the hotel as would have been customary, forcing everyone to seek solace from God in the temple. "God cannot enter here," he told the priests. "Take Him elsewhere." And when the family left for the gurdwara, Lal did not go with them.

The entryway of Amarpur's gurdwara was littered with chappals and shoes. Baba Singh hesitated, not wanting to enter. He looked up at the building, at the small golden dome above the door, a Sikh flag draped beneath on which was printed the image of a circular disc and two swords crossed beneath, like Yashji's swords. Finally, about to kick off his own sandals, he was stopped by two of his cousins who had come from Harpind.

"Do not go in there," one of them said. "Come with us." It was Ishwar, faithful and always serious. He was Baba Singh's age, but he looked older now.

"Where?"

"Just come," said the other, Tejinder with the missing front tooth. He looked different, too.

Baba Singh followed them around the side of the building toward the back where Ranjit was already waiting for them. The muffled sound of prayer came from inside as the priest read from the holy book. They could hear people crying.

"What are we doing here?" Baba Singh asked.

"Ask them," Ranjit said.

Ishwar shrugged. "Too much crying inside, don't you think so? It is better here." He suddenly grinned. "We have not seen you both in ages. I was just thinking, do you remember when Tejinder fell after running from that ghost in the cotton field."

"Oi!" Tejinder pointed at Baba Singh, pressing his tongue through the gap in his teeth. "You were the one making those noises."

Ranjit smiled. "You should have seen how scared you were."

Baba Singh also smiled. "Bebeji was so mad when she found out. Apparently, Sharan Uncle heard me, too, and ran off for a day thinking he was cursed."

They laughed.

"Bebe was only pretending anger," Ranjit said. "She was trying not to laugh."

"Your mother was good that way," Ishwar replied, leaving them all silent.

The last time Baba Singh saw his mother, Lal was pushing her pyre into the Ravi River. She was a white, undulating sheet of curves, angles, and shadows, the shape of a baby at her breast. And then his father set fire to her with a torch, and she was consumed by flames. Baba Singh watched her speed away with the current, dusk changing the light into tongued streaks of pink and orange.

In the silence at the hotel, after their family had returned to Harpind, the smell of death crept under the door from the room where Harpreet died. In the confusion and grief, no one had gone to clear it out and wash it down. Lal now ignored it. He took his opium pipe and retreated to his own room, the one he had once shared with his wife. The children were made queasy by the odor and looked desperately to Ranjit. Baba Singh would never know how his brother was able to do it, how he gathered the sheets in a single sweep of his arms, how he bunched up the white material caked with blood and rushed them outside to bury next to the dead dog.

The smell also permeated the porous wood of the furniture, so Ranjit flipped the two charpoys on their sides and dragged them down the hallway and out of the hotel's main door. He removed the chest and put it with the lamp and bed table at the side of the building to air. He tossed bucketfuls of water into the room to scrub down the walls and the floor. But still the odor would not lessen. Not even the smell of Desa's cooking—which she had been doing much of in the days since Harpreet's death, making feasts of cauliflower *subzee*, butter chicken, thick wheat roti, and blended mustard leaves with extra lumps of ghee—helped to dispel the scent of death. Finally Ranjit was forced to seal the room shut with plaster.

The days following passed in a daze. Ranjit returned to work, Desa stayed with the girls and Lal, and Khushwant and Baba Singh slumped about the hotel in stupors.

The nights were the most difficult. Kiran and Avani, usually exhausted and quiet during the day, cried pitifully for Harpreet as soon as the world became dark. They believed she was alive and that they must find her. They snuck through the hotel in a frenzied and desperate search as soon as the rest of them fell asleep. Or sometimes they remained on Desa or Ranjit's charpoy, staying awake long into the night, Kiran telling Avani tearful stories about their mother. Baba Singh's only hope was that they would eventually exhaust themselves into a fitful sleep.

~ ~ ~

The hotel, solid as it was, seemed instead like a skeletal

frame in the middle of the sweltering desert, casting ribs of shadow in which the Toors desperately huddled, trying to catch their bearings. Lal only emerged from his room when in need of the outhouse or more opium, refusing even to eat the food Desa left at his door. When they saw him, he was a terrifying image, his face sagging pitifully like roti dough, his long, frizzy mane of hair unwashed, unturbaned and wild. They never actually caught him, but they knew he took money for his opium from the tin in Desa's chest where they all deposited their wages. None of them spoke of it. He did not take much.

"I do not want to stay here any longer," Desa finally announced one morning, trying to mend a hole in one of Khushwant's shirts. "I am going back to Harpind. I can help Charan Uncle."

"You can't," Baba Singh replied.

"Why not?" she asked angrily.

"Desa," Ranjit said gently. "Ajmer is married now."

She flushed slightly and stood, picking up the kurta and bunching it in her fist. She spread it on the table, then folded and creased it meticulously.

That evening, before bed, Baba Singh knocked on Lal's door. There was no answer. Slowly he cracked it open. His father was sprawled stomach-down on his charpoy, arm hanging flaccidly off the side. A few feet from his hand was one of the chests Ranjit had made. Carefully folded and precisely laid within were his mother's few items of clothing—a sari and salwaar kameez—her broken-toothed wooden comb, and one ivory wedding bangle. Beyond the chest was her charpoy, sheet neatly spread, wrinkles smoothed away.

Lal roused, lifting his head an inch off the charpoy, looking at his son through wet slits, groggy and distant.

"Ajmer is married," Baba Singh told him. "Everything has

changed."

His father let his head fall to the sheet and again closed his eyes. "It is not what I had hoped for," he said, licking his dry lips.

~ ~ ~

A voice caused Baba Singh to stir in the middle of the night.

"Will she be there?" the voice asked hopefully. "Can we come?"

Hot, Baba Singh kicked off his blanket and was again pulled through a dark tunnel back into sleep.

Minutes later—or so it felt—he suddenly woke in a sweat. Something was wrong. Dawn lit the room with a dull ginger glow. There was a sound. Someone calling out.

"Kiran?" he heard Desa from the hallway. "Avani?"

Khushwant woke suddenly, disoriented. "What is it?" he asked Baba Singh, flinging off his blanket.

Desa called out again. "Kiran? Avani?"

Baba Singh went to the door. "Desa, what's wrong?"

Her eyes were big, alert with fright. "I don't know where they are."

Looking at her, he was also afraid. "They are probably somewhere close," he said, trying to keep calm as Khushwant pushed past him. "They must be searching for her again."

Desa held up Avani's elephant as if to say, *without this?* Her eyes were red, like she had been crying, the delicate skin around them swollen. "I think Avani dropped it."

"You didn't hear anything?" Baba Singh asked.

"No. I was…" She hesitated and bit her lip. "I was tired and fell asleep. They are always awake, and I can never get them to close their eyes, to stop talking and walking around."

"They cannot have gone far," Khushwant said, pointing into Ranjit's empty room. "They must be with him."

Relief softened the jagged-edged worry on Desa's face. "He didn't tell me," she said. "He should have woken me."

Khushwant pulled a sweetmeat from his kurta and flicked it at his sister, smiling when it hit her directly on the nose.

Startled, she opened her mouth to speak, then clamped it shut. She gathered her loose hair and tied it back, bending to retrieve the candy before glaring at him and leaving to prepare breakfast.

"What was that for?" Baba Singh asked.

"She is too worried all the time," Khushwant shrugged, returning to his charpoy. "It is much better if she is mad at me."

In the washroom, Baba Singh splashed water on his face and scrubbed his armpits. He wanted to wash away his dream. That same ominous dream he could never remember. Drying his face, he went into the lobby to wait for Ranjit. He chose his mother's reed chair, sitting in the silence of that empty room without moving, trying to feel her. He could not say how long he sat there. He was so drowsy. Perhaps he slept.

"Baba?"

Baba Singh started when he heard Ranjit's voice. His brother was kneeling in front of him.

"Baba, you were daydreaming."

Rubbing his eyes, Baba Singh took a deep breath, trying to orient himself. "Just a bad dream," he mumbled.

"You need to sleep. Come."

"Did you put Kiran and Avani to bed? Are they finally sleeping?"

Ranjit frowned. "No."

"They must be tired."

Desa came rushing down the hallway from where she had just delivered a plate of food to Lal. "Baba," she called out. "Bapu is not in his room either." She froze when she saw Ranjit. "Where are Kiran and Avani?"

"They aren't with you?"

"We thought they were with you."

Ranjit motioned for them to stay calm. "Then they have to be with Bapu."

"But Bapu is in no condition to—"

"Perhaps he is finally feeling better.

"Where were you?" Baba Singh asked his brother.

"No place," he said. "I could not sleep."

Baba Singh was uneasy. He could almost remember something important, but the details were hazy.

"Go," Ranjit told him. "You should not sit in here like this, afraid for nothing, staring into space." He smiled so warmly and with such calm that Baba Singh began to relax. "Go," he said again, "you have already missed too much work at the doctor's."

Amarpur was already beginning to warm in the late morning sun, and people were moving about. Baba Singh, however, did not go to work. Instead he paced the town, peeking into shops along Suraj Road to search for his father and sisters. At midday, he heard the train pull into Amarpur with a violent discharge of steam, like a beast exhaling. Peering down the road toward the station, he saw Dr. Bansal and Yashbir walking toward him, the doctor waving. He felt a sudden pang of guilt at missing so much work, and also at the thought of last week's package, still on his bedside table.

"We were on our way to see you, Baba," the doctor said. "I have been worried."

"Thank you," Baba Singh mumbled.

"We have just seen your father," Yashbir said, laying a sympathetic hand on the boy's shoulder and pointing to the train station platform behind them. "Nalin was delivering his package and found him up there with your sisters."

"My sisters?" Baba Singh asked, relieved that Ranjit had been right.

Dr. Bansal nodded. "Yes, they are there. But, Baba, your father is not well, and the girls would not come with us. We were hoping they would listen to you or Desa or Ranjit."

The train's whistle pierced the air, and the train began to move slowly along the platform. The click clack along the tracks quickened, and they could smell black coal smoke.

Behind them, at the end the road, a man stumbled down the station's platform staircase. "Bapu?" Baba Singh called, sprinting past the doctor and Yashbir who quickly followed. Lal was a disheveled and forlorn mess of hair and wilted limbs. "Bapu, where are Kiran and Avani?"

"They had more courage than I," Lal replied. "The conductor told me to go home. Get on or go home."

"We just saw them," the doctor said. "They were up there."

"Get on or go home," Lal said again. "They made their choice. Brave girls. They are brave girls."

Lal stumbled and Yashbir caught him by the shoulder, twisted him around. "Ji, did you send them away?"

"No," Dr. Bansal said. "Not possible. The station master would never allow it."

"Unless he did not see," Yashbir replied. He looked at Lal. "Tell us what happened?"

Baba Singh stared in sudden horror at the departing train receding in the distance. "What did you do?" he asked, his voice rising.

"I do not have to explain myself," Lal said, shrugging Yashbir off and standing unsteadily.

"Ji," Yashbir said firmly. "Where are they?"

Lal began to sob. He sank to his knees. "They are gone. I kept thinking that I should go away, too, that it was too much to look at you all every day, that it was too much to think of it all the time. But when the train finally stopped I could not get up. I just watched it. Where would I go? What would I do?" He wiped his nose with the back of his hand, squinting beseechingly upward.

Baba Singh gaped at the train, now a dot on the horizon, a pencil prick. He launched up the stairs three at a time, crying out, running, waving his arms in vain.

~ ~ ~

Yashbir tore away toward the telegraph office, Baba Singh close behind, shouting for help. The blacksmith burst through the door, startling the operator. "We need to send an urgent message," he said, "to the Amritsar train station."

Two young girls. Stop, the old man dictated. *Unattended, coming from Amarpur. Stop. Please hold them. Stop. We are coming. Stop.*

Minutes later the operator read the grim return message: *The train station serves thousands of passengers in one day. Stop. We will try, but there is very little possibility of locating them. Stop.*

"Get your brothers and sister," the blacksmith told Baba Singh, tossing aside the message and shoving the boy outside. "Bring them here. Quickly."

Wasting no time, Yashbir had a tonga waiting for them outside the telegraph office when Baba Singh returned with the others. "Up, up," he said, already prodding the horse forward as they scrambled to get on.

They crossed the train tracks and Baba Singh saw his father, still weeping, leaning heavily on Dr. Bansal, who escorted him toward the hotel.

"I knew," Desa said. "As soon as I found the elephant."

Khushwant held her hand.

"They will search for her," she mumbled. "They will search for Bebe everywhere."

Ranjit had a haunted look about him and did not speak.

The afternoon was hot as they plodded through the open plains toward Amritsar. They moved too slowly. The light was already changing, their shadows moving position. Baba Singh slumped. His eyes were open, but he could not focus on his surroundings. He pictured his father stepping up to the train station platform, Kiran and Avani following closely. The hanging oil lamps were lit, dimly illuminating the uneven wooden planks in the darkness before dawn. The girls began their search, peeking behind benches, laying their little bodies down, their heads hanging over the platform to check the dark tracks where Harpreet might be hiding. They called out, "Bebeji?" There was no answer. Avani began to cry, terrified without her elephant, begging for it as Kiran dragged her to join Lal so they could wait for their mother. They waited until the sky grew less dim and the train station master came and he tipped his hat and went into his small office. And then they waited more. Avani fell asleep. She slept until the train came. Kiran pulled at her and they jumped down off the bench. They glanced at Lal, who drooled and wept and covered his face, and then they went to search without him. They boarded the train, and Kiran asked the passengers questions, pulling Avani through the cramped cars, bodies pressed against each other, fighting dog-like for space. The whistle blew a shrill blast and the train began to move.

Baba Singh jerked out of his daze.

"It's okay, Baba," Khushwant whispered to him. "We will find them."

The city was dark when they arrived at Amritsar's train station. It smelled of auto fumes and greasy, fried foods. Baba Singh looked into the crowd with a sick feeling, at the moving rickshaw and car traffic outside the main building. He had never been to the city before, and though he had imagined it larger and more bustling than Amarpur, he was not prepared for the enormity.

"Stay close," Yashbir said.

The movement and flow of people inside the station was a gargantuan swell. Coolies in white dhotis followed the well-dressed wealthy with suitcases atop their heads. A million conversations in the chattering crowd melted into one colossal roar of activity. Families wailed and bid farewell as one of their own handed paper tickets to a conductor, who validated boarding passes with practiced efficiency. Train windows were flung open and a thousand hands waved desperately to their families.

"Excuse me!" Yashbir shouted, waving down an official. "Excuse me!"

"Yes," the man replied, his eyes wide with impatience.

"We are looking for the train from Amarpur."

"From where?"

"From Amarpur, ji."

The man frowned and began to flip through some papers. "Amarpur," he muttered. He paused, then looked up. "Already gone to Calcutta."

"Did you see two little girls?" Desa asked, indicating how tall they were. "One of them four, the other seven."

"I have not," the official said, then pointed off to the left.

"For lost luggage and persons, the superintendent's office is that way."

But the superintendent had not seen them either and suggested they buy tickets to Calcutta.

"But what if they got off?" Ranjit asked, frustrated.

The man gave him a blank look. "I do not know what you want me to do."

"Help us," Desa said, reaching out to the man. "Please."

"The ticket booth is there," he replied, ushering them out and shutting the door to his office.

They weakly looked around.

"I will go," Ranjit finally said. "If they are in Calcutta, I will find them."

Yashbir shook his head. "You cannot go alone."

"One of us has to," Ranjit replied, already stepping away from them and into the crowd toward the ticket booth. "Stay here. Look everywhere."

"Wait!" Desa shouted, thrusting Avani's elephant at him. "Take it."

Ranjit took the wooden toy. "I will find them," he said and disappeared.

The rest of them stayed in Amritsar until morning, until Yashbir told them they had to go back. They had no leads that could take them from the station into the city.

Desa refused. "*They* would not have given up," she cried. But when she stepped outside into the madness of morning traffic, she relented with dismay. Everywhere was simply too vast. She bent her head, and Yashbir led them home.

At the hotel, opium smoke lingered in the air. Lal was in his room.

Lying on his charpoy, Baba Singh was unable to sleep. Across from him, Khushwant was in a similar state, staring blankly and unblinkingly at the ceiling. Without a word, he turned on his side to face the wall.

Dr. Bansal's undelivered brown-paper-wrapped package still rested on the bedside table. Baba Singh picked it up and turned it over, touching the Calcutta address. He pulled on the strings and unwrapped the brown paper to reveal a greasy box crammed tightly with ladoos. Inside there was a note that read: *Mother, please forgive me. Your son, Nalin.*

A Coconut & a Sword
1911–1914

There were coconuts, and there were swords to slice them open. That is what Dr. Bansal had said about Calcutta. "They thrive in the city. Coconut wallahs sell them from their street carts. 'Fresh coconut, refreshing, fresh, fresh drink!' they shout while lopping off the tops with machetes. Right there in front of you."

The doctor palmed the hard, green coconut that rested in the center of the counter. He lifted it and affectionately began to pet it, like trying to mold its crown into a cone. "A man visiting from Amritsar was here recently and gave it to me. Have you ever tasted one, Baba?"

Baba Singh mutely shook his head.

"Climate here is not good for it. Too far north. But better to ask. Better never to discount the possibility."

Baba Singh regarded the coconut dispassionately.

"Would you like to try a piece?" Dr. Bansal asked, then abruptly put up his hand without waiting for an answer. "No, you do not have to speak. Of course you do. All children are curious about the undiscovered. It is what makes them healthy. Stronger than adults, I say." He tossed the coconut gently in the air and caught it with both hands, nearly dropping it. Still, he looked satisfied, blinking and smiling. "Let's open it up."

He stepped outside for a moment, propping ajar the door. Banging the coconut against a large rock outside, he grunted with the effort. There was a crunching sound, like stepping on loose gravel, and he returned in a hurry. "Oop, oop, oop!" he said as coconut juice dribbled down his hand to his wrist. Rushing the coconut over to a small bowl, he poured out a whitish liquid. "Machetes are much more efficient. Almost lost all the water."

The doctor split the coconut, now leeched of its juice, open into two halves and sat in his chair. He paused to push a platter of ladoos toward his silent young friend, like offering a balm intended to aid healing, then began to scrape out the innards of the coconut with a small knife. "Did you know that coconut is the most complete food?" he said. "It is life and survival. Meat, milk, water, and oil."

Baba Singh wordlessly watched him, absently taking one of the ladoos and pressing it between his thumb and forefinger until it crumbled into a pile of bits on his plate. They had received a telegram several days after Ranjit went to Calcutta. He told them not to wait at every train, that he would let them know when he was coming. After Calcutta he had gone to Hyderabad. Then Bombay. Then Jodhpur. Udaipur. Jaipur. They did not know how he lived, how he managed to pay for food, train tickets, or his telegrams. Perhaps he would search forever. Maybe he would never come back.

The doctor laid his knife on the counter with a clink and offered up a jelly sliver of coconut meat. "Try a piece," he said, shoving it at Baba Singh, who feebly waved it away.

"Take it," Dr. Bansal said. "It is life. Survival and all that. It will help."

When Baba Singh did not reach for the piece, the doctor set it on the plate next to the ladoo crumbs. He seemed to want to say something more, but hesitated. He glanced awkwardly at the burlap sack resting on the lower shelf by the entrance. "Baba," he said finally, "the train station master came by to see me."

More alert now, Baba Singh's eyes flitted guiltily to the sack. Preferring to keep the bag with him, he usually left it there when he came in; with all the rubbish in the doctor's office, he had assumed it would be overlooked. It contained a number of brown-paper-wrapped packages, all for Dr. Bansal's mother in Calcutta. He had been hiding them away, including the one he had opened and meticulously repackaged so many weeks ago. One for every week his sisters had been missing. After returning to work he had begun to collect them for luck, amassing apologies until Kiran and Avani came home. He had become convinced that sending the bulk of them together would mean more, that in greater number they would have more of an impact. A mother would not be able to ignore them like that. She would have to forgive her son.

Dr. Bansal pretended that he had not noticed the sack and continued scraping. "He was worried. I do not think he knows how to ask you directly. It is never easy to ask about loss."

Miserable, Baba Singh lowered his eyes.

"You should absolutely not blame yourself," the doctor went on. "For any of it. I know you think you could have stopped it, that you should have watched Kiran and Avani more carefully, especially after losing your mother. You think it is what she would have expected. Maybe you think that you should never be forgiven. But you should be. You certainly should be. Most importantly, you should forgive yourself."

He paused.

Baba Singh looked at him, then tentatively reached forward and took a piece of coconut. He put it on his tongue and closed his eyes, tasting the dull sugary-ness of it before swallowing it whole.

The doctor nodded, satisfied. "Good. Now drink some of this," he said, passing Baba Singh the coconut juice and waiting until the boy had a few sips. "Better?" he asked.

Baba Singh nodded weakly.

"Well then," the doctor beamed, removing a note from his pocket. "Forgiveness, especially of oneself, always brings great fortune. I was at the telegraph office this morning. The operator told me to give you this."

Baba Singh unfolded the telegram. *In Amritsar. Stop. Will be on the next train to Amarpur. Stop.*

For nearly six weeks his brother had pounded the ground of India. There was no hole, no dark place in existence beyond his scope. Ranjit was a champion splash maker. He had never let them down. He flew.

He was coming.

~ ~ ~

The train hissed to a stop. The packed-in passengers stared through the windows at the Toor family, mildly curious about this small-town stop en route to bigger cities. One of the cars opened to release a handful of people, among them Ranjit, who stepped from the train and onto the platform like a stranger.

He was thinner than Baba Singh remembered, but healthy. He wore the same maroon turban, but it was tied sharply now, the material ironed smooth, creases edged like stacked knife blades with a high twist at the front, like a dancer's flourishing hand. And his jet-black beard was tucked up neatly. His clothes were also different: a button-down shirt instead of his kurta, trousers instead of pajamas, laced oxfords instead of chappals.

Baba Singh smiled broadly, adjusting the burlap sack on his shoulder. Their good fortune was astonishing. After so much sorrow, Ranjit was here, finally standing before them with all the signs of a successful mission written on his rich clothing, the fierce glint of a warrior in his eye.

"Ranjit, you did it!" Khushwant said. "Where are they?"

His voice quiet, Ranjit replied, "I should have been more clear in my message."

Grinning, Baba Singh peered behind his brother into the train car, wondering where the girls were hiding.

"But I could not write it."

"Write what?" Baba Singh asked. He shot a quick look at Desa when his brother did not answer. She had paled, and he followed her eyes to see what she was seeing: Avani's wooden elephant in Ranjit's hand. His smile faded.

"It is such a big country," Ranjit said sadly, "and they are such small girls. I am sorry."

A short gust of wind blew gritty dust from the plains into their faces, stinging Baba Singh's eyes, causing him to stumble backwards. Ranjit reached forward to steady him, but Baba Singh turned away and began to run, staggering down the platform stairs and onto Suraj Road. The echo of his family calling his name dimmed behind him. All sound faded entirely. His thoughts stumbled.

He had not quite made it to Dr. Bansal's, hurrying past India Quality Cloth, when he saw the door to Mr. Grewal's money-lending establishment propped open by a steel chair. He halted, skidding in the dirt at the entrance in the dark shade of the building. His throat constricted. Confused and scared, he kneaded his forehead as though molding mud or clay, quickly glancing up and down Suraj Road. Practically empty, he observed, feeling unnoticed and alone. Everyone has gone home for lunch, he thought with detachment, then grimaced and began to cry.

Collecting himself, wiping his eyes on his kurta, he entered to see the moneylender.

"Mr. Grewal," he called out, glimpsing the shelf of debt ledgers behind the store counter. He had seen those ledgers before. He had been here once, with his father, just before they were forced out of Harpind.

Lal had been worried that day, anxiety all over his face as he hovered intently over one of the books. "But, Mr. Grewalji, these numbers are not right. There has been a mistake."

"No mistake," the moneylender replied, snapping the book shut and replacing it on his shelf. "The numbers do not lie."

"But I do not have enough," Lal said.

"No problem at all, ji," Mr. Grewal had assured him. A lie until he could arrange to send some men over. "For you, my friend, of course we can work something out."

So many lies.

Baba Singh firmed his grip on his sack of ladoos and circled around the front counter, searching for the ledger he thought might contain his father's debts.

"Is someone there?" Mr. Grewal said, stepping out from behind a shelf at the back. For one so cruel, the moneylender was such a miniscule, unassuming man. Bald and bony. He secured his spectacles higher up on the bridge of his nose and peered around the shop.

Baba Singh pulled one of the ledgers down from the shelf and came out from behind the counter. "I do not know what you did, but the numbers were not right."

Turning toward the voice, Mr. Grewal frowned. "What are you doing here? You do not belong back there."

"These numbers are lies."

"I am not sure I know what you mean, young man," Mr. Grewal said placidly, taking a step forward, eyes narrowing behind his spectacles as though trying to place the boy standing in the middle of his shop. Then he lifted his head in a slight nod of recognition. *Ahhh*, he seemed to say with a hint of disdain. "You could not pay."

"It wasn't done fairly."

"Those books will not help you," Mr. Grewal shrugged. "Everything is recorded precisely."

Baba Singh rubbed his eyes, but despite all his efforts, he could not stop himself from crying. The burlap sack of ladoos was a lead block in his hand. Moving forward, he let it fall to the floor.

Several packages came loose, skidding across the linoleum towards Mr. Grewal.

~ ~ ~

Running home, his lungs searing, Baba Singh was beset with flashes of something horrible. His hands. He could recall his hands, the sensation of his fingers closing around his sledgehammer, but as he ran he knew he had not been to Yashbir's that day.

Clutching his chest, he pushed open the hotel door, sprinted down the hallway to his room past Lal's opium smoke, and flung himself on his charpoy.

He closed his eyes, recalling a glint of light reflected in Mr. Grewal's spectacles. He covered his face. In revulsion he tried to shut the image out. "Fix the numbers," he was saying, holding the bald little man against the wall, shaking the ledger at him. "Make it right!"

The moneylender scowled at the packages scattered about his feet. "Pick those up," he said with irritation, struggling to free himself. He began to cough and sputter, a sudden panic behind the glint of his spectacles, unable to break loose as fingers closed around his windpipe.

Pushing aside the image, Baba Singh rocked on his charpoy, his hands pressed against his face, his nose crushed under his palm.

Sounds of a commotion came from the hotel lobby, and Baba Singh quickly looked up.

"Baba?" Khushwant called as he, Desa, and Ranjit rushed into the room. "Where did you go? We came here looking for you, and when we didn't find you, we—"

"Mr. Grewal was just murdered," Ranjit said breathlessly. He stood in the doorway, gripping both sides of the frame.

Baba Singh froze.

"The town is gathered on Suraj Road now," his brother said. "The police have arrested Dr. Bansal."

Stunned, Baba Singh asked, "The doctor?"

Desa sat on the charpoy next to Baba Singh. "Has everyone gone crazy?" She licked a tear from her lip. "He didn't have to do it. We all knew it upset him, that he had some personal attachment to you."

"What do you mean?" Baba Singh asked, his eyes flashing about the room.

"Yashji says it was because Dr. Bansal blamed Mr. Grewal for ruining our lives," Khushwant said sadly, sitting on his own charpoy and curling his feet under his legs.

"Yashji?"

"Baba, you don't look well," Ranjit said, stepping forward.

"Dr. Bansal would not have done something like that," Baba Singh said, trembling. He started to stand. "We should go tell the police before they take him away."

"No," Desa said, wrapping an arm around his shoulders. "Enough has happened today."

"But I know he did not do it."

"Yashji thinks so," Ranjit said. "The doctor was very outspoken about his views on moneylenders."

"The doctorji never spoke about moneylenders."

"He often told Yashji it was the most evil of professions, and that he would like to put Mr. Grewal out of business."

"We did not ask for this kind of help," Desa said.

Baba Singh looked around beseechingly. "Everyone is leaving."

"It's okay, Baba," Khushwant said, moving to kneel before his brother and taking his shaking hands. "Not all of us are gone. We are still here."

~ ~ ~

Yashbir was not in his shop.

Baba Singh whirled around. He had not slept well and was groggy. He wondered if he was still sleeping. The metal objects blurred around him as though under water. His shoulder was sore. Khushwant had squeezed it, trying to wake him because he had thrashed about on his charpoy all night. His back was sticky with salty sweat.

Attempting to call out, he choked on his words. "Yashji?" he said only slightly louder than a whisper. "Yashji, I need to ask you something."

He fumbled his way through the shop to Yashbir's

apartment, hesitating beneath the swords. There was a truth—a truth he could not decipher because of the nebulous shape of it. But the swords helped to steady his nerves because they held within their decorative hilts and polished blades the promise to protect him, to slice through his fear so that he could handle whatever it was he could not yet see.

"Yashji? Are you here?"

He leaned into the curtain, listening, but heard nothing. Pulling it aside, he saw that the room was nothing like he had imagined. No silk bedding, no hand-carved furniture, no ornate, engraved decorative metal plates. Only a simple charpoy on which was spread a thin mat and wool blanket. There was a wooden chair in the corner with no padding. And despite Yashbir's liking for all things artistic, there was no display of artwork. It was an ascetic's apartment, genuine and without pretence.

Not sure any longer why he had come in search of the blacksmith, Baba Singh released the curtain. On his way out, he paused in the middle of the room and lightly touched the handle of the sledgehammer that rested upside down against the anvil. It was like an object he had never touched before. It did not belong to him.

"Baba?" Yashbir said, entering the shop. He appeared harried, as though he had been running. Moisture ran down his temples from beneath his turban.

Baba Singh slowly moved his hand away from the sledgehammer. "What is it?"

Yashbir opened his mouth to speak, but no words came out.

"Something has happened," Baba Singh said, his tone flat. "I know."

"Yes," Yashbir replied, moving closer. "Something has."

Baba Singh wanted to step away but did not dare move.

"It is the doctor," said the blacksmith. "I thought you had gone there this morning. I was looking for you."

"They already told me, what he did to the moneylender."

Yashbir seemed relieved. "Yes, that is right." He took another step closer, his eyes sympathetic. "I know the doctor was your friend."

Baba Singh nodded, then shook his head. "No, he *is* my friend."

"You have to forget it now," Yashbir said.

"But he didn't do it."

"He *did*, Baba."

"You *know* the doctor. He is your friend, too."

The blacksmith moved yet closer. "I spoke with him before they took him. He told me everything."

Eyes wide, Baba Singh shuddered. "He confessed?"

Yashbir knelt and regarded the boy. "What do you remember?"

"I don't know. I remember waiting." That was all. He felt like he was still waiting.

"The evidence they found was strong," Yashbir said. "There is no doubt."

"What evidence?"

The old man's face took on a severe quality. "Packages to his mother. A number of them."

Baba Singh looked at Yashbir, his heart like a slingshot in his chest. "But you know that I—"

The blacksmith shook his head and reached out his hand. "You are a good boy, Baba. You always did your job. The doctor made that very clear."

Baba Singh slumped on the edge of the anvil. "Where did they take him?"

"To a prison post in Amritsar."

"What will happen to him there?"

"I do not know, Baba," Yashbir said sadly. "Perhaps it is best you do not think of it."

"I want to see him."

"He does not want that," the blacksmith said, wiping some dirt from Baba Singh's cheek with a firm thumb. "He is not a bad man, Baba. Mistakes were made, and now he only wants us all to move on. We should listen to him."

~ ~ ~

Dr. Bansal's shop was looted. Baba Singh himself had gone inside to check under the counter in the futile hope of finding one more final ladoo-packed apology intended for Mrs. Bansal. He shoved aside papers and journals, patient logs and empty vials, but he found nothing. Perhaps someone else had taken it, had eaten every single ladoo, munching on an apology that was powerless yet nonetheless spoke of unparalleled and unrequited love.

Eventually the shop was shuttered, and after a time, fueled by gossip, the building gained a reputation for being unlucky. By 1912 the doctor's story had acquired a tinge of myth. He was the eccentric protagonist—the fallen hero—in a fascinating tale of intrigue that residents recounted while shopping in the open market or while eating lunch at the temple. Soon, however, the growing outrage at the British taxes and racial tensions between Indians and their white oppressors overshadowed the doctor's misfortune. And then Dr. Bansal was forgotten entirely—by everyone except Baba Singh—as new waves of protest flooded the north.

More recruiters entered town in search of potential

nationalists, of desolate and outraged men willing to do anything for their freedom. They brought with them a feeling of revolution. Ranjit had been expecting them. He had been quiet in the months since his empty return, and Baba Singh later understood this was because his brother did not wish to be a presence in their lives, that he had known all along once these men came, he would leave again, that he would go with them.

"You will not go," Desa said flatly, snatching away the empty burlap bag Ranjit opened to pack his things.

He gently pried it from her fingers and put it on the lobby table. "I'm sorry, Desa," he said, a fanatic patriotism making his eyes flash. He began to fill the bag with items he had organized on the table: a comb for his black beard and long hair, an extra kurta from the tailor, a pair of trousers, and Avani's hand-painted wooden elephant.

"Stop it," she said angrily, reaching for his things.

He brushed her hands aside. "When I was away, I met a man," he told her. "I had not eaten for several days and my clothes were torn. I had not bathed in weeks. I told him what happened to Kiran and Avani. He gave me money and told me his plans against the British, against all the horrible things that are happening here and to Indians abroad. He said that even if I could not save them I could save others, that together we can stand up and do something."

"Fighting is for cowards," Baba Singh said.

"Come with me, Baba," Ranjit said, stuffing Avani's elephant into the top of the bag. "You will see it differently. You will see what I have seen."

Desa stood protectively beside Baba Singh and Khushwant. "If you will be stupid, then be stupid alone. They are too young."

Baba Singh pointed at the elephant. "That is not yours."

Ranjit cinched the bag. "It is not yours either."

"It is more mine than yours. You know that."

"You gave it to her. It was hers."

Baba Singh's voice rose. "You are just running away. It is not brave."

"Baba, there is something terrible happening out there." Ranjit pointed at the hotel's entrance. "They beat us. They call us names and take our land while we try to make a life in our own country. They send us away to other places, places very far from our families so that we can farm *their* land and clean *their* buildings. But when we showed them that we were hard workers and smart people, they got scared and beat us again. Sikhs suffer the most because of our turbans and our beards. They do not understand who we are, that we are a proud people. Guru Gobind Singh fought so we could have rights and freedom. He asked us to wear turbans, not to cut our beards so that we could be seen and respected. He said that we are warriors and that we should fight when attacked. We cannot ignore this."

"Give me the elephant, Ranjit."

A shadow passed across his brother's face, dampening his zeal. He threw the bag over his shoulder. "I spoke to the tailor. My job is yours."

And then the mighty champion splash maker was gone, gone on a two-hour train ride to Amritsar and then four days to Calcutta. Calcutta, where there were coconuts and coconut wallahs lopping open hard, green shells.

After that, Baba Singh did not know.

~ ~ ~

There was a two-year lull, a time when malevolent spirits slumbered. Most of it was a glow of color, of golds and reds, of grays and greens, hues of passing seasons. Though the nights were a heavy burden of recurring nightmares, Baba Singh could nonetheless recall a measure of contentment during the period from 1912 to 1914. As the monotonous days accumulated—a cyclical sequence of work with the tailor, then with Yashbir—it seemed an end of loss, no more pieces threatening to go missing.

Silence and smoke emanated from underneath Lal Singh's door, becoming odd comforts to Baba Singh for their regularity, their seeming permanence. It was enough, after all that had happened, to have that much. And he had Yashbir, who was a great source of selfless and dutiful reassurance, ready with a soothing word whenever Baba Singh expressed doubt and confusion, whenever his nightmares—of being alone and in danger—leaked into the daylight hours.

He and Desa spent most of their free time watching Khushwant and his friends dance bhangra, cheering when the performers spun about yelling "Brrrrrrrahhhh!" Their brother's twelve-year-old body was lithe, his movements practiced as his troupe prepared for the annual Basant festival to celebrate the harvest. They whirled around in a blur of color, wearing the bright red, purple, green, and blue kurta pajama outfits donated by the tailor.

Baba Singh often laughed while watching them, trying to conjure a joy he did not feel. Laughter ceased the tugging in his mind, the image of Mr. Grewal's spectacles that sliced through his thoughts and jolted him with fear, and also his intense longing for Ranjit to come home. Laughter meant he could forget, and so, for a time, he made a habit of it—both of the laughing and the forgetting.

A new moneylender had claimed Mr. Grewal's territory, the many-headed beast unremitting and somewhat daring in the face of the increased peasant disquiet. Resentment toward the heavy-fisted British escalated. Terrorist organizations commingled with and incited the tired, abused poor; there was talk around Amarpur of regaining control of stolen farmland. But this turbulence of the outer world did not affect the Toors during those two years. They ate well, dining on subzees and rotis flavored with onions, salt, and mustard seed, and tapped their feet in time with the music, dancing and laughing, until it was no longer possible to ignore.

Reports of an incident on the *Komagata Maru*, a Japanese liner transporting Indian passengers, flooded Amarpur in 1914, a roaring swell of news that left the region staggering with rage. The passengers, many of them Sikh, were refused entry into Canada. The Canadian Prime Minister, concerned his country and culture would be suffocated by the large influx of Indian immigrants, would not allow more Indians into the country. He had dispatched the liner back to Asia where it was then declined in both Hong Kong and Singapore. The passengers disembarked in Calcutta where the British then ordered them on a train back home to the Punjab. The Sikh passengers dissented, refusing to be shuttled around like children without rights. They marched in protest, holding their holy book aloft. The police, employing no other recourse, had fired on those unarmed men, killing many.

The incident was followed not long after by another wave of recruiters, and the return, once more, of Ranjit. He had been to San Francisco in America, where a group of Indians had gathered and organized to protest the sort of global racism demonstrated during the incident of the *Komagata Maru*.

"We are trying to stop it," he said, sipping tea Desa had

made. "I will not stay long, just for a moment. A party leader named Rashbehari Bose will be coming north to Amritsar. We are organized and ready, but there is much still to do."

"Are you expected to save the world?" Baba Singh asked, his tone mocking. "What little thing can you do?" There was still too much anger. He did not want to be so ruthlessly forced to be reminded of what had been lost. He did not want to always have to hold this constant sense of dread at bay.

Khushwant sighed. "You do not have to be cruel, Baba. He only just got here."

Ranjit stood and pushed back his chair.

"It is not time already, is it?" Desa asked. "Sit down and finish your tea."

"I really tried to find them, Baba," Ranjit said. "But I am just like you. I am no different. That is the reason I could not bring them back." He bent to kiss Desa's forehead. "Thank you for the tea," he murmured and left.

Baba Singh went to his room conflicted by the mixture of fury and sorrow weighing heavily in his chest, wishing he had the courage to ask his brother to stay. He opened the top drawer of his bedside table, and pulled out the vial of mint extract the doctor had given Harpreet. He had the habit of rolling it between his palms when he was upset, but now it did little to comfort him. He took a deep, shaky breath, clutching the vial, squeezing it tightly.

He found himself walking to a place that he had frequented these past few years. Everyone was scared of it, this particular building located on Suraj Road, scared of the ghosts that lived there, of the stories it told. Settling down on the pavement, Baba Singh leaned against the black, dust-coated façade, his knees pulled to his chest, finding solace in memories of Dr. Bansal. "Hey, hey, Baba, don't drop those tins. The odor released will cause a burst of hair to sprout from your nostrils. I tell you, long enough to braid. It happened to me once."

Baba Singh smiled, feeling the smooth glass glide between his hands. He would stay for a while, until night fell, until it was time yet again to go home, to climb in bed and be consumed by his dreams, one in particular that had taken clearer shape, and which he would never forget.

Whatever the doctor had done, it had not been with malice. It had been an accident. Yashbir had said so. "An unfortunate mess," the blacksmith often told him, "But the doctor looked as though he had made his peace with it. He was not scared, Baba. He was very brave."

~ ~ ~

Baba Singh clutched the edges of his charpoy. He was tumbling from a great height, tumbling from the black dome of the night sky until finally he landed hard in the dust on his hands and knees. Fear made his limbs tremble, made him sweat. Rivulets of it ran down his backside beneath his kurta. Far away down the path a man approached him in the dark, deliberately and slowly. Closer now Baba Singh could make out the man's rumpled dhoti, his chappals, his turban, and his well-defined naked torso.

The man continued forward. Closer and closer until Baba Singh could see that he was faceless. Shadows eclipsed his eyes, nose, and mouth. No longer advancing, the man waited. Panic pounded Baba Singh's insides. Dirt and rocks ground into the flesh of his palms and knees. He could see the musculature of the man's forearms, holding aloft a large coconut in one hand and a sword in the other.

Then Baba Singh understood, and he was no longer afraid.

He rose from the dirt, his body imbued with renewed strength, his own muscles developed and powerful. Eying the coconut greedily, he knew with infinite certainty that it was his salvation. Quickly he sprinted toward the faceless man. With one quick jerk of his wrist, he snatched the sword away. Eerily still, the man made no resistance and remained motionless as Baba Singh ran the sword into his naked chest. Staring curiously into the shadowy face, Baba Singh heard a gurgle as the man choked on his own blood and slumped to the ground.

Fear returned.

Alone now he stood in the faceless man's place, sword in one hand and the coconut on the ground before him. Desperately he began to hack at the coconut, striking it as he did metal on the anvil, over and over, again and again. But the coconut would not open. Something was wrong. Weeping, he continued. Blow after blow after blow that, had Khushwant not woken him, could have continued in perpetuity.

The Mighty Champion Splash Maker
1915–1919

From the edge of the pond, splashes resembled temporary soaring twigs of ice crystals. They were dewy, glimmering bubbles. A commotion. A shattering of smooth, reflecting surfaces, like bombs kicking cities up into dust. It was a grand spectacle that ended so quickly, leaving behind nothing of substance, nothing to show for such a build-up of spirited effort, the height of the jump, the warrior cry. Baba Singh thought it had always been so with Ranjit.

Off saving Indians from the world, his brother gained nothing for his efforts. He had gone to Amritsar a fully-fledged affiliate of the Ghadarite party to conspire with revolutionaries, but the police foiled every scheme his leader of the revolution, Mr. Rashbehari Bose, had formulated to derail trains and blow military posts sky high. The Ghadar party, with their grand promises, had yet to aid a single one of their countrymen. While striving for a momentous impact, trying to atone for a long-ago mess he had not been able to clean up, Ranjit had recklessly made a new one.

Life was not a pond back in Harpind, Baba Singh would have told his brother if Ranjit had not already been arrested and sent away to prison with his fellow cohorts.

But it was not only the revolution that was devastating the Punjab. Turmoil had spread to every corner of the globe, a great war, of which Great Britain was a central player, or so the townspeople and villagers of the region had heard. Royal British army recruiters made off with their sons like loot, like commodities stuffed into their back pockets. They had taken Baba Singh's cousins, Ishwar and Tejinder, offering a high wage in exchange for the risk to their lives, which was at least more than Ranjit had accomplished.

But, although his brother may have been a failure, he was apparently no traitor, even under duress, and it had saved his life. Residents of Amarpur searching for sons and cousins who had also joined the party reported that after its fall, many—particularly the informants—had been hanged in Amritsar for collaborating to create civil unrest. Because of Ranjit's silence, investigators had not been able to confirm his Ghadarite involvement, which was fortunate. Now he would simply need to wait, finish his sentence in penitent disgrace before someday returning home.

Desa packed a bag as soon as they discovered Ranjit was still alive. In her room, working efficiently and quickly, she folded a kurta and shoved it in, followed by some stale rotis and a tin of spinach.

"Where are you going?" Baba Singh asked from the doorway.

She regarded him with astonishment. "To see him. Aren't you coming?"

"They will not let you simply walk in for a visit. It is not so easy."

"How would you know that?" She found a small piece of rope and tied the bag shut. "Khushwant," she called out.

"The train does not come today," Baba Singh told her.

"We are taking a tonga." She stepped past him and crossed the hallway into his and Khushwant's room.

"What about Bapu?" he asked, following her. "Who will feed him?"

"Khushwant," she said again, ignoring Baba Singh. "Are you ready?"

Gathering some things together, Khushwant nodded.

"But we do not even know if the information is accurate," Baba Singh said. The tailor, who had just left, had relayed the news but had not been entirely positive. He merely told them that his son, who had also joined the party and later escaped, had a source.

Desa turned sharply to Baba Singh. "He is there. In that prison."

"I am not going," he said. "Ranjit has not done anything except make things worse."

Angry, she shoved him, hard. He hit the wall behind him. "You are too old to believe a person can be perfect," she said. "You are now his age when he went on a train to go find them. Would you have had the courage? He did not know what the world was like. None of us had ever left this place. You would blame him for the whole war if you could, for everything that has gone wrong. But he has done more than you or I. At least he tried."

~ ~ ~

The sky looked like rain, a sheet of it in the distance drawing nearer as Baba Singh sat on the edge of the train station platform, allowing his legs to dangle over the tracks.

Desa's words ate at him like moths chewing on stored winter blankets. He pictured Ranjit's jail cell. It was a place he had imagined many times before, a place where Dr. Bansal had been lost. The dankness must have been the worst of it. Seeped of warmth and wet like clammy, fever-ridden hands. Baba Singh did not want to go there. He was scared of being trapped and forgotten. Awful, awful memories would be loosened and freed. Avoidance was out of the question in a place like that. It was impossible to skirt around fears when alone for the duration of your life. Perhaps only at first, but sooner or later, the shameful things always made a stand and demanded to be noticed.

He glanced again at the rain, still far off. Cocking his head to the left, he dug a finger under the rim of his new turban, attempting to stretch it out. It was too tight, his ears pressed too firmly into his head, like he would need to peel them off later. Yashbir had insisted that he wear it. There was no specific age for wearing a turban, yet he was getting older and beginning to look absurd walking about with only a topknot. Even Khushwant wore a turban. He had for several years now, because Ranjit had taught him, as he had once tried to teach Baba Singh.

Watching the rain move closer, shame pressed a hard hand against Baba Singh's chest, because Desa was right. His brother had always tried.

It had only been a few weeks since Baba Singh learned how to tie a turban. Yashbir had resolutely directed him into his apartment, closing the curtain with the finality of a steel door. "Who will marry you like this?" the blacksmith asked, gesturing at Baba Singh, an overall gesture meant to suggest the pitiful tiptoe pace his young friend was making into manhood. His gaze ended somewhat reprovingly at Baba Singh's head. "Marriage is something you should begin to think about, Baba," he said as he unwound the sky-blue fabric of his own turban.

The old man's head appeared much smaller without the pillow of cloth, seemed fragile and wizened. His expression softened, and Baba Singh felt uneasy. Opening a drawer, Yashbir then pulled out a green turban, the color of spinach. "Marriage can be a new beginning," he said.

Taking the turban from Yashbir, Baba Singh removed the cloth of his topknot. Looking to the blacksmith for guidance, he bit the end of the six-yard-long cloth between his teeth as instructed, and together they practiced winding and folding, creasing and tucking until Baba Singh could manage it by himself.

When they were done, he scrutinized his reflection in Yashbir's small hand mirror. The turban was a little heavy, making his neck feel thin like a chicken's. It would take some getting used to. Gently placing his hands flat against the cloth to press the padding tightly against his head, he tried to get comfortable with the image. Staring at himself, he wondered who would wed their daughter to a young man who had been so often seen sitting outside Dr. Bansal's haunted building, who only had an empty hotel and a shrunken, withered family to offer his bride.

But Yashbir had already seen to that, perhaps had someone in mind all along.

Feeling the air grow brisk as the rain crept upon the edges of town, Baba Singh stood, ready for his new beginning. The sky darkened as he stepped down off the platform and onto Suraj Road toward the blacksmith shop.

~ ~ ~

Prem Singh had wary eyes circled by weathered lines. They were watchful hawk's eyes, and Baba Singh felt like prey beneath that hard stare. The man wore a cream-colored kurta and dhoti. He was tall and thin, like a rail, with lean calves, his feet bare, cracked and dirty. He possessed the ashy-skinned look of a farmer. A widower with no sons and four daughters—three of whom had moved away with their husbands—Prem Singh had only one unwed daughter remaining, his youngest, Sada Kaur.

"It was good of you to come, ji," Yashbir said, offering Prem a seat.

Lowering himself into the chair, the farmer regarded Baba Singh disapprovingly. "You did not mention he is so short."

Yashbir smiled easily. "Come, let us have tea."

Prem frowned dubiously and crossed his arms. "Where is his father?"

The blacksmith appeared relaxed when he spoke, but Baba Singh could see that he was irritated. "We have already talked about what has happened to Baba's family. Lal Singh is not available."

"For this I thought he would try to collect himself."

Embarrassed, Baba Singh could not meet Prem's eye. Yashbir's expression hardened.

"And what of the others?" Prem asked. "Where is his family?"

Yashbir stood abruptly, angry.

Instantly apologetic, Prem uncrossed his arms in a gesture of contrition. "Please, sit."

"As a farmer, you have likely witnessed similar misfortune befall your fellow villagers," Yashbir said. "In your position, it is not wise to interrogate Baba. He can help you."

Curious, Baba Singh now looked directly at Prem.

The farmer took a breath. His mouth tensed. "Has Yashbir mentioned that I may soon need to borrow?" There was a bitter edge in his voice. "I do not have much land, but I cannot manage it on my own. I need a son, and all the young men of my village have disappeared to the war. If I marry my daughter to someone of another village, she will go there. I will have no one. I have not found any family willing to help."

Baba Singh glanced at Yashbir, who had begun to pour tea into earthenware mugs. "It is a good match, Baba," the blacksmith said. "I have met her. You will like her very much."

Distant memories, filed away these past years, unfurled anew in Baba Singh's mind: the scent of rosewood and neem trees, soft clay under his feet, the whisper of wind gliding through wheat crops, the smell of burning molasses in the afternoons, Ranjit, Khushwant, Ishwar, and Tejinder sprinting with him through the village to the pond. He wanted to kick off his sandals, air the sweat off, feel the breeze between his toes, the clay of earth under his nails. There were things he could not get back, things lost forever, but some of it, a small piece, might be possible to reclaim.

"Sada is pretty," Prem said, studying the young man carefully. "She is also smart, a little educated and cooks very well."

Baba Singh had listened to Prem and Yashbir continue to discuss the possibilities of a match, but he had not immediately given an answer. He left that meeting uncertain, feeling a bit like Yashbir was too anxious to have it settled, too eager for him to go away. Doubts circled his thoughts. He did not know anything about Sada Kaur. Perhaps he would not like her. Perhaps a life with her would not bring about change but only more sorrow.

He also knew Desa would be angry, not simply for considering marriage without involving her, but for abandoning them and moving away, for whittling their number down one more. In the end, however, it was she who finally convinced him.

When she and Khushwant returned from Amritsar, she ignored Baba Singh when he told them about Prem and Sada Kaur. "Ranjit is fine," she said, sinking into one of the reed chairs, her expression haunted. "A little trouble getting in, but that was to be expected." She suddenly straightened, her voice taking on that same tone of zeal that had once consumed their criminal brother. "He wanted me to tell you that. He wanted me to tell you not to worry."

He could see that she was trying mightily to rescue this once great house of Toors, but the mortar was crumbling around her, threatening to bury her and take her whole life. Their family was beyond repair. Baba Singh knew that. He did not want to be buried with her.

"I will not be far," he told her. "Barapind is only a few miles outside of town. You can come any time."

"No more leaving," she said flatly, finally acknowledging him.

"Desa," he replied, trying his best to be gentle. "There is not much left to leave."

~ ~ ~

It happened quickly. Baba Singh did not have the time to reflect on his choice, which he would later admit to himself was deliberate. It was a plunge into cold water, a swift tear from his old life into a new expanse of possibilities. He did not recall much of the wedding, only a blur of color, being plied with turmeric paste by his family who had come from Harpind, the priest reading prayers, garlands of flowers, Khushwant dancing, Desa's forced smile—until suddenly he was here, alone with his bride, the two of them standing in his room in Hotel Toor, the simplicity of a single, sputtering candle and the silence between them a great contrast to the cacophony of the day.

He looked sidelong at Sada Kaur now as though peering too hard would crack her to pieces. It was not that she had the appearance of being fragile. She was actually rather stout in shape. She was also direct in manner. That much he could see without having yet exchanged one word with her. Her eyes made that clear. They pierced right through him, knowing him instantly. This both pleased and terrified him. He had the urge to scoop her up, to swing her around with abandon, to play a game perhaps, like old friends. Yet he also felt inclined to be sick.

In the middle of the charpoy lay a partition of rough wool blankets and feather-packed pillows he had earlier arranged. She sat softly on the edge of one side of the bed, smoothing out her wedding clothes before lying on her back to wait, her hennaed toes pointing upward and her painted hands and bejeweled arms crossed over the front of her beaded sari.

She had tremendously attractive feet, small and fine despite her sturdy frame. Her skin was equally as beautiful, luminous like a pane of glass or untouched water. In Amarpur's gurdwara, as he had pulled aside her wedding veil and beheld her for the first time, he had been instantly transfixed by her rouged cheeks that glowed with absorbed light.

He chewed the inside of his lip, embarrassed, and sat on the opposite side of the charpoy. She was otherwise agreeable, though not spectacular. She had round eyes, a snub of a nose that was out of place in a region where noses were generally quite large, and a severe, thin-lipped mouth that seemed to indicate she would not tolerate nonsense.

She peered around the bedroom, seeming to assess the items within it, the furniture Ranjit had built, the metal pieces Baba Singh had made and carved with Yashbir, the doctor's vial on the bedside table. He quickly snatched up the vial, putting it in the drawer, shutting it away from her.

Outside, they could hear the murmur of guests settling in for the night. He removed his shoes.

Finally, twisting around to face Sada Kaur, he said, "You do not like her."

"Who?" she asked. Her voice disquieted him, was young, yet as stern as her mouth suggested.

"Desa. I saw the way you looked at her."

Sada Kaur assessed him for a moment, then said, "She is very angry."

"She is not angry," he said sharply, feeling chastised.

"You both are."

He stood and she sat up, startled.

With deliberate slowness he said, "I am not angry." He had to speak calmly so she would believe him.

She did not reply, but he could see that she knew he was lying, that he was afraid. He again sat, slumping, allowing her to place a hand on his back. He did not return her touch, not that night, as was expected of him. He could not remember the first time he was with her, when he finally and gently stripped away her clothes, if it was soon after or much later. On their wedding night they had simply fallen asleep, with no more words, encased in all their wedding finery.

For the remainder of his years, Baba Singh would wade

through darkness to try and reach those first moments with Sada Kaur, that night of unblemished and dreamless rest. So slippery to hold, he would always lose it, that peace seeping like water between his fingers. But she would always be there, knowing he was lost, and he would always be able to see her, no matter how far she receded, an oasis of light.

~ ~ ~

During his first years in Barapind, memories came to Baba Singh sharp as needles, the sounds and smells of his past mixing seamlessly with those of his new life, threatening to undo his attempt at a fresh start. Prem Singh's two-room mud hut was so much like his home in Harpind that he sometimes saw the ghost of his mother cooking and cleaning, floating between rooms. There was an open shelf in the corner for pots and dishes, dhurrie rugs thrown on the floor, a coal-fire stove in the rear courtyard, soft light penetrating the curtained doorways. Outside, the bleating goats also haunted him, as did seeing farmers leading the bullocks to the village watering hole. He could hear children there, playing, cooling off, making splashes.

But Barapind was not to be entirely confused with the magical place of his childhood. This was a harsh place in a new age of India, where British rule had tightened, choking them with fear. Taxes were raised because of the war, because productive men had been recruited away from the land, because years of drought had yielded so little, all of which deprived the government. The people owed their dues, and the British intended to collect. They stationed officers throughout the country, men of great authority with the permission to employ their weapons liberally on any commoner—Sikh,

Hindu, Muslim, or otherwise—who fell short.

Prem rarely slept after planting season. When Baba Singh woke in a sweat from his usual nightmares, he could hear his father-in-law pacing about the hut long into the night praying for rain, praying for wealth, praying for another to suffer the bad luck of a ruined crop. For all his praying—and Desa and Khushwant's help selling their produce in Amarpur's market—their village had held up well, had met the challenges the British imposed under impossible circumstances—until the end of Baba Singh's second season when one of Barapind's number was defeated.

The farmers were coming in from the fields at dusk, making their way through the wheat crops when Baba Singh saw the silhouette of a British military officer against the setting sun and heard his sharp, booming call. "Ratan Singh, please come forward!"

Ratan, a gap-toothed, easily chagrined farmer with a shrew of a wife and a four year-old son, stopped cold as the officer unholstered his pistol to prevent any of them from fleeing. It was not a conscious movement, but Baba Singh found himself stepping back away from the farmer, as did the other men, rather than coming forth to defend him. He was not afraid for himself. Sada Kaur was at home, shuffling about the hut holding her back and rubbing her belly, which jutted out now past her beautiful, swollen feet. She was waiting for him.

The officer stepped forward and roughly grabbed Ratan by the arm. The poor man stumbled and began to babble incoherently in terror. "Come with me," the officer commanded, gesturing to the rest of them as he headed toward the village center. "There is something you all need to see."

Because of the pistol, they followed.

Without freeing his grip on Ratan, the officer kicked aside

the charpoys under the largest neem tree where the villagers often rested at midday. He then yanked the farmer's arms around the trunk of the tree, binding his hands with rope. Baba Singh watched in horror as the farmer began to weep, begging to be released, his face pressed against the bark.

The officer pulled a baton from the loop in his uniform and began to walk stiffly in a slow military march. He coldly gauged the crowd who had gathered to watch, and then, in one sudden motion, he swung around and struck hard.

The muscles of Ratan's back tightened. He screamed. "It will not happen again, sahib!"

Baba Singh's eyes widened in disbelief. He felt his knees weaken as the officer struck again. He had an urge to sink to the ground, to fall within the tide of other villagers. He observed their feet, the nervous twitch of their calves as their muscles tensed with the British officer's swinging arm. Like a dance, they moved in time with music.

Prem, watching his tormented neighbor, pulled his shawl tighter around his shoulders.

Eyes focused on the cane, Baba Singh concentrated on its swing around and over the British officer's shoulder, acutely aware of the white-knuckled grip that held it, the heavy-handed surety. He remembered his own hands. A flash of light cut across Mr. Grewal's spectacles. He clenched his fists, recalling something familiar. The nerve endings of his fingers tingled in protest. The air around him slowed. He no longer experienced the touch of the evening breeze on his face as he tried to comprehend the violence of the cane as an extension of the man who held it, the intention of the blunt force at the end of that arc. He opened his eyes, breathing hard now. The British officer made ready for another swing, even as Ratan slumped unconscious against the tree.

It was the fist, the ferocity in the officer's hand that made Baba Singh finally know it. He drew in a sharp breath and bent over, sick. Opening his palms, he shuddered and stared weakly at them, knowing now what they were capable of, remembering the day he had intended to return Dr. Bansal's packages, remembering that he had stopped at Mr. Grewal's.

"It was me," he mumbled, but no one heard him say it. Their legs continued to twitch rhythmically as Ratan regained consciousness and screamed again.

Baba Singh let out a choking cry, for himself, for his wife, and for his unborn child.

He straightened, needing to escape. He turned to Prem, his father-in-law seemingly unable to avert his eyes from Ratan. It was dread that Baba Singh witnessed in Prem's face, the dread of what they could not control. It was dread of the day when *he* would be strapped to that tree, a day that he believed was imminent and looming, and which they were all powerless to prevent.

~   ~   ~

The blacksmith's shop was brighter than usual. The sun had entered through the recently cleaned windows at just the right angle, like God peering in, illuminating every surface, every curve and dent of metal, every particle of dust. From where Baba Singh sat, the two kirpans crossed above Yashbir's apartment were flashing, frowning eye slits. Admonishing because of the lie, the one he had allowed himself to believe.

"Where is the doctor?" Baba Singh asked.

Yashbir was sitting at his desk. He caressed the various-sized chisels lined up in front of him with the tip of his index finger. He betrayed nothing. "This is not the time," he said.

"Think of your wife now, Baba."

Baba Singh clenched his fists. He squatted next to his friend. "I need to see him," he said quietly, looking up.

"Think of Sada Kaur," the blacksmith said again. "You cannot go chasing phantoms of the past while she is about to give you a family."

"Where did they send him?"

"He is gone," Yashbir replied.

"Where?"

"I do not know."

Rising, Baba Singh paced the room. "You should have told me. I would have stopped them from taking him away."

"He did not want you to."

Picking up several stray nails from a shelf, Baba Singh cupped them in his palm. "You must be in contact with him," he insisted. "You said Amritsar. I will go there."

"No. He does not want—"

Baba Singh slammed the nails down on Yashbir's desk.

The old man did not flinch. He collected the nails, some of which had fallen under his desk. He stood and placed them in a box containing a stock of other nails. "Nalin knew what he was doing. He was not happy here. There were things he understood he could never fix. When he realized what you had done, he came to me. He said he could fix this one thing. He wanted you to move on, to be happy."

"Tell him it did not work," Baba Singh said. "I have had nightmares. You know that. It was not worth it for him. Tell me where to find him."

The blacksmith's face fell. "He knew you would not want to do it this way, that you were a good boy. And then you did not remember what you had done. I was glad I did not have to tell you."

"Where is he, Yashji?"

The old man sighed mournfully. "He has been transferred somewhere. I have not heard from him in quite some time."

Baba Singh rang his hands. "I have to see him. We have to undo it. It was a mistake."

Yashbir looked at his young friend. "Sada Kaur is the most important now. And Ranjit. He is being released in a few days. You have been too hard on him. Apologize and bring him home. It is the best way to honor the doctor."

Baba Singh began to shake. "I think I knew the whole time. No one will forgive me."

Yashbir stood. "You never have to tell," he said, pulling Baba Singh to his chest. The old blacksmith smelled of something woody mixed with the soapy scent of his long beard. Baba Singh was not eighteen anymore. He was a boy again. He melted.

~ ~ ~

The train was jammed with luggage racks, double-height berth seats, and too many people as it jetted through the flatlands toward Amritsar. Baba Singh was squeezed against the wall of the boxcar next to Desa and Khushwant, a cramp in his side from not being able to move. A man above him was sleeping; his arm dangled through the iron bars of the luggage rack. Baba Singh rested his head against the glassless window frame and listened to the *teedoo teedoo, teedoo teedoo* on the rails as the train sliced through the air. It was his first time on the train; he preferred the slow jostling pace of horse tongas. Things at this speed passed by too quickly.

The wind whipped at his face, drowning and suffocating him. He yelled into it, "I am sorry." But all sound was carried away to the pinnacles of the distant Himalayan Mountains where it meant nothing.

Despite the nerves twisting his stomach, he smiled a weak, involuntary smile as he pictured Kiran and Avani on board, the way he preferred to think of them. Even now they hurtled through India, untouchable angels, laughing at how fast they could fly.

They arrived two hours later, pulling into Amritsar's train station, which was as loud and massive as Baba Singh remembered. Wafting in from outside the station were the heavy smells of oil, spices, and smoke from an army of vendors bellowing, "*Gharam chai, chana, chana*! Hot tea, chickpeas, chickpeas!" Motor rickshaws buzzed in swarms like insects, exoskeletons weaving in and out. Bike rickshaws were slower, but no less aggressive, lawless rebels tinging their tinny bells.

Baba Singh followed Desa and Khushwant on the long walk down Grand Trunk Road and onto Queens Road where they passed a number of government buildings until they reached the jailhouse. Several Indian guards were just inside the entrance, wearing turtle-green British police uniforms.

Approaching the head guard who was sitting behind a desk, Khushwant said, "We are here for Ranjit Singh Toor."

The guard gave a bored nod and rifled through some papers.

Baba Singh stepped forward, his heart thumping in his ears. "And doctor Nalin Bansal. I would like to see Dr. Bansal."

The guard stopped and glanced up irritably. "I only have release papers for Ranjit Toor."

Desa nervously pulled her brother back. "Yes, that is right."

Baba Singh pried her fingers from his arm. "I have to see the doctor," he said again. "He was brought here from Amarpur in 1912."

The head guard set his pencil down, his jaw tightening. "Crime?" he asked.

Baba Singh lowered his voice. "Murder."

The guard peered at Baba Singh momentarily. Then, nodding brusquely, he gestured to one of his men. "Vakash," he said. "Look up Bansal." He appraised them all, raising a menacing eyebrow. "Anyone else?"

They shook their heads.

"Ranjit is that way," he said, coming around from behind his desk holding a familiar hand-painted wooden elephant.

"Where did you get that?" Baba Singh demanded.

The guard tapped the elephant into his palm. "Ranjit had it on him. Personal possession." He turned to the other men and asked mockingly, "Should we give it back?"

"Should we?" one of the others laughed.

The head guard's face suddenly hardened. "Perhaps he does not deserve it. He is a traitor who conspired with other traitors."

"The government deserved it," Baba Singh said.

The guard tapped his uniform, a threat. "The government takes care of me," he replied.

"You can keep the toy," Khushwant said hastily. "We don't need it."

The head guard smiled with hostility. "Vakash, the key," he called over his shoulder as he led them down a corridor to Ranjit's cell.

"Baba," Desa whispered. "You have not seen him. He will not look like himself. He—"

"He was lucky," the guard said, overhearing. "We know what he did, but they say he is not a threat. Who are we to argue? We tried our best to get him to talk. We think the elephant made him look innocent. Terrorists do not play with toy elephants, right Vakash?"

"No, sir," Vakash grinned, jogging toward them with the key.

The head guard stopped in front of Ranjit's cell. "Right baby Ranjit? Ranjit baby?"

Baba Singh peered into the dark cell, his eyes slowly widening when he found his brother. Ranjit sat cross-legged on the cement floor against the far stone wall. His turban was off, crumpled in the corner. His hair draped down his back in frizzy clumps. He had lost an eye, a patch of scarred skin where the eye once was. His lips were cracked, his body—clothed only in a dhoti—was covered with half-healed scars from whip lacerations, and some of his fingernails were missing. His feet and wrists were chained.

"He never said a word, only cried like a baby," the head guard told them as Vakash loosened the chains. He then tossed Avani's elephant at Ranjit's feet where it landed with a clatter. "Oi, get out of here, Ranjit baby. Time to go, unless you want to stay for more."

Vakash nodded at Baba Singh. "No Bansals here," he said, following the head guard down the hallway, heels clicking on the cement floor.

"Baba?" Ranjit said faintly. "Did you come for me?"

Baba Singh's knees went weak and he grabbed the cell bars to steady himself. "God," he whispered, face to face with a fate that should have been his. "Wait," he cried out to the guards.

They stopped.

"The doctor was brought here in the year 1912," he repeated, his voice loud and panicked. "You might remember. He had a chipped tooth, and his hair was always combed, and he spoke strangely, his mouth was red from too much paan, and his favorite sweets were ladoos."

"Don't recall." The head guard shrugged and moved on down the corridor.

"Is this what I have done to him?" Baba Singh choked, turning back to his brother.

Ranjit picked up the elephant with his bloody fingers as Khushwant and Desa rushed in to help him stand. "No, Baba," he said, misunderstanding. "These were my choices. You were right. I should have stayed with you." He started to cough.

"What did I tell you, Ranjit?" Baba Singh said, standing next to his brother. "You were just running. I did not want you to go." He slid his hand around Ranjit's waist, speaking softly, "I am much worse. What I did was so much worse. And all this time I have hated you."

Ranjit smiled weakly. "I know, Baba. I have hated myself."

~ ~ ~

A son was not the sort of penance Baba Singh had expected for his crime, but when Manmohan was born he fully comprehended the enormity of what he had done. He had ruined his own child with a legacy of violence and brutality, had brought him into a world of greed and cruelty. Over the next two years, Baba Singh handled his son at a distance, watched him grow with an increasing concern that the social and political threats continuing to brew around them would one day turn Manmohan into the enraged and lost man that he had become.

And he could hardly bear his wife's discerning eyes, her intuitive understanding that something was wrong, that something had changed despite his obliging smiles. He had also ruined her, had sentenced her to a life with a murderer. He could not touch her the way he once had. He was tentative, worried that he would be too rough, thinking all the time that she would not be able to stand his hands on her if she knew.

Guilt for all measure of things now filled Baba Singh's days and months and years. He spent a great deal of time with Ranjit, asking questions about his search for Kiran and Avani, those sleepless nights in which he had huddled in corners, fending off rats, searching for leads, starving for food. He asked about his brother's time in prison, about those many meetings in San Francisco, about how the Ghadar party had incited poor, rash men to rise up without reason or logic, about how Ranjit had been led by rich men, equally as rash, who had caused so many to die, who had allowed torture without ever coming to rescue those who sacrificed everything. "Cowards," his brother muttered, touching his eye.

Every detail was critical, every second Ranjit had experienced hopelessness and sorrow had to be examined, pitted against all those years of Baba Singh's self-righteousness. Yet he eventually realized that Ranjit would rather not have relived any of it, that his brother shared his stories only to atone for what he believed were his own failings, and that too increased Baba Singh's guilt. He would have tied himself to a tree if he could have, would have beat his own body for the penalties he had not paid, for the dues he owed.

Indeed, it was his secret hope that the British officer would return to arrest him, would brandish his pistol and cart him away to prison. Yet, although the officer had visited the neighboring villages in recent years, he had no reason to set foot in Barapind. After Ratan, the villagers had agreed to work more cooperatively. Prem's insistence on sinking a new well and Ranjit and Khushwant's willingness to venture regularly into Amritsar—where the earnings for the harvests were better—had staved off further calamity for their small community. Still, they could sense another wave of unrest approaching.

Gandhi was touting peace even as British war recruiters continued to flash their shiny uniforms in Amarpur and the surrounding villages. After more failed monsoons and a major outbreak of influenza, they ruthlessly sponged up nearly every remaining, able-bodied Sikh peasant warrior willing to fight for the British crown. With many on the brink of starvation, peace was becoming more and more problematic to master. Farmers and peasants all anticipated glorious appreciation for their sons' defense of the British, but instead their problems were compounded by yet another unsympathetic increase in taxes and a resurgence of floggings in neighboring villages for nonpayment.

When the Great War finally ended in 1919, the countryside held its breath with collective relief, and grief for those who had died. Yet after the soldiers returned—expecting to be hailed, to be garlanded with flowers and riches—to discover their farms in ruin despite the savings they had sent home, pillaged by the British for whom they had just won the war, the mood again shifted. The people breathed steam and fire, enraged by too much abuse. They protested, burning post offices and banks and derailing goods trains.

Though a difficult task, Gandhi, with his considerable influence, managed to calm the public. He appealed to a purer sense of patriotism. Stop the violence, he reasoned. Join his peaceful march. Determining their voices would best be heard from the Golden Temple, Northern India's holiest of shrines, he called on them to assemble there, and over five thousand disillusioned Indian citizens began their trek to the meeting place in Amritsar.

"I have to go, Baba," Ranjit said. He had come to Barapind,

had asked Baba Singh to step outside the mud hut so they could speak. "Ishwar asked me. After what happened to Tejinder, I have to go. He thinks Tejinder died for nothing." He crossed the lane to stand in the shade of a small rosewood tree.

Baba Singh reached up to grab a tree branch, his kurta feeling too big around his shoulders when he stretched out his arm. He had not eaten much since Ishwar had come to tell them about Tejinder. "They will not allow this protest," he said. "After everything that has happened you should know that much."

"Khushwant is going with us," his brother replied.

Manmohan peeked his head through the front door curtain, searching for them.

Ranjit beckoned to him. "Come," he said, and the boy sprinted across the lane toward his uncle. "Baba, you should bring him. There will be many other children. Ghandiji's message is clear. None of us will have weapons. There will be no fighting." He smiled.

Baba Singh released the branch. "Ranjit, haven't you had enough?"

His brother made a wry face, picking Manmohan up and settling him on his hip. "I am not trying to save the world anymore, Baba. I just want a place in it."

Manmohan grinned happily in his uncle's arms.

Ranjit returned the smile, but after a moment it faded. "He is so little. Avani was this little the last time I saw her."

"I cannot remember what she was like," Baba Singh replied, his guilt returning. "Or Kiran. But I like to think they are still this little, safe and happy, on some great adventure, not here, never knowing what will come next."

"What about him?" Ranjit asked, indicating Manmohan.

"What will happen to him if he stays here in the middle of this madness? How can we do nothing for him?"

Baba Singh looked gravely at his brother's scarred face.

Ranjit pulled Avani's elephant out from a loose, hidden pocket in his kurta. "You can keep this until I get back," he told his nephew. "I will not be long."

Baba Singh watched as his son took the elephant. Then, with a smile, toy in hand, Manmohan offered it to his father.

"No, son," Baba Singh said. "It is your job to keep it safe."

The next day, Baba Singh—standing with his wife, his son, Desa, and Yashbir—waved to his brothers, Ishwar, and many others as they were carried away on tongas down the road leading to Amritsar.

~ ~ ~

Khushwant had lost his turban somewhere along the way home, but in his hand he clutched Ranjit's. It had taken him nearly a day and a half, following the train tracks to Amarpur on foot. He was dehydrated and blubbering, his face gritty and tear streaked. His feet were blistered as he crossed the threshold into Hotel Toor. Desa relayed an urgent message to Baba Singh, and when he and Sada Kaur arrived in town, Khushwant was shivering on his charpoy in Yashbir's arms, mumbling that he and Ishwar had been separated on their way back home. His clothes were stained a reddish brown and carried on them a familiar smell, assumed forever plastered shut in the back room of the hotel.

Gandhi's peace it seemed had been ineffectual against British General Reginald Dyer's order to fire indiscriminately into an unarmed crowd marching around the Golden Temple. Ceasing only when out of ammunition, Dyer left behind the stench of several hundred dead. The smell drifted with the breeze until it blanketed the Punjab flatlands. Ranjit's turban reeked of his own death, and also of gunpowder and metal bullets.

Desa was incapacitated by grief. She had always been quiet in mourning, keeping the intensity of her loss private, born from the intensity of her love. She lay in her room in a near coma, a trance that was broken only when Sada Kaur began to brush her hair. Then she began to silently cry.

When Manmohan asked where his uncle was, Baba Singh gently took away Avani's elephant and gave him Ranjit's turban. He hoped it would make the boy understand that his uncle was not returning. Manmohan held it for a moment, then dropped the cloth to the floor and ran to his mother.

No body to cremate, Baba Singh found himself in his old room with only the folded yards of Ranjit's turban and Avani's wooden elephant. He opened the drawer of his bedside table and pulled out Dr. Bansal's vial of mint extract. As he closed the drawer, he spotted the dark corner of something sticking out from behind the table and leaned forward to retrieve it. It was a leather book of some sort. He opened it and stared at the columns of numbers and names, of interest percentages scratched out and recalculated.

It was one of Mr. Grewal's debt ledgers.

He slowly closed the book, remembering now that he had taken it, intending to erase at least this small portion of the region's debts, to allow men to hold firmly to their land and to their families. He remembered the moment he had hidden it there, at some black point between running home and hearing that Dr. Bansal had been taken away for murder. He stared at the ledger, gripping it in his hand, confronted with the evidence about his own person, the sort who was not only physically able, but possessed the disposition to choke a man with his bare hands.

He took the ledger, the elephant, the turban, and Dr. Bansal's vial to Lal's room. Entering without knocking, Baba Singh found his father passed out on his charpoy, opium pipe on the bedside table, a line of spittle trickling from the corner of his mouth.

"Oi!" He shoved Lal with his foot, trying to nudge him awake. He kicked his father again, harder, but Lal was dreaming of something now, consumed by unconscious pleasures that reality no longer provided. Drool continued to trickle, oblivion apparent in his slack limbs. Lal had no clue of Ranjit's death; in his dreams his son was still tall and handsome. Baba Singh opened his father's storage chest and laid the items atop Harpreet's sari, salwaar kameez, wooden comb, and ivory wedding bangle. He carefully arranged everything neatly before securing the chest shut, closing in the scent of death and a hint of still lingering gunpowder and metal bullets.

Colonial Police Batons & Pistols
1920–1922

The flyers posted in Amarpur's open market were charcoal drawings of a turbaned Sikh constable astride a horse. He was dressed smartly in a police uniform—pressed khaki trousers and a knee-length, double-breasted overcoat with a thick leather belt at the waist—and his beard was neatly combed, the fierceness of a warrior in his narrowed eyes. In one hand he wielded a lathi, the iron-tipped bamboo baton brandished by policemen to maintain public order. In his holster was a pistol side arm, his other hand placed on it as if ready to draw. In Gurumukhi print, the flyers read, *Constables Needed.*

Baba Singh could not help but stare at the one tacked to the wooden post where he, his brother, and sister had positioned themselves to sell produce. He gritted his teeth, tearing his eyes away. Spreading a blanket on the market floor, Khushwant looked at the flyer and then at Baba Singh with unmistakable reproach. Their gazes fixed for one moment, then Baba Singh followed Desa to unload the tonga full of potatoes he had brought in from Barapind.

These particular flyers had been posted for several months now. Each time Baba Singh happened across them while on his way to visit Yashbir or the hotel, or to pick up supplies at the sundry shop, he found himself drawn to them. The severity of the constable's gaze cast spells, eyes twisting in kaleidoscopic tunnels. In his rigid spine, in the way his leather-booted feet held the stirrups taut, poised for battle, in the scrawl of words across the bottom that stated the impressively high wage of sixteen rupees per month, there was a promise of escape, of freedom. But it meant uniting with the enemy, with the men who had killed Ranjit.

Tempted to the devil, Dr. Bansal had once said.

Baba Singh carried in and emptied a sack of potatoes onto their blanket. He knelt down to help Desa arrange them, wondering how he would tell his family what he intended to do. They would have arguments against him joining: the Amritsar massacre would be their strongest, but there was also Ishwar, who had gone home to Harpind after the war to find his family besieged by taxes, and Tejinder dead, and Ratan strapped to that tree.

They would not see the greater benefits, the money Ishwar and Tejinder had earned as members of the British armed services. Unlike Ratan, who had recently fled, abandoning his wife and son to poverty and shame, his cousins had avoided borrowing from the moneylender despite the taxes, a pressing threat that Baba Singh and Prem spoke of daily. Sixteen rupees a month was a sound solution to their many worries, was a means to protect Sada Kaur and Manmohan, to protect the new baby that was coming.

"Baba," Khushwant said.

Baba Singh averted his eyes.

"How can you consider such a thing?" his brother asked as

Desa began haggling with customers.

Baba Singh brushed a potato clean. "We should not have to worry all the time, to wonder when—not if—we will be ruined."

"None of us are starving."

"Not yet."

Khushwant's jaw tensed. "Ranjit would not be happy."

"It is foreign patrol, police work, nothing dangerous. The war is over."

"Many would disagree."

Baba Singh lips tightened. He stood, ripped the flyer off the post. "Pride is not the answer. Pride is what killed Ranjit. This," he pointed at the wage, "is the only important consideration." He ran his finger down the list of requirements. "We have secondary school education. We are honorable, come from a race of warriors."

"No, Baba."

"What is the problem?" Desa asked.

Khushwant snatched the flyer from Baba Singh and gave it to her.

She took a moment to read it, then furiously crumpled it in her fist.

Baba Singh gently unclenched her fingers and removed it, careful not to let the paper tear. "I refuse to wait for another tax or drought. Or another war." He looked at his sister. "You told me once that Ranjit was better than us because he did something."

"I was wrong," she said. "It is not enough to do just *anything.*"

"There are no other solutions," he replied.

"What about your wife and children?" Khushwant asked. "And Yashji? How can you leave him now, after everything he has done for us?"

"I will talk to Sada," Baba Singh said, his tone blunt. "And Yashji knows why I need to do this."

But Yashbir had no patience for Baba Singh's relentless guilt. He had grown older, had begun to stoop and shuffle. His once sinewy arms were now frail, his hands spotted with age. "I need you to stay, Baba," he said firmly.

"I have a chance to make things right," Baba Singh told him.

"What you cannot face here, you will not be able to face elsewhere."

"That is not what this is about. I can prevent—"

"Life happens, Baba. You cannot prevent it. You might not come back."

"You told me to think of my family."

"I am also your family, Baba."

"Yashji—"

"I do not have lifetimes to wait," the old man said.

Baba Singh looked sadly at his friend. "I am sorry, Yashji. I have to protect them."

"I think you will find that Sada also sees it very differently than you."

Indeed, Sada Kaur felt much the same as the blacksmith. When Baba Singh showed her the flyer, she quickly skimmed it then folded it in half, ran her thumb and forefinger along the crease and said, "I do not understand. Singapore, China, South Africa, Fiji." She glanced at Manmohan who was asleep on a mat in the corner of their room.

"We spoke about this once."

"I do not recall speaking of this."

"You know what happened to my father. I cannot allow that to happen to us."

"But nothing has been lost."

"It always feels as though we are about to lose everything."

She straightened her arm toward him, the paper in her hand like a fluttering white flag. "We have been doing fine. It is not necessary."

"It will be too late if we wait," he said, attempting to reason with her. "I said I would do anything. I promised." He stepped close, touched her stomach, then took the wrist of her outstretched arm and put it around his neck. "It is because of you that I did not go sooner."

She looked at him with resignation, as if suddenly understanding that she had married a man who had always intended to leave, like it should not surprise her to be twenty-one and alone with two children. She leaned in and rested her forehead on his shoulder, tightening her arm around him, and he felt the hot breath of her sigh through the cloth of his kurta.

~   ~   ~

The British official made no pretense as his gaze moved slowly and critically from Baba Singh's sandaled feet up to his veined forearms and broad shoulders. "You are short," he finally said in Punjabi.

"Is being taller a requirement?"

The official tapped his cheek with his forefinger. "And pert," he said with a cold grin, then picked up a pen and scribbled something on a scrap of paper. "Come on this day to this address. You will need to pass training."

"Training?"

"War times were desperate," the official replied blandly. "The tide has calmed. This is not simple soldiering. You need skills."

As Baba Singh exited the government building, he folded the paper and tucked it into his pajama pants wishing Khushwant were with him, the both of them planning to go off into the greater world to save their loved ones together. There was a steady watchfulness, an acute loyalty about his brother's manner that Baba Singh had always found reassuring, especially after Ranjit's death.

Their relationship, however, had begun to change the moment Khushwant met Simran. His brother was getting married, and Baba Singh shamefully discovered as he headed home that he possessed a tiny sliver of jealously for the young woman who was to be his brother's wife.

The young couple had developed a casual friendship over the last year, often running into each other at the open market, engaging in many drawn-out exchanges regarding the quality of the corn or potato crop. Always accompanied by her father, owner of the largest sundry shop on Suraj Road, the mood between the two had been painfully restrained.

The marriage was not arranged by the usual course. No formal introductions were made, although Yashbir inquired once on Khushwant's behalf. Despite the blacksmith's good standing and his well-known informal adoption of the Toor children, Simran's father was not initially interested in pairing his daughter with Khushwant, hoping to attract suitors more socially appropriate.

"Tell that boy to stop flirting with her," Simran's father had told Yashbir with outrage. "She is refusing all others. She has locked herself in her room and threatened to run away."

"Certainly, ji," Yashbir replied mildly. "I will do my best, but it is difficult to control the young when they are in love."

"Love?" Simran's father sputtered. "That is ridiculous."

"Of course, ji."

It took some time, but Yashbir's words apparently softened the man, who was, beneath his intimidating and callous countenance a rather impassioned romantic. Unlike so many Indian family patriarchs, Simran's father had an abiding respect for the female sex and wished more for his daughter's happiness than a suitable dowry. So, together the two men had made arrangements for the wedding, which, as Baba Singh noticed when he again looked at the scrap of paper the British official had given him, was to take place just before police recruitment training.

Preparations for the nuptials took several weeks, during which time Baba Singh tried his best to be enthusiastic, despite feeling like he had lost something important. The event brought together people he had not been in direct contact with since before the Great War. So many had become faded images of their former selves. Like Ishwar. Standing with Khushwant at the entrance to the gurdwara just before the beginning of the ceremony, Baba Singh saw his cousin approaching with what appeared to be his usual rolling gait, drunken-like, full of amusement and mischief. But as he came nearer, Baba Singh realized he was wrong. Ishwar was limping.

He was only twenty-four, just two years older than Baba Singh, but he had the wrinkles of a middle-aged man, of one who had spent too much time tensing the muscles of his face. His loose posture suggested wariness, his body not relaxed but alert, prepared to pivot, to whirl around, to dodge bullets. His turban was wrapped tightly and compactly, more military than village.

Khushwant took Ishwar's shrapnel-scarred hand and smiled at his cousin. "It is good to see you again."

"Look at you, Khushwant. Not so little anymore," Ishwar replied, the lightness in his tone forced. "It has been a lifetime.

Baba, I am sorry I have not come by to meet your wife and son. I hear another one is on the way."

Baba Singh shook his head. "I am just sorry Tejinder is not here."

"Yes," Ishwar murmured. He smiled wryly. "It is terrible to admit it, but I was glad he was there with me, even though I know it is an awful thing to be grateful for."

"It is not awful," Khushwant said. "I know he felt the same way about you."

Ishwar glanced inside the temple where the guests were waiting for the start of the ceremony, then smiled again, this time more brightly. "Big day."

Khushwant grinned, and Ishwar grinned back.

"Shall we go in?" their cousin asked, and without waiting for a reply, he stepped inside the temple.

It was late when the festivities concluded. Many of the guests slept in the hotel, planning to return to Harpind the following day. Khushwant retired with Simran to the guest quarter he had once shared with Baba Singh. Manmohan stayed with Desa on her charpoy, and Baba Singh and Sada Kaur slept across from her, in the charpoy that used to belong to Kiran and Avani. Baba Singh could smell the faint scent of opium in the air.

Unable to sleep, he replayed the events of the day. He had not been able to stop watching Ishwar, the way his cousin had snuck off to the periphery of the celebration, with his darting eyes, his nervous shudders.

Sada Kaur moved closer. She leaned in and placed her arm over Baba Singh's chest. Soon she was asleep. Lifting her hand, he kissed the tips of her fingers, hating the doubts, wishing for hope.

~ ~ ~

Barapind's pond was smaller than Harpind's. Still, it was pleasant, set off into the trees where it was private. A room without walls. Baba Singh massaged his bullock's hindquarter where he had often gently jabbed at it. He then ran his hand along the rough line of the animal's protruding spine up to its head.

"Shall we?" he asked it. "I feel like I might like to swim today."

The bullock's eyes narrowed.

Baba Singh ruffled the smooth surface of the pond with his toe. Go on then, the animal seemed to say, looking away impassively.

Baba Singh stepped in with both feet, the water tickling his ankles. He removed his turban and then his kurta, placing them both on the grassy bank. He stared down at his lean bare-chested reflection for a moment, captivated by the sun sparkling on the water through the tree leaves. Bathing in sunlight.

Hearing a rustling in the reeds, he turned to see who was there.

"Baba?" Khushwant called through the small clump of trees.

"Yes," Baba Singh replied.

Khushwant pushed through the foliage. "I just came to say goodbye before I head back to town."

Baba Singh lifted his foot and patted the surface of the water with it. "So soon? Stay for dinner at least, for my last night."

"It is only training, Baba. I will see you in the morning. Simran is waiting.

"I see."

"Sada is wondering where you have gone."

Baba Singh undid his topknot and let his hair down. "I just needed a moment."

Khushwant nodded.

"It is hot today," Baba Singh smiled faintly, still tapping the water with one foot.

Khushwant returned the smile. "Even now that you are older and bigger, there is no way you can do it."

Baba Singh laughed softly. He dipped his foot back into the water, unsettling the mud and clay beneath the surface. "I know it. I would not even try."

"It is very strange without Ranjit."

"I was thinking about what Ishwar said," Baba Singh replied. "That he was glad Tejinder was with him. It was better having each other. I think Ranjit was also glad for you."

Khushwant was quiet. He pulled a leaf from an overhead branch.

"You know that I have never been back to Harpind," Baba Singh told him. "It would only take an afternoon on a tonga, but I have never gone back." He was quiet for a moment, gazing again at his reflection. Then he asked, "Do you think Ranjit would understand what I am doing?"

"I am not sure that I understand it."

"He could not save Kiran and Avani so he set out to save the world, or India, or maybe himself. I do not even know anymore. I could not save them either; none of us could have. But now I can protect my family."

"There is nothing to make up for. None of it was your fault."

"Some of it was."

Khushwant frowned, tossing away the leaf. "I still don't

understand."

"I have to go because of Dr. Bansal."

"The doctor?" his brother scoffed.

"He did something for me once, something I did not deserve."

Khushwant picked another leaf and tossed it in the water. "You make him sound so noble."

"He is."

"There is nothing noble about what he did."

"He did not do it," Baba Singh said, not moving. The water stilled, and his feet looked as though they had slipped into glass.

There was silence. Not even the trees whispered.

Khushwant's eyes widened as he began to comprehend Baba Singh's meaning. "That is not possible," he said. "We went after you."

Baba Singh took a step toward the edge of the pond where his brother stood, rippling the surface. "I did not even remember it until much later."

Khushwant sunk to the ground into the bullock's shadow. The animal lazily turned its head toward him, then looked away and snorted. "At the jail...I understand now."

Baba Singh nodded.

Khushwant's face flattened into an arrangement of indecipherable lines. "So now?"

"Now I make sure my children never get lost."

"None of us knew what would happen. You do not know what the world will be like for your children. You cannot prevent the things that will or will not happen to them."

"I have to do *something*."

Khushwant stared at the water for several moments. Baba Singh waited, his loose hair hot on his back.

He thought his brother would be angry or terrified or filled with hatred, but when Khushwant finally spoke, his voice was firm. "There were so many mistakes, one after the other. None of what happened was right. But I was there, and I know it was all too horrible to take." His expression softened, now resolutely gentle. He removed his own turban and kurta and set them beside Baba Singh's.

He waded into the pond, bending his knees until his dhoti was soaked and he was immersed up to his chest. Then he raised his arms and smacked his flat palms against the surface.

The next morning Khushwant climbed the stairs to the train station platform with Simran, Yashbir, and Desa. He carried a half-filled burlap sack. Simran's eyes were red as though she had been crying. Desa stood beside her, furious.

"I am coming with you," Khushwant said to Baba Singh.

Baba Singh looked at his brother with surprise, then glanced at Simran. "I would not ask that," he said.

"I am not sure what was worse," Khushwant told him as the train pulled into the station. "Being with Ranjit and seeing him die, or being here not knowing. I *wanted* to be with him. And whatever happened to them, even Kiran and Avani had each other."

~ ~ ~

It was August. Amritsar was shrouded in a heavy, almost solid mass of fog unusual for that time of year. It hung low, a gigantic mat of murkiness unfurled across the Punjab. Baba Singh felt like reaching up and scooping out handfuls as they entered the training facility. The weather made the inside of the building seem colder than it should have been, and darker, gray like hawk feathers.

"This is not what the flyer promised," Baba Singh muttered to Khushwant when he saw the conditions in which they were to live for the next three months. The other recruits, mostly Sikhs from the region, were equally disappointed, grumbling that there were no mess or kitchen amenities, and worse, no washrooms or outhouses.

"I do not know why you are surprised," his brother murmured as a uniformed British training officer led them to a barracks room.

"How will we wash and eat?"

His brother pointed bleakly outside over his shoulder at the street.

Baba Singh closed his eyes, trying to calm his nerves. "I am sorry, Khushwant. About everything, about this and Simran. Are you sure she is all right?"

"I shared some things with her about Bebe and Kiran and Avani. She understands. It was her father who was angry. He is more emotional than a woman."

The training officer assigned beds and asked them to leave their belongings before reporting for orientation. Baba Singh assessed the barrack. It was large and cave-like, outfitted with several rows of charpoys, sheets folded on each in tidy, creased squares. There were no pillows and no blankets. The only decorations were black and white photographs, one centered on each of the four walls. They were small, which made the walls on which they hung seem higher and wider. Baba Singh approached one of them. It was a picture of a Sikh contingent in Singapore. Uniformed, they looked much like how he remembered Ranjit: tall and princely.

"The guards at the prison wore something similar," Khushwant said from behind him.

"We are not like them," Baba Singh said, stepping away and

placing his burlap sack on the charpoy next to his brother's. "Ranjit said they were ignorant, that they were blind."

"Perhaps they were once like us," Khushwant replied as they were waved down to follow the other recruits to orientation.

"You Sikhs should be proud," the training officer told them when they were all seated. He appeared bored with his speech. "You are from a martial race that spans back through history to Guru Gobind Singh. Your people have an inborn, instinctive warrior's skill, and as such have been integral members of the Queen's army and Colonial Police Force for nearly one hundred years." He went on to explain the nature of their three-month training program and informed them that upon completion, they would each be required to take and pass a written examination. He did not speak as though he believed they were warriors.

On their first day, Baba Singh woke to the blare of a factory siren. It would wake him every morning, an unsettling sound that spoke of the city's grudging, bleary-eyed rousing. He pushed himself up and gazed down at the line of shifting bodies as the recruits came alive. The men dressed and filed out of the facility in search of breakfast. Finding a food stall nearby, they crowded around it to eat, swallowing stale chapatis and watery dhal full of spongy lentils, doubt cast across their faces.

"Stop watching me," Khushwant told Baba Singh that first morning as they forced down bites of food. "I am here because I want to be."

Baba Singh chewed on a chapati, his mouth dry.

During the course of their training, they suffered through a physical fitness program that tested the limits of their stamina. Some men vomited next to their charpoys at night, the combination of bodily strain and foul food doing them in. Many could not complete the training and were sent home with small stipends. It had thus far been a grim test, and the atmosphere began to stink with lost faith.

British officers taught them equestrian exercises, how to properly march the parade grounds, and how to disassemble, reassemble, and fire a pistol. They also enlisted a veteran Sikh officer to train them in the Sikh martial art of *gatka*. The British told them that it set their contingent apart, that they would possess an ability both prized and exclusive. Clearly the British understood the value of gatka, but Baba Singh felt they were too stiff to practice it themselves. There was a certain grace required, and most of the recruits who had learned to dance bhangra from childhood innately possessed it. Like the battle skills that made Sikhs such prized military material, the recruits knew how to spin and swirl, the deadly lathis in their hands more like streamers than weapons.

When not practicing gatka, the British instructed them on other uses of the lathi, which made Baba Singh uneasy. Applying it to a man's throat, or swinging it against a man's body—even in training—brought with it the all too familiar images of Mr. Grewal's spectacles and hacking at a coconut in the relentless dream that still haunted Baba Singh after all these years.

In addition to the physical component of their training, they endured hours of lectures. They would be posted in China where the British needed them most, either in Shanghai, where a large deputation had already settled, but more likely Hong Kong. The British training officer educated them on local Chinese customs and about police-community relations, instructing them not to interfere in Chinese business unless specifically to maintain public order. This was somewhat of a relief for Baba Singh. It would not be a considerably significant posting, just street patrol. Likely he may never be required to even remove the lathi from his pant loop.

The lecturer paced the room during those long, tedious hours, firmly encouraging them to understand the nature of their importance abroad. The Chinese respected the Sikh police officers. Sikhs were fiercely impressive, both in appearance and demeanor, and were a necessary part of the Empire's security and quality of life. They had been the root of British success in battle and were now a means to preserve order in other colonies.

"They think we are stupid," Khushwant told Baba Singh heatedly, getting under his sheet for the night. "They think we want to hear all that. They think that if they say nice things we will forget that we do not have latrines, that we have to wash up on the street wherever we can find water and still report for training on time. We do not need false praise from these murdering, condescending monkeys."

Despite the lecturer's flattery, at the conclusion of training, when the remaining recruits had passed their written examinations, there was no ceremony to mark their success or initiation into the British force. The men were cursorily thanked and given two sheets of paper each: a training certificate and a detail of their post locations with the date and time to report for duty. None of them left feeling like celebrated members of an elite contingent.

As they traveled back to Amarpur by rented tonga, Baba Singh pulled his certificate from his burlap sack, which now also held his new uniform: khaki pants, knee-high black leather jackboots, an overcoat, a wide leather belt, a bright white turban, a pistol, and a lathi. He stared at the certificate. It read: *Each officer should posses a character unblemished, humane, and*

*courteous, with a combination of high moral, mental, and physical qualities
to be used in the service of men.*

Khushwant was looking at him, holding the horse reins
loosely. He grinned then. "Monkeys," he said.

Baba Singh arrived home to Barapind late in the afternoon
after leaving his brother at Hotel Toor. His wife stared at him
helplessly when he entered the mud hut. She was rocking a
crying newborn. Manmohan was next to her.

"You missed it, Bapu," his son said. "A baby came."

"Satnam," Sada Kaur murmured. "His name is Satnam."

Baba Singh set his bag down and sat beside her. "He is so
tiny. Is he healthy?"

"He is perfect."

Prem had been watching them from his charpoy. "So you
did it," he said, indicating the lathi sticking out of Baba Singh's
sack. "I guess you will be leaving soon." He raised his cup of
water in a bitter toast. "But, if you recall, I allowed you to
marry my daughter because I needed you here."

"I will send money," Baba Singh told him, keeping his voice
even.

Satnam began to cry louder.

"When do you leave?" Sada Kaur asked.

"Next month."

"Where will you go?"

"Hong Kong."

Looking at him in astonishment, she gave Satnam her finger
to suckle. The room was suddenly quiet.

"For how long?" she asked.

"I don't know."

She stood and left the room. He quickly went after her. She
put the baby on a sleeping mat, sat on the charpoy, and
pinched the bridge of her nose. Satnam began to cry again.

"How is this different from Ranjit?" she asked quietly. "You hated him for leaving. You cannot guarantee we will be safe. You cannot prevent bad things from happening. At least with you here we can face those things together. I do not want you to go."

"I would like you to understand my reasons."

"I understand that you are running. I don't know from what, but you do not have to."

He sat beside her, reaching his hand under her salwaar. Angry now, she tried to shove away his arm, but he held it there. He found the bare skin of her soft back and caressed her softly. His face was only inches from hers, but he was acutely aware of the many future miles and years between them, separating their bodies by inconceivable distances of space and time. Even as Satnam was crying, she let him hold her, let him kiss her mouth, keeping her eyes open, seeing everything.

~ ~ ~

The month had passed so quickly, like the snap of freshly picked beans. Baba Singh packed a small sack of personal items: a wooden comb, an extra net to tuck his beard, an extra turban Sada Kaur had given him, a pair of sandals, and a small wad of rupee notes. His belt as well as his pistol and lathi were lying next to the sack on a small table. He smoothed the front of his overcoat, glancing around the room at the several chairs in the corner that had always seemed to crowd the small space, at Prem's charpoy against the left wall, at the drawing of the ten gurus on the wall opposite, at the open shelves jammed with pots and earthenware dishes, at the water jug by the door, at Sada Kaur's low stool where she made roti dough. He breathed deeply, inhaling the aroma of neem and dusty livestock.

The front door curtain was hooked open. Manmohan was outside, struggling with a clay pot of water.

"Where are you taking it?" Baba Singh asked him.

"Bebeji needs to clean the baby," his son said, panting and sloshing water over the sides, inching the pot through the doorway.

"Did she ask you for it?"

Manmohan looked up as though he had not thought of that. He frowned, two little wrinkles of confusion on his young six-year-old face. "No."

"You are wasting it," Baba Singh told him.

Manmohan stopped to catch his breath. He placed his hands on his hips and assessed the pot.

Baba Singh smiled. "Leave it for now. Are you ready to go?"

Manmohan shook his head.

Baba Singh strapped on his belt and inserted the pistol into the holster. "Let's get Bebe and your brother," he said, picking up the lathi and sliding it into the loop on his trousers.

"Are you going away?" Manmohan asked.

"I am."

Abandoning the pot, Manmohan approached his father. "Did I do something wrong?"

Baba Singh knelt down. "I don't know why you think that."

"Nanaji thinks you should stay here."

"Your grandfather will be fine."

"Are you ever coming back?"

Baba Singh stared at his son, at the cautious yet hopeful expression of one too young to grasp life's many cruelties. "Get your mother," he said, sending the boy away.

They stopped at Hotel Toor on their way to the train. Baba

Singh knelt on the floor beside his father's charpoy. "Bapu," he said gently. "I am leaving."

Lal mumbled something.

"I will think of you," Baba Singh murmured, kissing his father.

The train was there when the entire family, including Yashbir, gathered on the station platform. The engine was quiet as the crew unloaded supplies.

Khushwant stepped aside with Simran. They were holding hands. Her head was down, and Baba Singh thought he saw tears.

"Good luck, Baba," Yashbir said, taking the young man's hand.

Baba Singh put an arm around his friend. Yashbir's body was bony, muscles deflated by age. "Will you be fine without Khushwant? Who will help you with the shop?"

"I will," Desa said, taking the old man's hand. Her light, cotton chuni billowed out behind her as a breeze cut across the platform.

"I do not think I will wait here," Yashbir said, smiling at Baba Singh. "You can get on board without me."

Desa nodded in agreement. "I will go with you." She gave each of her brothers a quick embrace, not lingering long enough for them to say goodbye, then took the blacksmith's elbow.

Baba Singh watched them walk away down the platform. From behind, they looked like two people simply out for an afternoon stroll. Then the sky blue of Yashbir's turban disappeared as they descended the small staircase onto Suraj Road.

Avani's Wooden Elephant
1930

Junjie had the run of downtown Hong Kong, or so he made it seem.

"They love me," he often told Baba Singh with that crooked, mocking smile that thinned his pointy eyes into slits and showcased the top row of his uneven front teeth. "They love me for what I have and what they do not."

"What do you have?" Baba Singh asked him once.

"A purpose."

He was a street corner artist, his workplace a paved corner along Des Veoux Road at the narrow mouth of a dead-end alleyway. About the same age as Baba Singh, but unmarried with no children—at least none that were legitimate—he made remarkable use of his considerably unique talents. He painted animals and grass, but with such piercing strokes and fitting hues, his productions were magical. He also created impromptu charcoal portraits of curious passersby, smudges of life on paper. It was the shades of truth in their sooty eyes that brought these people back. They were stripped naked by his drawings. They were rendered vulnerable. They walked away confused at how he managed to see within them what they labored so hard to hide.

That was why Junjie was wrong. People did not love him. They hated him. Inevitably he would peer too deeply. He would expose too gratuitously. He had shamed them.

"What *is* your purpose?" Baba Singh wanted to know after Junjie had drawn him, upset by his own charcoal portrait, disappointed by his depiction. It was too melancholy. Everything was drawn downward, the corners of his eyes and mouth tipped not just in sadness, but in a severity that seemed foreign to him. His black beard was a series of downward strokes that spoke of rigidity, as could also be said of the length of his nose. Only his turban ascended, in gray, curvy smears of wrapped cloth, but it served to make everything else appear that much more elongated *down*. It was unfair. Baba Singh had felt a genuine hopefulness during those first months—even years—in Hong Kong. He had not felt as cold and as hard as he had been illustrated.

"*This* is my purpose," Junjie replied simply, holding up his brushes and charcoals. "I was brave enough to do it."

It took more encounters with the artist to determine his meaning, but Baba Singh eventually learned that Junjie's parents were members of China's wealthy upper crust. They had thumbed their noses at their son's obvious talent. And he did have it, undeniably.

Other artists faced with similar scorn might have drowned in alcohol or jumped into the sea to drown themselves that way. But not Junjie. He had taken what he interpreted to be a higher road. He had chosen to elevate himself, to regard his parents as simpletons, as he would come to regard everyone. According to Junjie, he had yet to meet his equal. He maintained this outlook even though it had sunk him down low, even though it had taken him into the void with everyone else who had ever gone missing.

~ ~ ~

Baba Singh looked over at Khushwant. They were walking side by side, their sandaled feet clapping hollowly on Amarpur's train station planks. His brother was smiling.

"Why are you so happy?" Baba Singh asked.

"Today?" Khushwant looked surprised, inhaling the Indian spring earth of the Punjab. "Why wouldn't I be? Why wouldn't we both be? We are home."

"It is so strange. It has been a long time. Much has happened."

"True. But some of it was fun, I think," Khushwant chuckled. "Remember the man in the alley?"

Baba Singh laughed ruefully, with both amusement and regret. He scratched his bearded cheek and shook his head, thinking of the year 1922. They had only been on patrol in Hong Kong for a few months.

It was the first time Baba Singh met Junjie.

~ ~ ~

Baba Singh stared hard through the mouth of the narrow alley to get a better look at the Chinaman standing in the middle of it. The air was cold as usual and had the tang of fish and sea. He hoped he would grow accustomed to these strange, unpleasant smells, sometimes wondering if he reeked of his new surroundings. He thought he could perceive it in his turban when he undid it at night. But it was hard to tell if it was his turban or if the odor had dulled his sense of smell.

The man in the alley was making deep guttural noises, but the two six-story tenement buildings that flanked the corridor and blocked the light made it difficult to see. "What is he doing?" Baba Singh asked Khushwant. "Is he drunk?"

"Singing?" Khushwant asked, dubious. "I was hoping to catch a drunk man singing today. What is that? It is definitely not Cantonese."

Baba Singh laughed.

Several feet away, a street artist, sitting cross-legged on the corner, stopped his work to look at them.

Baba Singh asked the artist, his Cantonese halted and broken, "You know that man?"

The artist regarded him seriously for several moments, then smiled broadly, almost stupidly. "No," he finally said, his smile instantly vanishing. He bent his head over his painting and continued to work.

Baba Singh stepped closer to the artist, who sat comfortably amid a collection of his paintings and drawings, a palette and brushes to his left, charcoal pencils scattered to his right. The artist was painting a woman reaching up to pluck a peach from a tree. Baba Singh was impressed by the intimate details, the elegant smallness of the woman's pale hand touching her fingertips to a fruit ripe with reds and oranges, a cascade of two green leaves pouring from the fruit's stem. The woman was desperate for the fruit, her face shaded pink with anticipation.

"Who is she?" Baba Singh asked.

The artist tapped his brush on the edge of his palette. "How do you know she is real?"

"Isn't she?"

"She is not."

Dipping the brush in black, the artist scrawled his signature in the bottom corner and placed the painting off to the side to dry.

"Junjie," Baba Singh said, reading the name. "It is a very beautiful painting."

"I know," Junjie said, pulling out a fresh canvas from a small portfolio.

Slightly affronted, Baba Singh glanced a final time at the painting, then moved away. There was no warmth or pleasure in Junjie's confidence. It was cold like a fact, sharp and painful.

Baba Singh again turned his attention toward the alley. Squinting at the drunkard, he said to Khushwant, "It does not look like anything illegal."

"Yes, but they are not supposed to be in there," Khushwant sighed, stepping into the dim corridor. "They always make a mess. We have to get him."

Closer, they heard the man make one final, remarkably impressive, guttural sound, low and rumbling.

"Hey," Khushwant said, but the man still did not notice them.

Taking a huge breath, the drunkard leaned back in an exaggerated arc. Like a bow releasing an arrow, with a *thwoo*, he shot a large gob of yellow mucus that smacked against the tenement wall in front of him. So awestruck by his own phlegm, he studied his spit closely, tilting his head to one side, then the other as though gauging the magnificence of its shine and amber tint.

Still not noticing the click of Baba Singh and Khushwant's boots on the cobblestones, the man then wiped his mouth on his sleeve and untied his pants to urinate.

"Oi!" Baba Singh shouted.

The man whirled around in astonishment, his genitalia hanging loosely over the hem of his pants. He stepped back, was startled when he hit the wall, jumped forward, and then fled down the alley and around a corner.

Baba Singh observed the smear of phlegm on the tenement wall, disgusted. "He backed into it."

Khushwant began to laugh.

~ ~ ~

"Was that when you first talked to Junjie?" his brother asked, still smiling as they descended the platform staircase onto Suraj Road.

Baba Singh nodded.

"What do you think happened to him?"

"I don't know," Baba Singh murmured as they stopped in front of Yashbir's.

"Things were a little wild at the end," Khushwant said, no longer smiling. "But I am sure he made it out."

Using the sleeve of his kurta to wipe clean a small section of the blacksmith's shop window, Baba Singh peered inside, but it was too dim to see much of anything.

Khushwant stepped back slightly and regarded the building. He shook his head sadly. "I still have all of Yashji's letters."

The old blacksmith had died five years before in 1925. Before that he had written constantly. He shared news of the entire family, made everyone real when the long days away had begun to flatten them into two-dimensional entities. He created scenes, built on moods, facial expressions, colors, and all the things left unsaid in Sada Kaur and Desa's letters.

The most memorable correspondence was news of Baba Singh's third son Vikram, born about eight months after his deployment. *This boy smiles at everything*, Yashbir had written. *I almost feel sorry for him because he cannot laugh yet as big as he wants to.*

128

Even now, Baba Singh still had parts of that particular letter memorized. It made him remember how he had made love to his wife before he left. They had gone to the canal. She was angry, but she let him lift her sari, insert his hands within the folds of cloth until he found her. He wondered if he had been too rough with her. He had not meant to be, had always been so vigilantly tender, but despite her willingness she was so removed. He panicked, pulling at her, terrified that she was already too far from him. Thinking of it had often kept him awake at night, particularly in the early years.

In his final letter, Yashbir had left his shop to Khushwant, who had no other means of support. Baba Singh had somewhat withdrawn from his brother after that, feeling displaced and disinherited. Sada Kaur and Desa's letters, which had always been lifeless in comparison, became even more so in the five years following. They contained only data. The children were growing and healthy. The farm was thriving thanks to the money he sent. The bathroom sink in the hotel had sprung a leak. But not to worry, they fixed it. Prem was tired. Lal was not well. Even when Lal passed away in 1928, it had been just another bit of information. Baba Singh knew they had tried, but he had read their correspondence without enthusiasm, frustrated with their inadequacy, with all the emotion lost while translating events to paper.

Baba Singh had written obligatory replies, and this is perhaps why he did not like the ones he received. He wondered if his wife had written them in the same dispirited frame of mind. How could he explain to her what it was like? How could he tell her about his job and his days and months and years in China when she had not experienced it with him? His letters, like hers, were perfunctory, businesslike, a list of changes. No life to fill them out.

Baba Singh turned away from Yashbir's storefront window. "It is too dark," he told Khushwant. "I cannot see much."

His brother jiggled the doorknob, but it was locked. "Let's keep going," he said. "I am sure Desa has the key."

They strode past Dr. Bansal's on their way to Hotel Toor. "Still boarded," Baba Singh noted with regret.

"No one ever replied?" Khushwant asked. "They couldn't tell you anything?"

"Some of the prisons replied to my inquiries," Baba Singh said, "but they did not know, or would not tell me, where he was."

Khushwant placed a gentle hand on his brother's back. "Let's go, Baba," he said, heading toward Hotel Toor.

The hotel was still ugly, yet affection rushed upon Baba Singh like the salty, stormy sea that drowned ships off the coast of Hong Kong. He had missed this derelict lump of stone and wood.

Simran opened the front entrance before they even had the chance to reach for the knob, a radiant smile on her face.

Khushwant grinned. Even after so much time, his wife was still young and glowing. She exhaled slowly, like she had been holding her breath for the past eight years, and took her husband's bag, placing it on the floor by the entrance.

Khushwant glanced toward the kitchen and sniffed the air. "Lamb?"

She laughed nervously. "We made a feast." She scrutinized them both. "You two have gotten old."

"You are still eighteen," Khushwant replied.

Simran's face was bright. She pulled her chuni over her hair and led her husband to the lobby.

"Hello Baba," Desa said from the kitchen doorway. Her voice was distant, as though she had spoken across a wide valley and he was only hearing a faint echo. She had patches of gray in her hair. He was sad to see that she was no longer beautiful.

"Nothing is the same as it was," he said, glancing around at the hotel, which truthfully did not seem so different. But it was the *sense* of the town and of the hotel, the absence of people that made it feel changed.

"For you I suppose." She looked over at Simran and Khushwant. "She wanted everything to be perfect. Ever since we got your letter. Sometimes I hated her. I could not understand her patience or her optimism. They are very lucky."

Baba Singh nodded tentatively, disturbed by the blunt indifference in his sister's tone.

She wiped her hands on a dishcloth, came close, and hugged him. She pulled away before he could return her embrace. "Why don't you put your things down?" she said. "I am almost done here."

He went to his father's room. Squatting next to Lal's chest, he paused for a second, laying his hands lightly over the wooden lid. He opened it. The scent of metal bullets and the faint hint of death drifted out and upward. Memories gathered in his mind like a crowd of mourners. He laid each item on the floor, his mother's clothing, her broken-toothed wooden comb, her ivory wedding bangle, the doctor's vial of mint extract, Mr. Grewal's debt ledger, Ranjit's maroon turban, and now Yashbir's chisels and his father's opium pipe. Desa had added those, he knew.

He frowned, searching for Avani's elephant. He checked once more inside the chest.

It was not there.

~ ~ ~

"Have you ever drawn anything?" Junjie asked Baba Singh, who made a habit of visiting the artist in the afternoons.

"When I was little. But nothing like that," Baba Singh said, indicating the artist's latest masterpiece, an old woman with youth and naughtiness etched in her fine wrinkles.

Junjie nodded at the compliment. "What did you draw?"

Embarrassed, Baba Singh hesitated. "Birds and trees, animals sometimes. On a slate board. All children draw."

"Did you like it?"

Baba Singh considered the question. He had loved it. He had perceived things more clearly when he drew. The world had been more logical when he dissected it and recomposed it in chalk. "Yes, I think so."

Junjie continued to work. "Then why did you stop?"

"Things changed."

"That is just an excuse."

"I am not an artist."

Junjie glanced up, wiping paint the color of milky Chinese tea on his tunic. "That is obvious," he said in that infuriating way of his. "Did you do anything else?"

"A carving once."

"What did you make?"

Baba Singh self-consciously adjusted the baton in his pant loop. "I carved an elephant. For my sister."

~ ~ ~

Baba Singh's eight-year absence gave the view of the flatlands a surreal splendor. Striding down the dirt path on his way to Barapind, he stopped for a moment to remove his chappals and grip the warm earth between his toes. He was glad to be away, from Hong Kong, the ships and trains, and even from Amarpur. The town had expanded; about ten new shops had lengthened the main strip beyond the open market. He felt the need to escape cities and towns, to find a reprieve in the eternal open air.

He had not stayed long at the hotel. Simran and Khushwant retired to their room after lunch. Baba Singh heard them laughing, exchanging stories. He was left alone with Desa, who had grown taciturn and cold. He had wanted to ask her about the elephant, but he had gotten the distinct impression she would be cross with him for implying she had been negligent, or for thinking he had any right to ask at all.

He kicked a rock, watching it bounce and roll into the weeds. He felt his body loose and free in the airy cloth of his kurta pajama, no longer confined by the strict fit of his uniform. His eyes adjusted to the plains, the yellow mustard seed flowers, and the slight dusty haze in the spring air.

The rough waters and the smallness of Hong Kong were two things Baba Singh had greatly disliked about the city. The only visible distance had been out over the water—beyond the confusion of sailboats and steam liners—to the horizon. He had often focused on the line itself—the cut of the world where the ocean met the gray skies—trying to achieve a feeling of home. But the cold and choppy waves had usually just reminded Baba Singh of his months at sea, the nausea, the diseased passengers, the raucous children, the maze of passageways confining him to a tiny bunk with Khushwant. It was good to be home now, to stretch his gaze over firm land glowing with golds, greens, and hints of red.

He had spent most of his time in Hong Kong patrolling Des Voeux Road, where Junjie worked. The street was lined with tightly-packed, two-story shop buildings, some of which had tall spires protruding up into the sky. White banners with Chinese characters hung from jutting poles and fluttered about in the wind. Wires crisscrossed above the street, and the double-decker trolleys attached to them clanged by on tracks gouged into the concrete, the veins of the city. People walked, cycled, and pulled carts alongside the tram tracks and shiny Model Ts, Model Ks, and Business Coupes. Fresh and dried catch hung in open storefronts, the manta rays flat and lifeless. Behind the shops rose tenement complexes full of families crowded into small spaces, the white plaster on the outside peeling into dirty black streaks of decay from the cool, salty sea winds. Even before the Japanese invaded, taking advantage of the riots that forced the British out of China—Baba Singh and Khushwant along with them—Hong Kong had been a constant chaos that often seemed to compress and squeeze his mind.

Now, his spirits brightened as the sweet smell of burning molasses coated the breeze, freeing him from Chinese smells, the heavy odors of fish sauces and urine that had seemed to permeate through his clothing and into his very skin. He rolled the sleeves of his kurta up higher to wash those smells from his body, to bathe in the air of molasses and mustard seed flowers.

He continued on barefoot. The day was getting warmer, his brow sweating under the open sun. It was nearly noon when he approached the outskirts of Barapind, his feet coated with gritty dust.

"Baba!" someone called out.

He shaded his face with his hand and squinted toward the voice.

"Baba!" a villager shouted again.

In the distance he saw several men running toward him through the fields.

"It is so good to see you, Baba!" one of them said breathlessly as they all came nearer.

Smiling, Baba Singh shook their hands. "And it is so good to see you all, so many familiar faces."

"You came back," said a man named Onkar, a faint hint of bewilderment and amazement in his voice. Sada Kaur had written that Onkar's son had also joined the British Colonial Police Force and was now stationed in Singapore.

Baba Singh adjusted his bag on his shoulder and clapped his friend on the arm. He understood Onkar's disbelief. Returning was rare. The world gulped the men of the Punjab down with an inexorable hunger. "Yes, I came back," he replied. He looked around, opening his arms expansively. "Everything looks the same. It is like I never left."

"It is not the same, Baba," one of the men said, shoving his way in front of the others. "The government extended another canal to Barapind as well as two other villages because of the drought."

Onkar seemed suddenly tired. "But the water bosses followed the canals," he said. "They guard the water and demand payment for something the government already taxes us for."

"No one told me," Baba Singh said, disturbed.

"What is the point for you to worry?" Onkar asked. "For you and your family it has been no problem."

"But doesn't your son also send money?"

Onkar picked some dirt out from under his nails and did not reply.

Baba Singh was reminded of the humiliation Ratan had long ago suffered. "I am sorry, ji."

Onkar shrugged, then forced a laugh. "Maybe I will move to Singapore."

Having no words for such futilities, Baba Singh nodded with pity, pulling away.

Navigating the footpaths past rows of mud huts, others waved and shouted to him. He searched for his wife, wondering if she would also come out to greet him, but he could not find her.

Turning around a bend in the footpath, he finally approached his mud hut. Three bicycles were piled against the outer wall, which had been recently sprinkled with water. Two sun-bleached wooden chairs he had not seen before were set under a small awning. A water pot was by the front entrance.

A young, grinning boy, perhaps ten years of age, flew around the opposite bend, coming from the village center. The boy's dhoti was soaked, and his topknot was logged with water. It dripped down his face and onto his adolescent chest. He stopped short and stared at Baba Singh with big, terrified eyes.

Baba Singh knelt slowly before the boy. "Did you come from the pond?" he asked in a low voice.

Still frozen, the boy continued to stare unblinkingly. Baba Singh waited, not moving.

"Bebe!" the boy suddenly cried out, darting into the hut.

Baba Singh followed him inside.

The boy was standing in the rear of the hut, in front of the open cupboard filled with spices and pots. His hands were clasped behind his back, and he glanced nervously at the door leading to the other room.

Baba Singh smiled. He sat on a chair and waited. He shifted his gaze to study the hut's interior. The same painting of the ten gurus hung on the wall, more faded than it once was. A picture of himself in uniform had been tacked up. He remembered sending it, nearly six years ago. He had forgotten how much he had aged since that picture was taken, a popping flashbulb capturing his younger self. Looking at it now, he felt much older than thirty-two.

Prem's bedding was now soft cotton rather than the rough wool he had once used. And Baba Singh noticed a shelf that had not been there before, installed by the front door. On it was a row of wooden carvings, a cow, a bullock cart, a rudimentary depiction of a farmer pulling it, one horse, and even what looked to be Hotel Toor.

"Are those yours?" he asked. But a movement caught Baba Singh's eye before the boy could answer, and they both turned as Sada Kaur stepped out from the other room. Her cheeks were flushed, and her hair had just been brushed and freshly tied back. He noticed a comb in her hand, which she discreetly set aside on a small shelf. She had a hopeful but guarded look in her eyes.

"Hello," she said.

Baba Singh pushed himself tentatively out of the chair. "Hello," he replied.

She did not seem to have aged much. She still reminded him in many ways of the girl he had married. She had that same youthful sparkle, the no-nonsense primness in her lips. He wanted to touch her, remembering the silk of her skin.

Instead, he walked over to the shelf. "What are these?" he asked.

"Those are Satnam's," Sada Kaur replied, inclining her head toward the boy. "Satnam, say hello to your bapu."

Satnam, doubtful, stared intently at her for reassurance.

A twinge of jealously surfaced. Baba Singh had gone away, had become an invisible hand stretched across continents to fend off moneylenders and water bosses. His children did not know him.

She pushed the boy forward.

"Sat sri akal, Bapu," Satnam said, bringing his arms around front. He had been holding an object and set it on the floor at his feet. Standing straight, he placed his palms together, looked up shyly and smiled. "So nice to see you."

Noticing the object on the floor, Baba Singh cleared his throat, trying to cover a sudden rush of emotion. "Is that yours?" he asked, attempting to sound detached.

Satnam looked at it. "Desa Bhua gave it to me. Do you like it?"

Baba Singh smiled weakly. "Yes. I like it very much," he said, pulling his eyes from Avani's wooden elephant.

He had made it when he was still a boy, perhaps Satnam's age, had dug out a small tree stump that Ranjit helped shape into a suitable block of wood. For several days he was not able to do anything with it, was not able to see what was inside. But Ranjit told him the answers would only reveal themselves after the first stroke, the first chink in the wood. So, with a small, stone-sharpened knife, Baba Singh finally began with the toes and the arcs of toenails, which then led to the feet as he imagined the weight of the animal upon them. He rounded out the legs and then the body, gave it wrinkles and large ears flattened against its head, like a chastened dog, and a slightly open, playful mouth. He then carefully shaped the trunk. The three-dimensional wrinkles at the bend of it had been his favorite, the highlight of his ten-year-old accomplishment. He had once thought that little bit had been the most realistic, although now it seemed trivial. When he grew bored of the elephant, he had given it to Avani.

"Would you like to see the others?" his son asked, bending to retrieve the toy.

Sada Kaur smiled encouragingly at her son and moved to the shelf. She pulled the figurines down one by one, setting them on Prem's charpoy. Satnam took a cautious step forward toward the bed. "Do not be shy," she said, waving him closer.

"This one," Satnam said as he approached the charpoy, setting the elephant down and pointing to the cow, "was my first. Cows are easy." He chuckled but would not look up to meet his father's gaze. "People are more difficult." With a grimace, he lifted the farmer pulling the bullock cart. "See? He looks like clay." His face dropped. "I gave up doing people."

Sada Kaur touched his cheek with the back of her finger. "You can try again when you are ready."

Baba Singh picked up the farmer. "What made you interested in carving these things?" he asked.

Satnam pointed to the elephant. "This one is so good," he said. "I thought it would be easy."

"It is not easy."

The boy shook his head in agreement. He finally glanced up at his father, hopeful. "But do you like them?"

Baba Singh regarded the carvings circumspectly. Truthfully, he did not like them. He did not think his son understood how to breathe life into them. Their essence was wrong. Satnam had not paid enough attention to what they really were before coaxing them out and giving them shape. But Baba Singh no longer understood how to do that either. Junjie had taught him that perhaps he had never known.

~ ~ ~

"I do not like it," Baba Singh said, tossing his charcoal portrait on the ground in front of Junjie. "It is not right. You have made me look too much like a police officer."

"Well, are you not?" Junjie said, brushing the portrait aside.

Baba Singh knelt. He could feel his pistol holster digging

into his side. His leather jackboots creaked. "I am a farmer. I come from a village in India. That is who I truly am. You boast all the time that you see people as they truly are."

The artist gave Baba Singh a withering look. "Baba, this is how I see you. That is not my fault."

"Please try again."

Junjie shrugged. "Yes, but you are expecting too much."

They met, as they had the first time, in the artist's one-room flat. It was a shabby space. Everything was the black-brown of grime. It was threadbare streaks and stains, the first hungry signs of nature slowly nibbling at the floor and walls. The room was dim. There was only one small window looking out into a tight shaft. There was a mat, much like those found in prison cells, on which Junjie slept. It reeked of mildew. A closed cupboard hung on a wall, which the artist opened to remove some fresh sketch paper and stubs of charcoal. There was one chair. That was for Baba Singh.

Junjie lit a candle and set it on the floor. He never bothered with better lighting, never fussed about specific angles.

Baba Singh had asked about this during his initial sitting.

"Turning one way or the other does not change who you are," the artist had replied. "And light does not tell the story. Light distorts it."

So this time Baba Singh did not ask where Junjie would like him. Without being directed, he sat in the chair.

Junjie positioned himself on the floor, spread his materials out around him, and began to work. Baba Singh watched him curiously, unsettled after a few minutes; the artist seldom looked up at him.

Doubt seized him like a hand clamped around his throat. The original sketch began to gnaw at Baba Singh. Perhaps Junjie would produce the same portrait and mockingly hold it up as if to say that you cannot be anyone other than who you are. Embrace it. Admit it, and then go sink yourself in the sea if you must, smash against the docks into a million pieces. When they find you and put you back together, you will not have changed. This stiff, stern policeman is what you will be.

His palms were sweaty. The first time they had done this, Baba Singh had groomed for his sitting. He had combed his beard with extra care and tucked it neatly. He had smoothed his eyebrows and fussed with his turban until it was perfect. Once in the chair, he had maintained a straight posture, had fixed an expression of pride on his face, with just the slightest hint of an amiable smile. Now he slumped in defeat. He could not hide.

Was he rigid? Was he so horribly severe? Was that *it*? Was there nothing else to balance him out? Certainly there had to be. He could recall being soft. He had a wife, whom he sometimes could not remember, but whom he had certainly adored. They had held each other. Many years before, he had whispered sweet kindnesses to her in the night. And what about Kiran and Avani? He had loved them. Love and loss ached so painfully. It was all inside. He had never let that go. So why was it missing?

"Enough," Baba Singh said, his chest constricted.

Junjie paused, his charcoal suspended over the paper. "I am not finished."

"I don't care. I do not want another one. The first was enough." He stood and swept past the candle, nearly snuffing it out.

Almost at the door, changing his mind, he spun on his heel. "Let me see it."

Junjie wordlessly handed him the drawing.

Baba Singh gaped at it in disbelief. "What is this?"

The artist casually stood and replaced the charcoal in his cupboard. "It is you."

But that was impossible. Baba Singh's beard had been shaded the white of an old man. His turban was missing and he had no hair. His eyebrows were bushy tufts. He was not twenty-nine. He was old and creased, sharp wrinkles branching across his face. He was withered and exhausted. The other portrait had conveyed a sense of searching. Beneath the stiffness there was desperation for a kind of nourishment, a seeking of answers. This self, this future rendition was finished searching.

And by the look of it, he had found nothing.

~ ~ ~

"Bebe!" another boy shouted from outside the mud hut. "He is here! Quickly, fix your hair! It looks like a nest. He is coming!"

Baba Singh tore his gaze away from the elephant in Satnam's lap to glance outside the hut.

Satnam chortled, covering his mouth as Sada Kaur carried in a tray of tea.

The other boy, also water soaked, flew breathlessly inside, stopping short when he saw Baba Singh. Then he burst out laughing. "I am too late," he said, slapping his knee. Assessing his mother, he nodded with satisfaction and gave her a thumbs-up.

She pursed her thin lips as she set the tray down on the small table. "Vikram, this is your bapuji."

"Eh, Bapu, was it a good one?" Vikram asked Baba Singh, wiping a wet clump of hair out of his face and squeezing water out of his topknot.

Sada Kaur threw him a towel. "Not on the floor."

"Good one?" Baba Singh asked.

"Your face was so shocked!" Vikram said. He nodded toward his mother. "Her hair hardly ever looks like a nest. It is the absolute truth. Look how beautiful she is."

"Vikram," Sada Kaur said, her voice firm.

He flung the towel over his shoulder and clapped his palms together, attempting to be more serious. "Sat sri akal, Bapu."

Baba Singh smiled in acknowledgement.

"I meant the floor," Sada Kaur said with raised eyebrows as she threw down several more rags.

"Oh," Vikram said, attempting to wink at Baba Singh, but actually blinking. He chuckled to himself.

Satnam put Avani's elephant on the table and jumped down off his chair to help his brother.

Baba Singh watched his sons, the deliberate way that Satnam cordoned off the water with a rag, the slow circular motion of his arm as he methodically wiped the floor, the way he politely gestured that Sada Kaur bring over the iron bucket that was resting by the cupboard, the way he wrung the excess water into it. It was so different from Vikram's haphazard flinging of his rag back and forth, not cleaning it up but rather smearing the water around.

Done, Vikram plopped himself cross-legged on the floor, the wet rag flung over his topknot. Satnam wrung the last drops out of his rag and hung it over the edge of the bucket. He then sat with his brother.

Sada Kaur gave Baba Singh a cup of chai. She held the mug with both hands and leaned forward slightly, as if presenting it to him. She smelled like mint and ginger, like she had been handling the herbs before he arrived. They scented her hair. His heart quickened and he smiled at her. "Thank you," he said, receiving the tea and taking a sip. She waited until he nodded, then sat in a chair across from him.

Swallowing another sip of tea, Baba Singh realized his sons were waiting expectantly, staring up at him. He crossed his legs and leaned forward. Mug cupped in both hands, he rested his forearms on his knee. "Are those your bikes?" he asked them.

"Yes," Vikram said, grinning. "The rusted one is mine. I rode it into the pond once. It never recovered."

"We will need to get him another," Sada Kaur said. "It barely makes it all the way to Amarpur now. Sometimes he walks it home."

"That is only because the seat is like a rock." He rubbed his behind.

Satnam smiled. "You are too skinny."

From where he was sitting, Vikram twisted around, trying to look at his bottom. "This whole time I thought everything else was too hard."

Baba Singh laughed, and Vikram wink-blinked at him again.

"Vikram is in the second standard," Satnam said. "And I am in the third. We study math, science, history, Gurumukhi, Hindi, and Urdu."

"And we dance," Vikram said. "We practice at the gurdwara."

"Your Khushwant Chacha used to dance for Basant," Baba Singh told them.

Vikram's eyes brightened. "Maybe we can dance together."

"I am not so good," Satnam replied a little morosely. "I usually come home and help Bebe wash the animals."

Baba Singh smiled. "That is also good."

Sada Kaur looked pleased.

They heard the snort of a bullock outside and the metal clank of tools placed in a pile. Prem and a teenage young man, sweaty and dirty from an afternoon in the fields, pushed through the curtain.

Baba Singh rose in astonishment when he saw Manmohan.

Prem sat on his charpoy. "Hello Baba. It is good to see you again."

"Sat sri akal," Baba Singh replied, inclining his head with a reserved respect.

"Manmohan, do you remember your father?" Prem asked. "You were big enough." He kicked off his chappals and began to massage his feet, making faces of exaggerated agony and relief. He had not aged well. His cheekbones were prominent, and his leg hair had thinned, the veins beneath purple and thick.

Manmohan nodded slightly. "Sat sri akal, Bapu."

"You look so much like someone I knew," Baba Singh said, thinking of Ranjit.

Vikram rolled his eyes playfully. "Manmohan is the smart man. He is finished with school. He knows everything now."

Manmohan flashed a boyish grin, lightly shoving Vikram with his foot. He was so much like Ranjit, with that same upward tilt of the eyebrow, amused and confident, yet the world had so far left him untouched.

"You are lucky," he told Manmohan. He glanced at Avani's elephant then turned to the others, speaking with deliberation, enunciating his words carefully. "You all are. I hope you know that, really know it."

Yet, as his sons all politely nodded, quizzically, like he had gone mad, he knew they could not possibly grasp the significance of what he said. They did not know what it meant to lead such fortunate lives, what it had cost to give it to them, to maintain it for them. They had not scrambled out of the valley only to discover that the world was much bigger and more frightening than they had imagined. How could they appreciate their privilege enough to protect it if they did not comprehend that it could be lost?

When the family prepared for bed that evening, Baba Singh felt empty thinking of their faces, their lack of understanding. He reclined on his old charpoy, uneasy, a guest in his own home.

Sada Kaur was in the main room with the boys, helping to get their beds ready. Baba Singh waited for her, fidgeting. He was not certain of her anymore. Earlier she had inspired in him a charge of desire. Now he was sick with anxiety. What would he say? How could he say anything, how could he *do* anything after his many nights alone with Bao Yo, who had known him longer, who knew, simply because she was there, what he had sacrificed?

~ ~ ~

Bao Yo laughed her throaty laugh. "An old man?" she asked, amused. Then noticing Baba Singh's distress, she quieted, patting the bed with a pout.

He climbed on, the overused springs making him wobble as he crawled over to her. She languidly reached her bare arm toward him. "Do not take it so seriously," she said. "Junjie drew you like that because he hates you, that is all."

"But we are friends," Baba Singh grumbled.

"Still," she sighed. "He hates you. He hates us all."

She drew back the covers to reveal her sagging body. The site of it had once made him cringe, but now he settled down next to her and cupped his hand over her breast.

Truthfully, she was the most unattractive woman he had ever encountered. When he had first come to see her, he could not imagine how she made her living as a prostitute. What right-minded man would touch her? She had black teeth, her hair was thin and oily, and her features were small and placed too close together, as if when she was a baby her mother had suctioned her face.

But she had grace.

Those narrow hips of hers swayed like ship masts on a calm day. They had fueled her reputation, and men came panting. She was also older and therefore not giggly like the other prostitutes in the house. Baba Singh especially liked the fierce aggression behind her luxurious movement. She would not hesitate to tackle any man to the ground who tried to cause her harm, as often happened to women in her profession. And the things she said often entertained him, strange things in broken Punjabi with a thick Cantonese accent. She told him she would like to learn to wear a turban for him, then wrapped her head with the long dress she had just stepped out of. She said she would mount him twice if he paid a little more so she could buy herself some wine and cheese and eat like the French for a night.

"How do you know Junjie?" Baba Singh asked her, moving his hand from her breast to caress her stomach.

"I know everyone," she smiled. "Except your brother. Does he know what you do with me?"

Incensed, he tried to pull his hand away, but she firmly gripped his wrist and grinned wickedly. "You wish you were in love, like he is. I know. It must be painful to see that kind of devotion."

He relaxed his arm, but turned away, ashamed. She forced his hand back to her breast and squeezed his hand around it, moaning slightly. He was not sure if she was mocking him.

"Do not be upset," she said. "Not everyone is so lucky.

Most women are terrible creatures. Junjie was thrown out like garbage and—although he pretends he is not—now he is angry and bitter. The love of his life ran away, like a startled little gazelle. She threw him out when she learned he had been cut off from his parents' money. And I knew his father. They had a lot of money. You should move on. Empty your head of it all." She pretended to spit off to the side, exaggerating her point.

"My wife…" he began, looking at her.

"I am sure she is no better," the prostitute said. "Cold like a dead fish." She brought him closer and wrapped a thin leg around his waist.

He clutched at her, roughly seizing her thigh, her flesh swelling between his spread fingers. He tried to remember. Sada Kaur was not cold, not when up close. Her skin had been hot when he touched it. It had burned into him.

But she was so far away. He gritted his teeth. She might not even have been real.

~ ~ ~

There had been warnings and signs.

Baba Singh wanted to roll his eyes at them now, at the red flags of his past telling him unambiguously that there was trouble. But he had missed them. What could be done about it now? Forward was the only direction—the only option—available.

He was pacing in front of Yashbir's shop. Desa was there, on a stool Khushwant had brought outside for her. She sat sloppily, like a man. She slouched, her forearms resting negligently on her open knees, her mid-length salwaar hanging in the space between her legs.

"Stop it," she said.

He reigned himself in, took a seat on the ground beside her stool.

There had definitely been warnings. Some of what he had disregarded was excusable, like his mother's constant cramping and nausea. How could he have known what that meant? And there was his father's opium. But Baba Singh had been dealing with his own grief. He had been too overburdened—and young—to fully grasp the extent of Lal's.

But maybe he could have been more diligent the night he heard Kiran's voice. That still bothered him. And there was Mr. Grewal, but he preferred not to dwell on that for too long. He still had nightmares. And truthfully, if he was absolutely honest with himself, he had known what would happen to Ranjit. He could remember the feeling he had when his brother left for Amritsar. That itchy sensation in his mind, an annoying mosquito he had just swatted away.

And Junjie. He had seen that coming, too. In all fairness, despite a growing dislike for the artist, Baba Singh *had* tried to do something about it. But in retrospect he had not made enough of an effort. From here, standing on the other side of the savage Hong Kong riots, he could clearly see how easy it would have been to rescue Junjie before the artist was swallowed by the enraged crowd. He could have forcibly dragged him away, whacked him over the head with his baton to sedate him.

"What is the matter with you?" Desa asked, although Baba Singh could tell she did not really want to know. He had been fidgeting, rolling his hands, one over the other, like washing off soap.

Flattening his palms against the ground, he asked, "Why did you give Satnam Avani's elephant?"

"Because he liked it. Because you are his father."

"He does not know that I made it. He does not know whose it was."

"You two have something in common," Desa said. "Why don't you tell him?"

An old woman dressed in a white salwaar kameez was passing by. Her chuni was drawn up, but when she turned her head to him, he noticed that her hair was shorn, stubbly, soft like white, cut grass. She came nearer, stopping in front of Baba Singh. She bent and jutted her face toward him like a pigeon.

Baba Singh inclined his head politely. "Sat sri akal, Auntiji."

"Reopening?" she asked, nodding at Yashbir's shop. Inside, Khushwant and Simran were organizing and cleaning.

"Yes," he murmured.

She leaned closer to him and he looked at her inquiringly. After a moment, she sighed and straightened, waving her hand as if pestered by an insect. "I thought you would know me," she said, indicating her hair. "I thought it would be obvious."

"Auntiji?"

"Your brother, Ranjit, once worked for me."

Desa's eyes widened.

The widow chuckled at their surprise, then glanced regretfully down the sunny road. "I should go now," she said. "It is nice out. But a shift in the weather could undo me. I thought the wars would change things. All these women alone here, I thought I could just be another one of them, but it seems I am special. This town will never let me out of my long-dead marriage."

"I am sorry, Auntiji," Baba Singh said.

"I was sad to hear of Ranjit's death," she said gravely. "I sometimes feel responsible."

Glancing away tiredly, Desa said, "What could you have had

to do with it?"

"He was with me the night your sisters went missing. He never forgave himself."

Desa stood abruptly. "He would not have done that."

The old woman reached out a placating hand. "We were only friends. He was grieving for your mother and I knew something about grief." She exhaled heavily. "He felt he was expected to save everyone, and then the girls got lost."

She adjusted her chuni. "He was such a nice boy," she said, smiling wistfully. "He felt everything so much more powerfully than most of us." She again looked down the road. "I am so glad to have seen you both. I wish I could stay longer, but there are clouds approaching." She bowed her head and continued on.

Baba Singh watched her go, remembering her manhoo, how Ranjit had spent too much time in that woman's unlucky shadow. But it was too late and foolish to blame superstition. There had been signs, little clues that, had he paid even the slightest attention, had he given the slightest credence, would have changed everything.

~ ~ ~

"Get moving, Junjie," Baba Singh said, roughly pulling at the artist's tunic. "They will be here soon."

Junjie pointed in exasperation at his latest painting. "I am not finished with this," he said, jerking his tunic free.

Baba Singh gaped incredulously at the artist. "I am trying to help you!"

"I do not need your help."

"Des Voeux Road is a main crossing. That mob is serious. The whole city is lost. You will be trampled."

"They are tired of not getting paid for their work," Junjie said, dipping his brush in a blob of yellow paint. "That is how your British bosses treat this country. They have a right to be angry. They have been told they are worthless."

"Junjie, at this moment the reasons so not concern me. Just get away."

"You do not have to worry about me. You should be worried about yourself. I will not be harmed."

Baba Singh pulled out his baton and stared down the road. He could see smoke in the distance, down by the docks. "How do you know?"

Junjie stroked his brush across the canvas. "Because they are not angry with me. They are angry with you. We are not on the same side, Baba."

~ ~ ~

Whatever side Baba Singh had been on, it was not the wrong one. That much was obvious. People died on the wrong side. Or went missing. He crawled onto his charpoy in the mud hut's second room and closed his eyes for an afternoon nap. He was so sick of righteousness. *He* had not gone missing. He was here. He was home.

Tired, he tried to rest. After the widow had disappeared down Suraj Road, he spent the entire day helping Khushwant, Simran, and Desa clean and organize the blacksmith shop. Tomorrow he would be in the fields with Prem and Manmohan. He was reentering his routine, settling back into his life.

"Bapu?" he heard Satnam ask from the doorway. "Are you sleeping?"

Baba Singh peeled his eyelids open. "You are back from

school early."

"I wanted to show you. Look what I made." Satnam came closer, holding a new carving in front of his father's face. "Do you like it?"

It was a man. Or it looked like it might be one. It was at least human.

"It is you," his son said, smiling.

Pushing himself up onto his elbows, Baba Singh looked more closely. "Is that a lathi?" he asked.

Satnam's face dropped. "Yes," he said. "I thought it was obvious."

Baba Singh sat upright, setting his feet on the mud-paved floor. "Can I hold it?"

Satnam wordlessly gave him the figurine.

Baba Singh turned the carving over in his hand. He thought of Junjie. Every one of the artist's pieces had been an experience, a tiny life, a contained universe. He could not explain that to his son. He did not have the words to express how he had felt when, long ago in his own childhood, he had drawn on a slate board, or when he had stared at a wooden block until an elephant had emerged. It was clear Satnam would not understand.

Baba Singh returned the man figure. "Maybe you should do something else with your time," he said, but his son did not fully grasp his meaning.

"I knew it," Satnam said, crestfallen. "I am no good at people. But I can do another animal."

"No, son," Baba Singh replied.

He heard Manmohan and Vikram toss their bikes against the mud hut before coming inside.

"Maybe a frog," Satnam said, brightening. "I have not tried that yet."

Baba Singh sighed. "Come with me."

He took Satnam to the main room. Vikram was sprawled on Prem's charpoy whistling tunelessly, and Manmohan stood over him, hitting him with a small pillow, laughing.

Sada Kaur smiled at Satnam from where she was stirring a pot of cooking onions. "Did you give it to him?" she asked.

Before his son could reply, Baba Singh picked up the bucket, walked the small length of the room over to Satnam's shelf of figurines, and swept everything off and into the pail, including Avani's wooden elephant. They landed, one by one, with a hollow, metallic thud.

"Bapu?" Satnam asked. "What are you doing?"

Baba Singh knelt beside his son, the bucket between them. "Too many people have ruined themselves with this kind of frivolous thinking. It is better you know now so you can focus on something you are good at."

But Satnam still did not understand.

Sada Kaur rose from her stool. "You did not like it?" she asked her husband.

"I did not."

"It is just for fun," she said, wiping her hands on her salwaar. "There is no harm."

Baba Singh clutched the bucket to his chest and slowly stood to meet his wife's strict gaze. "He is still young," he replied resolutely. "But he is old enough to hear the truth. I will not tell him that the world is easy or good. It is not. It is a hard, horrible place. It is much better to be realistic, to see things how they really are. He should not waste more of his time."

"Please give them back, Bapu," Satnam said, nearly in tears now.

Baba Singh glanced down into the bucket, his face bleak. "I will not."

When he again looked up, he saw that Vikram and Manmohan were both staring at him. They were disappointed, which he had expected, but they also pitied him, which he had not.

~ ~ ~

A horde of men pushed against Baba Singh, and he stepped backward, groaning against the pressure.

"Push them back! Use your lathi!" another officer shouted.

They had been assigned to defend the docks, to reopen the supply ship flow that had been suspended by a raging and discontented labor force. Khushwant's face was red with strain. He gripped his baton horizontally, shoving it hard against the front line of the mob.

Baba Singh felt a tug on his belt. Someone had taken his pistol. Shots were fired. "Stop!" he shouted to the rioting throng.

"Baba!" Khushwant called, pointing to a Sikh officer on the ground. The world froze momentarily. There was a swell, and then the masses trampled the body, surging forward.

Baba Singh whirled and finally pulled out and raised his lathi. "Stop!" he said again. But the crowd melted around him and swarmed the docks. "Khushwant!"

"I am here, Baba! Come this way!"

Baba Singh forced his way through the mob toward Khushwant, the crowd thickening around him like a swarm of violently buzzing hornets. A Chinaman leapt in front of him and screamed madly, spraying Baba Singh's face with spit, "Better pay, better pay!"

Without thinking Baba Singh cracked his baton over the man's head. A line of blood dribbled down the Chinaman's forehead and off the tip of his nose. Eyes wide with shock, he fell backwards into the swarm of the mob and was dragged away by his shoeless, white-socked foot.

Baba Singh ran. He heard the sharp pounding of Khushwant's boots behind him as they abandoned their post.

"Baba, we have to go back!" Khushwant said, panting.

"I have to find Junjie," Baba Singh replied, still running, slowing only when they turned onto Des Voeux Road.

The thoroughfare had been rampaged. Many storefront banners were ripped. A trolley had been tipped over. It lay like a wounded lion. Paper and torn banners littered the street. Baba Singh stumbled over a telegraph machine and a spray of glass shards. The machine had been thrown through a window.

Junjie's corner was desolate. The artist's paints, pencils, paintings, and charcoal drawings were scattered, stomped on, ripped, and broken.

He was gone.

~ ~ ~

Baba Singh held Avani's wooden elephant and raised his head to the open, night sky. There was a good chance Junjie survived. For one's life it was such a little thing to abandon everything and run.

Baba Singh shook his head. No, Junjie would not have done that. Like his sisters, like Ranjit, he would have clung on, to his lofty devotion to art, to a girl who had never really loved him, and to the pain of his parents' rejection. And then he would have been ripped away and mangled, lost like the rest of them.

He set Avani's elephant aside and lifted the bucket of Satnam's wooden figurines, dumping them into the hole he had just dug. He gathered dirt into his palms, like cupping water, and let it trickle over the carvings. Then, with wide sweeps of his forearm, he packed in the soil, patting the mound firmly when he was done.

Better for Satnam to let it go, for a better life.

Picking up the elephant, Baba Singh dusted it off and held it tight as he stood and began the long walk to Hotel Toor, where he would replace it in his father's chest.

Heaven Bound in Brown Leather
1932

There was another place where Baba Singh imagined he existed. Another him. Another life. It was not far, close enough to be felt, visible just in his periphery, but also so far that it vanished when he turned to see the whole of it. Sometimes he sensed it in his nightmares, a beacon of shelter where nothing bad happened, but where he was not allowed to go.

There was a book in his lap, unopened. He sat in his chair, his palms pressed down flat on the tattered, brown leather cover while his family prepared for bed, his sons laying out their mats. He had already looked through the book earlier in the day, had already stamped onto his mind the star maps contained within, the vastness of space calling to him, dimly familiar. *Geography of the Heavens*, a line in handwritten Punjabi script read at the bottom of the inside cover. The rest was printed in the slanted flourishing swirls of English, which he could not read.

He had acquired the book from the astrologer, although books of any kind were not common on his shelves. Opiates and pendants were his specialties, as well as answers about the inscrutable minutiae of existence, of senses and second lives, of karma and God, of all things possible beyond human reason. Or so the astrologer often claimed. Perusing the shelves of elixirs and animal skulls, Baba Singh had searched for the answers to his problems in this otherworldly realm, but they were not forthcoming, stubborn as a hot, overworked bullock. Then he had come across the book, tucked away on a lower shelf, forgotten.

It was a shop rarity that had apparently been tossed away some months before by a British man, donated with what Baba Singh imagined was a condescending snigger, a sneer at the backwards, countryside people of India who would not be able to understand it, but let them try. It was true that Baba Singh could not read the book, but he nevertheless did understand it. Some knowledge was far more significant than that which could be articulated or transcribed. The maps told him of greater distances beyond his imaginings where he was certain he had been before, long, long ago when time had no meaning. Petrified of moving forward, he had bought the book to serve as hard, tangible hope that all was well despite the disgrace of his wretched life. Indeed, a great wisdom worth achieving was the knowledge that all events—however monumental they may seem—were categorically trivial down here on this humble Indian earth, even murder.

The book, however, was no match for the guilt he had accumulated over the past decades, and he could not so easily dismiss himself. Tethered to an unfortunate episode of brutality, he was still the same boy he had been after bringing Mr. Grewal to an untimely end. It had seemed to him like such a courageous effort to marry and move to Barapind, but truthfully he had never really moved here. His growth stunted by remorse and shame, he remained, even now, at Hotel Toor, living in the whitewashed walls of his bedroom where he had slithered off after leaving the moneylender crumpled on the floor, the man's spectacles twisted by his head.

Baba Singh slid his palms over the embossed title, curling his fingers around the edge of the book. Earlier that day, Khushwant told him that he wanted to sell the hotel, that it was time for them all to release the demons of their past, but there were over twenty years between the thirteen-year-old boy he still was and now. It was such a long, perilous journey to catch up.

"Simran is pregnant, Baba," Khushwant had told him. "I cannot start my family here." He put his hand tiredly to his forehead. "We have been living with ghosts. None of us has ever really said goodbye."

It was the tone of his brother's voice that stopped Baba Singh from protesting, that resonance of a childhood fraught with perils and devastating losses. "I will try," he had said softly, unable to suppress a conflicting sensation of betrayal washing over him like the river flooding the banks during monsoon season.

The edge of the book pressed hard into the soft, padded flesh of his palms as he now thought about his future cut loose from his past, about the strength that would be required to purge his particularly foul demons.

"Bapu, can I see it?" Manmohan asked, breaking his father's reverie.

Slowly removing his hands, Baba Singh allowed his son to slide the book away.

"An astronomy book," Manmohan said, opening the cover and running his hand over a picture of a constellation, enchanted by the dulled luminosity of stars on the yellowing, worn paper. "It is about the universe."

"What do you know of the universe?" Baba Singh asked, his voice quiet, but gruff, resentful at the narrowly scientific assessment.

Manmohan lowered his eyes. "Not very much."

Vikram and Satnam crawled under their blankets for the night, whispering conspiratorially. Vikram laughed, then with a sharp look at his father, covered his mouth.

Baba Singh ignored them. He glanced at his wife kneading roti dough, her forearm muscles flexing as she pressed her fists into the sticky mix of flour, water, and ghee. She would not look at him. She never did anymore.

His sleep was fitful that night, like the days when his nightmares had begun, before he learned to steel himself against them. The collective mass of stars crushed him beneath their omniscient eyes as he plunged his sword into the faceless man's chest. Beams of light flickered behind his eyelids, the whole night sky flashing with lighting and squeezing down upon him as he struggled to chop open the coconut at his feet.

He woke with a start.

Light sputtered from the other room. Climbing out of bed, his heart beating rapidly, Baba Singh found his son's oil lamp still burning, hissing quietly. Manmohan was sleeping, his sharp, beautiful features softened by shades of fiery orange.

Son of a murderer.

Geography of the Heavens was open across the boy's chest. Baba Singh eased it out from underneath his arms, sitting cross-legged with it on the floor. He ran his forefinger around the centerpiece map, moving from one star to another, constructing bridges, links in space, from the bottom of the page to the top, searching. When he had touched every star, he let his finger move beyond the page, until it hovered in the air.

Then his arm went limp and he slouched over the map.

Just before dawn, he set the book by Manmohan's head, turned the knob on the lamp, watched the flame die, and went back into the other room.

~ ~ ~

The months rolled by relentlessly, bringing to fruition all the change that Baba Singh had been dreading. He avoided his brother and sister during this time, remaining in Barapind, toiling in the fields, his back aching as he tended his spring crop, sweat dampening his clothing. His return to the hut in the evenings made him uneasy; it was an empty, long walk through the village to his hovel of tension where his wife and children treaded so softly around him. Yet it was preferable to suffer through such endless days of discomfort than go back to Amarpur where so much of his history was disappearing. Postponing the inevitable, he waited until it was necessary to resupply their sundries before visiting the emptied Hotel Toor to see the renovations Simran, Desa, and Khushwant had made to Yashbir's, where they would now live.

It was much worse than he had imagined. Working in collusion with the unrelenting, forward course of time, Khushwant had made insufferable modifications to things that should have remained eternal. He had built a second story above Yashbir's, in the process altering the lower floor almost beyond recognition. This was made harder to bear when faced with the actuality of Hotel Toor's sale, which had been finalized. Desa and Simran had packed everything, had moved whatever of Ranjit's furniture they had not given away into the blacksmith shop where Baba Singh could no longer recognize it. How would he be able to find Ranjit now that his brother's spirit had been shifted about? How would he know which charpoy had been Kiran and Avani's?

"I am glad you came, Baba," Khushwant said, leaning against the doorframe of Yashbir's old room where Desa was sweeping. The room would be hers now. The curtain had been pulled aside, her things, most not yet organized, lined up against the far wall.

Baba Singh soberly surveyed the shop. There was now a staircase where Yashbir's desk once was. "You have changed everything," he said bleakly, yet trying his best not to sound accusatory. Walking slowly across the room, he picked up the sledgehammer from the corner where it had been moved with the anvil, too far from the iron stove. "This does not belong here. Yashji had a place for his things."

Desa continued cleaning. She would not be baited. "He is not here anymore."

"Neither of you understand what this place meant to him. You could never understand unless you had the talent with metal that he had."

Stopping to look at him directly, she replied, "You do not have it either."

Baba Singh put the sledgehammer down, suddenly exhausted. "He believed I did."

"You threw it away."

Khushwant shot Desa a piercing look, shaking his head.

Baba Singh closed his eyes momentarily. "What have you done with his things? There were metal plates. His art."

Desa set her straw broom aside and approached him, taking his arm. "Baba, it is all here. Stop fussing."

"You did not have to change everything."

Whatever sympathy she had for him instantly melted. She turned back to her task. "Just go away, Baba. Whenever you are here I feel like I am moving backwards. We all do."

When he turned to Khushwant and saw a similar sentiment reflected in his brother's eyes, he could not speak. The swords, still crossed above the entryway to the bedroom, cautioned him with a silent reprimand, asking him to leave.

Out on Suraj Road, he wandered to the places of his past. Some, like Yashbir's, had been renovated. The train station platform had been rebuilt, the wooden planks still raw wood the color of golden wheat. The station had a new master. The old one had taken his family to South Africa where he had been given a promotion serving just second to a white superintendent. Baba Singh would never understand the British, their loathing one moment, their regard the next. And Mr. Grewal's money-lending establishment had been whitewashed, the exposed brick no longer reminding Baba Singh of what he had done. The changes were hateful, especially this last, asking him to forget. He did not deserve to forget.

Other places had entirely crumbled. Dr. Bansal's was gone, the building demolished, the empty lot lying bare, exposed to weeds and the elements. The doctor's name and his tale of intrigue were no longer whispered along Suraj Road. His mark upon this town was thinning, vanishing as the years passed.

Hotel Toor had been the only place impervious to change, stolidly resistant. It had neither improved nor was it falling apart, which, despite everything, was why Baba Singh loved it. Entering the lobby, now cleared of its furniture, he wondered what he would do without these walls and rooms to which he had always retreated when the pain of his nightmares sharpened.

He turned to leave, unable to understand this shell of a building, unable to grasp its new meaning. But as he placed his hand on the door handle, he heard a noise from down the hall.

"Get out. Let's go," he heard someone say. "We will be caught."

Baba Singh peered down past the six sleeping quarters toward the washroom. "Vikram, is that you?"

There was what sounded like a tussle, and then Vikram stepped uncomfortably out into the hallway. "Bapu, I am sorry. I tried to stop him."

"What is wrong? Did something happen?" Baba Singh asked apprehensively, taking wide, quick strides down the hall. Broken bits of plaster littered the tiled floor, and he saw with disbelief that the room where his mother died had been forced open.

"He wanted to see it," Vikram said.

Baba Singh gestured toward the room. "There was a reason we kept it closed. Don't you smel—" He froze when he saw Satnam inside, coming out from behind the door where he had been hiding. "What have you done?" he asked the boy, knees weakened by the scent of death that had not dissipated in all these years.

"It is just a room," Satnam said, his chin lifted defiantly, trying to disguise his fear. It was clear he had not expected to be discovered.

"You do not belong in there. Get out. We need to close it again."

Satnam's jaw tightened. "No."

Baba Singh strained to keep calm. "I will not ask again."

"We are always doing what you say, and we hate it."

"You are too young to know that I have only wanted to help."

Satnam shook his head. He was such a small boy, so frail for his age. "We were fine doing whatever we wanted. We were happy before you came home."

There was a pause of shock as Baba Singh slowly swallowed Satnam's words. Without warning, he swung his arm around high, bringing his hand down solidly upon his son's cheek. Satnam stumbled backwards, losing his balance, landing with a thud on the floor.

No one said anything.

Face hard as rock, Baba Singh turned and left them there, his fists tight, strained and white at the knuckles.

Once outside, he fled, running, clutching his heart, sinking fast, mumbling to the wind.

~ ~ ~

She was by the river. She did not know that he watched her while she bathed, fully dressed, revealing only parts of herself as she soaped her skin in segments, rinsing off with handfuls of water. Even alone she was entirely modest. Nonetheless she was alluring, exposing first a wrist, then a forearm, a smoothly polished shoulder.

He was not skulking, but he remained in the shade of trees off the bank where she could not detect him. The sweat of panic had almost dried, his legs no longer burning from his long run, his breath finally even. Now he watched her peacefully, not thinking of his misfortunes, of his innumerable failings. Not thinking of her accumulated and reasonable hate. He thought of nothing but the image before him, the exquisite softness of the moment, the reflective droplets on her skin.

His reverie was broken by cries of distraught children coming nearer, closer and closer until they found her. There were two of them, young boys, holding hands, one of them in tears. She waded out toward the bank, dropping to her knees in front of the one who sobbed, tenderly turning his head to see the wound on his face. It was red, inflamed, scorched by fingers.

She pulled him close, held his head to her soaked clothing, her eyes shut with sorrow.

She released him, looked once more at his wound, and then slowly they made their way toward the village, the three of them, together.

When they had gone, he remained, staring into the river, the image of her beauty seared upon his soul where not even she could touch it or take it away.

~   ~   ~

The hot August sun beat down on the roof and stucco walls of Hotel Toor with feverish intensity as Baba Singh, Desa, and Khushwant gathered in front of it. There was a man with them, nearing seventy, not too tall, modestly wide in the middle, as though life had cushioned him against the turmoil of the last several decades. A retired judge, his hands were soft and without calluses. Ink and paper had been his livelihood, as well as his weapons of war. He had been a tinkerer of laws, an Indian minion of the British who never saw the front lines, never fathomed the impact of his statutes during his tenure in office.

He appeared lost as he surveyed the town, his eyes finally landing square upon the hotel, undisguised disappointment in the downward turn of his mouth. "It was never pretty," he said ruefully, squinting up at the building with distaste.

"Have you been here before?" Baba Singh asked, suddenly curious about the previous era of the hotel, its service to weary travelers, its life as a usefully functioning member of Amarpur society, when its guest quarters were filled with the bustle of passers-through greeting each other in the hallway on their way to the lobby for dinner.

The man tapped the sides of his legs with impatience. "My grandfather's masterpiece. He had no real sense of architectural continuity or harmony. I had forgotten his horrible lack of refinement."

"Your grandfather built this hotel?"

"When I was a boy and our family had entrepreneurial inclinations." The man put his fists on his hips, nodding toward Suraj Road. "This town is nothing like I remember. It is grittier. I am not sure I like it anymore."

Khushwant glanced around. "A lot has happened here."

The man frowned. "I suppose I heard that."

"Are you alone, ji?" Desa asked him.

His face fell. "Yes," he replied. "My wife should be here, but she died last year. We spoke about it, the quaint little town from my childhood, before my father learned how to play politics. A return to my roots, so to speak, peace in old age." He straightened, wiping the moisture running down through his short, thinning hair with a handkerchief. "I could not get away in time. There was always so much work." He looked once more at Suraj Road. "It really is not at all like I remember."

"It is a very big building for one person," Desa said.

"I do not plan to keep it," he said. "My grandfather was really very proud of himself, but I think it will have to go."

Baba Singh turned slowly to the man, disbelieving. "Tear it down?"

"Something more suitable, I imagine. A nice little house will do, perhaps with a garden where I can take tea."

~ ~ ~

The tiles were cold and hard as iron beneath Baba Singh's back, the night around him slick as oil. He had lain down on the emptied lobby floor of Hotel Toor, where the reed chairs had once been, ticking away the hours in darkness until the sun fired rays through the windows. Sleep had been intermittent, and his extremities were cold despite the morning's promise of another hot day. Dozing, he turned on his side, his shoulder bone pressing into the tiles.

There was another presence in his dream. He sensed rather than saw it.

"Can't you help me?" he asked it, looking down the dirt road beyond the faceless man, feeling so small beneath the black sky. "I do not want to hurt him anymore."

"Possibly," it replied. "Possibly not. I do not know. I am not there yet."

Baba Singh opened his eyes.

The front door of the hotel swung inward, cautiously, almost curiously, until Khushwant was framed in the entryway, silhouetted by the bright morning. Before coming in, he turned first to nod to someone outside.

"Have you been looking for me?" Baba Singh asked him.

Khushwant nodded. "Sada came this morning."

"Did she?"

"When you did not come home, she wondered about you."

"I see."

"Did you manage to get any sleep?"

"Not much. I did not intend to stay the night."

Khushwant appraised his brother, the disheveled turban, the rumpled clothing, the dark circles under his eyes. "This is not a good idea, Baba, being here like this."

"What have you done with Bapu's chest?"

"Desa has it. She knows it is important."

"I never thought it would be torn down," Baba Singh said. He took a deep breath. "I really wanted to fight to keep it."

Khushwant regarded him sadly. "You are always fighting."

Pressing his palms into his eyes, Baba Singh asked, "Don't you feel them?" The lobby was full of echoes, murmurs of memory, whispers from another realm, cotton blooms brushing lightly against his cheeks.

"Feel who, Baba?"

"They are all still here."

There was a small noise by the door. Baba Singh sat up when he saw his wife enter.

"I told her," Khushwant said discreetly, raising a calming hand when his brother flinched. "Not everything." He sighed. "This is all so unhealthy. I did not realize how little you had shared with her. Talk to her," he said, leaving the room.

Baba Singh straightened his turban as Sada Kaur approached, stopping several feet away in the center of the lobby, waiting for him to speak.

"I know you hate me," he said.

"I have never hated you," she replied, but her tone was not forgiving. "Khushwant did not have to say anything. I have always known."

"What have you known?"

She frowned with irritation. "Everything. Your losses: your parents, your sisters. I was there when you lost Ranjit. I have always understood you."

"Are you angry?"

"Yes."

"I cannot get free," he told her, trying to explain.

Stepping closer, she leaned over him. With that same

bluntness she used to express every rational, logical course of action, she said, "Stop trying."

~ ~ ~

Rising from his charpoy, Baba Singh slipped his feet into his chappals. Glancing behind him in the dark when Sada Kaur shifted away from him in her sleep, he waited for her to be still. She had brought him home that morning, had fed him breakfast, had waved him off—almost affectionately—as he left to join Prem in the fields. In the evening, they had gone to bed. There was no tenderness in it, no warm advances, they did not even touch. Still, it had been an eternity since she climbed into bed with him without waiting for him to first doze off. He had been grateful, almost happy.

He went to the other room. Holding his breath, he carefully took *Geography of the Heavens* from the shelf where Satnam's figurines had once been. Tiptoeing past his sons and father-in-law, he went outside to sit in one of the sun-bleached chairs, opening the book to the center astrological map. But he did not look down at it. Instead he turned his gaze upward toward the open and sparkling sky. Chilly, he wrapped his gray shawl tightly around him, the reality of the cosmos imposing and intimidating.

He trembled restlessly. He felt that there was some business he had not yet finished. Gently closing the book and tucking it under his arm, he rose from the chair. Hesitating, he spun around, seeking encouragement, but he was alone.

He began to walk.

The moon was his only light for the five-mile stretch of dark, unpaved road to Amarpur. His heart pounded as he strode purposefully forward, the field of silhouettes around him much like what he had been dreaming about for over twenty years. A faceless man was with him; he could sense his presence in the air.

The walk was long, and he was afraid. It was almost two hours before he came upon the edge of town. Striding down the sleeping Suraj Road, he saw the twinkle of oil lamps at the train station far at the end. Mr. Grewal's was to the right, Dr. Bansal's empty lot to the left, then India Quality Cloth and Yashbir's and the astrologer's, until finally he turned down the side street that led to Hotel Toor.

The way to the universe—to that familiar place he knew with certainty existed because he knew with that same certainty he had been there—could not be found by conventional means, by maps of stars and plot-point coordinates. It came from somewhere closer and much less precise. Mustering his courage when he arrived at the hotel, he pried open the front entrance and went inside.

Exhaling softly, he groped toward the center of the lobby, sitting, waiting patiently until his eyes adjusted to the darkness.

"Hello?" he said softly, not sure what to expect, not surprised when nothing happened.

Feeling foolish, he set the book on the floor as a symbolic gesture meant to express farewell.

As he stood, ready to go home, he perceived a shadowy box that had not been there the previous night, black as ink in the corner. Frowning, he approached it, realizing even before he was able to distinguish it clearly that it was his father's chest. There was a scrap of paper on the top and Baba Singh went to the window to read it in the faint starlight.

Goodbye, and thank you, it read. Three names were scribbled beneath: Khushwant, Desa, and Baba Singh.

His jaw instantly tensed and he dropped the note. Agitated

he paced up and down the room, accidentally stumbling over the book.

Bracing against the wall, he caught his breath, considering the chest.

After a moment, he squatted down and clenched his teeth as he heaved the weight of it onto his shoulders, intending to carry it the entire five-mile walk back to Barapind. The edge of the wood cut into his shoulder as he made his way, chafing his skin and bending his back. But he persisted, stepping relentlessly forward through the flatlands, followed closely by spirits.

When he finally arrived home, spent and weak, he hid the chest under a tarpaulin outside, then slipped his aching body back into bed to lie stiffly next to his wife.

A Two-Story House
1935–1937

The world yawned. Baba Singh could feel it, a gateway opening.

He squinted beyond the worshippers bathing in holy water, across the manmade lake at the Golden Temple, the tawny plating reflecting the honey-colored sunlight of early afternoon, as if it were catching miracles and transmitting them to the masses of Amritsar.

Baba Singh was here, he knew, standing before this great monument of serenity, because Khushwant believed it was an ideal place in which to share possibly distressing news. He was probably hoping that coming here would forestall Baba Singh's potential descent into yet another period of utter despair. It had not been, however, necessary to go to such lengths. Baba Singh was determined not to be affected by the letter Khushwant had just given him, discovered in an old tin of Yashbir's things that Desa had long ago packed away, and which had been received some time after the blacksmith's death. He clutched it in his fist with detachment. Despite the sweat of his grip smearing the scribble of ink on the unopened envelope, he was calm.

To Yashbir Chand, the front of it read, *From Dr. Nalin Bansal.*

Khushwant gently pried his brother's fingers open and took the letter, smoothing it over his forearm. "It is very peaceful here," he said.

"Is it?" Baba Singh replied, still gazing at the temple, finding it beautiful in spite of how much he resented it. "I thought it was full of bad memories."

"It was, but I have been here many times since Ranjit died, and one day I reminded myself that he came here for peace. I think he found it."

"I cannot imagine that to be possible."

"It was a horrible day," Khushwant agreed, continuing to iron the wrinkles out of the envelope. "The gunshots were loud and never ending. People were trampling each other in their panic. But I could see by Ranjit's face that he did not even notice all the feet and dust and screaming around him. People were kicking me, scrambling over my head, and I shouted at him, grabbing his hand, but he did not speak. He looked at me as if I was the only thing worth seeing. There was no fear, only peace."

He fell silent, not wanting to share more.

Baba Singh had many questions about what had come next. He did not, however, ask them. He stifled them, shoving them into the folds and creases of his memory.

Khushwant returned the letter. "You should open it."

"There is no need," Baba Singh said. "It is too late." He gestured at the temple. "Come. They will start soon."

They circled the lake to a bridge, unfurled like an outstretched, welcoming hand for the steady stream of pilgrims who numbered in the thousands. They entered the main complex through a gate, a portal from the roaring metropolitan hum to the sweeping quiet of reverence and the murmur of prayer.

They found a place to sit in the enormous hall, the priest's voice echoing through the cavernous space as he read from the Holy Book. Baba Singh set the envelope down in front of his knees and bent his head, praying not to God, but to that letter.

His two portraits came to mind, the two that Junjie had drawn of him and which had long ago been stampeded into Hong Kong's concrete footpaths, crushed under enraged feet, charcoal staining the pavement, paper ground into oblivion. Both drawings had spoken of a bleak future, a hunt for contentment and liberation, a hauntingly regrettable realization that neither would be found. Junjie had seen more than the people he drew; he saw that all of them were on trajectories, unable to veer to avoid calamity.

Still, perhaps it was possible to change direction, if one possessed enough strength and courage. Not all men were doomed, as Junjie would have had his subjects believe. There had to be those whose lives ended in good fortune, if for no other reason than to provide balance in the universe. Baba Singh realized that he would simply need to earn it, to force himself on a journey of absolution so he could be worthy of the many blessings in his life.

In the swell of prayer he saw clearly what would have to come next. He had been living the last twenty-five years as if with a fever, his wife and three sons so far from him, existing only beyond the fog of his illness. He slept in a mud hut like so many others, so commonplace, the walls surrounding him containing no record of the unique hardships he had endured. There were so many of these unremarkable dwellings, fanning out towards the fields, all of them brown and ordinary, caked in dung, easily melted by storms, easily washed away by the tide of time.

He needed to make a statement of perseverance, of longevity and durability. A vision of a new and distinguished house came to him. It would be two stories supported by blue pine brought from the base of the Himalayas. It would have high ceilings, cement floors, a fireplace for crisp winter nights, corrugated iron gates to partition the livestock and waste away from the house, a room for the boys, another for Prem, one for him and Sada Kaur, and one to store foodstuffs. There would be an elegant archway at the entrance, a balcony above for sleeping on hot nights, a row of charpoys comfortably arranged where they would be able to feel the cool breezes. The exterior was the most critical detail: lime-washed outer walls, bright like sunlight, easily identifiable from afar, washing its own reflected miracles over the flatlands. He would need that. He would need to be able to find it.

Khushwant lightly touched his shoulder, and Baba Singh raised his head, disoriented. Glancing around, he saw that the service was over. Worshippers were already standing and filing out of the temple. He watched them go as the world continued to yawn, its maw growing wider, beckoning to him. He would build his house, something solid and able to endure, and then he would leave again.

It did not matter where.

~ ~ ~

Barapind's pond was muddy. The potter had been there to collect clay while they were in Amritsar, stirring up the sediments, clouding the water into a brown soup. Baba Singh kicked at the surface with his sandaled foot, watching it ripple and stir, briskly wiping his eyes. Dr. Bansal's letter was still in his hand.

"Just open it, Baba," Khushwant said.

Baba Singh closed his fist harder around the paper. "Onkar is talking of going to Fiji," he said, remembering the last time he spoke with his neighbor, the two of them squatting under the rosewood across the lane from the Toor's mud hut. Onkar had been subdued, his knees pressed into his armpits, arms lazily dangling monkey-like to the ground as he traced patterns in the dust with his two forefingers.

"My son married a Singapore lady," the old farmer had confessed. Despite his poverty, he was a very clean man when not out in the fields, his white turban always starched, his simple clothing unwrinkled. When he spoke, even to relay his own misfortune, it was always with dignity. "He never sent much money. Now he refuses to send any. He says everything has its limit." There had been a grey look about him then, his eyes losing focus.

Khushwant shook his head, picking off a sliver of bark from a nearby tree. He was irritated now, his once boundless tolerance no longer boundless. "If you go, you will take it all with you, all these problems of yours."

"Fiji is full of Indians, more Indians than Fijians, they say. The possibilities are enormous."

Khushwant grimly regarded his brother. Baba Singh felt as though he was shrinking, melting into the mud beneath his feet, but he narrowed his eyes in feigned anger to disguise his doubt.

They heard the sound of a military-issue motorcycle engine, a quiet rumble in the distance. Manmohan was arriving.

Khushwant tossed away the bark shaving and pushed his way through the trees to the lane. "You have not seen him for months," he said, iron in his voice. "Say something to him."

Baba Singh followed, glancing in the direction of the motorcycle. "He has never listened. What is left to say?"

"The British chose only five out of three thousand to do his job," his brother replied as they walked home. "It did not surprise me when he was selected. I have never seen a young man work so hard to be just like his father. Be thankful that he was stationed here, with you."

The rumble of the motorcycle grew into a roar that echoed across the farmland as Manmohan finally pulled around the corner, meeting his uncle and father in front of the mud hut. He cut the engine, leaving behind a vacuum of quiet.

"Sat sri akal, Bapu, Chacha," he said, removing his helmet, swinging his leg over the seat, and stomping his booted feet to remove the excess dust.

"Successful run?" Khushwant asked him.

Manmohan grinned. He had just been out delivering sensitive government messages across the Punjab, a nineteen-year-old boy gone for months on end in an abyss of hostile land where the possibilities of adventure were endless. "Always," he said, slapping clean his uniform, which was much like the one Baba Sing had once worn as a police officer. He then sat on one of the sun-bleached chairs to unlace his boots.

"Good man," Khushwant smiled. "I will be waiting to hear about it inside." Pushing aside the curtain, he greeted Sada Kaur and Prem.

As Manmohan pulled off his boots Baba Singh approached the motorcycle and gripped one of the handles, imagining the rushing air, the speed that was far more intense than riding a train to Amritsar. Touching the leather seat, he had the urge to climb on, to pretend that he was flying through the countryside. There would be no thoughts of Dr. Bansal, of whatever painful kindnesses were undoubtedly written in his letter, of betrayal, of the excruciating, deep-down ache of missing his friend who had uselessly sacrificed everything to save him. No complications, no one else, just the wind and the growl of the engine.

"It is loud," he finally said, impressed.

Manmohan clapped the bottoms of his boots together. "I will walk it through next time," he said, misunderstanding, smiling with a forced politeness before disappearing inside the mud hut.

~ ~ ~

The shape of Baba Singh's new house wavered ghostlike before him in the space where he would build it. He knew now that he had always had the heart of an artist, but he had been stunted by the events of his life. Now he would change this. Just as he had once carved an elephant from a block of wood, he would sculpt his new house.

It almost made him want to stay.

But there was time yet. A house of this magnitude would take at least a year, perhaps longer, to construct with his own two hands, with the seasons dictating his progress. He decided to relish the slow process, to appreciate each detail as a prolonged farewell in which every second was precious, every spread of mortar a part of what he would one day return to when he properly deserved this place.

Not everyone, however, understood the need for this sudden change, and there was a sort of restrained, non-confrontational dissent within the household ranks. His plan to first tear down the mud hut's second room in order to make space for the house's frame—squeezing them all into one room—followed by a period in which they would all be required to live under the tarp-roofed frame of the partially-built structure while Baba Singh pieced the entirety of it together, was not received well. The boys nodded bravely at the idea of losing their childhood home, smiling joylessly, clearly pained. Prem pointedly mentioned his age and how the onset of so much turmoil would only further aggravate his back, which was slowly bending him over into a permanent slouch. And Sada Kaur remained bleakly silent, suspicious of his plans at the conclusion of the endeavor. Baba Singh had known she would not be fooled, and this he regretted very much because they had finally reached a tentative understanding after years of uncertainty.

"Why?" she asked him.

"Because I need to see the results of the life I have worked for."

"Is that all?"

He touched her hair, something he had not done since before going away to China. "I am only trying to make peace."

The mood was further soured when, once they had torn down the mud hut's second room and crammed the livestock into the small courtyard where Sada Kaur did her cooking—all in an effort to clear space for the building's frame—there was very little time for construction. It was the fall planting season, and Baba Singh was forced to spend most of his days in the fields. The others could not, or would not, contribute: Prem was in no condition for physical labor, Satnam and Vikram were both in school in Amarpur and not inclined to help when they got home in the afternoons, Manmohan was often on duty delivering military messages, and Khushwant was far too busy running the blacksmith shop. Negotiations with the carpenter in Amarpur were also proving lengthy. It took several months to obtain cement mix and wood to be delivered by train from Amritsar. And just as Baba Singh had finally managed to lay the foundation, winter arrived, forcing them all into the tight space of the hut's remaining room for warmth.

The monsoons of 1935 were brutal and frigid. The project was entirely halted, and the pile of blue pine Baba Singh had purchased seeped up moisture from beneath tarps that did little to protect it. The family suffered through an uncomfortable several months, during which time they huddled together in the hut's confining quarters. Baba Singh dreaded every inescapable, empty moment of this period, alone with the doctor's still-sealed letter that dredged up the sludge of anguish, sharpening his nightmares and making him sweat under his covers when he slept. He also dreaded the forced nearness of his family, which amplified all the things unsaid among them, the hostility, and the defensive anger lurking beneath the surface. They should be grateful for this house, he often thought whenever his dreams and the cold nights woke him.

"It will be better," he once told the family as they clutched mugs of hot tea before bed.

"We know, Bapu," Manmohan replied. "Thank you."

But he was quickly rebuked by a sharp look from Satnam.

"Can't you imagine it?" Baba Singh asked his son. "It is more than any of us has ever had." But he could see that for Satnam—for all of them—it was not true.

Sada Kaur began to unroll the boys' mats.

"What could be wrong with wanting to give you a new house?" he asked her.

"There is nothing wrong with it," she said. "I am sure it will be lovely. We simply did not *need* it."

When the ice began to thaw and flowers forced their green shoots through the saturated soil, Baba Singh freed himself from the hut. He was eager to begin again, to shake off the thick blankets and shawls and his family's unwarranted indignation that had been suffocating him.

His plans to begin the moment he had seeded the fields, however, were again postponed when an old friend of Yashbir's approached him to propose a marriage between his granddaughter and Manmohan.

"Yashbir spoke of you," the man said to Baba Singh. "I cannot imagine a better life for my granddaughter than one with a family he loved as his own."

"It is a good match," Baba Singh told Manmohan.

"If you think so, I am happy to marry her, Bapu," his son replied.

"Yashji was a good man."

"I remember," Manmohan replied, which discomfited Baba Singh. He had forgotten that his children had once called the blacksmith their grandfather.

The girl's name was Jai, a tiny and demure sixteen-year-old creature, pretty in a plain and industrious way, her features square yet soft. She had dark, smoothly matted skin, the only mark on her face a small mole on her chin.

The wedding was scheduled for May, and after another month of preparations—during which time the foundation of the new house remained untouched—Jai and Manmohan were married in Amarpur's gurdwara. After she had moved into the mud hut, Baba Singh discovered that, despite her petite size, his son's new wife was surprisingly tough. She brought water in large clay pots from the well in the village center, seemingly without any effort at all, her breath as even as it had been when she left with the pot empty. She lifted heavy spice bins and carried them out back where she could more easily mix masala for curries, never asking for help. And her smallness more easily allowed her to maneuver the crowded hut that now housed seven people, lifting and leaning charpoys along the wall to create space for sitting, cooking, and weaving.

They were all fond of Jai, particularly her poised and unruffled gentleness in the face of Prem's constant diatribes about the delicacy of his age and condition and the disrespect of being forced to live in such uncomfortable circumstances. She was quiet and unassuming, but provided strong and certain reassurance, her presence easing tensions that had long ago affixed themselves to the heart of the family.

By the time she settled in, spring was well underway, and although the season was warm and fresh, they had only until June before the monsoons arrived again, which did not allow much time to work on the new house. Row upon row of crops needed harvesting, after which the ground needed to be plowed and seeded. Baba Singh made small steps in the evenings by the light of hurricane lamps. By the end of spring he had managed to tear down the mud hut's last remaining room, lay the rest of the foundation, and finish erecting the house's frame.

"What will happen after this?" Sada Kaur asked him as he secured a tarp over the roof.

"We will have a house," Baba Singh said as he climbed down.

"It is too big. We will be separated by all these rooms."

He sat on one of the charpoys Jai had set near the future pantry. "It will be beautiful."

"You can stop any time," she told him. She spoke softly, tapering her usually stern tone.

He gestured around him. "We cannot live like this."

"There has never been a problem with the way we live."

"This is not what I want for you," he replied, lying down,

exhausted.

She lit a flame under her cooking pot. "Do you know what I want?"

But he had already turned over, pretending to be half asleep because he was not able to answer her.

By 1936, the house, supported by beams of blue pine, had finally developed flesh of Punjabi mud brick and mortar. Several months later, at the turn of another year, Baba Singh finally gave the house a roof and doors and filled it with furniture. He used his wife's old spinning wheel as a decorative piece in the main sitting room and bought Sada Kaur and Jai an imported sewing machine for their needlework. Opposite the spinning wheel was an empty trunk carved ornately with panels of Sikh battle stories, reminding Baba Singh of his many losses, but also suggesting a glorious future victory. Sada Kaur and Jai spread several chairs across the main sitting room for receiving guests, including a comfortable, cushioned reed one for Prem outside his ground-floor bedroom, above which hung his tattered, old picture of the ten gurus.

Vessels filled with flour and spices flanked the door leading to the foodstuffs pantry where there was a large, loose pile of red maize flour on the floor and stacked burlap sacks of rice along the walls. The kitchen had ample counter space and open shelves for plates and cooking utensils that led to an enclosed courtyard in the back where Sada Kaur made flatbread in her new clay tandoor. In the center of the courtyard Manmohan planted a mango tree and a garden of jasmine, chilies, and herbs.

Upstairs the two sleeping quarters were furnished with cotton mattresses in lieu of charpoys, both leading to an expansive balcony that overlooked the entire northern side of Barapind, the ring of mud huts thick around the center, the hint of the well beyond the neem trees.

Baba Singh stood on the balcony facing his village, his clothes splattered with paint, his hands calloused, his nails broken and frayed, like this land that was still being ravaged by the British, by their mongrel moneylenders, their recruiters, their soldiers who soaked the soil in so much death and anguish. He was sorry for all of it because he loved his village so much.

The sun struck the newly lime-washed house with brilliant force, and his face felt hot as he gazed out into the distant fields, knowing that when he was out there he would never lose his way back.

Satisfied, he went inside to the room he shared with Sada Kaur. He was alone. Lal's old chest was shoved to the corner, still covered with a dhurrie rug. He threw the rug off, thinking that he might look inside. But seeing it now, he realized he had no desire to sift through the items within. It was enough to possess them, to have them here with him.

He removed the doctor's letter from his pocket. It was still sealed, but the envelope had been softened over the years, the edges torn, the paper thinned.

"Is the elephant in that chest?" Satnam asked his father from the bedroom doorway. "Is that where you keep it?"

Baba Singh turned and saw his son—that poor, subdued young man too soft and meek to survive this village—and a mighty wave of resignation, like the giant stormy swells breaking against the Hong Kong ports, flooded his bones. He had the compulsion to speak candidly to Satnam, to confess something important. "How did you know I kept that one?"

"Desa Bhua told me about it."

"It was never supposed to be yours. It was not hers to give."

Satnam hesitated, and then he said in a timid voice that he no doubt intended to sound brave, "What happened to your sisters?"

"I would rather not talk about them," Baba Singh replied, folding the letter and again putting it in his pocket. He could not start at the beginning. Instead, he gestured that Satnam join him on the balcony and pointed at one of the village huts. "A girl is interested in you. Her father would like to have us over for tea."

Eyes set uneasily on the potato crop beyond the village, Satnam stepped close to the balcony's rail and rested his forearms on the warm wood.

"Kuldeep's daughter, Priya," Baba Singh told him. "She likes you, and Kuldeep seems to think that you like her."

"I am not sure about marriage."

"Marriage was my best chance to start over."

"Did it work?"

Baba Singh thoughtfully pulled on his lower lip, suddenly wary, now worried that he might betray too much. "For a time it did," he said. He regarded the view, the sky a hazy blue, patches of clouds on the horizon. "But now I think it is time again for something else."

Satnam nodded behind him at the house. "Is that why you built this?"

Baba Singh regarded his son carefully, searching the boy's eyes for something, and then he said, "I built this house so that it would always be here, even if I was not."

~   ~   ~

"I will not go with you," Sada Kaur said flatly. She looked stunning in her purple and green sari, but she was tired after the tonga ride from Amarpur's gurdwara where they had just celebrated Satnam's wedding. And she was angry.

She unwound the yards of fabric, tossed the sari aside, and stood before him in her tunic and petticoat. Baba Singh led her to a chair in the corner of their bedroom and kneeled beside her. "Fiji has a large community of Indians. We will be very comfortable. Onkar went. He is there. Families are starting businesses and trading."

She shook her head. "You do not even truly want me to come, or expect me to. You only ask because you hope to disguise the fact that you do not want to be near the things that could possibly make you happy." She pulled her hand from his. "What were your reasons for leaving the first time? Was it to give me what I wanted, to give your sons what they wanted, to give us something that you did not have?"

"Yes, of course."

"No. It is what you have always told yourself, that it was about me and about them, but it is not the truth, and I can see that you know that now, that you are not lying to yourself anymore. It was always for you, to make up for some loss of your own."

"I wanted to give you all safety so that you could avoid my losses."

"But you wanted us to do it your way. There was no room to exist outside your losses. We have always existed within them." There was reproach in the cut of her single eyebrow. "What is so wrong with the life we have here?"

He stood and strode across the room, pacing. "Everything is wrong with it. Nothing is right. There is so much bad feeling."

"That is not our fault."

"I do not want to be here and farm and have this life, acting like none of it ever happened."

"Like *what* never happened?" she asked, standing to face him, the toes of her bare feet peeking out from under her petticoat. "Would having a life elsewhere change anything that has ever happened?"

Feeling hot, he removed his turban and tossed it on the bed. The air was cool on his scalp through his thick hair. "I do not know," he replied.

"I know you will ask them to go with you for the same reason you have asked me," she said, lowering her voice. "I will not, but they will go."

This surprised him.

"They would do anything for you," she said. "I know them, each one of them. They think that if they go, they will finally hear that you approve."

"They hate me," he said quietly.

She glared at him. "You want them to hate you. But where there is hate, there is a need for love."

She then shoved his turban off the bed and climbed in. He did not move for a while, and she lay there with her eyes wide open, staring up at the ceiling. Finally, looking regretfully at his wife, Baba Singh dragged a chair out onto the balcony. Lighting an oil lamp, he thought that if someone were observing him from a mile away, he might appear to be a star hovering close to the earth.

He pulled out Dr. Bansal's letter from his pocket and stared at it for a moment before finally tearing it open in frustration.

My dear friend Yashbir,

It has been a while since I have been able to write. I am sending my best wishes from

Calcutta prison. It seems that after so much moving around, I have made it home after all. My circumstances have been ironically fortuitous. My mother has come to see me. I never stopped writing to her, and once she knew that I was home, she finally came to make peace. It was not easy to move beyond our regrets and unhappiness, but she is sorry for all the years we have lost. I am very happy.

I will not write again. It is time to let go of Amarpur, but I am grateful to have known you. Please, if Baba remembers anything about what happened, tell him that this life works so strangely. I do not want to be found, and he does not need to worry. There have been very difficult periods, but my choices have also given me so many blessings. Guilt is a waste. He should know that we are only able to bear so much, that sometimes things are so heavy that we burst. But even what seems like the worst can be forgiven. He should do everything possible to release his guilt. Tell him to eat a ladoo. It always helps.

A happy life Yashji,
Nalin

Refolding the letter and reinserting it in the envelope, Baba Singh was flooded with a rush of relief. He smiled faintly, remembering the animated, brimming spirit of his friend.

Stepping inside, he glanced at Lal's chest under the dhurrie rug, thinking that this time he would take it with him. When he was ready, he would abandon it out in the world where the history inside could no longer touch him. He would do as the doctor had said and release his ghosts, returning unburdened to his village.

Sada Kaur had fallen asleep. He approached the bed and moved a strand of loose hair from her face. Bending, he whispered with conviction into her ear, "I will come back."

Part II
Manmohan
Greater Suva, Fiji

Plastic Toy Tools
1947–1948

The kitchen cupboard was a portal, an entry to a black hole, like the ones Manmohan had read about, that sucked even light into its vacuumous mouth. He stared helplessly up at it, gathering his courage, one hand gripping the kitchen counter, the other poised on the knob of the cupboard door, until finally, in spite of himself, he pulled it open. A store of memories flooded forth when he saw, there on the top shelf, the handmade plywood box that he had not opened since 1945, just after Darshan died, and which contained the few trinkets of his son's short life. That was how black holes operated. They dredged up even the most deeply buried feelings until there was nothing left but emptiness.

"Let's fix, Bapu," his son used to say. "Let's go. Let's play." Let's. As in, let *us*. Manmohan missed that.

He still had Mohan, but his oldest son did not seem to need him the same way. Manmohan had hoped losing Darshan would bring them closer, but even now, at nine years of age, Mohan possessed a clear sense of self-sufficiency, an ability to cope that Manmohan never had and greatly envied.

This was particularly evident on the one-year anniversary of Darshan's death, after they returned home from the memorial service at the Sikh temple in Suva. Manmohan had thought it would help to spend some time with Mohan after the service. But the moment they arrived home, his son scooped up his soccer ball and headed toward the front door.

"Wait," Manmohan said. "Where are you going?"

"To play a game with Narain," the boy replied.

Manmohan sighed. "I thought we could sit together for a while."

Mohan glanced impatiently at the front door. "Sit?"

"We saw a lot of sad people at the temple today. Maybe you want to talk about it."

"About what?"

"Don't you miss your brother?"

Manmohan would never forget his son's expression then, the perplexity, the discomfort and confusion. But they had both lost someone. They were supposed to be mourning together. "Well, don't you?" he asked again.

He could not recall his son's answer, only that Mohan had gone to play his game of soccer.

Now, staring up at the top shelf, the loss of togetherness Manmohan used to share with Darshan pinched his heart. His hand tensed, ready to shut the cupboard, intending to leave the box there for eternity, or at least until the solar system had reached its end and the box would be disintegrated in a roar of planetary collisions.

But it was, however, necessary to open it. Jai had gone into labor that morning. He had already checked her into Colonial War Memorial Hospital. He could not imagine meeting this new person, welcoming him or her into the family without at least trying, after all this time, to say goodbye.

He reached up and pulled the box down, marveling at how light it felt. For some reason he had expected it to be weightier, but he supposed it made sense. The effects of a boy who had lived only three years would not be very heavy.

The box brought to mind his father's chest that had come from Hotel Toor, the one that had been hidden away under a dhurrie rug in the years before they all traveled to Fiji. It was now shoved in some corner of the house on the outer island where Baba Singh lived with Satnam. He suspected that the chest was full of sad memories, that it contained a number of sentimental artifacts, proof that people who were now gone had been on this earth; keeping their possessions meant still having a small remaining sliver of them that was tangible. It surprised Manmohan to realize he shared this with his father, that he could relate to the propensity to do such a thing.

Taking a deep breath, he carried the plywood box past the chrome-rimmed kitchen table and vinyl-upholstered chairs where Mohan was eating his cold lunch of lentils and roti. "Hurry up. And you better change your clothes before we leave," he told his son, who nodded obediently.

On his way through the living room, Manmohan was conscious of the black-and-white family portraits hanging above the couch between a framed painting of the ten gurus and a black and gold tapestry of Fiji's main island. The portraits were serious, unsmiling faces captured with his flash-bulb camera. The photograph just left of the center was the only picture he had ever taken of Darshan. It was hard to see the detail of it from where he now stood, but he knew that picture well. The snap of the flash had made Darshan laugh. His son had been looking directly into the lens, the only smiling face on the wall. Manmohan had taken it one morning while testing out the camera he had just purchased. After that, there had not been enough time for more pictures.

He shoved aside the sheet that curtained the glass door leading to the backyard and stepped out onto the cement patio. Sitting on one of the two wooden chairs he had built the year they moved in, he placed the box between his leather-booted feet.

Regarding his boots, newly buffed but worn after years with the Fijian police force, he thought that he should go change out of his uniform before heading back to the hospital. He had already been dressed for work when Jai's water broke and had been in a rush after that. He had to send a courier to the outer island to fetch his father before rushing to check Jai into the hospital. He had to get her settled before driving to the ferry to pick up Baba Singh—and unexpectedly, Satnam's wife Priya as well. He had to drop them off at the hospital before pulling Mohan from school and bringing him home for a quick bite of lunch. The thought of going to the bedroom now, unlacing his boots, undressing and redressing seemed unnecessarily tiring after the morning's running around. The snug feel of his boots was comforting. He did not want to take them off.

He flipped up the box's metal latch, the lid squeaking on its hinges as he lifted it open. Darshan's soft, grey hospital-issue blanket was at the top. Unfolding it, he held it to his face, disappointed that it smelled of wood, remembering how difficult it had always been for Jai to put Darshan to bed. His son had never wanted to sleep.

Draping the blanket over his shoulder, he frowned slightly at what was underneath. There they were, the two halves of a coconut shell. He had never been able to determine where the coconut had come from, or why it had been tucked under Darshan's arm. Although he knew that Hindus regarded the coconut as an object of worship and offered them to their deities, coconuts had no major significance for Sikhs. The doctor had been a Hindu, but Manmohan had long ago dismissed the idea. The doctor had never been alone with Darshan. Perhaps it was Baba Singh, who had been the last one in the room before Manmohan went in to find Darshan no longer breathing.

The recollection was disquieting, especially now. His father had been talking lately of having vivid dreams. He said they were messages.

"You will have a boy," Baba Singh had told him several times over the last few months.

That alone was not particularly unsettling, though admittedly strange. What troubled Manmohan was that, because of those dreams, Baba Singh insisted that the baby's name be Darshan. His father behaved as though he knew something the rest of them did not, but Manmohan had never known his father to be wise, only rigidly distant. It was best, however, not to argue the matter. He would pay for it dearly— as he always did when he disagreed with Baba Singh—with shame and embarrassment. Nevertheless, it annoyed him to feel so inconsequential in the issue of naming his own child, to feel so compelled to obey.

Setting the shells on the cement next to the box, Manmohan peered down at the last item within, a cotton sack filled with plastic toy tools. Resting his elbows on his legs, he scrutinized the sack as though touching it would reduce it to dust.

Just then Mohan flung the curtain aside, joining him on the patio, crumbs of his lunch at the corners of his mouth. "What are you doing out here, Bapu? You did not eat anything."

Manmohan pursed his lips in exasperation. "You have not

changed your clothes."

Mohan glanced down at his Samabula Government Boys School uniform. "You said we were in a hurry."

"There is a little time."

"But you haven't changed either," Mohan replied, bending down to peer into the box. Then he glanced questioningly at his father. "I remember those tools, that bag he used to carry them in."

"Yes." Manmohan nodded, tugging the blanket off his shoulder. He carefully folded it, squaring up the corners and hems.

"Can I open it?"

Manmohan eyed his son for a moment, until finally he gave in. "Just be careful."

Mohan pulled the sack out and sat cross-legged on the cement. He shook out the wrench, the hammer, the two screwdrivers, and shovel, all of the tools landing with a hollow clatter on the cement.

"Be easy," Manmohan said, gently laying the blanket on the bottom of the box and nesting the coconut shells on top of it. He took the empty cotton sack from Mohan, an onset of apprehension making him want to stop this nonsense. "Maybe it is better if we put these away and get going." A large drop of rain struck the soil just beyond the patio. He gazed up into the darkening sky.

Mohan brandished the hammer. "Can I keep this one?"

"What would you do with it?"

The boy shrugged.

Manmohan hesitated, considering the hammer in Mohan's hand, the brown paint of the handle meant to give the impression of wood, the line down the middle where the plastic had been cut on some assembly line. His son waited hopefully, stirring Manmohan's sympathies at the idea that this was an expression of the boy's grief.

"Please do not lose it."

"Thank you, Bapu."

"Maybe you and I can so something together when we get home."

Brushing aside several hairs that had come loose from his topknot, Mohan asked, "What do you suppose?"

Manmohan collected the remaining tools and replaced them in the cotton sack. "You have any ideas?"

"I hadn't thought about it."

Manmohan set the sack inside the box, closing and latching the lid. "We should go."

When he replaced the box on the top shelf of the cupboard, knowing that it was not possible, he nonetheless imagined a slight change in its weight: a short life minus a small piece.

The day's tropical rains began to fall, first in thick, sporadic droplets, then a rushing sheet battering the corrugated tin roof of the front door overhang. It pelted them sharply as they ran toward Manmohan's used World War II truck. Flinging the vehicle doors open, they clambered into the solid steel cabin, drenched. As the downpour hammered the windshield, and the humidity entered through the ventilation slits in the side panels, Manmohan glanced behind him at the six-foot cargo bed, wishing he had not forgotten to throw the tarp over it. He was fond of his truck, had purchased it the year the war ended. With its walking beam suspension and locking differentials that had made it such a useful off-road vehicle during the war, he easily traveled the poorly paved roads throughout the island. Noting the rust along the steel bed, he thought that he would have to treat it soon.

As abruptly as the rain had begun, it stopped, leaving the

ground wet and steaming in the heat. Adjusting himself in his seat, using the hem of his shirt to dry his face, Manmohan inserted the key into the ignition. "Ice cream?" he asked as they pulled away from the curb.

Absently tapping the plastic hammer against the dashboard, Mohan grinned, his face bright and wet. But then his expression fell. "Bebe is waiting for us."

"There is always time for ice cream," Manmohan replied, although he was not entirely certain about it.

The diesel engine grumbled as they drove down the hill away from their house in Tamavua toward the hospital in Suva, past large palm trees and verdant jungle that blanketed every inch of soil. The last vestiges of ocean view disappeared as they descended toward the small city.

They had been living on the island now for nearly ten years, which often astonished Manmohan. He had truly believed they would be back in Barapind by now. After their initial weeks on the quarantine island of Nakulau where immigrants were taken for processing, forced to eat rice crawling with worms, and sleep on the hard ground like animals, Manmohan could never have imagined one day calling Fiji his home. Jai had been nine months pregnant with Mohan. He hated to see her eat that food, but she merely smiled and picked out the bad parts. She never once complained.

Even after they had cleared processing and docked in Suva, it was Manmohan who had the most trouble with the constant tropical rains, the mosquitoes that made his legs and arms swell. The Toors spoke Punjabi, Urdu, and Hindi, but Indians on the island spoke an unfamiliar dialect of Hindi that had been initially bewildering. It was too distorted. They were too far from home.

And he had hated the little shanty they all initially shared in the city the first few years: he, Jai, Baba Singh, Vikram, and Satnam and Priya. Squeezing into that tiny shack, sweltering in the humidity before saving enough money to live civilly again had been one of the hardest and longest periods of adjustment.

In the beginning, he also disliked the natives, a tall, dark-skinned, seemingly fierce people. He had been affronted by their strict unwillingness to associate with Indians, an attitude that had sharpened during World War II. Jai, however, had pointed out that the segregation worked to their advantage because they were free to maintain their cultural inclinations with little outside interference or influence. "It is hard to tell if we are in *desh* or *pardesh*," she had once joked. *Home or away from home.*

In many ways, she had been right. An array of Indian-run shops stretched along Victoria Parade, comprising a commercial district of grocers and tailoring enterprises. The stores, many of them wooden structures erected in the early 1900s, were like those Manmohan had frequented in Amarpur. A chemist's shop—much like the astrologer's—sold painkillers and balms. Spice shops perfumed the streets with cumin and chili. The men who gathered near the seaport to watch the tall masts of ships approaching from Sydney and Auckland—a mix of Hindus with red-stained mouths from chewing betel leaves, Muslims wearing their taqiyah caps, and turbaned Sikhs—reminded Manmohan of the men in Amarpur meeting to chat at the open market.

The Indo-Fijian community was sizeable on the island, perhaps equal to that of the local Fijian's. Although primarily Hindus, Madrassis, and Muslims, the Sikh community—established before the turn of the century—was nonetheless strong. Like the other Indian groups, the Sikhs had their place of worship, a gurdwara centrally located in Suva on a hill across the street from Mohan's school. There were also a decent number of grocers and textile shops run by Sikhs. Despite the stark differences between the dry, flat plains of the Punjab and the rolling green abundance of an island thick with ferns and cane palms surrounded by swells of blue ocean, Manmohan had come to appreciate that at least the faces were familiar.

Though Suva was similar in some regard to Amarpur— both towns comprised of wood, iron, and corrugated tin— Suva was larger and hillier, more populated by cars, an infant metropolis. Manmohan wove through the one-way streets past the colonial wooden buildings along Victoria Parade, around the angled intersections and contorted loops that he once found confusing but now navigated with confidence, coming to a stop at Raj's sundry shop.

"Let's not take too long," he called to his son, who had already jumped out without waiting, slamming the door and darting across the street toward the shop.

A bell chimed as Manmohan stepped inside the store to find Mohan already rummaging through the freezer.

"Sat sri akal, Raj," he nodded to the shopkeeper. "A kulfi stick for him."

"My wife says it is almost time," Raj said, leaning his elbows on the counter.

"Yes. Almost."

Mohan held up a cardamom-flavored ice cream bar.

"I will also have one," Manmohan said, taking a stick from his son and pulling off the wrapper. He bit into the cold cream, his teeth aching. "Tasty," he told Raj.

The shopkeeper smiled. "On me."

"No, no." Manmohan shook his head, leaving some Fijian dollar notes on the counter. "I have to pay for Jai's shopping the past month."

Raj momentarily checked his books. "I had almost forgotten," he said, putting the money in his till.

"What about your wife and daughter?" Manmohan asked, taking another bite. "Are they well?"

Raj lit a beady and inhaled. "Oh yes, very well, thank you. They run my life like queens, and I always obey."

"And the shop? Everything is good?"

"Bapu," Mohan said, halfway through his ice cream. "Bebe is waiting." He wiped his sticky hands on his school uniform.

"Yes, yes, we are leaving," Manmohan replied, quickly finishing his kulfi. He waved to Raj.

"Good luck," the shopkeeper said, taking another puff of his cigarette.

Back in the truck, Manmohan continued on toward the hospital, the ice cream heavy in his stomach.

He made a sharp turn off Victoria Parade and drove up a small hill. The terrain of the island often caused him to miss the freedom of his motorcycle cutting through the silent plains of northern India. That was the only lingering dislike he had for the island. Riding his bike had felt like he was embracing the whole landscape, gathering everything across the horizon into his arms. Here, there was no space. Something was always in the way.

He also missed his mother, particularly today. He had written to Sada Kaur to tell her about her latest grandchild, but as usual she had not replied. The last he heard from her was after Darshan died. She had sent a short note that read: *I am very sorry, Manmohan. I wish I had known him.* Though its brevity could have been misunderstood as curtness, he knew her. She was simply spelling out a regrettable truth, which had made him feel worse about being away.

Gripping the steering wheel, the truck hydraulics bouncing

205

him slightly in his seat, Manmohan recalled the day they boarded the train to Calcutta nine years ago. Baba Singh told her that he would send money and occasional updates. She had looked away. Their farewell seemed like two strangers completing a business transaction. It was stiff and formal, like one of them had been swindled out of a fair price, although Manmohan had not been able to tell which of them had been cheated.

Sada Kaur had nodded to each of her children, dispassionately, without any love at all, or as he understood later, too much. Vikram bent over and pressed the back of her slack hand against his forehead before stepping onto the train and sitting beside his father. Satnam whispered something in her ear and lightly kissed her cheek before boarding. Manmohan returned her nod, attempted a reassuring smile as if to suggest the whole circumstance was absurd. "Sat sri akal," he had said, as if he would see her the next day. "We will be back soon."

"You do not have to go," she had told him.

"What kind of son would I be? What will Bapu think of me if I stay?"

She had smiled weakly at him. "I know that is how you see it."

"Why don't you come?"

"Your grandfather needs me now. And I am not interested in chasing after your father's phantoms."

Then, one year after they had come to the island, World War II broke out and ship travel between India and Fiji was suspended. The Toors had been forced to accept the island as a more permanent home, and over time, settled more deeply into well-paying jobs. It became harder to leave, even when ship travel was reinstated in 1945. They had never made this much money in India, had never felt so secure. It was difficult to relinquish. It was why they had come.

Time steam-rolled forward, and earlier just this year in 1947, India gained its independence, which had grave and devastating consequences for the Punjab. The line of partition dividing the country in two had cut directly through the region. Large pieces of Manmohan's homeland that he had once traversed on his motorcycle—now part of Muslim Pakistan— were forever closed to him.

Hindus, Muslims, and Madrassis had marched through Suva celebrating and chanting, "*Jai Hind*. Long live India," waving the three-striped saffron, white, and green flag of a new nation that many Indians in Fiji had never even seen. But Manmohan, along with the other Sikhs on the island, could not celebrate. They heard stories of massacres in the Punjab. Muslims crossed over into Pakistan, and Hindus and Sikhs into the new India in mass migrations because none of these groups could coexist any longer. It broke Manmohan's heart to think of his home like that, of Guru Gobind Singh's efforts to protect that land for future Sikh generations. Manmohan often wondered about his mother, alone in a two-story house since Prem had passed away, in a region now only a sliver of its once historical greatness, no longer the home he would recognize.

"The ocean will swallow all of you whole," Sada Kaur had told Manmohan. She had known all along what would happen. She had known so many things.

He should have returned to be with her, and yet—although it caused him a great deal of distress—he still cared, after all these years, what his father thought. When Baba Singh had first returned from China, Manmohan was so full of awe. Despite his father's sometimes odd and stern manner, his experiences abroad endowed him with a mix of mystery and valor. It was

Manmohan's goal to one day embody those same qualities. He believed that following Baba Singh to Fiji would change everything. They would find common ground, bond over police patrol stories and how much they both missed India. His father would one day acknowledge that Manmohan had achieved precisely what they had all set out to accomplish on this island: a stable, wealthy lifestyle that even the British would never be able to undo.

He drove past Spencer's department store, where his ambitions to please had taken firm root. He had started by getting a job at Spencer's, cramped in the rear stock room. The largest business on the island, Spencer's was two stories high with a total of five large rooms stocked with clothing, sundries, knickknacks, and lanterns. He had been responsible for organizing boxes and registering weekly inventory. His wages were decent, enough to live on for a short time while the family settled into their new life, with enough remaining to save for his own autonomous and economically successful enterprise that would certainly rouse his father's admiration.

His savings then doubled when Baba Singh, with his history as a colonial police officer, got all three of his sons employed on the Fijian force. Yet just as Manmohan had begun to feel comfortable on the island, living in a modern, westernized house in Tamavua replete with the accoutrements of success— an electric icebox, aluminum barrels of spices and foodstuffs, running water and flushing toilets, his World War II truck parked on the well-paved and well-lit street outside, and money accumulating for that day he could start his own business and finally satisfy his father—Darshan had died.

~   ~   ~

Baba Singh was waiting for them outside the hospital as they pulled up to the parking lot. In the years Baba Singh had been in Fiji he had barely aged at all. At nearly fifty years old, he had only a handful of gray hairs, unnoticeable under his turban or in the thickness of his beard that was tucked neatly up into the black net tied around his chin. He presented well in his starched turban, khaki trousers, and blue button-down shirts, always pressed and washed. Standing outside of Jai's ground-floor hospital room, his hands were laced together behind his back, his shoulders straight. He was a stone sentry. A statue. He never changed.

Manmohan shut his truck door and approached the hospital wall, his boots crunching on the gravel. The humidity seemed to have lessened, and the air now felt clean. He glanced through the room's window, which had been cranked open. There was an empty space where Jai's gurney had been earlier that morning; she had not yet returned from delivery. The yellow walls inside were peeling. An empty glass vase rested on a wooden bedside table. The tabletop was slanted slightly, and its single drawer was missing. The water inside the vase was cloudy, like it had not been changed in some time.

"What took you so long?" Baba Singh asked. "You might have missed it."

"Hello, Dada," Mohan said to his grandfather.

Manmohan rested his upper arm on the window frame. A splinter of wood poked into his skin. "We're on time," he said, bothered by the lack of conviction in his voice.

Baba Singh pointed his chin at his grandson. "You should not have brought him. He is too young for this sort of business."

"What sort of business?" Mohan asked.

Manmohan scuffed his boot heel along the edge of the wall.

"Have you gone inside at all?" he asked.

"I prefer the fresh air out here."

"How long has she been gone?"

"Several hours. She should be back soon. Priya is with her."

"Very good," Manmohan muttered, trying not to seem sarcastic about it. Satnam's wife had come to help Jai through the delivery despite missing her weekly women's gathering with a sorority of wealthy, affluent Indian ladies. Referring to them as ladies was, in Manmohan's view, quite generous. It was really an afternoon of tea during which they all slung thinly veiled insults at each other like barbarians, smiling viciously. Jai called them mango heads because all they had up there was pulp.

"It is a pity," Priya had said to Manmohan when he dropped them off at the hospital that morning. "My friends will miss me terribly. But perhaps my being here will do some good. God knows I have been an exceptional mother to my little Karam." She had pointedly stressed the word exceptional while staring down her nose at Jai, then dabbed a tissue to her eye at the mention of her son, who was only a year younger than Mohan. "Young boys need the gentleness of their mothers if they are to grow into respectable men." She turned to Jai. "Just some friendly advice, one mother to another."

She was probably the worst of those mango heads.

Mohan jumped up to get a better look through the window, clutching the plastic hammer, dried ice cream all over his hands. After a moment, unable to see anything, he kneeled in the mud and collected a number of rocks into a pile. He then slammed the hammer down, splattering them in all directions.

Baba Singh noticed the hammer. "It has been a while since I saw that. I had almost forgotten about those toys."

Manmohan lowered his arm, rubbing it where the wood splinter had been digging in, trying not to feel so chastised.

Leaning against the wall, he crossed his feet and adjusted the baton on his side. Down the hill in the distance, Pacific Robins were amassed and perched on Suva's buildings, chirping in post-rain merriment. Mohan gathered more rocks into a pile, scraping them across the mud with the head of the plastic hammer.

"Last night, I had the same dream," Baba Singh said.

"It is just a dream, Bapu. Isn't it just a dream?"

"I have learned to listen to my dreams. It is more than a dream."

Manmohan stared at the electroshock therapy facility across the street, saying nothing more.

Soon they heard the squeaky wheels of Jai's gurney and quickly turned toward the window. A nurse was pushing her into the room, Priya trailing behind them.

"Gharwala?" Jai said, her voice grainy like sandpaper. She tiredly lifted her head and looked toward the open window, searching for her husband outside. The baby was cradled close to her chest, wrapped in a blanket.

"I am here," he said.

She smiled when she saw him, resting her head back onto the pillow. The nurse pushed the gurney as close to the window as possible.

A boy?" Manmohan asked her.

She nodded sleepily.

He looked at Baba Singh, whose expression was calm, like a knowing, sage guru. But he was not a guru, just a smug old man.

Stretching his arm inside, Manmohan touched his wife's hand. Her hair was matted to her forehead, but he could not reach far enough to wipe the sweat from her brow.

Priya sat on the edge of Jai's bed and peered critically at the baby. "His eyes are quite close together. I think they were a bit rough with the forceps."

"His eyes are fine," Jai said, covering the baby's head with the blanket.

Mohan reached up and clutched at the window frame for leverage in an attempt to jump higher. "Bapu," he said, still unable to see anything. "It is too high."

Manmohan lifted him.

Mohan's hands tightened on the frame, and he nearly dropped the plastic hammer inside the room. "Hello, Bebe."

She smiled.

"What is so important?" he asked.

She pointed at the baby. "This is your new brother."

"Where did you get him?"

"Come," Manmohan said, lowering his son back to the ground. "We can see more inside."

When he was standing beside his wife's bed, Manmohan took the baby in his arms and gazed at the red, sleeping face, bending over momentarily so Mohan could see. "My father had that same dream again," he told Jai.

"What dream?" Priya asked.

Manmohan ignored her.

Jai nodded. "It does not matter about the dream or the name," she said. "Whatever we call him, he is who he is."

Manmohan looked outside. The window framed the back of his father's turbaned head. Baba Singh did not seem concerned with what was happening inside. He seemed only to be waiting for them to decide what he believed had already been decided. Manmohan wished he knew if doing what his father wanted would make any difference. He wished he knew if it mattered at all that he was willing to give the name of the person he had loved most to a new person who might never comprehend its importance.

Sighing, he sat on the edge of his wife's gurney, still cradling his new son. "Maybe the name will teach this boy something important," he said. "Maybe just by having it, he will know what it cost me to give it to him."

~ ~ ~

"It is too hot for that," Jai told Priya, who was kneeling over the baby. Darshan was sleeping on a mat in the center of the living room. His cheeks were pink in the heat. Although the back door had been propped open and the curtain pulled aside, the air still did not move.

"I am not hurting him," Priya replied drearily. "I just want to see him."

Jai bent forward in her chair and looked hard at her sister-in-law. "You are too close, and it is too hot for that. Give him space."

Priya stretched languidly out on the linoleum-covered floor beside Darshan. "Shouldn't you be down here with him? You are his mother."

Jai opened her mouth, but Baba Singh put his hand up as he relaxed into the couch beside Manmohan. "Enough," he said. "Is fighting always necessary?"

She restrained herself with difficulty. Priya tried not to smile.

Manmohan eyed Satnam, who was on the floor resting against the wall just under the window. His brother had been regarding the tense exchange with disinterest, his expression blank, like he was bored.

"Say something to your wife," Manmohan told him.

"What should I say?" Satnam asked indifferently.

"Satnam is right," Baba Singh said, clasping his hands over his stomach. "Leave it be."

Manmohan's jaw tightened.

Vikram was sprawled out on the floor. Mohan and Karam ran toy trucks over his body. Karam's eyes narrowed as he drove his vehicle toward his uncle's stomach. As the front wheels made their approach, Vikram began to laugh, as if it were too much. Rolling onto his side, he curled himself into a ball. "Stop, stop," he pleaded.

"Does it tickle, Vikram Chacha?" Karam asked, grinning, and he and Mohan threw themselves on top of him, trying to reach his most sensitive spots. In spite of his frustration, Manmohan smiled. He knew Vikram was not very ticklish.

"Not too rough," Priya said. "Karam bruises easily."

"He bruises the same as any other boy," Jai said, still irritated.

Sitting up, his turban askew, Vikram threw his hands in the air, defeated. "Okay, okay, I surrender."

"Now you have to do what we tell you," Mohan said.

Karam nodded. "You can be our horse and take us through the house."

"But first," Vikram said, "perhaps we should get everyone some ice water."

Mohan shook his head. "Horse first."

"Are they always so demanding?" Vikram asked his brothers.

Manmohan grinned. "Only when you are here."

Vikram laughed. "I suppose it is an uncle's job to be the entertainment." He stood and crossed the room to the kitchen.

"Horse first, horse first," the boys shouted.

Vikram chuckled. "It is too hot just now. When the sun sets. I promise." He pulled some tumblers down from a cupboard. "Bapu, why don't you tell them about your idea?"

Manmohan turned curiously to his father.

Baba Singh made a face and shrugged. "A dairy farm is for sale near Veisari. I mentioned to Vikram that we should all buy it."

"Hmm," Manmohan said cautiously, pretending to mull it over. "Such a big time commitment, Bapu. Have you heard from Bebe?"

"I have asked her to join us."

Satnam glanced up in surprise.

"The war is over," Baba Singh continued. "Your grandfather is gone, and she is alone. After what happened with independence, she will change her mind. This time she will come."

"It is just that I think she is waiting for us to go back to her," Manmohan said, taking a tumbler from the tray Vikram was passing around. He took a sip. The cold water felt good in his mouth.

"I am not going back," Priya said, sitting up, an edge in her voice. "It is better here, especially now. I heard what happened there. Trains full of dead bodies." She shuddered.

Manmohan set his tumbler on the floor to roll his slacks up to his knees. The air was not very humid today, but the temperature was high, and he was sweating. "What about the farmland?" he asked, retrieving the tumbler and reclining again.

"I have no plans to return just yet," Baba Singh told his son. "Khushwant has been doing a fine job with the land."

Satnam shook his head. "I am perfectly satisfied with my job. I am not a dairyman. Patrolling suits me. We do not always have to change things."

Baba Singh regarded Satnam for a brief moment, and then he said, "Think about it. Let me know what you decide."

Manmohan looked sharply at his father, then quickly took another sip from his tumbler to hide the incredulous resentment he knew was written clearly in the flat, hard line of his mouth.

Baba Singh turned to address him. "And you?"

Slowly swallowing his water, Manmohan covered his mouth with his fist and cleared his throat. "It is a bit unexpected," he said, attempting a smile.

His father regarded him with impatience. Or was that eagerness? It was so difficult to tell the difference.

Manmohan held his smile. "But, yes, it is a sound idea," he said. He could feel the tight pressure of the leather watchband on his wrist. He had gotten it while serving as an army signal. It had not worked properly since just after his son died, which was why he liked to wear it. It was comforting to feel that he was not bound so strictly by time, that he had eternities to sort through all that confused and upset him.

Vikram gestured his agreement, sitting again on the floor with the boys and setting the empty tray beside him. "Is this not why we came to Fiji? Certainly not to be policemen."

Addressing Satnam, her tone wheedling, Priya said, "Gharwala, let's not miss out on this opportunity. You can keep your job and work on the farm during your free time."

Satnam looked away from her, his attention fixed on the water tray beside Vikram.

"Is that a new toy?" Karam asked Mohan, pointing to the plastic hammer.

"Yes," Mohan said, gripping the tool closely to his chest.

"Can I play with it?"

"No."

Priya wrested the hammer out of Mohan's grip.

"Hey…"

"Do not be so greedy," she said. "You should share your toys."

Manmohan abruptly stood. "Give it back."

Priya hesitated, looking up at him. Then she smiled ingratiatingly. "Of course," she said sweetly, returning the hammer. "It is just that I teach my Karam to share. It is a bad habit to allow children to be greedy. Karam would have shared."

Manmohan slowly lowered himself back down onto the springy cushions of the couch.

Jai beckoned Mohan over. "Come sit with me for a little while," she said. She made room for him on her chair and rocked him slightly, wrapping her thin, strong arms around him. He pouted and glared at his aunt.

Manmohan raised his cup to his mouth.

Priya smiled, lightly, as though she had already forgiven the outburst. She tucked her legs under her knees and addressed Baba Singh. "The dairy farm is such a good idea. My friend's husband started one several years ago, and their family now has such a beautiful house."

"Priya—" Satnam began.

She waved a dismissive hand at her husband and laughed. "What is not to love about it? Naturally we will contribute."

Manmohan caught Baba Singh intently watching Satnam. He turned away and focused on the cold tumbler grasped firmly in his hand, hating that look on his father's face, that expression of apology, of sympathy, and of unmistakable concern.

~ ~ ~

The Toor family dairy farm was located far down from the

hills of Tamavua, south of Suva in a jungle clearing off the island's main road. Though the twenty-five acres of pastureland and eighty cattle—fifty-eight cows, two bulls, and twenty calves—had been advertised as a functioning dairy farm, much of the equipment was rusted beyond repair, broken, or damaged. The shack housing the water tank balanced precariously on its rotten frame. Another, slightly larger shack—for the double-boiler stove, the generator-operated milking machine, the refrigerator, and pasteurizer—was a cramped and untidy space in which to operate the machinery. The only structure on the farm of any quality was the shelter where the animals slept at night, and even that, as Manmohan knocked on the supporting beams, looked as though it would soon need reinforcing.

As he surveyed the property, meandering through the clumsily built structures, Manmohan could not understand the appeal, why this was so much more preferable to the alternative, which was simply to return home to his mother as promised with the small fortunes they had accumulated. He wondered if she was still waiting.

He tried to picture Barapind in its current state. It must now be a no man's land where Sada Kaur wandered, empty and depleted. So much feeling once lived there, so much love and anger, hope and frenzied fear. Now all that remained were echoes of laughter and shouts in the wind. How did he get here? Why was he waiting for his father to finally decide to go home?

Baba Singh commenced work on the farm with the construction of a fourth building, a small cottage where he would live with Vikram. It was a modest structure with only two rooms and a tarp overhang out back shielding a metal stove for cooking. It was so simple in its layout that it did not take more than four days to complete. When they had hammered in the final nail, Baba Singh considered it. "Perfect," he muttered darkly.

"There is no room for Satnam to sleep," Manmohan remarked. "He cannot travel every day from the outer islands."

"No," Baba Singh said. "This place is also his, but his strengths lie elsewhere."

And Manmohan was hurt because still he did not understand.

The farm had gotten a strong start, which required an unrelenting pace, particularly during its first year. Manmohan was forced to retire his police uniform, commit himself entirely to his father's venture. After they had torn down and rebuilt the sheds and replaced or repaired the broken machinery, the farm opened to almost immediate profit. Baba Singh had already introduced himself to shop owners in Suva and had arranged for milk, butter, and cream delivery to those who preferred his lower prices to the larger, well-established dairy farms in the area. The Toors were also the only Sikh dairymen in Greater Suva, and community loyalty swung Sikh customers in their direction, without abatement. Often out making deliveries in the year since the farm's opening, Manmohan saw these customers more than he did his own wife and sons.

He daydreamed now, all the time. When driving through town with milk loaded in his World War II truck, or when he was with the cows, the soft skin of the udders in his fists as he monotonously squeezed milk into iron buckets, he thought of his boys. If they were together now, he would take Mohan to the cinema to see *Ek Mahal Ho Sapno Ka*; his son would snicker whenever Ramu cut the tension with comic relief. He would find Darshan and walk with him along the back of the house near the garden. The boy had taken his first steps, had a practiced, rolling gait.

How different this boy was from his namesake, this Darshan so quiet and unassuming. The other was eager and ambitious. In the long hours working on the dairy farm, Manmohan sifted through his memories, comparing, making distinctions. The first had been driven to *do*. But this Darshan was an observer. He watched.

~ ~ ~

The evening was still relatively young, Manmohan released from his duties early for the first time since opening the farm. He pushed the front door in, happy to see Jai, who was comfortably snuggled on some floor cushions in the living room, stitching a hole in a pair of his trousers. She glanced up at him from her sewing and smiled. Setting aside the trousers, she went to make a pot of tea for their evening together. As she passed, she lightly squeezed his hand.

Mohan was also there, his back to the door, kneeling in front of the couch where Darshan was seated. When Manmohan called out to him, he did not turn around. He was focused intently on his brother, who appeared slightly agitated.

"Oi, Mohan," Manmohan said. "I am home early."

Still his son did not acknowledge him.

Removing his boots at the door, Manmohan tried again. "Mohan?"

Darshan began to whimper with frustration. Mohan finally swung his head around, his chin on his shoulder, his chest leaning into the couch cushions. "He won't take it."

"Take what?" Manmohan asked, joining the boys on the couch. Then he saw the plastic toy hammer lain like an offering between Darshan's plump, outstretched legs.

Mohan gestured at the hammer. "I am trying to give it to him. It is a gift. But he won't take it."

"Why did you think he would?"

"I don't know. He never takes it."

"You have tried it before?"

Mohan nodded.

Manmohan moistened his lips, wondering how to respond. Finally he said, "*This* Darshan does not like them. You understand?"

Mohan watched uncertainly as Manmohan lifted the hammer. "I think it is time to put it back, don't you?"

For a moment, he thought Mohan might challenge him. His son, however, said nothing. His expression was bewildered, like he was losing something significant, but was not certain what.

LPs on the Gramophone & a Cabinet Radio
1949–1952

The faint odor of engine grease permeated the air of Pali Bhatia's mechanic shop. It was one of Manmohan's favorite particulars about Suva Auto Repair. Walking through the center aisle toward a door at the rear, he waved at the store clerk on duty as he passed, glancing around at the iron shelves laden with parts and all manner of equipage for vehicle repair and maintenance, the merchandise covered in black fingerprint smudges from mechanics' hands.

"Is he out there?" Manmohan asked the clerk, gesturing toward the door.

The clerk nodded. "Just got in."

Entering the main garage, Manmohan took a deep breath, savoring the smell of oil and metal much like Jai often inhaled the scent of the freshly cut plumeria and morning glory that grew along the edges of their house. The already large space of the high, wood-ceilinged garage was made larger by the rolled-up sectional tin door that opened to an expansive back alley courtyard where several rusted vehicles had taken root. Parts and tools were strewn around two cars, one bus, and several motorbikes. Mechanics—some Hindus, some Sikhs, and one Madrassi—worked on repairs while listening to Hindustani love songs on the radio, transmitted across the local Fijian airwaves. *Kuchh Na Kaho* from the movie *1942 Love Story* echoed from the black box, the female vocalist's high-pitched, melodious voice sharpened by the radio's antenna wires spread in a V.

Manmohan approached one of the motorbikes, delivered several weeks ago by ship from Auckland. It was a dull, black color. He reached out and placed his hand on the torn leather, double-passenger saddle, the bike standing firmly on its kickstand.

"She is old, but a classic," Pali Bhatia said, clapping Manmohan on the back and kissing his puckered fingers. He was known around the island as Junker Singh, a moniker the mechanic cherished, conferred upon him because of his love of beat-up vehicles he believed still had life.

Manmohan smiled at his friend. "German. Puch 1934. It will need anodizing, a good coat for the paint to prevent rusting. Four-speed gearbox. Double-piston engine, 284 cc."

Junker Singh nodded, impressed, but not surprised at his friend's knowledge. "The engine needs replacing," he said. "But she's loud once she is running."

"Yes," Manmohan murmured, patting the seat. "Why would you ever want to sell her?"

Junker Singh pointed to his bad knee. "I am too old and fat to keep her," he said with no trace of self-consciousness.

Manmohan chuckled.

"You bought that 1937 last year if I remember," Junker Singh said, "which you allowed to rust beyond repair in your backyard. You hardly rode her. You would not dream of letting the same thing happen to this one?"

"Dairy farming has kept me too busy to ride her."

"Beginnings are always like that," Junker Singh agreed. "They empty you out."

Manmohan stared listlessly at the bike. "There is more time now," he said. "Things are better." He missed the air piercing through his beard, and although he preferred the flatlands of the Punjab, he nonetheless also missed the green and gray blur of jungle and road streaming by like splashed paint as he flew around the island toward the openness of the sugarcane fields on the northwest side near Ba.

Junker Singh rested his rough hands over the top of his stomach, the buttons on his shirt straining against his belly. He inclined his head toward the motorcycle. "She is yours if you promise not to let her rust. My heart would not receive it well if you allowed that again."

Manmohan remained quiet for a moment, thoughtfully tapping his lips with two of his fingers. *Kuchh Na Kaho* came to an end, followed by a commercial announcement on the radio: *Buy two salwaar kameez, get one tailored suit for husband at discount price. Only at Suni Ganesh Saris and Spices!* When he finally spoke, he found that he had trouble looking his friend in the eye. "It is not for me. It is for Mohan. I am worried about him."

The laugh lines around Junker Singh's eyes softened.

Pulling a piece of paper from his shirt pocket, Manmohan unfolded it. It was his son's latest grade report. He handed it to the mechanic. "I thought a bike might be good for him. He seems to like them. Something to encourage him to work harder."

Looking at the report, the mechanic whistled softly and shook his head. "Ji, I know how much you like books. You are a reading man. But this is not a big problem. Not everyone is meant for school."

Manmohan winced, like he had been roughly jabbed. "My wife said the same thing." He walked around the bike and grasped the throttle, thinking of the conversation he had with Jai the other day. She had never been formally educated. Neither had Junker Singh. They did not understand the growing necessity for education in this new age of the world. His wife had been so dismissive, and, irritated, he had tried to explain to her. "Knowledge is an important advantage. The world is changing, and a man can do as much now with his mind as he can with his hands."

Jai had regarded him carefully then, with that same resolute manner that always characterized her loyalty to him. Brow furrowed thoughtfully, taking him more seriously, she had replied, "Perhaps he needs some motivation."

Picking at a hole in the bike's saddle, exposing the foam, Manmohan glanced at Junker Singh. "I have seen Mohan look at my motorcycle, like he is trying to sort out what is wrong with it. He sometimes takes a rag to it, trying to polish away the rust. He does not realize that rust changes the metal, that it cannot simply be wiped away. You have to change it to fix it, to repair the damage."

Junker Singh witheringly raised an eyebrow. "Now, you see, that is what is so tragic about rust."

Manmohan smiled faintly. "He is eleven this year. I remember when I was eleven. At his age I sometimes saw the British drive cars through Amarpur, and I imagined myself behind the wheel, racing through the country." They had finally found common ground, something they both loved.

"Yes, I was the same," the mechanic replied. "And when I was eleven, I did not do my schoolwork either. It is normal."

Manmohan shook his head. "Mohan does not have to love

it like I did. Why is it not enough that I ask him to improve? I am his father. Shouldn't that be the most important thing a son can offer, to always do his best?"

Junker Singh's expression changed, his mouth tipping downward in sympathy. He stuck his hands in his pockets, which made his paunch seem even larger and rounder. "He is a boy, ji. It is what boys do. I was sometimes disobedient. Remember that and do not be so hard on him."

Manmohan looked away, into the bright sun of the courtyard beyond the garage, the rope used to pull down the sectional door dangling in his periphery. It was hard to admit to his friend that he had never been that sort of free-spirited boy, rebellious or badly behaved, and that he could not understand or condone such behavior. He had always done as he had promised, had always done exactly what he believed would make Baba Singh proud.

~ ~ ~

Mohan gaped at the motorcycle as Manmohan wheeled it into the backyard, positioning it near his old bike where weeds had started to grow around the base of the flattened tires. Resting it on the kickstand, he stepped back to admire it. His son rushed over, touching the steel frame and the torn saddle, gliding his hand over the bike's surface, over the bumps of rust, the rough, unpolished metal, the glass of the speedometer, the broken side mirror that hung limply.

"Come over here, Mohan," Manmohan said, going to the patio and lowering himself into one of the chairs.

"It is bigger than the other. Is it faster?" Mohan asked, following his father.

Manmohan wordlessly pulled out the grade report and

handed it to his son.

Mohan's face fell.

"I believe you are a smart boy," Manmohan told him. "I have no doubt about what you can accomplish. That is how I know you are not trying."

"But Bapu, I am working so hard. Nothing I do makes any difference."

"I am sure that is not true," Manmohan said gently. "But you have to study. That is what I tell you all the time. It is wrong to disobey your parents, to tell them one thing and do another."

"I really *am* trying," Mohan said, near tears. "But nothing comes out the way it is supposed to."

Manmohan put an arm around his son's waist and pulled him close. "I think you are saying that just to make me happy. You think it is what I want to hear. I even believe you mean it when you say the words. But what would please me most is to see results, to see action follow your words."

"But, Bapu, I don't know why—"

Manmohan put up a firm hand, finished with excuses. "I understand that school may not be your favorite thing, so I have decided to balance what you do not like with something that you do." Pointing at the motorcycle, he smiled. "We can work on this bike together, and one day, when you are old enough, perhaps if you deserve it, you can have it."

Mohan glanced at the bike, but he did not seem excited. Perhaps he was sorry. That was good.

"But you have to promise me that you will make real improvements," Manmohan continued. "Do not just say the words."

Mohan hesitated for a moment, still regarding the motorcycle. "Bapu," he began, turning hesitantly back to his father. Then he took a deep breath and spoke with more confidence. "I promise."

"I will hold you to your words," Manmohan said. He kissed Mohan's cheek. "Go. Help your mother with dinner. We will start tomorrow."

Mohan loosened himself from his father's arm and ran inside the house. Manmohan watched him go. After a moment, feeling satisfied, he stood to clear a space opposite the cucumber garden where they would work on the bike.

With Mohan's help the next day, after the larger rocks had been moved and a small square of land prepped, Manmohan staked a gray tarpaulin to the ground and nailed another over tall four-by-four pillars of lumber that he pounded into the dirt. During the following days, once the pillars had been reinforced with concrete, they built a row of shelves for parts and tools and set it as a wall in the back of the tarpaulin shed, the finalizing touch on their makeshift auto repair shop.

Over the next several months, Manmohan rolled out the cabinet radio from the living room so they could listen to the Hindustani station while they worked. He took great pleasure in restoring the analog gauge and barrels, the carburetor, and the leather bench seat while humming along with the music and sipping an occasional cold beer. During his few years in the army, the Amritsar barracks were often quieted by the voice of one of his bunkmates who sang beautiful love songs while polishing his boots. The music from the radio reminded Manmohan of the harmony and simplicity of those days, when he had been pulled away from all that made him restless and insecure at home.

And on some days, when the air was dry and not humid and it seemed to fit the mood, he wound up his gramophone and played the Duke Ellington LP he had run across in a shop on

Victoria Parade. His favorite recordings were "Sepia Panorama" and "Bojangles." When he listened to them he was young again, but having never heard jazz when he was in India, the songs made him feel young without the ache of nostalgia.

Though Mohan was not particularly skilled with tools— holding them awkwardly—he engaged in each task with absolute focus and a clear desire to accomplish it well. Watching Mohan strip the paint off the bike's metal frame in order to coat it with an oxide layer before repainting, Manmohan could not fathom how one so capable of hard work and dedication could have ever done so poorly in school.

Mohan had taken a greater effort with his schoolwork since their motorcycle project had begun. Each evening, before they opened up the tarpaulin bike shop, Mohan was required to complete his school assignments, solve mathematical equations and write essays on the history of India and Indians in Fiji. Manmohan offered to help once, but Mohan did not want it, adamant about doing it on his own.

So Manmohan would read one of the books from his great collection while he waited, Duke Ellington wound up and sweetly melodic in the background. He loved the musty smell of his books' yellowing pages. He drank in the paragraphs. He wanted to know everything about the world. They were perfect evenings, both of them learning, embarking on journeys of the mind, together. Sometimes Mohan studied for so long there was not time for the bike. He would eat dinner and slump off to bed, looking utterly drained. For Manmohan, these evenings were great successes.

Nonetheless, many of the evenings during those last months of 1949 ended with the clank of tools being returned to the shelf of the tarpaulin shed, the silencing of the radio or the scratch of the needle as it was pulled off the LP, and a twist of the knob on the Coleman lantern by which they had been working after the sun set. As Mohan would head inside, smiling and wiping the grime from his hands, Manmohan would stare out into the darkness of the backyard, listening to the crickets and feeling the hint of ocean breeze on the back of his sweaty neck, Duke Ellington still playing in his head. Jai and Darshan were usually already asleep by the time the two of them trod heavily to the washroom to rinse the grease from their bodies. They would eat the meal left for them on the kitchen table and then drop onto their beds, the day feeling like a series of accomplishments worthy of their exhaustion.

~ ~ ~

It is always good, Manmohan thought, clinging to the happy evenings with his son, the two of them out in the backyard, the pleasant music and the sweet, agreeable smell of grease. That was exactly what he needed now. An evening with Mohan and the bike to remind him what sort of man he was, and what sort of father. Standing outside his house, he took a slow shaky breath. Jai was likely in the living room playing quietly on the floor with Darshan, the house smelling of freshly prepared roti and bean curry. And Mohan had no doubt been working diligently on his homework, was now finished and had seen him pull up in the truck. He had probably run to his room to change out of his school shorts and button-down shirt, putting on the clothes he had designated as his mechanic's gear: a raggedy black pullover shirt and an old pair of trousers that he said made him feel like he was allowed to get dirty. This last thought made Manmohan brighten, a momentary elevation from the bitter mood he was steeped in, relieving some of the pressure in his chest.

Taking another breath, this time slower until his lungs tingled with the pressure, he then released it like he was exhaling a steady stream of cigar smoke. He had just left the dairy farm, and though he tried his best not to think of it, not to let it consume him, the memory of Satnam standing around all day doing nothing made him sick.

Sinking to the ground, Manmohan rested his back against the house by the front door.

Satnam and Priya had spent the entire day on the dairy farm for the first time since its opening because Priya had said they wanted to learn about what she called "the family trade."

"We've got to know what it's about," she said. "We cannot just sit around at home and expect to make a profit if we do not know our own business. What if something happens to any of you?"

Manmohan stared at her for a long moment. He wanted to laugh hatefully at her, but she gave him that infuriatingly wide-eyed stare that, for her, meant sincerity.

"Well," she said, "show me what it is you do around here."

"It has been three years," he finally replied, the weight of the two bucketfuls of milk he was holding straining his shoulders.

"Well, yes. I was talking it over with the ladies. Our friend's husband simply collapsed while milking a cow. Now she's got nothing."

"You want to learn to milk a cow?"

She laughed. "I wouldn't do that *this minute*. Observation is eighty percent of learning, isn't it?"

Not pausing long enough to wonder where she had heard that, he turned and walked away toward the pasteurizing shed where Satnam was talking quietly with Baba Singh.

"I'll just see what you do next," Priya said in a cheerful,

singsong voice. "To the shed, is it?"

"What kind of game are you playing?" Manmohan asked her, setting the buckets down by the shed door near Baba Singh.

"It was my idea," Satnam told him. "I wanted to come."

"Why now?"

"I thought—"

"As I have told him so many times," Priya replied, adjusting her chuni over her severely pulled back hair. "We have got to participate. We have got to play our part."

"It is their place, too, Manmohan," Baba Singh said, taking one of the buckets inside.

"They have been here all morning and haven't done one thing," Manmohan said, heat rising to his cheeks.

"We have every right to observe," Priya said.

"Of course you do," Manmohan replied with sarcasm. He turned to Satnam. "While I *work* you can *observe* all you like."

"Leave him alone," Baba Singh said, stepping protectively in front of Satnam, annoyed. "Do you always have to pester him?"

Glancing behind his father at Satnam, Manmohan spoke slowly and evenly, tension in his jaw. "I just mean that if he wants to learn, I am about to start the boiler."

"He did not come for that," Baba Singh said quietly, taking the second bucket inside.

"What did he come for?"

But no one had answered him.

The front door of his house cracked open. "Gharwala?" Jai said. "What are you doing out here?"

"Enjoying the sunset," Manmohan replied.

"Will you come in soon? I have been waiting."

He scooted over and patted the ground. "Come sit with me

for a minute."

He had to steady her as she lowered herself down awkwardly. She was pregnant again. Being pregnant always made her look so much tinier than she already was.

"I am a good husband to you," he said. It was not a question, and he was not really speaking to her.

She took his hand.

Sighing, he squeezed, the smallness of her palm engulfed by his large one, making him feel protective and less tense. "Why have you been waiting?" he asked.

"Mohan's grade report," she replied. "He brought it home with him today and went straight to his room. He said he was sick from the bus fumes. I have told him many times not to sit in the back." She gave the envelope to Manmohan. It was unopened. "I have not seen it yet. I waited for you."

"Is it already January?" he murmured, always struck by the oddity of Fijian summers beginning in what had been winter in India.

Gently releasing her hand, he ripped open the envelope marked *Fourth Standard Completion*, his mood lightening a little. He unfolded the paper, smiling. "I am sure when Mohan sees this, he will feel much better."

But as the print at the top of the report registered in his mind, his smile fell. The black ink was stark against the white of the sheet, unwavering and clear, telling him that Mohan had failed every single course.

He crumpled the sheet in his fist and gave it to Jai who unwrinkled and assessed it, frowning. Never in his life had Manmohan known trying, doing, then failing. If a person tried, inevitably he would succeed. If he did not eventually succeed it was because he simply did not care.

Jai placed a hand on his shoulder. "You deserve his

respect," she said somberly. She struggled to stand. "Talk to him. I will have dinner waiting."

Manmohan pushed her up, watching her step out of the darkness and into the light of the open door. After a moment, he followed.

Mohan was on the couch, watching Darshan play with blocks in the center of the living room. He was afraid, as he should be, fidgeting with the hem of his shorts. "I am sorry, Bapu," he said without waiting for his father to speak.

Manmohan sat next to him on the couch. "Explain it to me."

"I don't know what happened. Every time I thought I was prepared, when I would sit down to take the test, the words looked funny. Everything was backwards and I would start sweating and—"

"Now you are making up stories. How can words change on the page? How can they stay the same in your books but not on the test?"

"When Mr. Gupta is talking in class, I understand everything. And it is not just the tests, it is in the books, too. Sometimes, if I focus really hard, I think I can read it, and then—"

Manmohan shook his head. "No. I do not know what you have been doing. You told me you did not need my help, that you could do it by yourself."

"But Bapu, I only wanted to—"

"I always give you so much: toys, visits to the cinema, ice creams, and now that motorcycle. And so many times, even if you are disobedient, I ignore it because I tell myself it is what boys do. People are always telling me that boys are sometimes badly behaved or rebellious. But I never did that. I never disrespected my father."

Mohan's eyes began to water.

Manmohan kneaded the back of his neck, just under the rim of his turban where his muscles were tight. "You cannot continue to have something for nothing. That is *your* lesson. *My* lesson, which has been a hard one for me to understand, is that trust must be earned. Words have no meaning without actions to support them. I should never have given you anything before you earned it. Do you understand me?"

"Yes, Bapu," Mohan replied in a shaky voice.

Manmohan stood. He ducked past the curtain and went outside to the backyard. He remained still on the patio, frozen in his anger, listening to the sounds of the island, the whisper of water and of leaves. He glanced at the motorcycle under the tarpaulin shed. The anodized metal frame still needed a coat of shiny black paint, but the bike was otherwise restored. Approaching it, he realized that what he wanted most now was to be on the saddle, in the darkness of the island where no person could find him. Rolling up his sleeves, he swung a long leg over the seat. Flicking back the kickstand, he pushed his feet along the dirt to roll the bike down the side yard of the house.

When he was on the street he started the engine. It rumbled low and loud. He turned around and saw Mohan in the house staring at him through the window. Looking away and toward the paved road ahead, Manmohan pulled the throttle and sped down the hill toward Suva, the bike sounding like a thousand growling lions racing through Fiji.

~ ~ ~

It was well past midnight when Manmohan got home. He tiptoed through the house to bed, his family already sleeping.

He had gone to the beach, gazing out into the water where the horizon was impossible to discern because the black sky merged so completely with the black sea. He sat there wishing for India, especially for the time of his life when he was fatherless: the pond, his mother's voice as she read from the Holy Book, and Vikram's yowls while chasing bullock fearlessly through the fields. He remembered Satnam as a young boy carving wood and the gentle way he helped their mother serve dinner, saving the largest portions for everyone else. Strange that he had thought of that, to recall his brother once being so selfless. Satnam had grown so much out of that virtue.

Manmohan had not stayed long at the beach. Growing restless with nothing but darkness in front of him, he had sped away from the shoreline through Suva to the main road that cut into the jungle. But somewhere around Veisari, just past the dairy farm, he had turned back, prickled with guilt. Maybe he was not seeing the situation from the right angle. Maybe he needed to reassess.

His bare feet were quiet now on the linoleum floor. Grit was on his cheeks and lips from the ride. He stopped in the washroom to rinse off, patting his face dry with a clean towel.

On his way down the hallway toward his room, he peeked in on Mohan. His son was flung face down on his bed, still fully dressed. Sighing, Manmohan carefully closed the door and tiptoed on. Climbing under the covers next to his wife, he decided they would have a talk tomorrow evening to clear up all the misunderstanding.

The next day, however, his son did not come home.

"He did not go to school today," Jai said, shoving a note from Mr. Gupta at her husband.

It was written in the scribble of a man who had been annoyed when writing it: "Your son failed to attend classes today. His marks, as you are aware, need serious improvement. I do not think he is studying at all. If there is some family matter that requires Mohan's absence or that is affecting his progress, please keep me informed as I cannot plan for his best interests without this information."

Manmohan flung the note aside. "That boy must hate me," he said, slapping the table with his palm.

They waited over an hour, sitting stiffly in the kitchen. Neither spoke, saving their words, their lips pressed into knife slits. They knew Mohan would come home, eventually. If it were something awful, they would have heard about it from the neighbors. It was a small island.

Darshan tugged at Manmohan's leg once, wanting to be lifted, but Manmohan did not respond. Jai gestured the boy over.

Without warning, the front door swung violently inward, banging against the wall. Their Hindu neighbor Mr. Ram Seth entered the house, eyes wild with outrage. Raising his fist he shouted, "Your son is a misfit troublemaker!"

He shoved Mohan roughly inside by the shirt collar. "I do not want him near my son again."

"What happened, ji?" Jai asked.

"They got into an accident," Mr. Seth screamed. "On that stupid motorcycle of yours. They did not know what they were doing! Narain was almost killed. Don't you watch your children?"

Manmohan nodded, not betraying his surprise, his face still hard. "I am sorry, ji. I did not know. We will talk with him."

"You *should* have known," Mr. Seth said, pivoting on his heel. He yanked the doorknob, slamming the door on his way out.

There was silence.

With a loud groan on the linoleum, Manmohan pushed his chair back and stood with deliberate slowness. He approached his son who was rocking unsteadily in the archway that separated the living room from the kitchen. Glancing around vacantly, Mohan smiled foolishly. There was a gash on his cheek.

Manmohan sniffed. Alcohol, potent like a spilled bottle. He grabbed the boy roughly by the chin and bent forward to smell his mouth. Grimacing, he pushed Mohan away.

"I have seen *you* drink, Bapu," his son said, indignant.

Manmohan grabbed him violently by the arm. "Not like this!"

Jai coolly examined Mohan's cut. "He seems fine."

"It is not so bad," Mohan replied, his speech slurred.

"What happened to the Seth boy?" she asked. "Is he all right?"

"Narain?" Mohan chuckled. "He is fine. Fine, fine, fine."

Jai dabbed at his cut with a cloth and he waved her away. "Bapu, I had to try it." He staggered then caught his balance, suddenly smiling. "We did it! We fixed the old thing! There is something I can do right!" He laughed.

"Stop it," Manmohan said sharply. "What is wrong with you?"

Mohan stopped laughing, and his eyes grew very large as he considered the question. "I do not know, Bapu."

"Get yourself together."

"It rides nicely," Mohan said. "It was perfect. Although we did not get very far." He pointed toward the street, stumbling backwards.

At this Manmohan snatched up his truck keys and went out. He found the motorcycle in a ditch at the bottom of the hill, just before the road turned into Suva. Using the two-by-eight ramp of wood he always kept in the back to heave up large crates from the docks, he rolled the bike onto the truck bed. One of the motorcycle's side mirrors had broken off, and there was a deep dent in the fuel tank. At home, he chained the bike to one of the tarpaulin shed's wooden posts. And for good measure, he kicked it, watching it wobble on its kickstand.

He went inside to discover Mohan had passed out in his room.

Idiocy, Manmohan thought, winding up the gramophone, turning the handle quickly, releasing his rage. The Duke was still on the table and he placed the needle on *Dusk*.

"Bapa," a small voice said from behind him.

"It's *Bapuuu*," Manmohan replied, looking down at Darshan.

"Haaaan," Darshan said. *Yes*. It was his first word, and he used it for everything.

"Come," Manmohan said, his anger subsiding, leaving behind the dull pain of disillusionment. He lifted the three-year-old into his arms and went to the couch. Darshan's breath smelled like cumin seeds. The boy touched his father's beard with a small, clammy hand.

They stayed there for a while, and soon Darshan was sleeping. Manmohan listened to The Duke until the very end. When the gramophone quieted, he put his son to bed and locked up the cabinet radio, ignoring the growling of his stomach. He had not eaten dinner.

Jai was still awake when he brought the gramophone into their bedroom. She said nothing, but watched as he opened the closet door and tucked the machine away, followed by the key to the radio and a box containing his LP collection, Duke Ellington and his Famous Orchestra on the top.

He did not touch his music for the next two years.

And he did not touch the bike, either. It developed a rash of orangey-red that spread like a disease. The overhead tarpaulin collected pools of water until it finally tore and collapsed under the weight. For the next twenty-four months, it covered the bike like a shroud.

~ ~ ~

There was a great deal for which to be grateful. Manmohan had only to look at the accomplishments of his life, at the course on which he had so resolutely stayed in order to make something of himself. He had been waking long before dawn, sleepily strapping on his watch that told him he had eternities. It took two more years of diligence, of backbreaking labor to sustain the family dairy trade, of sweat and grit, of animal waste and patience, holding his tongue while Satnam did nothing and Baba Singh loved him anyway.

It had, however, been worth it. In Veisari, not far from the farm, there was a lumber mill once run by a family who had since returned to India, and now it was his, the fully operational business smoothly transitioned into his possession. He had already hired help, a few Hindus and also Onkar, an old villager from Barapind. He had already bought two Caterpillars, another World War II truck from Junker Singh, two flatbeds to haul wood across the island, and new machinery to treat felled logs transported from his several acres of backland to the mill where he would treat them in his kiln. Because the need for lumber was steady but not excessive, the business was valued as only moderately lucrative, as Baba Singh had noted several times since Manmohan signed the Fijian government's one-hundred-year lease. Nonetheless, it was his, "as long as he could still contribute on the farm," his father had told him.

Manmohan had built a sprawling new house in the lumber mill's circular clearing, the entirety of it raised up on stilts to protect it from the lowland's regular tropical flooding, with five bedrooms, a living room, as well as a room for his ever-growing book collection. The kitchen was magnificently large and sensibly arranged with abundant counter space and a walk-in pantry where Jai had already begun to store dried dhal, sundry condiments, spices, pots and pans, flour for roti, and medicines. He had even built furniture to fill the house: cabinets; tables; bed frames; chairs; shelves for curios, for his books, and for clothing.

Yet, wandering through his emptied and already-sold house in Tamavua, his sandaled heels scraping gently on the linoleum, Manmohan found that although he had so assiduously sought a means to assert his independence and successfully achieved it in every logistical sense, now living and breathing a business wholly his own, he could not help wondering if he had made a mistake.

Baba Singh seemed to believe so. Out in the jungle, removed from Tamavua's westernized housing and lamp-lit streets, their new home in Veisari was dramatically different. In the jungle, the Toor family would now live a life more similar to that of the village in India. No central plumbing, they would instead use an outhouse. An electric generator buzzed nearby, but it only supplied electricity to the mill in order to operate the kiln and saws. The house itself had no power source. Jai would need to cook by the heat of wood-burning ovens, and when it grew dark she would need to light the grounds and rooms with candles and lanterns. After listening to Baba Singh's disappointingly reasonable argument that they had come to Fiji for a life of modernity and opportunity, he wondered about her reaction to their changed circumstances. Despite his doubts, however, she seemed truly happy with the transition, returned to a life with which she was most familiar, an Indian life.

He let his eyes roam the nakedness of his Tamavua bedroom, stopping at the closet where he once stored his police uniform, which had collected a layer of dust in all the years he had not touched it; where he had once kept his leather boots; where he had hidden away his gramophone, his LPs, and the key to the cabinet radio. He had tried so often to shut the music out of his mind, yet he still sometimes craved it, which was why he had not thrown anything away, why it was all tucked up in the rafters of the mill house where he now stored all things forbidden: the plywood box, unlabeled bottles of alcohol used for medicinal purposes, and the old knickknacks from India that reminded him of happier times. It sometimes seemed excessive to him, to shut the music out entirely, but then he thought of Mohan's rebellious nature, his blatant whip-like contempt these past two years, his voice full of acid, his son, who should adore him without question.

Mohan was probably somewhere with his friends now, lounging on the beach, drowning in beer or rum. That first taste he had the night he ran off with the motorcycle had not been his last. He and his friends lapped it up like dogs, tripping over themselves, hooting clownishly, listening to the transistor radio they stole from Manmohan's truck before he had a chance to bring it inside. Manmohan had seen them once, had crept to the edge of the beach behind the mangroves to watch. He had never seen Mohan so uninhibited, his head thrown back in the throes of laughter. It looked like joy.

Manmohan had taken revenge for the stolen radio, for the

hours of amusement it had afforded when at home he had prohibited such revelry. Last year when Fiji Airways had announced it would land the first jetliner on the island, marking 1951 as the first time the country had ever seen such a massive commercial airliner, Manmohan had refused to let Mohan go. He went alone on the three-hour drive across the island to Nadi airport. He stared at the apron through the chain link fence with all the other onlookers, at the whitewashed stone paths connecting the apron to the terminal, watching defiantly as the plane landed, forcing his eyes to swallow up the entirety of it, taking in the details and storing them away, remembering every second of what he had forbidden Mohan to see. But it was foolish. He discovered later that Mohan had gone with Narain.

He poked his head into the other emptied bedrooms, checking for anything left behind, and then he went to the living room where the discolored squares of paint on the walls indicated where the family portraits had once hung. The photos were the only items left unpacked in the new house. He had not allowed Jai to hang them. He was considering new pictures, the old ones imbued with too much history.

He went outside, glancing at the two tarpaulin-covered, rusted motorcycles parked across from his cucumber garden. Junker Singh had been devastated when he saw the second bike. "At least tell me it was an offering to God. *That* I can understand, ji, because God would be most impressed with her."

The tarpaulin rustled, and a movement caught Manmohan's eye. A small head with a topknot of hair peeked out from under the tarpaulin. "Oi!" he called. "I can see you."

The small head quickly ducked down.

"Boy, I said that I can see you," Manmohan called. "What

are you doing out here? You are supposed to be in the truck with your mother."

Darshan stood. He was a gangly five-year-old, too tall for his age, arms sheepishly clasped behind his back. "I was just checking, Bapu," he said. "I don't want to leave anything behind."

"Is your sister with you?"

Darshan glanced guiltily down behind the canvas. "She was helping."

Peering over, Manmohan found his two-year-old daughter Navpreet covering her head with her arms. She did not move.

Darshan tapped her shoulder. "He can see you."

She slowly lowered her arms and looked up, her eyes wide. "No," she said.

Manmohan squatted next to one of the wooden posts that had once held up the tarpaulin bike shop and beckoned his children over. "Come around here."

They approached slowly, Navpreet petulant. "Do as you are told," he said. "Get in the truck. We do not live here any longer."

Navpreet hugged the post and began to cry. Manmohan felt that she cried quite a lot. He loosened her grip from the post, prying her fingers off, and she screamed and pounded her fists into his chest as he carried her away. "No, no, no, no."

"Is this the only word you know?" he muttered, tucking her under his arm like a rolled-up carpet while she continued to flail. "Darshan, let's go."

Jai was already waiting in the truck, holding their infant daughter Livleen. Scooting over on the bench seat, she made room for them all. Released, Navpreet crawled to her mother, and without warning pinched the baby.

"Enough!" Jai said, slapping Navpreet's hand.

Darshan squeezed in next to his sister, and she leaned against his shoulder as Manmohan steered away from the curb, his mood sour.

They arrived at the mill shortly after. As Manmohan entered the clearing and navigated his way toward the house past a row of tamarind trees, he sensed Jai stiffen. Beyond the trees he saw Mohan waiting at the top of the staircase by the house's main entrance, wearing a turban. Manmohan wondered with a stab of regret who had taught him to tie it.

Pulling to a stop, Manmohan jumped out of the truck onto the soil, soft from the recent rain. Appraising the house momentarily, Manmohan then crossed the clearing and climbed the stairs. On his way inside, he nodded curtly at his son and said, "Come to steal something?"

"I thought I should be here today."

"I do not see how it matters," Manmohan replied, noticing several empty boxes stacked just inside the main entrance. It took a moment for his eyes to adjust after the bright sunshine outside, and then he saw the family photos he had not wanted to unpack. Next to the black velvet scroll map of Fiji was one of the pictures he hated most, that unsmiling image of himself standing between Satnam and Vikram who seemed so much more relaxed than he.

In another photo he was seated next to Jai on one of the wooden chairs on Tamavua's backyard patio. In another, he was with his father, on opposites sides of a cow. Some were more recent, shots of Navpreet and Darshan in the cucumber garden, and of them playing games in the living room. The shots of him and Mohan working on the bike were missing, which fueled Manmohan's anger. A person could not simply cancel out their wrongs by excluding them. And then he saw the one he hated most, the only photo of his dead son, hanging above the couch just like it had in Tamavua, that smiling three-year-old face.

"What is all this?" Manmohan asked, pointing at the walls.

"I thought it would make things feel more like home," Mohan replied.

"Why aren't you out with your friends?"

"You never told me about this place. I did not want to be left behind."

His son appeared so sincere, Manmohan almost believed him. "I wanted to wait, to decide for myself what stays and what goes," he said, pulling Darshan's photo off the wall. "I did not want to see all this, all these stupid mistakes and bad memories. I did not ask you to do this."

He abruptly left the room to go to the kitchen. There was a ladder against the far wall. He moved it under the entrance to the rafters and climbed up, pushing the door in. The plywood box was off to the left. He dragged it close, opened it and shoved the picture inside, slamming the lid down tight, pressing the latch in firmly.

Mohan was still in the living room when he returned, his head hung as he began to remove the photos from the wall.

"Leave them," Manmohan told him. "But add the others, the ones you did not hang, the ones of us."

Mohan stopped, his hand suspended near one of the frames he was about to take down.

"And stay," Manmohan told him, his voice stiff, "if you mean it, if you really do not want to be left behind."

~ ~ ~

Later that year in July, for perhaps four days, the island was suffocated by humidity unmatched in all the fourteen years

Manmohan had been in Fiji. Logging slowed somewhat. He had pulled a number of employees from their lumberjack duties to haul water in the World War II trucks to the backlands to ensure no one fainted of heat exhaustion or dehydration. Conditions inside the mill were so unbearable because of the added warmth generated by the kiln that they had to shut it down. Yet, Manmohan did not want to risk halting operations entirely, so the loggers continued to log and fresh tree trunks piled up in the mill's clearing because they could not be processed.

Bathing was pure futility. He did not have the energy to carry water from the river to the bath chamber upstairs and pour it in the aluminum tub. But this did not matter. He was always wet anyway. After bathing he could not get dry. And Jai fed everyone cold, leftover curries without roti because she refused to start the oven. During the day, the children retreated to the river to play, but in the evenings they barely moved, lounging about in the main house living room, limp like ragdolls.

"Why doesn't it *rain*?" Mohan asked desperately, pointing at the dark clouds above the jungle while holding Livleen. She had been sleeping all morning, her head sweaty, her hair matted.

Manmohan watched as Mohan gently wiped the baby's face before giving her to Jai. Ever since he had chosen to stay with the family, Mohan made Manmohan decidedly uncomfortable—and suspicious—with his newfound and determined loyalty, with his many contributions to the mill and his affection for Darshan and the girls.

Glancing out the window, he replied, "It should come very soon." The sky was nearly black, but nothing stirred. He closed his eyes. Day four had undone them. He felt beaten and drowsy. There had been nothing left to do but wait, so he finally succumbed and shut everything down before midday. The family had gathered in the house for lunch, but their plates of cold food were scattered about the floor, untouched.

Now, something cool brushed Manmohan's face. He opened his eyes and looked around. They had all felt it. The air was finally moving. He rushed out to the deck like a starved man desperate for one tiny, wayward crumb. Everyone hungrily followed.

Navpreet gripped the bars of the railing and pressed her face between two of them so that her mouth stretched clown-like.

Jai fanned herself with the hem of her salwaar.

Darshan struggled with a chair, dragging it out from the living room and setting it next to her. She smiled at him before sitting in it like a melting ice cube, Livleen in her arms.

The rest of them sank down, sprawling out on the wooden planks of the deck, focusing only on the slight movement of air that teased the tops of their sweaty bodies.

It came slowly, took nearly an hour, but finally it began to rain.

The storm hit hard. The sky had overstrained itself, and each drop was a bucketful. Mill workers scattered like insects, running toward their homes to secure their families and their possessions from the inevitable flooding. The door to the main house was only feet away from where they sat slumped on the deck, but Manmohan, Jai, and the children could not move fast enough. They were all soaked by the time they made it inside. Navpreet began to cry at the crack of thunder. She threw her little body down on the floor and lay on her stomach, spread flat like a floorboard. It was only midday, but the room was dim. Jai lit a candle. They again settled themselves on the couch, in chairs, and on the floor to wait out the storm, which to their disappointment had intensified the indoor humidity.

"Bapu, Bebe, look!" Darshan shouted urgently. He was standing on a chair by the window, watching the downpour.

Rushing over, they saw a cow float down the swollen river, its eyes wild with terror.

"Is that one of Dadaji's?" Mohan asked.

Manmohan laughed.

"Me," Navpreet said, holding her arms up to her father, wanting to see out the window. Manmohan absently waved her away. Navpreet reached out to her mother. "Me," she said again.

"It is gone," Jai told her, holding Livleen closer to the glass so that the baby could tap it with her palm.

Navpreet lowered her arms and moved away.

A mattress floated past, then more debris, mostly tree branches and pieces of broken wood, likely from houses and bridges. The river continued to rise, overflowing and rushing through Manmohan's young garden and under the house, crashing against the stilts. The water splashed and sloshed the rest of the day and long into the night.

The following morning Manmohan and Mohan went outside and surveyed the clearing. The call of roosters and the barking of dogs in the distance broke the eerie quiet in the wake of the storm. Manmohan's boots sunk into the mud as he staggered toward a group of employees who had gathered at a messy pile of logs strewn next to the flatbed trucks. Kicking away branches and other jungle debris, he called Onkar over.

"Are the trucks all stuck?" he asked his old friend.

Onkar nodded. The humidity seemed to have aged him. He was wrinkled, like fingertips soaked too long in water. "The wheels are sunk in. We are trying to figure a way to get them all out and moving again."

Manmohan absently kicked the tire of one of the flatbeds. "We can lay down a path of two-by-fours out to the main road. There is a stack of them there to start." He shook his head at the state of the lumber they had treated before the humidity, all soaked and bulging.

He turned at the sound of men calling out from behind him, two officially dressed Fijians, their small afros like fluffy halos.

"Is everything all right?" he asked them, thinking they had been stranded.

"The bridges are out," the short one replied, panting slightly from his exertion through the mud.

"Yes, I thought so. The river was full of debris."

"*All* the bridges are out," the other said. "We need wood."

The shorter one spoke, glancing around, making assessments. "We have been advised that while the other mills of the island suspended business in the days before the storm, you continued to log. We understand that you have a large supply of pine," he gestured to the piles of logs around the clearing. "We will take it at a fair price."

"Of course."

"We need you to prioritize this over all other commissions for lumber and wood," the other continued, "but there are also a large number of houses and shops that have been ruined. They should be second on your list."

Manmohan nodded and gestured at his trucks. "If you can send your own vehicles, I have dry lumber in storage. I can have more by the time you get here. By then, hopefully my own trucks will be out of the mud."

As the officials turned to leave, the shorter one said, "We will get the paperwork for your contract later to you in the week. We have commissioned others, but their supplies are low. You are now our primary supplier."

As the two officials turned to leave, Manmohan saw that Mohan, who had already joined the mill workers to start organizing a team for laying the wooden pathway, had stopped and was looking at him. His son grinned and shot him a thumbs-up before bending his knees to lift a two-by-four out of the mud.

~ ~ ~

Good fortune twinkled in the candlelight along the deck railing that curved all the way around to the front of the house. Manmohan murmured a silent prayer of thanks into the dusk settling over the mill. The months since the flood had been very good.

Junker Singh was with him. His friend leaned his forearms on the railing, the rings on his thick fingers glimmering against the flame of the candle nearest. "I have never seen such a big fuss," he said.

Manmohan chuckled. "It is not yet over."

The day had been both chaotic and momentous. The government had just proclaimed Suva Fiji's first city. Residents had paraded through the streets lauding the growth and prosperity of a place that had once been a clump of mangrove fields and a small row of shops but now had a downtown composed of three- and four-story buildings. For the first time, Manmohan had seen Fijians celebrating openly with the many Indians of the island. He marveled at how enthusiastically they shared in the festivities. It was an acknowledgement that although Indians had taken over much of the island's business, the growth of the city was a success they all shared. The natives had put on a great display of their culture rarely seen in Suva. They walked over hot coals and ate fire, and village chiefs invited Indians of the city to sit in yaqona circles, in which coconut shells fashioned as cups were filled with grog and passed around to drink.

Like Junker Singh, Manmohan was already exhausted by the day, his head a little light from the grog. But the party for the Diwali new year, which this year happened to fall on the exact same day, was just beginning. "We are getting old, Pali," he grinned at his friend.

"You are old, not me."

The chatter within grew louder. Guests were still arriving to the main house: Satnam, Priya, Karam, Vikram, and Baba Singh. And Manmohan had invited his nearest neighbors Dev, Kalyan, and Paandu, and their wives, as well as his favorite mill workers—Onkar, of course, but also Chandan, Sabar, and Vasant. His closest friends from the city were also coming: Upinder Balil, who owned Motherland Books, and Raj the sundry shop owner.

"I suppose I should go in soon," Manmohan said. "But it is such a nice night."

"What was that jazz record you once told me about?" Junker Singh asked. "Ellson, or what is his name? He was a duke I think."

"Duke Ellington."

"That is the one. I tried to find another copy of that LP, but I never could."

Manmohan nodded. "I suppose I should have pulled it out for tonight." He thought that maybe it was time for it again. "I do not know much about jazz, but that duke used to make me feel good, lighter somehow."

Junker Singh looked amused, slapping his paunch like even

Duke Ellington could not make him lighter.

"Maybe I will remember it for next year," Manmohan murmured.

"It does not matter, ji. Your wife has set a fine mood without this duke." The mechanic indicated the candles lit around the main house and the few flickering out in the clearing. "October is my favorite month, Diwali my favorite holiday. She has made it even better." He straightened. "I am off now to find your wife so I can kiss her hand." He grinned. "Then to find mine so I can kiss her lips."

Manmohan laughed.

Junker Singh pointed at the mill. "It is quite an accomplishment." He clapped Manmohan on the back. "Happy New Year, ji." And then he disappeared into the house with the other guests.

Manmohan tapped the railing with his fingers, smiling. He gazed into the darkness at the shadow of the new diesel tank that stood aloft on its iron frame, at the used flatbed he had recently bought to replace his old one.

Satnam joined him, clearing his throat in the doorway. "Happy Diwali," his brother said, stepping out onto the deck.

Manmohan's smile faded and he nodded curtly. "To you as well."

"Do you remember how we used to celebrate in Barapind, before Bapu came back?"

"No, I do not."

Satnam leaned his bottom on the railing between two candles, crossing his arms. Manmohan saw that he was very thin. He had not noticed that before. His brother's turban seemed too large for his head, and his thick beard made his cheeks look out of proportion with his sunken eyes.

"I think you do remember," Satnam said quietly.

Manmohan sighed and with one last tap of his fingers on the wood, turned to go inside.

"We used to scare the other villagers at night," his brother said, "the ones who wandered to the river to lie down in the reeds doing sexy things. We used to pretend we were animals. Do you remember how hard we laughed?"

Manmohan regarded his brother. "Is it really so important now?"

Satnam shrugged. "No, I suppose not."

Manmohan went inside the house. He did remember. They had even managed to anger the frogs—or scare them—into silence. He had always liked that, the silence, and also the glint of the moon on the water through the reeds. Baba Singh had been away in China. They had not even known who he was.

As he muttered *sat sri akal* to a number of people gathered in the living room, Jai pushed her way through the small crowd. "Gharwala, have you seen Darshan?"

"No, not since he was with you when you were lighting the candles."

"I cannot find him anywhere," she said.

Having overheard, Raj the sundry shop owner approached with his teenage daughter, Lehna. "Darshan is with Mohan. I saw them outside as I got here. They were coming in from the clearing."

Manmohan smiled at his wife. "Nothing to worry about."

"But what were they doing in the clearing at this time of night?" she said with irritation. "The party is here. It is pitch dark out there. There are not enough candles."

Manmohan frowned.

"Can you please go get them?" she asked. "Darshan wanted to help pass around the sweets. I promised him I would not forget."

"Excuse me, ji," Manmohan said, shaking Raj's hand and smiling at Lehna. "I will be right back."

Shaking several more hands, he made his way toward the front door and went outside. He surveyed the dark clearing, searching for his sons. The stairs sounded hollow beneath his feet as he descended. "Mohan, Darshan?" he called out from the bottom step. "Your mother is passing out sweets."

He waited, then cupped his hands around his mouth. "Mohan? Darshan?"

A hushed, urgent voice came from somewhere underneath the house. "Be big and brave," the voice said. "It is not so bad."

Manmohan ducked slightly so that his turban would not rub against the underside of the house's floorboards. People were moving around upstairs, the light through the boards dancing shadows across the darkness. "Mohan? Is that you?" He spotted them near a stilt close to the front staircase.

Darshan sniffled and whimpered. "Bapu," he said, holding out his hand, "I got burned."

"Come, both of you. Let's get out from under here. It is too dark for me to see anything."

In the light of a candle Manmohan assessed the small but severe and already-blistering burn on Darshan's index finger. "How did this happen?" he asked.

Mohan shrugged sheepishly, palms up. "I took him for a walk to see the lights on the other side," he said. "He touched the metal net of one of the lanterns."

"It hurts," Darshan said, crying.

"You should have watched him more carefully," Manmohan said. "He is only five. He does not know any better, but you are supposed to."

"I didn't mean anything by it, Bapu. It was an accident."

"Mohan," Manmohan said evenly. "You have been such a responsible young man lately, and it has been good to have you home and see such positive changes, though I cannot yet say with confidence that there is no other motive for this newfound wholesome behavior. Why would you take him into the jungle at night without telling anyone?"

"But I did not think I had to. We were just looking at the lights. There was no harm."

"And yet, see what has happened? While you are here under the house, worried that you will get into trouble, his finger is in pain and might get infected."

Mohan's eyes widened. "I did not realize."

Lifting Darshan in his arms, Manmohan began to climb the stairs. "You have a history of just disappearing, of not listening. You cannot expect me to forget that overnight. Your mother was scared."

Mohan sat heavily on the lowest stair.

In the kitchen, Manmohan soaked a towel in the water basin and applied it to his son's wound. The boy winced, but he stopped crying.

"What is the problem?" Satnam asked, strolling into the kitchen, a cup of tea in his hand.

"Just a burn."

"What happened?"

"Mohan."

"Mohan burnt him?" Satnam asked, astonished.

"Not on purpose. He simply did not think."

"Where is he?"

"Outside, hopefully considering his part in all this."

His brother left quietly, but Manmohan was too distracted to notice. It was the last he saw of Satnam at the party. When everyone had gone home after the new year, Manmohan discovered that his brother and Priya had taken Mohan with them to the outer islands. Jai had found a note from his son that read *I am living with Satnam Chacha now.*

~   ~   ~

What Manmohan really wanted to do was stalk the house in a rage. But he could not lose his composure in front of the children, so instead he fumed quietly, his teeth clenched as he slammed the door of his World War II truck, twisted in the handbrake to release it, and headed toward the Suva docks to commission a boat to take him to see his brother.

He rumbled down the makeshift loose-lumber driveway that they had kept since the flood. The planks settling and unsettling under the weight of his rolling vehicle sounded clunky, and the clutch smelled faintly of burnt rubber as he headed toward the main road.

It was well past one in the morning when Manmohan reached Satnam's. His brother's house was a long way on foot from the smaller island's dock. "Satnam, where is my son?" he called out, pounding on the front door.

He noted with distaste the manicured perfection of the yard. It was too dark to see clearly, but he had been here before and knew that every single leaf had been arranged. He always hated that, preferring nature have some say.

The door swung open. Satnam held a candle in one hand and a mango in the other. He had not changed out of his clothes or removed his turban for the night. In the flicker of the single flame he appeared like a sick old man. "You will wake everyone," he said.

"Where is Mohan?"

Leaving the door wide open, Satnam casually backed inside.

He took a seat on his couch. It was upholstered in that peach-colored fabric that Priya loved. Setting the candle on an end table, he bit a hole in the mango's skin, then spit the skin piece into his palm. He began sucking the mango pulp through the hole.

"Where is my son?" Manmohan asked again, refusing to enter. "I am taking him home."

"You treat him like a fool," Satnam replied, wiping his mouth with the back of his arm.

"Sometimes he acts like one. But I am his father, and I decide how to treat him."

"I know what it is like, to see a father hurt his son simply because he refuses to understand him."

"And you know him better?" Manmohan scoffed.

"I do. We talk."

"You behave as though I have done something wrong. But you have no right to judge me, just because you have always been so important, just because you were never held accountable for your mistakes."

"What mistakes?" Satnam asked, setting the half eaten mango on the table. "What do you know of my mistakes?"

"I know you are lazy."

Satnam shot him a curt, forlorn smile. "I don't know. Maybe I am. But you are not flawless. You give up too quickly. You expect a lot, and then give up when you do not get it."

"You do not know how long and how hard I have worked to make Bapu proud of me."

"I know nothing of the troubles between you and Bapu. I was talking about Mohan. He is too scared of you to ask for anything. Last year when he needed help with his turban—"

"It was *you*?"

Satnam shrugged dispassionately. He again picked up the

mango and peeled back a sliver of skin to eat the meat.

Manmohan glanced around the living room. Like the flowers out front, it was all very arranged, not one curio out of place. It seemed as though the vase on the shelf, the chairs set in a semi-circle around the couch, and the transistor radio on the coffee table were glued down. Controlled. But it was pointless. If any one item were moved, the whole room would crumble.

His eyes lingered for a moment longer on the radio. He had not listened to one in years, although he meant to before Mohan had stolen his. Now he wished he really had taken out his gramophone during the party and spun Duke Ellington. He wished that it was not too late.

Returning his gaze to Satnam, Manmohan said, "If you think you can do better, you can have him." And then he turned back toward the docks.

Pasteurized & Homogenized
1957

Manmohan recognized the neat formation of Punjabi characters, tidy and compact, on the front of the overseas mail in Baba Singh's hand. He had gotten just enough of a glimpse to catch the April 1957 postmark across the bottom before his father folded it in half and shoved it into his trouser pocket.

"Post from Barapind," Baba Singh said in an oddly monotone voice.

"What news?" Vikram asked from where he was bent over rinsing out several large milk pots at the water pump just outside the open door of the pasteurization shed.

"She is not coming," Baba Singh replied tersely, finally receiving the answer to a question he had asked ten years before. The muscles around his eyes and mouth were tight.

Vikram released the handle of the pump and straightened, water spattering mud onto his ankles until the flow eased to a drip. Manmohan set down the sieve through which he had been pouring milk.

"We know, Bapu," Vikram said gently.

"She is not coming," Baba Singh said again.

Manmohan checked his broken watch, aware of all the passing years stored within. It gripped his wrist like an admonishing hand as he saw his mother's lifeless body floating down the Ravi River, alight with fire, none of them there to properly send her off, to say farewell.

"Just leave it be," Baba Singh told them. He switched on the boiler to pasteurize the milk and pulled out the temperature gauge.

He had already assessed the quantity the cows had yielded that day. He had already determined an amount for making butter, setting aside several buckets of pure, untouched milk to refrigerate. In the cold of the icebox, the cream would separate into a top layer, which they would later churn and sell in Suva's open marketplace. The rest he would set on the double boiler for pasteurization, to be heated to one-hundred and forty-five degrees, cleansed of unhealthy microorganisms, making it safe for human consumption. "It kills the bacteria and some of the enzymes," Baba Singh had explained in the beginning, standing on a stool, pouring a bucketful of unprocessed milk into one of the huge pots on the stove.

Manmohan never doubted that pasteurization was necessary, but he nonetheless felt the process was regrettable, loving the flavor of fresh milk just as it came, straight from the cow. Pasteurization resulted in a disappointing taste. All the fine flavor, everything about milk that made it enjoyable to drink—the creamy, thick, satisfying feel of it, especially sweetened with almond shavings—had been boiled away. One hour on the stove was all it took. One hour to destroy perfectly good-tasting milk.

Vikram passed Baba Singh several buckets until both pots were full. Steamy condensation edged its way up the outside of the aluminum receptacles in waves as the pasteurization process began.

The boiler hissed. Metallic hardware clanked as they tidied the milking shed littered with sieves and strainers. They worked without speaking, the clatter of their movement shaping barriers between them. Manmohan had not known anything about his mother since coming to Fiji, how she lived, what she dreamt about, who she talked to. He found himself now wondering what her favorite foods had been. He had once read in a science journal that a person's palate changed every seven years. He had not seen her for nearly twenty.

Her silence had caused her to become strangely infinite in his mind, immortalized on Amarpur's train station platform. He riffled through his memories to bring to the forefront the image of that long-ago day in 1938. He studied the memory of his mother's eyes carefully, remembering what she had said, her jet-black irises full of regret: the ocean will swallow you whole.

Needing air, Manmohan backed away from the stove, bumping into the shed's center counter and causing a sieve to brush across the surface, leaving behind a trail of milky droplets. He turned, searching for a towel, something with which to clean it, but the towels were on the shelf behind his father, and those he could not reach.

"She knew it," Manmohan told Baba Singh.

The old man raised his eyebrows, heated, feeling challenged. "What did she know?"

"That we would never go back."

His father shot Manmohan a tight, angry grin. "You should not speak further."

Vikram placed a hand on Manmohan's forearm, giving a squeeze. "Let it be," he whispered.

Manmohan stared at his father for a long, stony moment,

and then he let his eyes fall and went home.

The warm smell of freshly made roti with butter wafted from the main house as he approached in his truck, smoke from the stovepipe drifting upward into the sky. Manmohan wove his way into the lumber mill's clearing, his stomach suddenly burning with need.

Pulling into the carport, he saw Mohan perched at the top of a large pile of logs, his face set in its usual expression of sardonic disdain. Something between them had broken with finality when Manmohan left him with Satnam that night. He had not really believed his son would so stringently prefer his uncle over his own father, had not really believed he would stay away for over a year. Mohan had returned sometime just after the following Diwali, which he celebrated with Satnam and Priya in what Manmohan later discovered was a rather oppressive party of Priya's women's group and their gutless husbands. Priya had bullied Mohan into serving snacks and drinks, excusing her own son from such duties with the assertion that it was Karam's home and he would not be a servant in it.

When the boy had walked through the main house front door after all that time on the remote, isolated island, there was a note crumpled in his fist. Priya had written that Mohan had been a bad influence on Karam, that he was always contriving to distract her brilliant son from his studies, and that since the moment Mohan had moved into their home, his innate stupidity had been rubbing off on his cousin. Announcing his return to the mill, Mohan had slammed the note to the living room floor in a weightless, dissatisfying scuff of paper against the wooden floorboards. No words, just pent up and inexpressible rage that even now, four years later, had not been purged.

Manmohan had felt sorry for his son then, and although there were often times when he was overwhelmed by a stab of fatherly compassion, he could not help but feel uneasy and wary in Mohan's presence, like his son was constantly pondering and perfecting a plan of vengeance, fueled by the cheap alcohol he drank.

Parking, Manmohan yanked the hand brake tight and climbed out of the cabin. "I told you not to sit up there like that," he called out. "You are too heavy. That pile will roll out from under you."

Mohan nimbly skipped down the pile, a gangly-legged nineteen-year-old of medium height with disproportionately wide shoulders, his thick turban and beard making him appear top heavy. Leaning against the pile of logs from which he had just scampered down, Mohan said in a controlled, intoxicated slur. "You do not look well, Bapu."

Manmohan trudged up the stairs, wondering if somewhere in the fog of drink, there was sympathy in Mohan's eyes, if maybe the drink made it honest. He caught another whiff of the cooking smells settling over the clearing and put the uncertain idea from his mind. Jai was waiting upstairs for him. He let thoughts of Amarpur and the train station platform loosen and ebb away. Shielding his brow with his arm, he looked skyward, as though watching the memories of Sada Kaur join the smoke from his wife's cooking, spiraling up in tendrils until it was nothing at all. When he entered the house, his mouth was already watering for Jai's creamy spinach with ghee, and also for a taste of her chai, fragrant with cardamom, cloves, and a hint of black pepper. Soon he would be sitting on a stool to watch her stir food in pots and slap her hands on her apron to clean off the flour while he sipped the warm tea from a mug. He would tell her what had happened, and then he would never talk about it again. She would serve him a plate, knowing that the best thing for him would be a bite of her food.

~ ~ ~

The beach was a twinkling landscape of trash fires. It was beautiful from afar in this half-light time of day before night. Baba Singh knew his family would be looking for him, but he wanted to stay for a while.

He had told himself he would release his sorrow, replace the dark part of him that had allowed murder with something beautiful and forgiving. Yet his whole life he had clung to his grief like a buoy in a vast and infinite sea, the choices and years behind him merely a series of dishonest attempts at making his losses, both immutable and immense, cease to feel so empty, at making his unrelenting guilt not weigh so heavily upon him. This was why he had brought his father's chest with him to Fiji. He had waited all these years for the moment when he would be ready to open it again, dump its contents into the waves that lapped against the Fijian shores, watching as it floated to the ocean's horizon and over the edge of the world. It now sat in his room in the shack at the dairy farm, reminding him of Sada Kaur and what she had always known, that he was lost and that he had lied to her about it, had lied to himself.

He took off his chappals and ran his toes through the sand, holding a coconut in his cupped palms. Darshan had given it to him earlier that day. Baba Singh had been sitting at the back of the mill's main house against one of the stilts, kinking the end of a coiled black-rubber hose. He had been there for nearly an hour, staring blankly at the rushing river, listening to the muted sounds coming from upstairs: the footsteps and voices of friends and family who insisted on paying their respects even though they had never known his wife. Gazing toward the river where the crickets communed in the brush of the embankment, he had spotted Darshan skidding down the verdant hill beyond the river through the thick mass of ferns. The boy gripped a coconut in his hand, held aloft, maneuvering the narrow pathway the children had carved out with all their many footraces from the crest down to the water where they loved to swim.

Baba Singh shuddered. When Darshan had reached the base of the hill, stepping over the taro, cassava, and chilies that Manmohan recently planted, for one fearful second his grandson appeared like the faceless man in his nightmare.

"For you, Dadaji," Darshan had said simply, stretching his arms forward to offer the coconut.

Baba Singh studied his grandson's face, trying to erase the apprehension he felt at being reminded of his dream. The smile around Darshan's almond-shaped eyes was gentle, and his light brown cheeks were flushed with pink. It was a nice face.

"What is it for?" Baba Singh asked.

"I thought it would make you feel better."

"You really thought so?" Baba Singh replied. His voice carried an edge that he had not intended.

"I know it is not much."

"Then what is the point?"

Timidly, Darshan said, "I don't know."

Baba Singh tried to relax, sensing the boy's unease. He patted the ground next to him.

Encouraged, Darshan took a seat on the soft earth and explained, "When I am tired I eat a coconut. Gives me energy."

"Someone once told me that a coconut has everything a man needs for life."

"That must be it then."

Baba Singh put the hose down. "Do you ever have strange dreams?"

Darshan placed the coconut between them. "I usually cannot remember my dreams."

Baba Singh recalled the damp of the soil underneath his palms as he had sat there with his grandson. Pressing down, he had made impressions in the ground, not letting his hand get too close to the coconut. "I have dreams," he had said.

"What about?"

"About many things. One of them was about you, before you were born."

Darshan considered the implications of this information. Finally he asked, a little concerned, "Was it a good dream or a bad one?"

"Neither."

Darshan squinted as though studying something down by the river, wrapping his thin arms around his ashen knees. Baba Singh wondered what his dream about the boy meant, wondered about his grandson. Darshan did not say anything, so he did not press the subject and for a time they listened to the river and the jungle sounds around them.

Regarding the coconut, Baba Singh finally asked, breaking the silence, "From the ground, or the tree?"

Darshan glanced at him, confused.

Baba Singh pointed to the coconut palms at the top of the hill. "Did you get that from the ground at the base of the tree? Or did you go up and get it from the tuft?"

Darshan shifted his eyes away guiltily. Baba Singh knew his grandson was not supposed to climb the coconut trees, especially the ones at the top of the hill. He reached out to pick up the coconut, quickly, like tearing a bandage from a wound.

"It is more valuable then," he said, "from the top of the tree. It is a gift you worked hard to give."

"I suppose so." Then Darshan grinned. "But it was also fun."

Baba Singh smiled faintly. "It is good to have fun. Otherwise life will swallow you whole, Darshan. That is what your grandmother knew; it is what she told us before we left India."

"Are you having fun?" his grandson asked.

The question had unnerved Baba Singh, shook his very core, and the whole of his life had caught in his mouth as he shook his head.

Now cupping the coconut in his hand, the grains of sand were cool on his feet. The ocean wind whistled in his ears, and the beach trash fires became brighter and more orange. Khushwant's letter was in his trousers, folded into squares. He walked over to one of the smoldering fires and pulled the letter from his pocket. He unfolded it and placed the paper in the sand next to the smoking pile of garbage, not setting it directly into the fire. He wanted it to burn, but he could not bring himself to watch as it did. He weighed the letter down with the coconut so that it could not escape with the wind, to keep the news of his wife's death near enough to the flames so that it would eventually burn and turn to ash, the remaining carbon compounds of it making their way into his dreams where they would shower down from the dark dome of night sky over the Punjabi plains.

It was time to go back to India.

~ ~ ~

The smell of milk permeated the shed, its faintly sweet

scent pleasantly lingering in Manmohan's beard, in his clothes, his skin, in the wooden walls and floor. He was alone now, appreciating the solitude. His friends, who had already expressed their condolences, were still concerned for him, but he lacked the energy to speak with them about it, to sort through the complicated nature of his loss, to feign sadness when all he felt was empty.

He brooded over the homogenization machine, hoping some feeling of hurt would well up deep within him so he could catch it, pull at it until it rose upward and out. Then he would be consoled by his own humanity. But after analyzing himself for a moment, searching, he discovered nothing but fury for his father, who had told him, after all these years of waiting, after a broken promise of the greatest magnitude, that he was finally returning home.

Adjusting the tubes on the homogenization machine, Manmohan slammed one against the inside edge of the aluminum tub. After an hour on the double boiler, when the milk had cooled, the machine would squeeze the pasteurized formula through small, tapered tubes in order to disperse its fat evenly throughout. As the pressure built up, the fat globules would break apart, making the milk consistent in texture, smoother on the palate. But what difference did texture make when taste had already been lost?

"I am not coming back," Baba Singh had told him, peering outside through the open door of the empty cowshed where they had been standing, watching as several of the cattle languidly made their way across the grazing field to huddle under a tree in the shade. "We have enough employees on the farm now so that it will run itself. I have given it to Satnam. You have always been so devoted to your own endeavors."

Flicking on the homogenizing machine, Manmohan's hands

shook with fury. The generator revved up, humming loudly. The tubes soon grew taut, strained with the pressure of fat emulsifying. The spray of milk into the homogenization receptacle sounded like a water faucet running into an empty aluminum tub.

For as long as he could remember, it had been like this. During their first days in Fiji Baba Singh had excused Satnam from helping with the task of finding them all a place to live. Poor Satnam had been the sickest from the long voyage at sea. And when they needed to find jobs, Baba Singh had given Satnam the time to consider his options, to find something that suited him, while Manmohan's job at Spencer's supported the entire family. In 1944 Manmohan and Vikram had voluntarily gone with Baba Singh to help build a Sikh temple two hours northeast of Suva in Nassinu. It took a month to erect the temple and prepare it for its first prayer, but Satnam never joined them. He was too busy, or too tired, or else disinclined. Baba Singh had accepted every one of those excuses without judgment or reprimand. But only for Satnam. The rest of them had to scramble and hoist and toil and labor.

When the homogenization receptacle was full, Manmohan took a large metal pole with a masher on the end and roughly thrust it into the milk. He jabbed it in several times to break up the unwanted assembly of stubborn fat microns that insisted on clumping together even after shoved through tubes clearly meant to tear them apart.

It was dusk when he finally came out of the shed. Baba Singh and Vikram were sitting on chairs outside their shack nibbling on dried, spiced peas.

"Come sit with us," Vikram said, standing to pull out another chair.

Manmohan shook his head. "It's late. I am tired."

His brother offered some peas, smiling. "Just for a moment."

"Why aren't you angry?" Manmohan asked him. "Hasn't he told you?"

"I told him," Baba Singh said, raising his head from his bowl of peas.

"Manmohan, please sit," Vikram said. "We have a lot to discuss."

"You should be angry," Manmohan told him fiercely.

"I am going with him," his brother said. "I am going back."

Manmohan stood frozen for several moments. Then he tersely turned to go.

Vikram threw up his hands. "Do not leave," he called. "Let's talk."

Climbing into his truck, Manmohan started the engine. He adjusted the rearview mirror, moving it slightly so that his father came into view. He watched Baba Singh eating his peas and Vikram standing there, defeated. Then he pressed his foot to the gas pedal, steering down the dusty drive toward the main road.

He watched them recede in the mirror, getting smaller and smaller, further irritated when he saw Baba Singh finish his peas, stand, and step into his shack without any satisfying indications of regret. No long gaze as his son drove away, no hand on his forehead lamenting his mistake and the inequity of his decision. Nothing at all but stepping out of sight into his shack where he was likely beginning preparations for dinner, firing up the stove out back, pulling aside the tarps and tying them with string so the smoke could escape, then heating food that Jai had sent over. After dinner he would stretch out on his mattress and fall asleep.

Manmohan slammed down on the brake, causing the truck

to skid and jerk sharply forward. A cloud of dust gusted up from under the tires. Slipping the gearshift into reverse, twisting his body around, gripping the bench seat, he made his way back to the shack, which now loomed larger in his rear window as he sped nearer. Again stepping firmly on the brake, he shoved the gear into neutral and jumped out, leaving the truck running. He walked purposefully toward a stack of corrugated iron panels he had purchased for their plans to expand the milk shed. The panels had lain untouched for several weeks, and they were beginning to rust.

From the corner of his eye, Manmohan saw Vikram signal him to stop, then give up as if knowing it would not help.

Rushing outside and following Manmohan to the panels, Baba Singh said sharply, "Enough!"

Ignoring him, Manmohan lifted the edge of two panels and dragged them toward the back of his truck, the corrugated iron making a trail of crimped furrows in the ground.

"Put them back," his father said.

Manmohan hoisted the panels awkwardly into the truck and went back for the last two.

Spitting his words through clenched teeth, Baba Singh said, "You are behaving like a child."

"Should I behave like you, Bapu?" Manmohan asked, his voice loud, the edges of the other two panels digging into his palms. "You who abandoned his wife? Like Satnam who is lazy and who stole my son, only to let his wife treat him like a slave and then send him back to me like garbage?"

"You know nothing about your brother, or about me."

Manmohan shoved the two remaining panels into the truck. Catching his breath, he asked, "Why did you wait until after she died?"

"Why did you?" Baba Singh asked, his voice powerful and

quiet, ruthlessly intimidating.

A sudden rush of love and regret came upon Manmohan, weakening his anger. "I wanted to stay with you, for as long as you were here." He shook his head. "Why did you even come to Fiji?"

"Put the panels in their place, Manmohan."

"Why should Satnam have them?"

"He needs them more than you do. He has always needed more."

"Because he is *weaker*?" Manmohan asked, incredulous, finally understanding.

Baba Singh's fists tightened. "Do not call him that."

Manmohan climbed into his truck. "You have made him worse, Bapu. Not better."

The panels vibrated against each other as the diesel engine rumbled down the road toward the mill. A memory surfaced as he drove, guilt as always beginning to prod at him. The rich smell of soil stimulated his nostrils as he remembered the canal on the outskirts of Barapind. He was eleven years old. He had fallen and his knees were bloody. Rolling over, he wiped the mud from his face, blew on his scrapes, flapping his hands in an effort not to feel the sting.

"Are you hurt?" Satnam shouted, running toward him, crashing through the reeds.

"No," Manmohan said, but it was a lie, and he was afraid.

His brother grinned then. "You are too fast, not looking in front of you."

"I know. I wanted to win."

"Can you walk?"

Manmohan winced. "In a minute."

Satnam pulled a cloth from his pocket and wrapped it around one of his brother's knees.

"Why do you have that?" Manmohan asked him.

His brother shrugged. "I always have one with me, just in case."

"In case you get hurt?"

"In case you do, or Vikram," Satnam replied. He had only been six years old.

The truck hit a hole in the ground and the panels jumped and slammed down into the bed. Manmohan turned to look at them, sighing with pity for his brother.

~ ~ ~

"That is impossible," Manmohan said loudly, waving the document in the British official's face. "When we received this lease, we were told—"

"Whatever you were told was inaccurate," the official said, turning over a sheet of paper. He flicked his eyes up from where he was seated at his small desk. His expression was bland, like the whitewashed wood and mortar around him had dulled the color of his face after years of working in that office.

"You cannot simply take away a family's livelihood."

The official clasped his hands together over the papers on his desk and focused his attention impatiently on Manmohan. "Your father is the person of record on this lease. It is non-transferrable."

"But he will be gone in just a few weeks. We were told—"

"Perhaps a local Fijian working at the leasing office told you something that you did not then verify with the administration. The Empire has the final say here."

An assistant, a native Fijian man, middle aged with dark skin, his kinky hair pulled back into a band, was standing at attention to the left of the desk. A flash of annoyance crossed the dull whites of his eyes. Affronted, he adjusted his shoulders, pulling them back straighter.

"We have heard all this before," a man shouted from the back of the small room. By the rugged creases in his face, darkened by hard labor, he looked to be an oil worker, and a Muslim from the cap on his head. "Do not waste your time," the man told Manmohan. "We have been trying to get the British to understand that we cannot live on the pay they give us. It has been years, and they do not seem to care that we are starving. They only want to bleed us dry."

Trying his best to ignore the oil worker, Manmohan began again, keeping his tone even. "I was an army signal for the British, and for many years my brothers and I were colonial police officers, as was my father who served in China. My brother needs this farm."

The British official looked away as if bored. "If you wish to appeal it," he said, "we are open to listening. The appeals office is down that way."

Manmohan glanced toward the assistant as if to ask for help. Despite what had been a long segregation of Indian and Fijian races on the island, Manmohan could see that this native sympathized with him. The assistant pursed his lips and shook his head slightly, suggesting that an appeal would be a waste of time.

When he exited Suva's parliament offices, Manmohan balled the lease that had grown damp from his sweaty palm and tossed it into the street. He walked away past the courthouse guard, the lease soaking in a puddle from the recent storm.

"Why did you go there?" Jai asked when he got home. "It is Satnam's problem." She was in the living room, sitting on a footstool, hand-grinding spices into a small wooden bowl.

Manmohan leaned back into the couch. "I don't know."

She stopped and looked at him with irritation. "After all this time, you feel sorry for him?"

He stood from the couch to sit on the floor next to her stool. Touching her wrist, he was about to speak, then closed his mouth, instead bringing her hand to his bearded cheek. He kept it there for a time, inhaling the freshly ground mustard seed at her feet and under her nails, until finally she sighed and let it drop.

Manmohan spent the next several days in the backlands supervising the loggers, trying to clear his head. He had felt the need to remove himself temporarily from his family's reach, to go to a place where the only sounds were the loud crash of trees falling into the jungle underbrush and the rough gnash of the saw's teeth on wood. Baba Singh and Vikram would be leaving soon, and this confused and unsettled him.

When he returned to the mill, he was exhausted from the steady and hard work of collecting the felled logs and roping them to his flatbed trucks. He strode slowly and heavily up the stairs to the main house. Pulling the workman's gloves from the back pocket of his trousers, he set them on the table by the front door as he entered the living room.

Satnam was on the couch.

"I did not expect to see you here," Manmohan said.

"I have been checking in. I heard what you did with the lease."

Manmohan cleared his throat uncomfortably. "Is Priya here?"

Satnam shook his head. "She is upset with me."

Manmohan sat on a chair opposite the couch.

"A lot has happened in the last few days," his brother said, gripping his knees, arms stretched out, elbows locked. "I have decided to go with Bapu."

"I see," Manmohan said, not surprised.

"Priya does not want to go. But it is all right. I never wanted the farm. I could stay, but…" his voice trailed off uneasily. He sighed. "I should go with him."

"You do not have to do that anymore."

"I think I do."

"You were different before Bapu came back from Barapind."

"That was a long time ago. I remember it, the images I guess, but I don't remember how it felt. You were different, too."

Manmohan leaned forward. "Would you like some chai?" he asked. He wanted Satnam to stay for a while.

"No, no," his brother put up a hand. "I just came to tell you. And Vikram will come by. He has his own plans. He will stay a while in Barapind, then go to England for school. He wants to be a professor at Oxford."

Manmohan smiled, but his smile quickly faded, realizing he would be left in Fiji, that he was never going back. "Yes, I suppose that is what he would be good at."

"What about you?" Satnam asked.

"Will I go?"

Satnam nodded.

"No," Manmohan said, his voice firm. "I do not think so. Not this time."

~ ~ ~

The dairy farm was still. Manmohan was struck by the dead sound of the place without its usual generator hum. Nature sounds were more audible, the rustling palm leaves and the skulking footsteps of small animals. He had come for a look around, to retrieve anything he might need for the mill before the government reclaimed the land. He pushed open the door to Baba Singh and Vikram's shack and went inside. It was small, with only two rooms, each with a cot. Vikram's room had been emptied of personal possessions. But Baba Singh's room still looked as if he would come back. His bed was neatly made, and his few belongings were still arranged as they had always been since moving here.

They had traveled by jet, departing from Nadi airport, Baba Singh boarding a plane at age fifty-three, not at all intimidated by that unknown. Manmohan had been a little envious of them, watching through the chain link fence as they accelerated down the runway. He tried to imagine what they would see from up there, how big the ocean and the earth and how small the island.

Clinging to the fence as the plane lifted into the sky, Darshan asked, "Will we see them again?"

"I don't know," Manmohan replied, glancing over at Mohan, who was squatting on the ground, squinting at the plane. Things were clearer now after talking with Satnam. He hoped maybe he could make it right with Mohan. He wanted to ask if his son believed that another chance was possible. But he was not able to form the words. Maybe it was enough that he had thought them. It was a start of sorts.

"I want to go to India, too," Livleen said, smiling dreamily with a five-year-old's imagination.

Navpreet jammed one of her loafered toes into a chain link hole. She was wearing a sundress, and her black hair had been washed that morning, slicked back into a rubber band and braided. Rolling her eyes at Darshan, she had said, "Maybe *you* will never see them again, but *I* am going to India some day."

Standing in Baba Singh's room, Manmohan was not sure

what would happen. The reality of the Toors dispersed across the globe just as some things were beginning to be clear gave him a hollow feeling, like being hungry but not wanting to eat.

Against the wall, next to Baba Singh's bed, Manmohan was surprised to see his father's chest. He knelt and opened it, releasing the musty scent of things long closed in. He discovered a few items of women's clothing and an ivory bangle, a broken-toothed wooden comb, a hand-painted wooden elephant that he recognized as Satnam's. There was also a faded, moth-eaten red turban, an old debt ledger with pages and pages of markings in neat columns and rows, a vial made of green glass with liquid inside, chisels, a smoking pipe of some kind, and a dented tin containing all of Khushwant's letters.

With the exception of the letters and the elephant, Manmohan knew they belonged to people who had died, important people. He tried to imagine what of his mother's he would add, but he did not have any of her possessions, nor did he remember the things she had called hers. He knelt beside the chest, leaning heavily over it, clutching the sides. Smiling, he decided that he would place the memory of her black irises within, and also the quiet fortitude that had sustained his happy and carefree life as a child.

Something about the maroon turban was very familiar. He held it close to his nose, breathing in deeply the dulled scent of gunpowder and metal. Closing his eyes he saw a one-eyed man speaking softly to him, walking with him through the winding lanes of Barapind. Manmohan realized then that he also knew the elephant. Long before Desa had given it to Satnam, this one-eyed man had given it to him for safekeeping.

I do not think we will see them again, he thought, in answer to Darshan's question.

279

Replacing the turban, Manmohan closed the lid and carried the chest to his truck. At the main house he heaved it up the ladder and into the rafters where he then slid it into place next to the old plywood box.

Malady & Mutiny
1959

Fevers heat the body, cells boiling into riotous, chilling shudders. They heat the mind, creating a torrent of babbling thought, brain synapses loosened and wild. Manmohan traced his finger slowly over the lines of text in his medical journal, reading, contemplating. He snapped the book shut. But they cool the spirit, he thought. To ignite the body and the mind, they drain the spirit of its warmth, leaving it cool and dark.

A quiet, wintry fear had returned as he sat vigil outside Livleen's room, his daughter plagued by the same illness that had long ago taken his son. Odd, unintelligible murmurs escaped her, flushed out by the heat. He listened hard, his own spirit depleted, cooling with hers.

He had not been to bed in two days and slept in a chair in the hallway. He again opened the book, trying hard to focus on the medical terminology that grounded him, words he could hold and dissect, but his neck hung, his mouth went slack, and the journal slipped from his thick fingers, falling with a rustling of pages to the floor.

He woke with a start. Junker Singh was covering him with a blanket.

"I am not cold, ji," Manmohan told him with bleary eyes, struggling to lift his head.

The mechanic insisted. "You were shivering."

"Is she awake?"

"No, ji, not yet. Jai is with her. You should go in. Do not stay out here."

Manmohan closed his eyes again. He could not go inside. He did not have the courage. "Who is this girl?" he heard himself say, but the house was empty and it was only him, sobbing in his chair. "Who is she? Is she mine?"

"She is yours," someone said. "But I know you do not want her. I know you do not want any of them."

"I want them. I am here in this chair. I want them."

"Sitting here like this only makes you believe that you want them. Nonetheless, she will be fine. The same events cannot happen twice."

It was his own voice in his own mind, he realized, half asleep, aware of his stiff body in the chair, aware of his aching neck. He woke again, wearily rubbing his eyes. Listening through the door, there was no sound coming from Livleen's room, no more mumbles of distress.

His medical journal was gone, and there was a bowl of rice and spiced taro for him on the hallway floor. Someone had laid out a sleeping mat. Pushing aside the food, he thankfully crawled onto it.

Sometime later, his mind once again pulled through the tunnel of deep sleep into consciousness, he sensed movement about him, people stepping into and out of the sickroom, but he did not open his eyes. He listened, for panic, for grief, but heard only muffled speech through the door, the sloshing of water in a bucket, the snap of a sheet as someone shook it out. Then he felt a shadow hovering near, kneeling beside him, and he groggily peeled open his eyelids.

"Bapu," Mohan whispered. "Come see. Livleen is awake."

"Is it over?" Manmohan asked.

His son nodded, his expression a mixture of relief and a question, asking why he had never been loved this much.

"I want to see her," Manmohan said, pushing up off the floor, shakily standing.

Mohan grabbed hold to steady him. "She will not be the same. She will have pain for a while. The doctor said she might never fully recover, that her heart has been damaged."

Manmohan faltered.

"But she is smiling," Mohan told him, holding open the bedroom door. "She wants to go to school."

Livleen was sitting up in her bed, encircled by white pillows and fresh-smelling sheets, her complexion pallid. Her dark hair had been combed and hung loose about her shoulders, a young royal amongst her devoted subjects, bestowing blessings and well-wishes with her encouraging smile. Jai was beside her, cleaning out the hairbrush. Her eyes had sunk deep, were dark and haunted, but there were signs of optimism in them now. She only needed rest. Junker Singh sat at the foot of the bed, Navpreet and Darshan beside him, leaning into him, both uncertain and bewildered.

"I hear you are already determined to go to school," Manmohan said, smoothing down the front of his beard with both hands, astonished by the resilience of youth, the bright, sharp eyes, the determined will.

Livleen nodded rigidly against the still painful rheumatoid lingering in her joints. "I missed the first days. Now everyone knows more than I do."

Manmohan stood next to Jai, placing a hand on her shoulder. "It is a very long way to school. You are not strong enough to walk that far."

"I will be," she said quickly.

"We will see," he told her, and this seemed to satisfy her. She snuggled into her pillows, her eyelids heavy, sweat glistening around her hairline. Jai squeezed a sponge into a bucket and dabbed the sweat clean.

"I can carry her," Mohan said. He spoke with such pleading that Manmohan saw a different sort of fever, of anguish and hope churning together, of a desire to be smarter, to have made different choices, to return to school, to open books, to read with fervor, his cheeks flushed with a desperation to be important, his spirit made cold because he did not believe he was.

~ ~ ~

A squeal in the distance jerked Manmohan from his reading chair.

"Stay calm," Junker Singh told him.

Bolting for the window, a sense of dread dropped like an iron ball in Manmohan's stomach as he cursed his friend who had convinced him that young people recover quickly when they are happiest. "Just let the boy carry her," the mechanic had said. "Let them enjoy it."

But there had been small riots in recent days—short, angry bursts of indignation against the British. The *Fiji Times* made events worse with its reports, escalating fear and panic. Although there had been no incidents of violence and the riots had been contained near the docks, Manmohan worried that the children would be caught on the streets at the wrong time, swept up into a rush of protesting men and women.

The mechanic joined his friend by the window and said, "There is no reason for alarm."

Pressing his face close to the pane of glass, Manmohan searched the curve of the wood-paved drive that turned toward the main road until he finally saw Mohan come around the bend, approaching the house with Livleen in his arms like a stack of firewood. Her legs dangled limply, and one of her arms was flung around his neck, her head thrown flaccidly back. Oh God, he thought.

But she was laughing.

Inhaling slowly with relief, Manmohan stepped out onto the porch to greet them. The aroma of cut lumber and wet earth from the river was strong. A cacophony of sounds came from the clearing in front of him and from the house behind him: the men chatting while working around the disorganized piles of plywood littered everywhere, the squabbling chickens, the roosters who seemed to think every hour was dawn, the barking dogs, the bleating goats, the clamor of steel and aluminum pots from the kitchen as Jai prepared tea and meals for the workers.

"What is the joke?" Junker Singh called down, placing his hands on stiff, sun-dried clothing hanging over the rail.

"My shoes are still shiny!" Livleen shouted up to the balcony, grinning. "All the other girls got theirs dirty."

The staircase creaked as Mohan climbed up. "She has a personal mule," he said playfully. Grunting, he set his sister down in a chair by the front door. "Heavier than she looks," he smiled. "You comfortable?"

She nodded.

"How was school?" Manmohan asked. "What did you learn?"

"We have an English teacher," she told him. "And I pet a lizard. And we had math."

Mohan sat on the top step of the porch, placing his forearms on his knees. "We had fun, too."

Livleen stuck out her red tongue. "See?" she showed them. "Mohan bought me a frozen juice stick on the way home. I was worried about passing Penitentiary Hill, but he told me that the men in there will never hurt me. He knows the person who keeps the keys, and that person would never open those gates without Mohan's permission."

Manmohan touched his daughter's limbs, examining her elbows and ankles. "How do you feel?"

"Fine."

He gently pressed her knee. "A little swollen," he murmured.

She mimicked him, reaching forward to press his knee. Junker Singh nodded at her with approval.

"What is happening in town?" Manmohan asked his son.

"The streets seemed a little quiet, and the bus took longer than usual."

"I don't blame the oilmen," Junker Singh said. "They know a fair wage. They know they are not getting it."

"They are spreading their complaints, making the British angry," Manmohan said resentfully. "Everyone is affected. People are going mad."

Junker Singh raised his finger in disagreement. "My shop has no parts because they are too expensive or not coming on the cargo ships. That is not their fault. Smells like the British. People deserve to go mad." He paused, considering. "But they leased you extra land. Perhaps it is not all bad."

"Perhaps, ji," Manmohan replied, still uncertain. The logging rights for an additional one-thousand acres in the backcountry had been very good for the mill. With the additional income, Manmohan had bought two more Caterpillar tractors, four more electric table saws, and a brand-new Bedford flatbed, seven tons of hauling power he filled with petrol from a pump he had installed next to the diesel tank. He built two more carports for all his vehicles. And the benefits of good business began to reflect on the house. He added rooms, creating a maze of corridors roofed with corrugated-iron panels held down by an abundance of heavy, loose lumber. He bought seeds for a number of new fresh vegetables in his garden—cucumbers, squash, taro, pepper—and planted fruit trees at the back of the house by the river: tamarind, with their stiff brown pods of sticky sweet and sour meat, apple, guava, and mango. Jai kept busy with the additional livestock, feeding the animals, milking the recently purchased cows and goats, and slaughtering chickens for curry.

The undercurrent of unrest on the island, however, concerned Manmohan. The additional lease had not been easy to obtain. He had to petition the British administrators in Suva's government buildings three times, threatening to cut their lumber supply before they had finally relinquished the land. The officials argued that Indians were thriving too much on the island and that the local Fijians needed some say about how their land was distributed. But whenever Manmohan had to stand in line with roomfuls of people, he heard them all muttering darkly under their breaths, Indo-Fijians and natives together, saying they were sick of the abuse, of being forced to accept insufficient payment for their hard work, of being suppressed when they wanted to grow.

"It is like 1943 again," Junker Singh said, "when the Colonial Sugar Refining Agency went up against the British."

"We should do something like that," Mohan said. He held

up a flyer from the Wholesale and Retail General Workers' Union. "'Never before in the history of this country has the need for unity been so great,'" he read. "People are tired of being underpaid. First the cane farmers, now the oil workers. In a few years it will be others if we do not do something."

"I have seen that," Junker Singh said, indicating the flyer. "But those cane farmers protested by burning all their cane. What good was that protest when they had nothing left to sell? In any case, it would not matter. The Fijians have never been interested in uniting with Indians on political issues."

Manmohan shook his head. "That seems to be changing."

"People should not take less than they deserve," Mohan said. "That is what happened with Dadaji's dairy farm. They took it away, a family's hard work."

Manmohan glanced at his son, surprised by his vehemence.

Mohan lowered his voice. "People should be treated with fairness." He looked at the flyer one last time, then folded it in half and placed it on the small table near where he was sitting.

Junker Singh responded with a slow, tired shrug.

The smell of cardamom being boiled in milk drifted into the living room.

"That is very nice," the mechanic said to no one in particular, a hint of a smile on his lips as he took a deep breath, enjoying the scent. "These things always have a way of working themselves out. There must be a balance. Sometimes people can push too hard and then there isn't anything anyone can do to ever make it right again, like trying to fix a broken vase. I was young, but I remember India. I am tired of that sort of thing."

~ ~ ~

In the days and weeks that followed, however, Junker Singh was proved wrong. The tension around the island finally heightened to a call for action. That December, just days before Darshan's twelfth birthday, the union organized three hundred workers employed by the Shell and Vacuum oil companies into a full-scale, peaceful strike. Much to Livleen's disappointment, Suva's schools and businesses were closed when police assaulted the protesters with tear gas grenades and the strikers subsequently retaliated by stoning the police. The violence further escalated when anti-police protests led to the shooting of a section leader when two Indians and two Fijians tried to snatch his rifle. The union's focus lost, nearly the entire population was now on strike, refusing to provide services, and many rampaged through Suva, damaging property.

The industry-wide strike put a full stop to business on the mill. Petrol and diesel were inaccessible, making logging and deliveries impossible. Concerned for his friends in the city, Manmohan used the last of his fuel reserves to take one of the World War II trucks into Suva. Driving through the city, he saw the many marching troops that had recently arrived from New Zealand to aid the British and stifle the strike. Men screamed for their rights and slammed bottles of alcohol into the pavement. Others scuffled with the soldiers, who wrestled them to the ground with batons. Fijian villagers and Indian farmers lined up by the open market, freely handing out money, rice, and sugar to the strikers, demonstrating an unprecedented cooperation between the two races, another clear indication that the island as a whole was outraged by Colonial abuse.

Spencer's was closed, the windows boarded, the doors chained. Stores that had once sold Matsushita transistor radios, hi-fi sound systems, cassette players, and smokes were now trashed and empty. Motherland Books, owned by Manmohan's friend Upinder Balil, had been ransacked. Torn pages were scattered on the sidewalk outside the open window like confetti, which Manmohan found more upsetting than all the glass shards and blighted storefronts. The value of books was the knowledge they contained to store in the mind. He could understand—if not condone—stealing them to read. There was not much purpose in taking them simply to tear them apart.

Following an alternate route and parking several blocks away from the main streets, Manmohan walked toward the road-blocked Victoria Parade. He did not encounter trouble, these side streets quieter than some others, conflicts isolated in certain pockets around the city. On the main thoroughfare, Manmohan found Raj's sundry shop abandoned. But Junker Singh was out in front of his auto parts store, the glass doors boarded with large pieces of plywood. His friend had a bucket of dried beans at his feet.

Only mildly surprised at seeing a familiar face approaching, Junker Singh momentarily raised his brow, then glanced down into his bucket. "I will have to get more soon," he said. "The last strikers who came through here took most of this one."

"Junkerji, go home," Manmohan said, annoyance skirting the edges of his voice. He felt ineffectual, and he did not like seeing his friend this way.

"No."

"It is not safe."

"I was lost without my shop. I thought all the bad days of India were returning. But when my wife filled this bucket and I saw how much she wanted to give to other people who needed it, I understood that this is not the same, that this is a simple thing. It does not have to be a fight, and we do not have to run away."

Junker Singh had not intended to be admonishing, but Manmohan nonetheless felt shamed by the truth of his friend's words. He bent, cupped some beans in his hands, and stood next to the mechanic to wait with him. They remained there until the next wave of rioters sped through, hungrily emptying the bucket, fearfully looking behind for patrolling police. There was some dignity in the doling out of food to men who appeared to have been ravaged by defeat.

The two friends did not speak again that day, not on the walk back to the truck, not even when they saw the fresh dent on the hood, made perhaps by a hammer, and not on the way to Junker Singh's house, where Manmohan dropped him off. They had both lived through enough of these events to know that talk was unnecessary, that saying little or nothing at all said more.

The strike dragged on for the better part of December. Onkar had retired earlier in the year, and Manmohan's many workers, including his favorite loggers, Chandan, Sabar, and Vasant, were at home waiting like he was, waiting like the rest of the country for some sway in the strike's standstill.

Every morning Manmohan bathed, dressed, combed and twisted his hair into a bun; wrapped up his turban; and tucked his long beard into a net. Though it was pointless, he then stepped outside for his routine walkthrough of the mill. He checked the generator first, which had not been running since the final logs had been cut into lumber and run through the kiln. Then he checked the oil in all the trucks and tractors despite the fact that none of them had been driven since their fuel gauges dipped to empty. The quiet allowed him to notice details he had not seen before. The World War II trucks were older than he realized, the strain of deliveries worn on their scratched and dented frames, and the bodies of the flatbeds were rusted through with holes. They had seemed healthier with the motion of business.

The futility of his routine usually struck him mid-morning, after he had wandered around the undelivered piles of lumber, their tags reading, "Ba" or "Nadi," cities on the other side of the island. He would then head back to the main house to read one of his many books, perhaps a science or religious text because they were his favorites. But even reading, something he had always loved passionately, had become tedious. The redundancy and inertia of the days drained Manmohan's energy, and like the trucks, he noticed his body aging. At forty-three, his joints had begun to ache. He felt it mostly in his wrists when he tried to keep busy with repairs, twisting a wrench under the hood of one of the trucks, or slicing lumber with the handsaw to make a new piece of furniture.

The only element of his daily life that had not been affected by the strike, for which Manmohan was infinitely grateful, was Jai's habitual movement around the house. She lugged clothes and dirty dishes to the river for washing. She carried water from the river to the house for cooking and bathing. She refilled the kerosene lamps at dusk, though now she rationed the kerosene, lighting the lanterns only when needed. She refilled glass and tin jars of grains and spices after grinding them in her new Steinfield grinder, a clever wooden contraption with a crank handle and a drawer that collected the powder. She pickled mangoes from their trees, saving the green ones to serve with salt. She firmly pulled aside Darshan and Navpreet to scold them when they became too rowdy down by the river. She read to Livleen who stared wistfully outside her window from her confinement in bed. His wife appeared impervious to the strike, continuing inexorably on the same path daily, a beacon of the normal that he hoped would one day return to him.

The strike continued on down a dark and endless passageway. Sometimes a flicker of light brought on premature hope when the latest union negotiations appeared promising, but these were quickly extinguished by the many accusations and insults that concluded each session. The monotony ate at them all, and even the very house seemed displeased, the hushed creaks in its joints, the air ringing hollowly with idleness, until finally they were pulled out of their stupor.

Creosote had begun to accumulate in the kitchen's woodstove chimney. The black, oily residue silently and slowly thickened along the interior walls of the iron flue whenever Jai ignited firewood for cooking, collecting unnoticed for years at every meal.

One afternoon Manmohan wondered about the odd smoky odor and the burnt taste in the kitchen's air of late, but distracted by an eagerness to do something, however futile, that would make him forget about the strike, he ran outside with the idea of organizing the perpetually chaotic piles of lumber strewn about the clearing. He spent the remainder of the afternoon outside, and the taste on his tongue faded in the humidity and with the heavy breathing of his labor. When night fell, he climbed wearily into bed next to Jai, rolling onto his side, a sense of satisfied accomplishment from the day's work lulling him immediately to sleep.

While the Toor family slumbered, the remaining firewood in the stove, not fully extinguished, had been left to smolder. The embers flickered lazily, the blackened wood pulsating a reddish orange. A slight breeze crept through the cracks in the house's timber walls, wafting gently through the kitchen, making its way to the stove. It caressed the cinders encouragingly until small licks of flame bloomed, then intensified, lengthening upward. Their tips grazed the chimney opening and ignited the creosote until the chimney's interior was a contained cylinder of fire. The fire heated the flue that stretched up through the rafters, through the ceiling to the sky outside. It heated the metal until the outer wall of the kitchen caught fire, which was roaring by the time Jai woke up.

"Smoke, Gharwala," she shouted.

Manmohan sat up and sniffed the air. Eyes widening, he threw off his blankets. "Get the children," he said. "Go!"

But she was already through the door and sprinting down the hall.

Shoving aside the bed sheets, Manmohan scrambled across the mattress and jumped toward his safe. Spinning the combination lock, he flung open the door and grabbed the lease papers for the mill, the contract for his extra thousand acres of land, and the delivery logs. The documents tucked under his arm, he then circled the room frantically searching for more valuables. In the dresser, he pulled out his wife's gold jewelry and a wad of Fijian dollars. He threw everything onto a crumpled bed sheet, then hastily wrapped it into a makeshift knapsack before running down the hallway shouting, "Fire! Fire!"

From the living room he could see wildly sputtering shadows through the kitchen door, a flurry of orange and yellow light reflecting in the glass of the framed family photos. The hot wind gusted and the flames roared. Ahead of him, Jai dashed out of Livleen's room, the girl in her arms. He was startled by how quickly she moved with their daughter. She was screaming at him, but dazed, he could not hear what she was saying.

"Get out!" he finally heard Jai's words take shape in the confusion as she ran toward the back door. But he could not move. The horror on Livleen's wide-eyed face as she clung to Jai's neck caused him to freeze. The magnitude of her terror weakened his knees. In that moment he knew they would all burn, that they were already burning.

Mohan jumped out of Livleen's room, nothing in his hands as he quickly darted outside. Navpreet bolted from her room and raced after her brother with a bulging sack flung over her shoulder.

"Gharwala!" Jai shouted from the doorway, cupping her free hand so he could hear her through the tunnel of the hallway. "Get out!"

Her voice finally rousing him, he began running, the breeze outside a cool rush as he descended the stairs two at a time. At the bottom he found his nearest neighbors, Dev, Kalyan, and Paandu, tossing water onto the outer kitchen wall. Having seen the flames and heard shouts of alarm in the distance, they had already been to the river to fill their buckets.

"Is everyone safe?" Kalyan shouted as he hurried up the stairs to fling water at the house.

Manmohan dumped the blanket of valuables in the dirt. "Yes, everyone is out!" he shouted and dashed under the house with Jai and Mohan close behind him, weaving through the stilts to find more buckets. He saw his hose, but that would not work. Not enough pressure. Snatching up a pail, he ran toward the river, seeing Navpreet and Livleen sitting a safe distance away. In the light of the fire, he saw Navpreet laying out the contents of her sack, accounting for all her dolls and carved wooden toys.

Halfway to the river, Jai suddenly cried out, "Where is Darshan?"

Manmohan and Mohan had already filled their buckets and were running toward the house, but both turned to her in shock.

Eyes darting back and forth in the dark, Manmohan searched for some sign of his son. But he was not there. He whirled around to face Mohan, sloshing water from his bucket. "Where is he?"

"I don't know," Mohan said. "I didn't see him. Didn't you get him?"

"Me?" Manmohan said, his voice pitched loud with panic as Dev, then Kalyan ran past toward the river to refill their pails. "*You* didn't get him?"

Breathing hard, Jai said, "Mohan was in Livleen's room, and Navpreet was in the hallway. I never saw Darshan."

Manmohan tried to piece the frenzied string of moments together. He dropped his bucket and grabbed Mohan's arm. "If you were with Livleen, why didn't you get her? Why did you wait until your mother got there? Why didn't you tell her you had Livleen so she could check to be sure everyone else was out?"

Mohan pointed to the sack of valuables at the foot of the back staircase. "While you were getting your valuables you didn't save anyone!"

"Those papers are our lives," Manmohan shouted, as the neighbors raced once more up the stairs to empty the water onto the flames.

"There!" Jai said, pointing toward Darshan standing on the back porch.

"Bebeji, Bapuji! What are you doing?" Darshan yelled. "There is a fire up here! We have to put it out!"

"Darshan!" Manmohan cried out, his heart still pounding. "Darshan, get down from there!"

The boy descended the stairs, jogging over to stand before the towering figure of his father. Manmohan brushed soot from his son's shirt. "I did not have time," he said, kneeling in front of Darshan. "There was no time. I don't know how it happened, how any of this happened, but I couldn't. It was not possible."

Darshan did not speak. He remained still, a small figure framed by the looming, smoking shadow of the house. He glanced around as if slowly realizing they had all left him for dead.

Voice shaking with outrage, Mohan said, "If I had known, I would have gotten him out. Everyone here knows how much I love my family."

"Oh God," Navpreet exclaimed, wringing her hands and looking frantically down at her dolls. "I hope nothing is ruined!"

Mohan turned desperately to Livleen, shouting over to her. "No one can say I do not love my family, right Livleen? Don't I love you?"

She looked at him from the ground where Jai had left her. Dev called urgently to them, "We need more! A few more buckets!"

The fire was nearly out, but in the fading light of the flames Manmohan could see that Livleen was still frightened. Nodding carefully, hugging her shoulders, she said, "Yes, Mohan, you do."

~ ~ ~

The commotion of that night amplified the quiet of the following days. This was a new and different quiet. Not forced upon them, but necessitated by exhaustion.

The pounding of Paandu's hammer striking wood echoed throughout the clearing and bounced off the river. "Can you believe they are saying that we hate the British? They are saying we went on strike because of hate," he told Junker Singh.

The strike had ended a few days after the fire, Fiji subjugated by another influx of troops from New Zealand, but the island, too, was hushed, sulking and slow to resume business.

Manmohan watched his neighbors work. They were all so at ease after everything that had happened: Paandu, Kalyan, and Dev. They worked on the house like its repairs were merely cosmetic—a nail there, a piece of wood here—like there was not a gaping hole in it, exposing its insides.

"Many people do hate them," Junker Singh replied, pulling a nail out of his mouth. "Including you." He was lying down on his large stomach on top of the corrugated-iron roof. His head was near the edge so he could look down over the side to watch the men putting up new posts. He should have been at Suva Auto Repair, but since reopening no one had come in.

"Maybe that is true," Kalyan said, shrugging, taking the nail from the mechanic. "But it was not about hate. It was about fairness, getting what is appropriate for hard work. Now they have turned it into another issue. There are Europeans on this island who fought for the same reasons the oil workers did. It was never anti British. It was anti poverty."

"Now they are saying we will have separate trade unions for each race," Dev said, straining to hold a piece of wood in place so that Kalyan could secure it.

Shaking his head, Paandu replied, "Now that it is over, they want to keep everyone segregated, make sure it never happens again."

"I cannot believe it is over," Kalyan said. "Seems like it just started. I went to bed last night thinking we were making progress, woke up this morning feeling like the union just gave up. The oilmen got almost nothing. And everyone else truly did get nothing."

Manmohan murmured his agreement. From his position on the ladder, he saw Darshan carrying pieces of wood through the clearing and into the jungle.

"How much damage?" Junker Singh asked, knocking his fist on the iron roof to get his friend's attention. "Did you lose anything important?"

Manmohan leaned into the ladder so he could free his hands for a moment, his grip causing his fingers to ache uncomfortably. He rubbed them together. "Just this wall and the stove. Nothing of value."

The pantry was intact, all of Jai's spices and foodstuffs still neatly stacked. The rafters had been untouched except for the small hollow behind the chimney. Baba Singh's chest, the old gramophone, the cabinet radio, and the plywood box were unharmed, only dusted in a thick coating of ash. The rest of the house was fine.

Dev pursed his lips. "The way they were arguing when we were calling for more water, I am surprised the house is still standing."

"Arguing?" Junker Singh asked, raising an eyebrow.

"Never mind," Manmohan said. "It was just the confusion."

"Where is Mohan today?"

"I never know where he goes."

Junker Singh passed Kalyan another nail, and Dev released the post that had been secured into place.

Darshan's small figure wove through the stacks of lumber, wood scraps in his arms. He had come to see Manmohan in the mill yesterday to ask if he could have them and some tools to borrow.

"Why do you need them?" Manmohan had wanted to know. "Are you building something?"

"Yes," Darshan replied.

"A fort?"

"I suppose it will be."

Manmohan licked his dry lips uncertainly, reaching out to lay a heavy hand on his son's thin shoulder. "About the fire, there was not time. I thought—we all did—that you were out."

Darshan silently nodded, but he did not seem convinced.

"Where will you build it?" Manmohan asked.

His son pointed at the line that separated the clearing from the jungle, a place where the mill and their home ended and the palms and ferns began.

Manmohan had felt a sudden impulse to ask Darshan not to leave, not to go out there where he could not be seen or heard. It seemed to him that something had finally risen to the surface and bubbled over. He could almost feel the sticky, starchiness of it seeping into the cracks and crevices of his life. And despite scrubbing up the mess, sweating with the effort, no matter how hard he worked, it was impossible to fully clean it.

From the ladder, Manmohan glanced at the mill, remembering how quiet it had been in there yesterday with his son. No ringing noise of saws scoring through dried logs, it was just him and Darshan, surrounded by peace and warmth and shafts of yellow light coming in through fissures in the wood, softening the look of everything, their spirits chilled through.

Ankylosing Spondylitis
1960

Colonial War Memorial hospital had an airy feel, like the best days of summer. Sea breeze and the scent of plumeria gently tunneled down the cool, linoleum-floored hallways. Black-and-white photos of Fiji islanders partaking in joyful rituals hung dusty and crooked on the soft yellow walls, as in an abandoned museum. Rays of sunlight poked through patient rooms. The paint was chipped—on the walls and on the wood-trimmed doorways and windows. But that was its charm. It was relaxed; the photos, the glass cabinets behind the reception desk, the waiting-room chairs, the very walls were all lounging and comfortable rather than standing stiffly at attention. It was a lovely place except for the rush of scuttling nurses, the occasional moan of patients abandoned in the hallways on rusty gurneys, and the Fijian and Indian physicians striding past them with purpose.

The doctor had just left for another appointment, and now Manmohan sat in examination room three, alone. Shirt off and hanging on the back of a chair, he peered down at his stomach, noting without either satisfaction or distaste that it was still relatively flat at forty-four years of age, but no longer firm. The lingering cold circles of the doctor's stethoscope on his back and chest bothered him. They felt like disconnected parts of his body, like unwelcome strangers touching him too familiarly. Placing his hands on his stomach and chest to warm his skin, he enjoyed the sensation of soft hair between his fingers. The cold circles soon faded.

His arthritis was mild, which was not uncommon at his age. It was not this, however, that troubled him. It was the doctor's other diagnosis, the Ankylosing Spondylitis that had been discovered in his back. Over time, perhaps in the next ten years, his upper body would be forced forward, the disease leading to the eventual curvature of his spine. He imagined himself an old man with beady eyes that struggled to look up against the downward pull of his body, his forehead etched deeply with wrinkles as though he was perpetually surprised.

He was afraid. To flush this fear out of his system, to let it drain away, he stood, appreciating his full height of six feet, two inches. He momentarily reveled in the beauty and strength of his naked upper body, noting the muscles along his spine that contracted and released with each movement, allowing him to be straight and dignified. He adjusted his trousers before reaching for his shirt, swinging it around over his shoulders with an exaggerated slow whirl, feeling the rotation of his scapulae before stretching his arms through the sleeve holes. He buttoned the shirt, tucked it into his slacks, then picked up his broken watch from the table and put it on, making sure the old leather strap was secure. Leaving the examination room, he trod down the hallway toward the exit, oblivious to the nurse who ducked into a room just ahead of him, and only vaguely aware of the Fijian woman stretched out on a gurney, sweat beaded on her upper lip, her once kinky hair now mutinously lifeless, oppressed by whatever illness had invaded her body.

In the parking lot, he climbed into his truck and sat for a moment in the hot cabin, staring at the electroshock therapy facility across the street where he would receive his preventative treatment. It was a square building, once intended for a schoolhouse but later converted into an extension of the hospital. The sight made him feel stifled in the truck cabin, and he cranked the driver's side window down. Still, the air did not move. He leaned over to crank down the passenger side window for a cross breeze, relieved by the pressure that released when he opened it. Then he saw, resting in the sun on the bench seat, the latest letter from Vikram.

His brother had gone off to England, writing that Oxford was bitterly cold and that school was often a frustrating challenge. "They do not like Indians at Oxford," Vikram had said. "They would run me out, but it is because they have trouble admitting that we Indians have more life in us, more color and vitality, perhaps even more intellect." He wrote that the family was well. Of their father and Satnam, Vikram never said more, and although curious Manmohan never asked. He imagined their lives in India now, Baba Singh sleeping alone, shuffling aimlessly about the village, Satnam working the land while Priya cared for the house, cooking from the clay oven, laundering the clothes in the canal. This was the life of Barapind. There was no other. But it was not their life. They had forced themselves into it, squeezed their existence into circumstances that no longer fit. Manmohan knew there was no way for Vikram to write this.

Faced now with the task of responding to this latest letter, Manmohan suddenly understood why his mother had chosen never to write. The last time he saw her she represented the unruffled strength of motherhood, and she stayed that way in his mind. But the reality was that she had gotten small all alone in that house, had shrunk to a little being that she could not bear for her sons to know it. It was the same for him now. He did not want to mention this latest news. In his letters to his father and brothers, he wanted to always be tall.

Firing up the engine, Manmohan pulled out of the hospital parking lot and drove through Suva back home to the mill. He moved slowly, crossing town by means of a more circuitous route, avoiding Victoria Parade. Finally entering his property, the truck lumbering over the wood-plank drive past the diesel tank and petrol pump, he pulled reluctantly into the carport.

Shutting off the ignition, the truck sputtered into silence, and he could hear Mohan's angry voice echoing across the clearing, as had become normal these past months. Resting his forehead on the steering wheel, he closed his eyes, futilely covering his ears.

"Shut your mouth!" his son shouted. A woman began crying, and an infant wailed.

Sighing, Manmohan got out of the truck, kicking a pebble and squinting up at the house. Through Mohan's bedroom window, he saw his daughter-in-law bent over, arms protectively covering her head.

Their marriage had begun in scandal. Raj the sundry shop owner had discovered his daughter Lehna against the back wall of his storage room, her skirt hiked up around her waist, legs locked around Mohan, breasts gripped fiercely in his hands while he bit her neck, his buttocks pumping disgracefully. They had only been missing for five minutes before he found them, but her torn shirt and splintered back had provided enough pleasure for a lifetime of change. There were moments when

Manmohan could not put the image of it out of his mind, the flesh and violence of it, their joint pain. He had never loved like that.

He had arranged their marriage shortly after the unfortunate realization that Lehna was with child. He had intended to restore honor to Raj's house, had hoped that two people so passionately engaged would find happiness together, that this would perhaps revive Mohan's lost faith. The wedding night, however, had been an angry tussle, furniture knocked over, a broken oil lamp, Lehna's cut lip. Manmohan understood too late that it had never been love, only loss, only hate. Most afternoons since that day Mohan took a bottle of alcohol to his room, and by nightfall, his voice could be heard across the mill.

Manmohan had tried once to reason with his son before the baby arrived, rushing down the hallway to discover Lehna curled on the bed, sobbing hysterically, shielding her belly.

"Leave it be, Bapu," Mohan said dangerously, spinning around to face his father. "She is *my* wife."

"But look at her," Manmohan said.

Mohan refused, covering his face, muffling his words when he spoke. "It is not what I wanted. I cannot do it. I did not know she would do this." He had slammed the bedroom door, leaving Manmohan staring at varnished wood and Lehna screaming within.

After Amandev was born, it only became worse.

Manmohan shut the truck door with a weak click, the hinges rusted stiff. He heaved his body against the door, giving a sharp shove to push it into place. Affectionately patting the metal frame of the cabin, he then made his way to the house.

"She is too loud!" Mohan bellowed. "I cannot think. Make her stop!"

As Manmohan entered the house, the baby quieted, causing

a sudden and loud silence to radiate from Mohan and Lehna's bedroom.

Navpreet was standing to the left of the kitchen entrance, holding her earlobes. Even from the doorway he could tell that they were red. When she saw him she stepped quickly away from the wall where she was not supposed to be resting. Still holding her ears, she raised her elbows up firmly like chicken wings, wincing.

"What did you do?" Manmohan asked her, his voice tired.

She shrugged.

"How long is your mother making you stay there?"

"Until she feels like telling me to move."

"Gharwala?" Jai said, sticking her head out through the kitchen entrance. Her hands were wet, and he could see a faint trail of soap running down her arm. Glancing at Navpreet, Jai breathed hard, her lips puffing out in exasperation. "Were her arms dropped?"

He nodded.

"The dishes again. I asked her to do them, and she refused."

Indicating Mohan's room, he said to Navpreet, "Sometimes you are just like him. He never listened either."

Navpreet lowered her elbows and raised her voice. "I am not!"

Jai slapped her daughter's arm. "Up. It is supposed to be hard; otherwise it would not be a punishment."

"Stay there," Manmohan said, his face tightening. "I will be back to check on you in a minute. If your arms are down, even a little, we will do it the hard way and you can hold your ears with your arms tucked under your legs. You understand? She is soft on you. I will not be. And after, you will help your mother."

Fear shaded her eyes, and she nodded. Jai disappeared back into the kitchen.

Entering the dim hallway, Manmohan slowly made his way toward Livleen's room, again allowing himself to feel the finer points of muscle along his spine, focusing on every tendon and vertebra.

Knocking gently, he opened the door. "Livleen?"

"Yes, Bapu?"

"Everything all right?"

"Yes, Bapu."

He crossed the room and pushed the window out to let in some fresh air. "How was school?" he asked.

She remained silent.

"You must be tired. Are you feeling well?"

She nodded.

"You can skip tomorrow if it hurts too much. I can stay home with you. We can study together."

"No," she said.

He regarded her for a moment, concerned. She had grown so melancholy since the fire, so taciturn and dark.

Manmohan glanced across the hall. "I know he yells a lot. It must be hard for you."

She stared out the window into the dusk. "He never yells at me. He takes me to school and brings me back, and he never yells." She raised her eyes, and he saw fear there. "He loves me."

"I will talk to him."

"You don't have to." She sank down into her bed covers.

He sat beside her, feeling her elbows and wrists, checking for inflammation. But her body was fine. It was her spirit that had never recovered.

~ ~ ~

Mohan was sprawled out in the bed of one of the World War II trucks in the shade of the carport. The truck had recently broken down, and despite all Junker Singh's best efforts to save it, the old vehicle would not start again. Mohan's bare feet hung over the end of the truck bed. His slacks were rolled up to his knees, and his hands were crossed under his turban, pulling up his untucked shirt to reveal his belly button. Manmohan remembered how muscular he was at the age of twenty-two, not soft like Mohan who was gaining weight, his stomach beginning to hang gelatinously. His son had also recently gotten into the habit of leaving his beard loose, no longer bothering to tie it up into a net. It was black and frizzy against the light gray of his shirt.

"It is not your business, Bapu," Mohan said to his father.

Manmohan was leaning against the side of the truck, gazing at the men working in the clearing. He saw Darshan scrambling over some logs with a thick length of rope to help secure a load. Pushing his body off the truck, Manmohan said stiffly, "You are too old now for rebellion." He kicked his boot against the back tire.

"I am Lehna's husband, and a husband should be given the same respect given to God. It is my right to make that demand."

Furious, Manmohan gripped the edge of the truck. "You take too much for granted. What have you done to earn it?"

"I suppose nothing," Mohan replied, his tone sardonic. He curled his toes upward, stretching his calf muscles languidly. "But a husband is a husband, and a wife is a wife."

"It is my house you live in," Manmohan said. "You cause so much discomfort for us all. Livleen is scared now."

Mohan propped himself up onto his elbows, intent. "Is that what she said?"

"She is upset for Lehna."

Mohan relaxed, reclining again into the bed of the truck. "It is not anyone else's business."

Manmohan lowered his hands to his sides, infuriated. "I do not want you taking Livleen to school. It does not make her happy. It is too hard on her."

Mohan sat up and scooted forward until his calves dangled from the back of the bed. "I thought it was important for you, all this learning and schooling," he said with a trace of disdain. He stretched, scratched his stomach, then stood to walk away.

Manmohan grabbed his shoulder. "Why are you so angry?"

"I am not angry, Bapu."

"You are very angry."

Mohan spun around, violently shaking off his father. "Lehna cannot give me what I need, what I deserve, what is my right. It makes a man angry."

~ ~ ~

"You think it is me?" Manmohan asked his wife. It was night, and they were alone in their bedroom.

Jai shook her head. "That boy was never going to listen to anyone, and when there were consequences he was always going to blame someone else."

"I look back to when he was a child. I cannot understand what happened."

She set her earrings on the dresser and approached her husband, appearing as though the whole matter with her son was beside the point. "You should not worry so hard about it. It might take him longer to learn than others that there are other people living in this world besides him. The time it takes him, that is something even a father—or a mother—cannot change."

"What about Lehna and Amandev?"

"Lehna comes to me when she needs to."

He looked down at her. The way she had to bend her head back to look up at him was reassuring. She looked so wise and handsome at forty-two. Her skin was beginning to wrinkle—just slightly—from all her time in the garden. She had strands of gray now, easy to see with her hair pulled back into the same bun she had worn her entire life. Her lips were still full and slightly pink. She was slender; anyone who did not know her would assume that she was frail.

Comforted, he opened his mouth to speak, then, uncertain, he again closed it.

"Gharwala?"

Pulling his eyes away from hers, he directed his gaze over her head, letting the dresser behind her go out of focus. "There is a problem with my spine."

Her voice softened with concern. "What is wrong with it?"

"A disease." He looked down at her again. "I will be stooped over."

She frowned. "How long?"

"Perhaps in ten years."

She smiled then, as though to say they still had time. "Do you remember," she asked, "that jazz LP you always used to listen to in Tamavua?" She began to hum one of the tunes from Duke Ellington and his Famous Orchestra.

He was staring intently at her, and she stopped, embarrassed. "The tune is wrong."

"No, it is good," he replied, beginning to hum the melody where she left off, taking her hand.

Her voice joined his. She began to swing her hips, just slightly so that nothing else moved and her bare feet did not shift. He could tell that the motion was instinctual, that it was impossible to make the music and not dance to it. Catching the rhythm, he followed her, his movement equally as slight as hers, the two of them swaying like reeds in a soft breeze.

~ ~ ~

Darshan sat on the edge of the seat in Manmohan's remaining World War II truck, his thin legs stretched out so that they barely touched the truck's foot pedals, his chest shoved against the steering wheel, his neck straining to see above it through the windshield. He revved the engine. The fan belt squealed, and the gears ground in protest. The truck jerked forward and the engine died.

"Release the clutch slowly," Manmohan told him, uncomfortable on the passenger side, the bench springs too firm, not shaped to his bottom. "Balance it with the gas. Try again."

Darshan reignited the engine. They were in the emptiest part of the mill clearing and had about thirty yards in front of them before the jungle started. Carefully releasing the clutch, he gently pressed the gas, and the truck began to inch jerkily toward the tree line. He sped up a little, shifting to second gear, then eased up, pressing in the clutch again and braking to a slow stop.

"Better," Manmohan told him.

Darshan turned off the ignition. "Anything else, Bapu?"

"No, I suppose that is enough for today," Manmohan said, feeling that Darshan was now at least moderately ready for those many drives through Suva to the electroshock therapy ward. "You can go."

Darshan jumped out of the truck. He waved without smiling and went into the jungle to the shack he had built. That boy always did what he was told: chores, homework, errands. He never asked questions, like why he was learning to drive when he was only twelve years old, his legs barely long enough to touch the pedals; why Junker Singh did not drive his father to the hospital; why it mattered so much that he do it. He never asked the reasons for anything. Manmohan watched him go, curious about what he had built deep in the trees, but too afraid to go see for himself.

He clamped his hand over the heavy metal of his watch. The brown leather of the band was now worn and shredded at the edges. The face was scratched, and the stainless steel push-and-wind knobs that spun the analog clock hands were nicked. Though it was shabby, he could not bear to be without it, but he knew the doctors would take it from him before affixing nodes to his body and jolting him through with electricity.

He did not offer it to the doctors at his first session, entering the chamber in his hospital gown, the watch still on his wrist. A nurse opened her palm disapprovingly, and as he sat on the padded, cold vinyl bed, he removed it, placing it in her waiting hand, watching as her fingers curled around it, taking it away from him, setting it on a tin tray. Gritting his teeth against the stick they had wedged into his mouth, that tray was where he focused all of his energy. As the currents flooded his body, the sight of his watch was a tangible link to sanity, to a moment when he would fasten it back on and go to the parking lot where Darshan was waiting to take him home.

Week after week he lay on that gurney, tiny amps of electricity replacing his arthritic aches with a tingling sensation, with a droning hum in his bones that was not at all musical. He rarely slept now, lying in bed awake at night, gazing upward, not seeing the corrugated iron ceiling, just a blank nothing that vibrated behind his pupils and threatened to consume his whole mind. He craved alcohol, a hot chug of bourbon to numb his body. Always he clutched at his watch, a solid object that grounded him in the dark, not telling him the time, but telling him he was here.

One evening he could not bear the idea of moving, of bouncing along the potholed roads that only added to the odd and uncomfortable sensations coursing through him. He made Darshan stay in the parking lot, not speaking, as he waited for the buzzing in his bones to abate, to stop ringing so loudly in his ears. The mill was dark when they finally returned home, lit only by a single lantern placed at the top of the stairs next to the front door and the truck's headlight beams as Darshan steered through the clearing.

The boy helped him up to the house and seated him on the couch. "Would you like a glass of water, Bapu?" he asked, bringing in the lantern and placing it on the floor in the middle of the living room.

"No. I am fine here."

"Are you sure?"

"Go on to bed. You have school in the morning."

"If you need anything—"

"Yes, I know."

When Darshan's shadow had disappeared down the hallway, Manmohan stretched his fingers wide, trying to shake off the residual electricity. He shook his wrists, then stood and paced the living room, making wide, quiet strides around the lantern before extinguishing it. The pictures on the walls, dark square and rectangular shadows, seemed to float about the room.

There was a sound of a doorknob click from down the hall, someone going to the outhouse. Approaching the hallway, he saw a bulky silhouette coming from Livleen's room.

"Mohan?" Manmohan asked.

The silhouette stiffened, caught by surprise. Apprehensive, it asked, "Bapu?"

"Mohan, what were you doing in Livleen's room?"

"I thought I heard something. I thought it was a nightmare. But she is fine."

A cold feeling trickled slowly up Manmohan's spine. "Mohan. Wait."

The silhouette turned to go. "Everything is fine, Bapu. I am tired. I am going back to bed."

Manmohan's heart began to pound, the chambers rapidly contracting and expanding, and he no longer perceived the electric hum in his bones. He realized that he knew something terrible now, that he had known it for a long time. A suspicion too terrifying to confront or examine made him tremble with cold and fear.

Walking briskly toward his daughter's room, he stopped outside the door, trying to slow his breathing. He placed his palm over the doorknob, turned it, and cracked it open. "Livleen?" he whispered.

He heard a whimper.

"Livleen, can't you sleep?"

Fighting the urge to run, he slowly walked over to touch her forehead. She shrunk into the pillow. She was sweating but had no fever.

"Where does it hurt? Your wrists? Knees? Is it your heart?"

He tried to touch her chest, but she shook her head, the whites of her eyes faintly visible in the moonlight.

"Is it Mohan?" he asked, and even as he spoke he did not

recognize his own voice, the flat and mechanical quality of it.

She stiffened. "He loves me. He tells me how much."

"How much?" he whispered.

"Without me he will do awful things. He will ask to let them out. They would come for me."

"Who?"

"The bad people, in jail."

"But I don't understand," he said, the thudding of his heart drowning out all other sound as he walked away from her. As if from a great distance, he heard a deep, furious cry, dimly aware that it had come from his mouth.

"Gharwala!" Jai screamed, running down the hall as Manmohan threw open the door to Mohan's room.

Lehna jumped from their bed in alarm, grabbing Amandev from the basinet and backing against the far wall, her eyes large with fear. The baby began to yowl and screech. Mohan was standing by the window, his shoulders bent forward, crying, tears soaking into his beard. Lunging forward, Manmohan hit the turban off his son's head and grabbed Mohan's topknot.

"Gharwala!" Jai screamed again. Mohan stumbled and fell, but Manmohan did not let go of the hair clenched in his fist, dragging his son down the hallway. Mohan flailed and slapped at his father's arms, scrambling and clambering through the living room and out to the balcony where Manmohan finally released him.

"Get out!" Manmohan heard himself scream. "Get out!"

Lying prostrate, Mohan reached for his father's ankle. "Bapuji, I am sorry!"

"What have you done?" Manmohan asked with rage and pain. "I trusted you to care for her!"

"No, Bapu," Mohan wept. He got to his knees and pressed his hands together as if in prayer. "You pretended to trust me because Junker Uncle told you to. People always had to tell you that I was worth anything, but she loves me! She tells me how good I am!"

Manmohan raised his fist, shaking.

"Stop, please!" Jai cried. "What is this about?"

"Tell Lehna to pack a bag," Manmohan told her, lowering his arm and unclenching his fist.

She did not move.

"You tell her to pack a bag."

After one more moment of hesitation, she scurried away down the hall, stopping only to push Darshan and Navpreet away from the living room and back to their beds.

Mohan stood, again reaching out his hand, still sobbing. "Bapuji, I am sorry."

Manmohan slapped his son's hand away and shoved him backward against the rail.

Then Lehna was there, stepping outside into the chill of the night with the baby. "Bapu," she said tearfully. "You can see he did not mean it, whatever he has done. I do not want to go."

"Lehna, I am sorry," Manmohan said, his voice raspy and dry.

Jai returned with a few items tucked into a burlap sack. She wordlessly handed it to her husband who tossed it onto the balcony.

Lehna moaned imploringly, stepping close to Mohan, caressing her daughter's head.

Manmohan shut the door, leaving them out in the dark. He bolted the lock, and Mohan banged on the wood. "Bapuji! Please!"

Turning to Jai, Manmohan wiped his eyes and said, trying to reassure her, "They will go to her father."

The lantern had tumbled over, a pool of kerosene on the

floor beneath it. Jai straightened the lamp, moving it away from the spill. She found another lamp and lit it. In the light Manmohan noticed the glint of his watch near the couch. Touching his wrist he realized it had come off in the commotion. He bent to retrieve it and sank into the sofa's cushions.

"Please go be with Livleen," he told his wife.

She nodded, then nervously left the room.

Manmohan remained there in the living room, alone, listening to Lehna crying and Mohan banging on the door, begging forgiveness. After a time there was the creaking sound made by their bodies descending the stairs. Then silence.

Secrets in the Rafters
1962

Pathogens deployed and probed for weaknesses along Manmohan's spinal column, slowly yet triumphantly conquering vertebra by vertebra. But they affected more than just his back. The disease was contagious. It transcended his body, reaching outward to infect his children, bending them forward under a great downward pressure that he himself had brought upon them.

The doctors told him to have hope, but he could sense the uselessness of his electroshock therapy sessions. The time he spent on that vinyl hospital table was wasted. It had blinded him to the catastrophes taking place within his household. Events had escaped him.

He sat now on his bed in his undershorts, slumped with an unwillingness to dress, hugging his naked shoulders, his hair loose, his turban on the dresser.

"It was an obvious place," Junker Singh told him, holding up a pair of trousers. "Anyone searching for that sort of thing would have found it."

"I never thought she would go up there," Manmohan replied weakly. "I never knew she was looking."

"What is important is that she is fine now."

"She is not fine."

"She is alive."

Manmohan closed his eyes, the sound of his bare feet slapping on the wooden floorboards last night still sharp in his mind, the brush of the walls against his shoulder as he skirted down the hallway, his breath heavy and quick.

"Get a handle on yourself," Junker Singh said firmly.

Manmohan rubbed his sore knees. "If you had been there, you would not assume things to be so easy."

Junker Singh traversed the room to the window. He rested his elbows on the sill and cupped his cheeks in his palms, staring pensively outside. He crossed one ankle over the other so that his large body looked like it was balancing on one foot.

Manmohan flexed his toes, focusing on them, trying his best to remain calm, to put it out of his head.

"Gharwala!" Jai had called out the previous evening, tearing his attention from the book he had been reading. "She is not breathing!"

Jumping from his chair, rushing around the corner from the library and stumbling through the living room, he had fallen once, his hands slapping ape-like on the floor for balance. Running into the kitchen, he flung himself hard onto his knees next to the unmoving figure of Livleen sprawled on the floor, her head in Jai's lap, the corners of her mouth heavy with white, foamy spittle.

A pillbox of his arthritis medication, an unmarked bottle of alcohol, and an empty tin tumbler were on the floor nearby. He remembered thinking how strange it was that those items had been so neatly placed, the pillbox positioned next to the bottle and tumbler as though she had been arranging trinkets on a dresser or flowers in a vase. The ladder had been set under the wide open door to the rafters.

Flexing his toes again, Manmohan scratched his beard, his fingernails rubbing hard against the skin underneath, trying to shake off the images. "We had to hold her upside down to get it all out," he murmured to his friend. "We hung her by the ankles over the balcony until she threw up." He remembered the coughing, retching sounds Livleen had made, the vomit in her hair when they pulled her back onto the deck.

Junker Singh listened, his body rigid.

"When it was over, I told her it was stupid," Manmohan said.

"Well, it was."

"She apologized."

The mechanic pushed off the window, and after a moment he turned around. "Get up," he said, handing over the trousers and a clean shirt.

"This is not a joke," Manmohan said. "I want to stay here."

"I love that girl, too, but being depressed and hopeless never fixed anything. It will not fix her."

Manmohan reluctantly slipped into his trousers and put on the clean shirt. Junker Singh led him to the kitchen and picked up the pillbox and the unmarked bottle that were still on the counter, holding them out, one in each hand. "Put them back."

Lugging the wooden ladder from the wall to set it under the rafter opening, Manmohan reluctantly complied. He was aware of how heavy the ladder was, how dense the wood, how weighty the metal bindings, and of how determined a ten-year-old girl with aching joints had to be in order to move it. He climbed the ladder and shoved up the swing door, laying it down carefully. Using his palms on the rafter floor to steady himself, he hefted his weight through the opening and sat on the edge, his feet resting lightly on the top rung of the ladder.

"Here," Junker Singh said, extending his arms. "Take them."

Manmohan reached down to receive the pillbox and bottle. He then held them together in his lap, scanning the crawl space. Rays of sunlight beamed through the walls, and sparkles of dust floated languidly in the dim light. He reached up to touch the hot, corrugated iron ceiling with his fingertips, already feeling the perspiration on his upper lip from the heat. He could see the chimney toward the back, the shaft running through the rafter floor and up through the ceiling, everything blanketed with cobwebs. There were tin cans scattered about, some empty, some filled with forgotten flour and spices, Jai's old spice grinder before she got the Steinfeld, the gramophone, his box of LPs, and the broad rectangular shape of the cabinet radio farther to the rear. He momentarily lifted Duke Ellington's LP from the box, then tiredly let it fall back.

Baba Singh's chest and the plywood box were to his left. There was a tarnished tray to his right, another unmarked bottle of bourbon resting on it, and the remainder of his arthritis medications, the only items Livleen had disturbed. Wiping the dust from the top of the plywood box, he found himself wishing for more evidence of her presence here, that despite her mission she had been curious enough to delay it and examine the objects of his life. He wished she had seen them as he saw them now: a record of Toor history, hidden away, perhaps tragic but still powerful and passionate.

He put the empty pillbox and bottle on the tray. Spinning the screw top off the other bottle, he took one sip of bourbon—always only one—then lifted it to admire the amber color of the glass as he held it up to the muted light. Thinking of Mohan, he felt it was peculiar that the substance used to alleviate his physical aches and pains was also the thing that could damage people when they applied it to their sorrow.

"Hi Junker Uncle," Manmohan heard Darshan say from below. He peered down between his knees to see his son curiously looking up at the open rafter door.

The mechanic extended his hand for a shake, pulling the young man into a bear hug.

Darshan laughed. "Good to see you, Uncle."

"You are home early," Manmohan said.

Darshan glanced up, his smile faltering. "A little."

Setting the bottle on the tray, Manmohan descended the ladder, hands empty. "Chandan needs help," he said. "The inventory."

"Okay, Bapu," Darshan said, waving as he went out. "I will take care of it."

"He is a good boy," Junker Singh said, watching him go. "You will make him very happy when the Falcon arrives."

Manmohan pushed the ladder off to the side. "Yes."

Junker Singh helped fold the ladder and lean it against the wall. "You have something to say to him, I can see it. Giving him a car is not the same as talking to him."

"I do not have anything to say."

The mechanic sighed. "Okay, ji."

Manmohan wiped his dusty hands on his shirt.

"Perhaps it is inappropriate given the circumstances," Junker Singh said wistfully, "but a tall drink of whisky would be nice. I always knew the Muslims had more willpower than us Sikhs. Islam says a man cannot drink, and so they do not drink. We are not supposed to either, but half the Punjab stumbles around like newborn calves, slurring all the time like babies."

"Don't say that. It is bad," Manmohan muttered. "It is a

very bad thing."

Junker Singh shrugged. "We should drink, you and I, put on some music and sing on the balcony, serenade our wives. They would grumble at us for being so wild at our age, but they would also smile because sometimes they really like us that way. It does not have to be bad. It does not always have to be only this way or only that way, so black and so white. Sometimes a thing means sin and death, but other times that very same thing means virtue and living."

~   ~   ~

Manmohan pushed through the dense growth of taro plants clumped at the bank of the river. The plants flourished here in this small section at the narrowest part of the waterway where he had not cleared them. He made his way toward the bridge that Darshan had built to replace the old one, seizing a clump of the broad, deep green leaves to steady himself. He squeezed, feeling moisture from the plants released into his palm, stopping momentarily to glance up the hill on the other side of the river. Puffing with exertion, he hated that he now had to pause to regain strength for something that had once been so easy.

Taking one more deep breath, he moved on, finally reaching the edge of the bridge, noting as he always did when crossing it how sturdy the frame felt beneath his feet. The narrow structure was well built, with rails that angled up and out, creating a slightly wider space for the body and providing easy gripping while crossing.

Following the footpath leading to the crest of the hill where a clump of coconut trees grew, he slowly climbed, occasionally stopping to catch his breath. It started to rain, beginning with a sprinkling of large droplets that quickly thickened into a cascade. He welcomed the relief of water soaking his clothes and washing away his sweat. When he reached the top, he looked down, shielding his face from the thick sheet of rain, noting with distaste how small he had once thought this hill was, how trivial this walk had once seemed. It was much steeper than he remembered, the house and his garden below appearing so insignificant in the span of jungle around him.

He regarded the cluster of coconut trees on the hill. Wiping the water from his eyes, he then followed the path to the tallest one. Peering high up, he saw Darshan's bare, long-toed feet dangling from the tree's palm tuft. "Darshan," he called, his voice a roar above the storm that was now pummeling the jungle. "Darshan!"

The boy's feet froze, and he poked his head through the tuft. Manmohan gestured at him to climb down. Grabbing hold of the narrow trunk, Darshan gripped the bark with his feet as he sidled downward, landing lightly on the ground.

"We have deliveries," Manmohan said. He studied his son's face, always so full of apprehension in his presence. He admired the almond shape of Darshan's eyes, the brown of his water-streaked skin that was very similar to Jai's, the soft feathery look of his mustache that had recently grown in, the turban they had practiced tying together. His son had chosen a navy blue fabric, had faced the mirror with a subdued acceptance of his manhood, obediently watching and learning. The turban was now wrapped precisely as he had been taught.

Holding his palms up into the rain, Manmohan said ruefully, "But I suppose deliveries will have to wait."

"Whenever you are ready, Bapu."

Indicating the tree, Manmohan asked, "Don't you think you might fall one day?"

"It really is not bad," Darshan said a little too earnestly, bending to retrieve a fallen coconut, clearly not sure if he would be punished.

Manmohan looked up at the tree, wondering if he should say more about it. He imagined the view from that height: the volcanic ranges toward the island's center, the thick jungle fanning out toward the ocean, the city of Suva like a vast clearing in the verdant thickness, made of tall buildings and buses releasing exhaust from tailpipes. He believed it was beautiful up there, quiet, and he was tired of so much conflict, so he said nothing.

Darshan tossed the coconut up, catching it deftly. The way he held it, for one moment Manmohan believed he intended to offer it to him, but he let it roll off his fingers and back to the ground. A little regretfully, Manmohan watched it land with a splash in the mud and tumble away.

"Your mother made lunch," he said loudly over the storm, waving Darshan onto the path. "Let's get dry and go eat."

By the time the two of them had begun to descend the hill, the river was already swollen, licking at the logs strewn haphazardly along the bank nearest to the clearing. Manmohan steadied himself on the trail that was now slippery with mud, making a mental note not to keep the logs so close to the water next time.

Without warning, Darshan swiftly brushed past him and sprinted down the path.

Startled, Manmohan called out, "What happened?"

Already far ahead, his son could not hear him above the roar of rain.

Manmohan watched as Darshan skirted over the bridge and ran toward the logs, soon realizing what the boy intended to do. "No, Darshan! Don't!" he cried, sliding and skidding down the hill, forgetting his aches and earlier fatigue.

Jai had also seen, bolting from the main house and darting through the garden, frantically waving her arms. Manmohan could hear the muffled sound of her wail in the distance.

Cupping his hands around his mouth, he futilely called out again, but Darshan had jumped into the water, his lean body slamming into a log that had finally been loosened from the bank and was floating downriver. The boy went under for a moment, his legs pushing upward in the current. Pausing, Manmohan held his breath, waiting. After several moments, Darshan came up, sputtering and coughing, his turban lost. Incredulous, Manmohan watched as Darshan then reached out with his free arm to grab at another log, but unable to retrieve it he instead paddled hard, edging his way to the bank where Jai was waiting for him.

Running now, Manmohan crossed the bridge in two wide strides, racing through the rain toward his son.

"Bapu, I saved one!" Darshan shouted triumphantly over the storm, his face streaming with water and blood. He dropped to his knees, coughing, and Jai pounded him on the back.

Manmohan grabbed him by his shirt, pulling him up to standing, and swung his arm wide around, planting an open-handed slap on Darshan's behind, the smack through the wet shorts hurting his hand more than his son's bottom. The boy's eyes widened in shock.

Jai roughly seized Darshan by the arm. "One log?" She put a finger up for emphasis. "*One* log?"

"I was trying to help."

"You could have drowned!"

"Is that what you think?" Manmohan asked. "That your life is worth *one* log?" Water was streaming from his turban onto his face and into his beard.

"No," Darshan said. "I—"

"We would *never* ask you to risk your life for even a hundred logs!"

"But—"

Manmohan furiously turned away, "No father would be proud of such stupidity."

Darshan chased after him, the mix of water and blood from the cut on his head trailing onto his white shirt. "I thought you would want—"

Manmohan stopped, and with an exaggerated shrug, the gesture heavy with scorn, he said, "I do not understand why you do not know what I want, why it is so difficult to be your father."

~ ~ ~

"What *do* you want?" a voice asked.

"I thought it was obvious," Manmohan replied, turning over in his bed, staring at the calm face of his sleeping wife.

"Each man is a different universe, separated by light years and matter and darkness."

"What are you talking about?" Manmohan asked.

"I don't know. Didn't you read that somewhere?"

"Maybe," Manmohan said. "What does it mean?"

"I thought you knew."

"But I don't."

"That is too bad. I was hoping for some answers."

"Is this what happened to him? Will I be with him now?" Manmohan asked.

"What are *you* talking about?"

An itchy, scratchy feeling rose in Manmohan's throat and

he sat up, coughing. He clasped his hand around his neck and bent forward. Tears welled up in his eyes, his vision blurring.

Jai woke and began to firmly pat his back. "I'll get water," she said and climbed out of bed.

He nodded, unable to speak.

She returned with a cup and he drank, first just one small sip, then a gulp, and another until he was tipping the tumbler upside down over his mouth. Jai removed the cup from his hand and set it on his nightstand.

"It is just the fever," she said, touching his forehead. "It is almost passed. Lie down and sleep some more."

~   ~   ~

The sticky residue of stale sweat coated Manmohan's entire body. By the incandescent light trying to press through the windowpanes, he knew the sun was strong outside. He sat up, placing several pillows behind his back. Pressing the heels of his palms into his eyes, he took a deep breath, his joints throbbing.

"Bapu?" Darshan asked. "How are you feeling?"

Removing his hands, Manmohan saw his son tentatively peering at him from the corner of the room.

"How long have you been in here?"

"Not long," his son replied, moving forward out of the shadows, trepidation on his bandaged face. "I am really very sorry, Bapu."

Manmohan waved him over. "Come sit here."

"I don't want to disturb you," Darshan said, heading for the door. "I am just glad you are getting better."

Manmohan reached out a hand. "Wait. Don't go. Sit."

Hesitantly making his way to a chair positioned near the

bed, Darshan slowly lowered himself into it.

Manmohan picked up his watch from the nightstand. "It is okay Darshan. I was just scared. You scared me."

"I know. I am sorry."

"Sometimes…" Manmohan began, his voice weakening, thinking of the plywood box, wanting to say what was in it and why it existed. "There are reasons why I do things, reasons I say things." He waited for Darshan to ask what he meant, but his son only looked at him uncertainly. The words and stories Manmohan had hoped to share suddenly caught in his mouth. "Just think first next time."

"Yes, Bapu," Darshan said, rising. "Can I get you something? Water?"

"No, I am fine. I will be out soon."

Manmohan dressed himself unhurriedly, grimacing as he eased his legs into his trousers. He was still weak. In the living room, he found his wife sitting on the couch, cupping a mug of chai.

"You slept for three days," she said.

"Three days," he murmured, dragging a chair to the window, but not sitting in it.

"How do you feel?" she asked.

"A little tired. Was it bad?"

She shook her head. "I have seen worse. There is water for a bath."

"Not now."

"You should eat something."

Manmohan rubbed his stomach. He was not yet ready for food. "Later," he replied. He eyed the mouth of the hallway. "How is Livleen?"

Jai sipped her tea, eyes focused on the mug. "She will be fine."

"Resting?"

She nodded.

"I am going for a walk," he told her. "I need some fresh air."

"That's good," she said, resettling the mug in her lap. These happenings were beyond even her strengths. He could feel her watching him go, and even when he was outside he sensed her still looking, waiting for direction, wondering what to do next, but he had no answers.

When he reached the bottom of the stairs, a gleam of chrome caught his eye from the shade of the carport across the drive.

"Junker Uncle brought it," Navpreet said, indicating the Ford Falcon Futura parked next to the World War II truck. She was playing jacks on a piece of plywood at the edge of the port. "Bebe wouldn't let me see inside."

He made his way slowly over. Running his finger along the brand-new chrome rim, he wished he could drive it, feel the one-hundred-and-one-horsepower engine, the rear-wheel drive, and 3M transmission yield to his every nudge of the steering wheel and change of gear shifts. "Did you see Darshan?" he asked. "He was just in my room."

"No," Navpreet said, catching the rubber ball and looking at him. "Can I see it now?"

"I want to show it to him."

"It's his, isn't it? He never did anything to deserve it, and I just want to see. I am twelve. When he was twelve you let him drive."

"Where is he, Navpreet?"

She inclined her head toward the jungle. "What did he ever do for it?"

"He takes care of me," Manmohan told her.

Navpreet let the ball drop from her hand into the pile of jacks, scattering them over the edge of the wood and into the dirt.

Jai had come outside, watching them from the balcony. She waved, nodding at the car and smiling.

Caressing the smooth paint of the Falcon's hood, Manmohan sighed impatiently. He wanted to shove his way through the jungle towards Darshan's shack and bring him here. But he could not go to that place, the one room on four sturdy stilts that he had only ever seen in his imagination, with its desk where his son studied, with its Coleman lantern hanging on a hook for late nights, with its pile of pillows for long, daytime naps, and its shelf for books, water, and snacks. It was a star in the universe. They all needed a place like that, a place separated by light years and matter and darkness.

~ ~ ~

It was the middle of the night, and again Manmohan could not sleep. He had been lying there, clinging to his watch, his body tense with alertness. He swung his feet around and out of bed, the floorboards cold.

Jai stirred, pulling the sheet to her neck. "Do you need something?" she asked drowsily.

"No," he whispered, but she had already fallen back to sleep.

He went out into the hallway toward the rafters. It was always hot up there. Even at night when the island cooled pleasantly, the heat in the rafters was the warmth of day accumulated and trapped, making him sweat. It was uncomfortable, with no place to lie down and curl up. Yet this was where Livleen had gone to undo herself, the space packed with pieces of a tarnished life. But it was his life, all its flaws, everything that was beautiful but melancholy, ugly but necessary. There were answers there, even if he did not know how to identify them. He went there now because he needed a place, and this was his.

Rounding the corner into the living room, he discerned the faint light of a lantern flickering from the kitchen. At the entrance he found Darshan halfway up the ladder, his hand poised on the door of the rafters.

Manmohan's eyes widened, and he quickly backed around the corner before being seen. His legs still weak, he slid down the wall until he was sitting on the floor. Listening, he heard Darshan scramble around up in the crawl space, making scuffing noises, dragging heavy items across the ceiling. It soon grew quiet. It was quiet for a very long time, until finally there was movement again, more dragging, heavy, exerted breathing, and then Darshan climbed down. As his son folded the ladder and moved it slowly and softly across the floor, Manmohan stood, pressing his heels into the floorboards, his back skimming up the wall. When he was steady on his feet, he silently snuck away, escaping into the corridors of his dark house.

Psalm of Peace
1965

The musty odor of Motherland Books was sharp in the back, unlit corners where Manmohan often lingered, browsing for additions to his collection. Embraced by a wealth of words, the high, varnished shelves packed with manuscripts eased the charge of adrenaline in his system. He skirted around a shelf into the next aisle, his fingers gently dragging and bumping along the book spines. Murmurs of quiet speech came from the front of the bookstore where Darshan and Upinder Balil were conversing.

He stopped to examine a familiar volume, small and thin. Tilting it out from the shelf with his forefinger, he read the gold-embossed title on the front cover. "Psalm of Peace," he silently mouthed, an English translation of Guru Arjun Dev Ji's religious cantos.

"Bapu," his son called from the front. "Are you ready?"

Manmohan paused, holding his breath and remaining silent. After a moment he heard Upinder and Darshan resume their conversation, and he relaxed.

Opening to the foreword, he scanned the lines: *Unity is the light-winged dream of humanity, but when this dream is to be turned into intention, few followers remain.*

"Bapu," Darshan called again, entering the aisle. "We will be late."

Manmohan ignored him, letting the pages flip under his thumb, stopping at a familiar passage, one his mother had often quoted when he was a child: *This "Psalm of Peace" is the knowledge, the praise and the Name of God; / The man who gives it a place in his heart becomes an embodiment of all excellences.* Knowledge of God, however, had been wiped from Manmohan's heart, to reside in his mind only; he possessed an intellectual awareness of divinity, gathered from various world religion texts, but no longer a spiritual one. Without God in his heart, he embodied nothing. Indeed, he felt disembodied, floating aimlessly, emptied of excellences.

His mother had always read from this Psalm during the morning hours, when the dew was thick over the field of crops and the animals were still sleeping. God, channeled through the guru's words and into Sada Kaur's clear voice, could not be denied during Manmohan's childhood. And then one day, after alighting so disruptively into their quiet, fatherless lives, Baba Singh had begun to join them in these prayers. It was then that the recitations had lost their ability to penetrate and Manmohan's connection to God was severed.

With his father sitting next to him on the floor of the mud hut, the act of devotional reading became imbued with a secondary, shameful meaning that was in direct conflict with the Psalm's intended message. It was a need for his father's good opinion, which had come to mean more than God's. Manmohan turned to canto three, stanza three and read the lines that thereafter haunted him during those hushed morning readings: *A man may surrender his life at a holy place of his own choice, / But pride and vanity will not cease to invade his mind.*

"Bapu," Darshan said again, stepping farther into the aisle. "The hospital…"

"I know."

"Bapu."

"Yes?"

"Mohan is gone."

Manmohan looked up from the book. "Okay," he said.

They had seen Mohan on the street, not more than a half an hour earlier. They ran into him after stopping to pick up cumin and turmeric from the spice shop on their way to the hospital. As they exited, a sack of spices under each of their arms, a Hindi movie poster taped to the display window caught Manmohan's attention. The woman in it was smiling coyly, lipstick thick, a sparkly *bindi* placed between her eyebrows, her midriff exposed, wind blowing her hair back, her chuni fluttering off to the side. Her outstretched hand was pressed against the bare chest of a man standing beside her, suggesting his advances were unwanted, yet her come-hither expression seemed to say something else entirely. Open me up, she was saying. Ravish me.

"So much has changed," Manmohan had muttered to Darshan. "There is no shame anymore."

"The movies were always like that," Mohan said from behind them. "Even the ones you took me to see when I was young."

Disgust welled up in Manmohan's chest like oven-rising dough at the sound of that voice, once spoken from a dark hallway in the shape of a silhouette that still haunted him during sleepless nights. Turning around, he braced himself against the sudden nearness of the enemy, the years of unspoken, agreed-upon distance that had now been breached.

The mass of body fat that had collected around Mohan's midsection was more repulsive up close. It sagged heavily, pulling him downward. There was a sordid quality about his eyes, in the way they narrowed at the corners, assessing and prodding. Lehna was standing near, her skin gray like ash. Manmohan detected a scar along her left temple that she tried to cover with her chuni, and he could see that two of her lower front teeth were missing by the way she nervously suctioned her lip into the empty space. A boy of about two was resting snuggly on her hip, and Amandev, now four, clung to her pantaloons.

"Lehna," Manmohan said stiffly, addressing his daughter-in-law.

She nodded in acknowledgement.

"You look well," he told her, wanting to be kind but regretting it instantly when she flinched. His expression remained stony so as not to betray his embarrassment.

"How is the mill?" Mohan asked, smiling with self-satisfaction.

"How is yours?" Manmohan replied. "I have heard it is a great success. Is your father-in-law impressed by his investment in you? Does he know you run your business solely to put me out of mine?"

Mohan flushed, his smile gone. He roughly nudged Amandev forward. "Say hello to your dada before we go."

Squatting next to his granddaughter, Manmohan extended an open palm, and she rested hers tentatively upon it. He smiled gently at her to allay her fears, suddenly overcome by affection, but she seemed about to cry. Staring helplessly at her quivering lower lip, memories fluttered up in his mind like bird wings, a commotion of events jumbled together. He felt the sudden and powerful urge to stretch time on a table, smooth out its wrinkles so he could better see how one thing had led to the other, how all of it had led to this.

"Say hello, Amandev," Mohan repeated, a threat at the edge of his words.

"Hello, Dada."

Hers had been such a sweet voice, like the music of the old days, like Ellington and Hindi love songs. Manmohan had fled from it, jetting across the street into Motherland Books.

He slid the *Psalm of Peace* into his back pocket and pulled out his wallet for some Fijian dollars. He handed the money to Darshan. "Give this to Upinderji."

"Shall we go?" his son asked.

Manmohan looked down the aisle, through the big glass window at the spice shop across the street. She was still there, that woman in the aged and faded poster, her hand still pushing the man away. He reached toward her, his chest leaning forward into her open palm, reading the words he perceived in her expression. Open me up, he believed her to be saying. Ravish me.

And he did. Manmohan was sure of it.

~ ~ ~

Nausea came in waves in the aftermath of Manmohan's electroshock therapy session as he watched Jai from the living room window. She was in the clearing distributing lunch to the workers, efficient with her movements, no energy or time wasted. After, she would make her way to the mill to oversee the jobs on the kiln and electric saws, another task she had accepted into the fold of her many other responsibilities whenever her weak, diseased husband could not manage them.

Agitated, he pulled his eyes from her, finding Darshan amongst the crowd of workers stacking more logs on an already overloaded flatbed that his son was scheduled to take to Ba that afternoon.

His mood worsened when he saw Darshan jump off the truck and scrutinize the strain on the tires with noticeable misgivings. Rapping the corner of the hardbound *Psalm of Peace* on the glass pane, Manmohan then sat in a chair by the window and opened the book. But still looking outside as the men struggled to rope down the load, he did not read. Instead he felt the pages, lightly touching them, trying to discern the minute raise of the inked letters under his fingertips, but the words were level with the paper and indeterminate. Flattening his palm over the cantos, he then tried absorbing fresh insights and new meaning from the text through his porous and ready skin, yet all he perceived was the grain of paper growing damp from his sweat.

Outside, Darshan gestured at the men to stop. Once more assessing the load, the young man then dropped his coil of rope and began to cross the clearing toward the house. Manmohan set his book aside, rising from the chair to his full height, ignoring his cane resting against the wall.

"It will be fine," he said the moment his son entered the living room.

"The truck will not make the hills," Darshan replied.

"It will."

His son stood there a moment longer, then finally turned to go, doubt etched deep into the lines on his brow. Manmohan heard him jog down the wooden steps, saw him again come into view through the window as he returned to the flatbed. Chandan and Vasant, both of whom would also go on the delivery, each spoke, and Darshan shook his head in reply, bending to pick up two large blocks of wood. He set them in the truck's cabin and wiped his hands on his trousers. Chandan glanced once toward the house, and although the urge to move away from the window was strong, Manmohan remained resolutely where he was.

~ ~ ~

Manmohan dozed on the couch, halfway between sleep and consciousness. His sensed his tongue, a dry, meaty wedge in his mouth like a thick sheaf of sandpaper. An insistent finger jabbed at his shoulder, but he was not sure if it was real or from a dream.

He recognized an urgent voice. "Manmohanji," it said.

Swallowing, trying to generate some lubrication in his mouth, Manmohan opened his eyes to see Chandan standing over him. "You should be with Darshan," he said, slowly sitting up, confused. He searched around for his book.

"Ji, the truck broke down."

Finding the *Psalm of Peace* on the floor, Manmohan bent to retrieve it. "Say again," he said.

Chandan paused to catch his breath. "She stalled around the bend of a hill about five kilometers west, just shy of a ravine."

Manmohan slowly turned his gaze to the millworker, eyes sharpening. "Impossible," he said flatly.

"Ji—"

"What did he do to her?"

"Nothing, ji."

"He pushed her too hard," Manmohan said, standing, reaching for his cane, irritated that he was not more surprised by the circumstances. "He did not ride her slowly enough."

"No, ji. He—"

"She can manage in second gear if you take her up slowly. He rushed her up the hill. I have told him never to do that."

Chandan tightly shut his mouth, anger dancing in his flushed cheeks.

"Get Sabar and the other flatbed," Manmohan told him, waving him off. "Now is not a good time to miss deliveries."

They approached the site, turning around the bend of the steep rise to see the rear tires of the overloaded truck resting precariously against the two wooden blocks Darshan had packed. The front tires were suspended an inch above the pavement, the weight of the load threatening to flip the vehicle in a back somersault down the ravine.

"Bapu!" Darshan called out from where he was perched on the hood of the vehicle, attempting to balance the weight.

Manmohan climbed out of his truck and looked down the ravine, at the craggy rough surface of it, then assessed the pressure on the back tires of the flatbed. He quickly turned at the sound of another truck pulling up the hill, which grew louder from around the bend until finally he recognized Vasant signaling from the passenger seat and saw the large, heavy outline of Mohan behind the wheel.

Gently pulling to a stop, his eldest son lumbered out of his seat to greet them.

Manmohan spun sharply to Darshan. "You should not have sent for him."

"Oi," Mohan said loudly, coming toward the broken flatbed.

Manmohan stepped in front of him. "They are *my* customers."

"I did not come to take your customers," Mohan replied, his expression indecipherable.

It took Manmohan a second to understand, and then he violently shook his head. He shoved Mohan, hands sinking into that soft flesh, satisfied when his son stumbled backwards. "It was not me. I did not send for you. I will never give you even the smallest chance to fix it."

Rage and hurt boiling in his eyes, Mohan stiffly and slowly shrugged, offering a condescendingly conciliatory smile. He retreated to his truck and backed away down the hill.

Without hesitation, Manmohan turned to Darshan and the millworkers, his face grim. "Redistribute the weight."

Darshan stared incredulously at his father for several seconds. Manmohan stood ready for a fight, until finally the young man looked away and called out to Chandan. "Take my place," he said, helping the millworker onto the hood. "Do not move. Sit here until I say so."

With Chandan secured on the hood, Darshan, Vasant, and Sabar transferred half the logs onto Manmohan's truck at a painstakingly slow pace until the front wheels finally groaned back onto the pavement. Testing the engine, the truck sputtered to life when Darshan turned the ignition.

"There is nothing wrong with her," Manmohan told his son. "You rode her too fast."

Shutting off the engine, Darshan said, "We should go back. Junker Uncle should look at her."

"We go to Ba."

Darshan's mouth tightened.

"Vasant rides with you," Manmohan told him. "Chandan, Sabar, and I will follow."

Both trucks set off together, cresting two more hills, and despite the slow progress, Manmohan was reassured by every inch of distance gained. They descended the last rise, the worst of the steep inclines behind them, but as he glanced with relief at the edge of the gully, Chandan shouted in alarm.

"Manmohanji!"

The tailpipe of Darshan's truck was spluttering black fumes, and as some of the exhaust cleared in the breeze, Manmohan cried out. The vehicle was speeding away down the hill.

Ahead of them, Vasant waved frantically out of the passenger window. There was a loud creaking noise and then a pop, like an internal explosion.

"His brakes!" Sabar shouted.

There was a long screech as Darshan's truck approached the bottom, grinding against the emergency brake. The vehicle pivoted to the right and slowed a little, skidding, the tires burning with acrid smoke until it finally stopped beyond the base of the hill, all the weight leaning to the right, the left half of the truck lifting off the ground. It hung in mid air for an eternity. Dust swirled. Then the whole vehicle finally shuddered to the ground on its tires, the engine smoking badly.

As Chandan pulled up close, Manmohan leaned into the dashboard and squinted at the smoke, catching a glimpse of his usually mild-tempered son jumping out of the cabin with a wrench in his hand. A gust of wind tossed the smoke to the far right, and he had a clear view when Darshan kicked the front tire, then swung the wrench against the side metal panel, leaving a huge dent. Manmohan clenched his fists, feeling his arthritic joints resisting.

"One of the engine valves is busted," Darshan bellowed heatedly, wildly brandishing the wrench. "And the brakes are out."

Chandan parked alongside the damaged vehicle, and Manmohan eased his body out of the truck. "Go find help," he told the millworker.

Chandan nodded, put the truck in gear, and sped off.

"You should not have gone to him," Manmohan said, his voice quiet but tense. "He is not your brother."

Darshan stared at his father in shock.

"He has done horrible things," Manmohan continued, steeling against the rebellion he knew was coming. "He is not a part of this family anymore. I never thought it was possible to truly break with family. There always something that connected us, even across the ocean and all the land from here to India. I never believed it could happen. But it can. And when it does, it is not temporary, and it is not just with one of us. Mohan broke from us all."

The rigid, angry tension in Darshan's shoulders thawed into resignation. "It was not me, Bapu." He nodded toward the millworkers. "I sent them both for you, but I suppose they had other ideas." Then he pointed to the dented panel with the wrench, as though overcome, like he no longer cared, and said, "I will fix that."

~ ~ ~

The river nearby, behind the clump of taro, was calm as Manmohan rested under the shade of a banyan tree. Jai wrapped a piece of rope into a figure eight around one of their cow's rear ankles and set a bucket underneath the udders, then hiked up her pantaloons and sat on the milking stool. The cow snorted and shifted uncomfortably, rolling its eyes. She patted its haunch.

Darshan was away. There was an inlet in Sigatoka where he and his friends could jump off an old pier and swim in the calm waters hugged by mangroves. Manmohan looked toward the river, remembering his children splashing there, playing beyond the ferns and taro. They did not play there any longer.

He imagined those young men with Darshan now, laughing and free, their nakedness and the long strides of their thin legs as they ran down the pier to plunge into the water, the Falcon parked off to the side, waiting to bring them home.

As Jai milked, Manmohan leaned his head against the tree trunk. The *Psalm of Peace* was in his back pocket, the rectangular shape of it against his bottom. He still had not read it. This morning he forced it onto one of his shelves that was already bulging with hardbacks, paperbacks, and sets of encyclopedias. He had hoped to forget about it, to lose it in the multitude of his many other books crammed onto the ceiling-high shelves. But an hour later he picked it up again, slipping it into his pocket.

Lifting his head slightly off the tree, Manmohan observed his wife, the pulsing of her grip on the udders, the forward bend of her back as she concentrated, the almost imperceptible movement of her lips as she whispered something soft and encouraging to the cow. Just beyond his wife, he could see his old broken-down World War II truck parked and abandoned off in the bushes. The growth had overtaken the now flat tires, and the metal frame was pockmarked with large jagged holes where the rust had eaten away at it. He had almost put the flatbed there with it, but at the last minute had decided to give it to Junker Singh. Although Darshan had repaired the dent, the engine had been irreparable. It was probably disassembled now, parts strewn across the mechanic's shop floor. It would have been foolish to leave it in the clearing, to delude himself into thinking he might one day have it fixed. He knew he would not.

With some difficulty, he stood. Slipping his feet into his sandals, he approached the cow and laid a hand on its back. "Do you need anything from town?" he asked Jai.

She shook her head.

He felt around in his front pocket for the keys to his other World War II truck but changed his mind when he walked past the carport. He no longer drove much, only occasionally in the window between his doctor's appointments, when the lingering sensation of the therapy sessions cleared out of his bones. And it was good to be on his feet, to be reminded that although he was forty-nine and not the same physically fit man he had once been, there was still some remaining strength left in his body. Leaving his cane against one of the house's stilts, he continued on down the drive, stepping carefully over the uneven planks of wood until he stood under the rickety stand that served as one of the main road's bus stops.

He waited a little more than a half an hour before the bus arrived, already packed with riders, the window tarps curled upward to give the people some air. He climbed aboard and pushed his way to the middle, settling onto the edge of a bench already occupied by two other men. The bus, the feel of bodies pressed against him, crowded in on the ripped vinyl seats, bouncing along the badly-paved roads, the springs digging into his bottom and his back, was a rare and welcome change from the normal. He never took the bus, and the discomfort of it grounded him; it was oddly consoling in its remoteness from all things customary.

The bus made its final stop, and Manmohan allowed the rushing stream of passengers flooding down the aisle to push him tide-like toward the front and outside. Everyone dispersed toward the city, and the bus rumbled across the street to park in the terminal, leaving him all alone to stare up at Penitentiary Hill.

He had intended to lose himself in Suva, in the small clusters of men chatting outside electronics or sundry shops on

Victoria Parade, sharing news from abroad. He had thought that perhaps he might also visit Junker Singh today. But instead he gazed upward at the prison, thinking of Livleen. He saw the prison as she had once seen it. She had been a small girl, perfect and sweet and only eight. She had been told that the only thing between her and the locks on those prison doors was one word from a person she trusted would never utter it.

He began to climb, his aching knee joints carrying him up the hill, consumed by a sense of dread as he moved upward. But he had to continue, to dispel the demons.

Approaching the gray building, he touched the cool, stucco wall and paused to catch his breath. Glancing around, he was strangely disappointed. There was a small tower with cables running from it, and the windowless penitentiary building was not as massive as it had appeared from below. Far more imposing from down on the street, at the top it was unremarkable.

A slat opened in the door to Manmohan's left. A man with a mustache addressed him through the bars. "Do you have an appointment?"

Manmohan straightened. "No."

The guard began to close the slat, but Manmohan stopped him. "Are there many men here?"

"Some."

"And what have they done?"

The man's mustache rose as his upper lip curled in an expression of boredom. "Not much. Theft and the like. The bad ones are taken off the island."

"I see."

"That all?"

"Yes," Manmohan said. "No, wait." He removed the *Psalm of Peace* from his back pocket and pushed it through the bars.

"Here," he said.

The guard took a moment to glance through the book. Then he pushed it back. "There is nothing like this here."

"Just keep it."

"No one will read it."

"Maybe you will like it."

The guard shrugged. "Okay." Without another word, he shut the slat.

Manmohan turned away from the door, the clarity he had hoped for still eluding him.

He glanced around one more time. The hill was not as high as Darshan's coconut tree, but the view was adequate. He could see most of the city, the children's school two kilometers east, the gurdwara and Hindu temple across from each other in the north quarter of Suva, the elaborate Colonial headquarter buildings to the south. He could see all the way out toward the docks, the tips of the ships' masts, and the horizon beyond.

He began his descent, pausing occasionally to look around at the changing altitude of the city around him, until at last he was standing on the flat surface of the street to wait for the bus back to Veisari.

A Shack in the Jungle
1966

The name Ranjit Singh Toor carried with it mystery and glimmers of memory. There was the scarred skin of one missing eye, and the kind, reflecting gaze of the other in which Manmohan had always been magnificent and loved. There was also a maroon turban that had possessed within its cotton fibers the perfumes of India—the clay of the earth and the spices of curry—until one day the cloth had absorbed a new and frightening smell. Manmohan had been only three when his uncle died, and this was all he remembered of their walks through Barapind. But later, when his aunt Desa had determined him old enough to hear them, she told him stories of the mighty Ranjit.

What Manmohan had come to understand from his aunt's accounts was that Ranjit's world was too small in that unassuming Punjab town, in those humble villages where families had nestled for centuries. Thus he had ventured outward from the rural nucleus into which he had been born, at first because he had no other choice, but later because he needed to escape in search of something that might ground him. "We were cast out," Desa told Manmohan when he asked what had become of his uncle. Firmly holding his chin, she had searched his eyes. "We were sent away from our land, and he, like your father, like us all, was set adrift."

Floating in the middle of a vast ocean, the air about Manmohan pulsated with yet another coming change, another imminent journey. One pencil and three blank university applications were arranged in a row at the top of Darshan's desk: Oxford, University of Sydney, and UC Berkeley. Manmohan gazed down at them, his fingers lightly tented over Oxford. The light was strange on the paper, cutting in through the windowpanes and leeching the color from everything.

He peered outside into the jungle in the direction of Darshan's shack, then opened one of the desk drawers. Finding it empty, he closed it with a hollow wooden clatter. He looked around his son's room, the bed the only other piece of furniture. Nobody lived here. Nobody had lived here for a very long time.

"I knew this would happen," Manmohan had told Darshan's teacher the other day, sitting in the classroom where his son had spent so much of his time.

Mr. Gupta had frowned. "You have always wanted this for your children."

"I know he should go. I know the mind is—"

"You have always valued the mind."

"But he will not come back."

His tone blunt, Mr. Gupta had replied, "Beyond this island the changes occurring are monumental. The mind cannot flourish here. You will simply have to trust him."

Lifting the corner of the Oxford application, Manmohan delicately held it up, tilting his head to examine it more closely.

The promise of enterprise had brought the Toor family to Fiji, but even then he knew that one day this would not be enough. He knew that one day only an education, only books, would carry the young forward. Yet, for all his reading, for all the expectations that his children firmly grasp this truth, he had not anticipated being left behind.

"Bapu?"

Startled, Manmohan dropped the application. It slipped off the desk and onto the floor under the bed. He watched it disappear, unable to bend to get it. Darshan went down on his knees, reaching to retrieve it. He then set it back in place on his desk.

"You left these here," Manmohan said.

Darshan nodded toward the jungle. "They will get dirty out there."

Manmohan pulled one of the blankets from his son's bed and wrapped it around his shoulders. "Have you decided which one?"

Darshan sat at his desk, picking up the pencil. "Not yet."

"There is not much time left."

"I know."

Manmohan sank onto the mattress. "I was just thinking about your great uncle Ranjit. Our lives are very simple in comparison. The consequences are not as severe as they were for him, but still he knew what he wanted in the most difficult of circumstances. He battled a kingdom, fought for his family, went on impossible missions, lost an eye, was tortured, starved in train stations, and traveled far and wide. He sacrificed everything to protect his countrymen against the evils of racism and oppression. He was a warrior."

"Where did he go?"

"To America. To San Francisco." Thinking of Desa,

Manmohan's expression hardened. "Maybe to you this does not seem like much, but it is very far. In those days, for village people in India, it was so remote it was considered the end of the earth. They did not even know it existed."

Darshan clicked his pencil on the desk. "Times are not like that anymore. Today there are no warriors. We are not fighting for anything. The answers are not as clear."

"Perhaps not," Manmohan said. "But whatever great quests he embarked on, no matter the complications, clear or unclear, your great uncle never forgot his home or his family. In the end, he went back. To them."

~ ~ ~

Manmohan studied his profile in the washroom mirror. He was fifty now, still too early to visibly see the manifestations of his Ankylosing Spondylitis, but there was nonetheless pain in his spine, a dull and persistent ache. He inched closer to the mirror, pressing his forehead against the two-by-two-foot square of glass propped on a wooden shelf to scrutinize his naked torso, searching for even the smallest outward indication of the disease, but he found nothing. His forehead left a greasy imprint on the already chipped and dirtied mirror. The aluminum tub behind him steamed with fresh, hot water. Jai had poured his bath.

Stepping carefully into the water, one foot, then the other, he sat on the stool placed just outside the tub, bent over and splashed and rubbed his face. He soaped his beard and hair, then lathered his underarms. Standing, using a small container, he scooped up and dumped water over his head, rinsing the soap away, splashing the tiled floor. When he was finished, he sat again and watched the sudsy dirt of his body flow to the drain in the center of the room, his eyes going out of focus as he thought of his children.

The whiny pitch in Navpreet's voice, forever resentful of any small measure of work she was asked to contribute to the family, often ground like chalk on his nerves. Livleen quietly roamed the house like a lost spirit, making him feel withered and awkward in her presence. And Mohan roused such fury and bottomless sorrow. Manmohan could not comprehend his life now without Darshan in it, to be left with these others who gave him no comfort.

He reached for a towel and patted down his body, already knowing without having to be told which school his son had chosen. Despite all of Darshan's doubts and reservations, Manmohan had seen a spark of fascination for Ranjit's story on his face, for this morsel of Toor family history, a small piece of which had taken place in America.

Wiping the condensation from the mirror, Manmohan assessed himself once more; his tucked beard still held water, his loose, wet hair clung to his back, his nose and cheeks were shiny, eyes resolute and bright with sudden and desperate hope.

~ ~ ~

The green of the freshly-cut grass beneath Manmohan's sandals was almost florescent, as if the sun itself had burrowed inside each blade. The earth was soft, healthy and reassuring, relieving the aches in his knee joints as he stood waiting with the families who had gathered on Mahatma Gandhi Memorial high school's soccer field for the senior class commencement ceremony to begin.

At last the headmaster crossed the field, wearing a new

pullover for the occasion, appearing stately and academic. He cleared his throat and, without the formality of first giving a speech, promptly began to call out names in a booming voice too loud for the small assembly of twenty-two students and a few of their family members. The graduates stood alert, listening, walking toward him with an awkward, unripe dignity when called upon to accept their diplomas. Unaware of the greater world into which they would now be thrust, they grinned foolishly as the headmaster bestowed upon them thin foldable leaflets indicating the year of their achievement.

One by one, the line of waiting graduates shortened, until at last, finishing off the list, the headmaster called, "Darshan Singh Toor."

Manmohan watched as his son approached to receive his diploma. Darshan wore, as did all the graduates, a newly washed uniform: khaki trousers, polished black loafers, a blue sweater-vest over a white short-sleeve shirt. But in other ways he was distinctly different from his classmates. Whereas they were playful and self-conscious, Darshan was serious and reserved. The only Sikh in the class, his beard was getting longer, curling around his jaw line. He walked with an easy grace, his posture, as always, straight. His eyes were direct, respectful but not challenging as he gravely turned to wave the certificate at his family.

The headmaster smiled. "Congratulations to you all," he bellowed, concluding the commencement. The group began to disperse, and Darshan joined his family.

Navpreet snatched the document from her brother. "Whatever happened to Oxford?"

He shrugged.

"I suppose if you insist on going to America, we will never see each other again," she said, "since I am going to Oxford."

Jai carefully took the diploma from Navpreet, regarding it with pride.

Livleen was quiet, sitting cross-legged in the grass, staring out into the field where the graduates had excitedly clumped together. Manmohan followed her gaze, then looked back at her. She absently pulled a small, isolated daisy from the ground and tossed it aside, then began plucking out single blades of grass.

A movement beyond the crowd of graduates caught Manmohan's attention, a long arm waving over the students' heads. "Darshan!" Mohan called.

"What is he doing here?" Jai asked in a hushed whisper.

Darshan's eyes flicked toward his brother, then away as if pretending he had not noticed.

"Come, we are leaving," Manmohan said, already moving across the field toward the Falcon parked on the street.

"When Darshan leaves, can I use the car?" Navpreet asked, kicking an invisible ball to the rusted metal goal posts.

"No," Manmohan said.

"But why not?"

Jai held her daughter back a step. "For what purpose?" she asked.

Navpreet sulked. "I have perfect marks in school, which is better than him. Bapu always says how important school is."

"You do not need a car to get there," Manmohan said as they approached the Falcon. He gestured for her to get in the backseat.

A priest from Suva's gurdwara was waiting for them outside the main house by the time they arrived home. He had come early to set up the holy book in the living room for the kirtan Manmohan had arranged for Darshan's accomplishment. Jai went into the kitchen with Livleen and Navpreet to prepare for the lunch they would later serve, and Manmohan and Darshan set about moving all the furniture into the bedrooms and laying cushions and sheets over the floor. When the room had been emptied, they screwed hooks into the wall beams and hung a silk overhang in the front of the room. Satisfied, the priest arranged the holy book beneath it and seated himself comfortably, readying for a long reading. He opened a bag and took out a flywhisk, torpidly waving it several times over the book, then waited for the guests to arrive.

Junker Singh was the first to enter the house. Saying a quick hello, Jai brushed past him on her way outside to help his wife bring up the sweets they would later pass around.

The mechanic shook Manmohan's hand, then turned to Darshan. "When do you leave?" he asked.

"One week."

Raising his eyebrows, Junker Singh replied, "So soon?"

"There will be a lot to do before school starts."

The mechanic positioned himself on the floor across from Navpreet and Livleen, who were already sitting cross-legged by the makeshift aisle of red cloth Jai was using for the guests to approach and pay their respects to the holy book. "It is much sooner than I expected," he said.

Darshan sat next to him, and Junker Singh took his hand, holding it close to his chest. Darshan made no move to withdraw it. Manmohan watched the two of them, stepping back several feet to leave them be, lowering himself onto a floor cushion.

The neighbors, Dev, Kalyan, Paandu, and their wives soon entered, bowing before the Guru Granth Sahib and taking a seat. The millworkers, Chandan, Sabar, and Vasant joined, and finally, after several of Darshan's classmates and their families arrived, filling the room, the priest began to read in a droning, singing voice. Manmohan was struck by the powerful nature of that voice, by the command for tranquility in it. The reading was rhythmic and undulating despite its monotony. It was a voice that carried men with it.

He looked at Darshan, observing the way his son's head was bent slightly forward, eyes fixed on the priest, listening. Wincing slightly, Manmohan tried to pull his legs underneath him. He was in pain but did not wish to retreat to the rear of the room and sit unobtrusively on a chair the way the old men of the village had done in Amarpur. But Darshan, catching his father's movement from the corner of his eye, rose without a word to get a chair from one of the other rooms. Manmohan watched him go both gratefully and resentfully. Sighing, he stood and, careful not to step on hands and feet, wove through the guests and took his place in the chair Darshan had positioned near the entrance to the hallway.

Navpreet observed her brother from across the room, then rolled her eyes and slowly mouthed the words "show" and "off."

After another hour, at last the priest raised his voice to bring the prayer to a close, singing, "Saaaat sriiiii akaaal. Waheguru ji ka khalsaaaa, waheguru ji ki fateh."

Bodies stirred, and people began to stand and stretch, the men making their way to the balcony and the women into the kitchen. Soon the smells of lunch being warmed wafted through the house. Jai had prepared stuffed bitter melon and kidney bean curry, both Darshan's favorites and testaments to her skill in the kitchen. People ate ravenously, afterwards lingering over cups of warm chai. Soon the afternoon clouds darkened the sky prematurely, threatening rain, and they began to slowly go home.

When the last of the guests had gone, Manmohan looked

about his house at the remnants of celebratory prayer, at the cushions and crumpled sheets in corners that no longer covered the floor, at the empty tin cups left on the window mantles, at the awning under which the holy book no longer rested. Some of the wives had offered to help tidy and restore the house, but Jai had sent them away. She, like he, enjoyed the quiet aftermath of such events, the echo of happiness, the memory of laughing voices in the air.

Drowsy from the food and in good spirits, he went in search of Darshan, who had earlier gone outside with several of his friends to say goodbye. From the balcony, he saw his son under the carport, resting on the hood of his Falcon.

Manmohan carefully descended the stairs to join him, leaving his cane at the bottom of the banister. Approaching the carport, he saw that Darshan held a rectangular metal box the size of a lunch tiffin in his lap and was gazing down at it somberly, his face shadowy in the fading light.

"Everyone has gone home," Manmohan told him.

Darshan lifted his eyes to look directly at his father. "You must be tired."

"A little."

His son looked down once more at the box and then held it up. "Junker Uncle gave this to me. He left. He told me to say goodbye."

Manmohan took the box, opening the lid to discover a small tool set, complete with two screwdrivers, miniature hammer, pliers, nails, and screws. His throat constricted. "When you were young—" he abruptly stopped himself, memories confused: the daily ritual of constructing houses made of brick in the backyard, the hollow tap of a plastic hammer on a hard surface, repairs to be made, a sturdy bridge over the river, and a shack in the jungle that no boy should

357

have ever been able to build alone.

"Bapu?"

Manmohan took a breath and shook his head, clearing his thoughts. "It must be strange to leave. Everything you know is here."

"Yes, I suppose so."

"Are you nervous?"

Darshan slid down the hood of the Falcon, careful not to scratch the paint. "Maybe."

As was his habit, Manmohan touched his watch. "That is good. It means you are alive. Maybe it even means you are ready." He brought the face of the watch close to his ear and listened. It ticked, loudly and with strength, like blood pumping in his ears. Lowering his arm, he unclasped the band. "Give me your hand," he said.

Darshan's eyes widened as Manmohan gently took hold of his son's wrist and fastened the watch around it. "I had it fixed. It is a bit loose, but it will not be long before it fits."

Shaking his arm so the watch shimmied down into place, Darshan tentatively regarded it, waves of emotion flickering across his face. Manmohan watched him, seeing the shape of his own wrist wrapped around his son's, wondering what would come next.

~ ~ ~

"It cannot be real," Navpreet said in awe, nudging Livleen with her elbow, astounded by the size of the jets parked along the tree-lined apron of Nadi airport.

Livleen squinted down the runway and gave a slight, uninterested nod of agreement. "Yes, they are very big."

Jai looked skeptically at the planes. "Will you be safe?" she asked Darshan.

The airport had changed since Manmohan had last been here with his father and brothers. Several more gates had been added to the apron, and the runway had been lengthened to accommodate the larger, louder-engined airliners. And not just one, but three airplanes taxied the runway. "He will be fine."

Darshan squeezed his mother's shoulder reassuringly, then looked at Manmohan. "Can you drive back?"

"I will be watching him," Navpreet said, her hands clinging to the chain-link fence through which they would watch Darshan take off. "You are not the only one who ever did anything."

"Here," Jai said, handing Darshan a cloth full of parathas. "To eat on the plane."

"Thank you, Bebe," he said. He was dressed in a new tailored suit. His tie was neat at the collar, pulled out over the vest, the end of it tucked into his trousers.

An outdoor loudspeaker at the top of a thin pole crackled. "Flight to San Francisco, boarding in five minutes."

Manmohan glanced up at it, then tucked a wad of American dollars into his son's palm. "Do you need anything else?" he asked, pulling his hand away as Darshan tried to return the money. "Do you have everything?"

Darshan patted his bag. "I think it is all here."

"Will you miss me?" Navpreet asked.

"I am sure I will."

She gave him a haughty look, like she did not believe him.

"I will miss all of you," he said.

Jai gripped both of his arms. "Study hard, and write us as soon as possible. I will be waiting."

"I will," he replied, adjusting the bag on his shoulder. "I should go."

"Darshan," Manmohan said, then hesitated because he was not sure what else to say. "Let me know if the battery in that watch stops."

"Of course, Bapu."

After Darshan had disappeared into the building, so dark inside compared to the bright sun on the tarmac, Manmohan left the rest of them at the fence. "I will be in the car," he said.

"Don't you want to see the plane take off?" Navpreet asked.

"I have seen it before."

Perhaps twenty minutes later, leaning on the hood of the Falcon, the rush of turbulence was loud as the plane tore into the clouds above, but still Manmohan did not look up. He waited until the echo of the engine had dissipated into the atmosphere, and then he tilted his head back toward the sky.

~   ~   ~

Carefully navigating the thick underbrush and verdant tangle of trees and vines, Manmohan pushed through the jungle, his cane dangling from the crook of his elbow. He had not been certain how far in Darshan had built his shack, but it was very near. Turning around to look at the main house through the trees, he realized that if he had been standing on the front balcony, squinting hard enough, he could have perceived at least a corner of the shack's roof from there.

The building was a bit worn, but Manmohan marveled at the durable stilts that had allowed the shack to weather the heavy storms that had blown across the island over the years.

A ladder rested against the open doorway, and Manmohan wondered if Darshan had been here that morning before leaving. He climbed up, and when he reached the blanket-covered door, he was more than a little surprised to hear the soft voice of his friend from within.

"I thought you would come," Junker Singh said.

"How did you know about this place?" Manmohan asked.

"I have always known about this place," the mechanic said, a little surly. "I helped him build it."

Manmohan nodded slowly, feeling shame now. "I knew someone had to. He was too little to do it on his own."

"But he knew what he was doing."

Rubbing his aching finger joints, Manmohan peered inside the shack. There was a blanket crumpled in the corner on top of a sleeping cot. Junker Singh was sitting at a table on the only chair. There was a tin tumbler next to his arm, condensation on the outside indicating it was half full of water. A collection of treasures lined a shelf: magazine clippings of cars and pictures of foreign countries, notebooks and candies, a slingshot, a compass, and one fresh coconut. An oil lantern was hanging from a nail above the table.

"Are you coming in?" Junker Singh asked. "Or will you stand there in the doorway?"

"It is much bigger than it looks from outside," Manmohan said, stepping all the way in, reaching up to touch the ceiling with his fingertips before taking a seat on the cot.

Junker Singh passed the tumbler of water to his friend. "I brought it up myself."

Manmohan took it, wiping the condensation off on his shirtsleeve. He was not thirsty.

"Why didn't you ever come see it before?" the mechanic asked.

"I thought it was private."

"Darshan would have wanted you to come, but he never would have asked."

"I do not understand why not."

Junker Singh laughed, slapping his palm against the table. "You never made any sense."

"Did he ask *you* to come here?"

"He did."

"That is entirely different."

The mechanic smiled broadly. "It is."

Manmohan stared down into the tumbler, at the clear liquid within. He tipped it slightly. The water was so pure and clean against the silver of the tin. "I never knew you both were out here. You never said a word."

"There were no secrets. It was your choice. He wanted to talk to you. It is a bit regrettable because that boy was always thinking of you."

"I was too worried. The children always worried me."

Junker Singh rose from the chair. Taking one last look around, he stepped toward the door and pushed aside the blanket.

"Where are you going?" Manmohan asked.

"I said my goodbyes. But you should stay." Junker Singh glanced at the ladder. "I tried to convince him to put stairs in, but he said this would help me exercise." He held his breath like he was about to duck under water, and then the curtain fell closed and Manmohan could hear his friend grunting slowly down the ladder.

When the mechanic was gone, Manmohan placed the tumbler on the floor and pulled his legs up, stretching out on the cot. He covered himself with the blanket to wait for something important to happen. He thought maybe he was waiting for acceptance, like the goodbye Junker Singh had achieved. Or perhaps it was something else, like peace.

He lay there, and then he lay there longer, but nothing came to him.

Impatient, he sat up, touching the empty place on his wrist and swinging his feet back onto the floor.

Part III
Darshan
Bay Area, California

Ford Falcon Futura
1969

Darshan was cold. Outside Kaiser Hospital, the wind tunneled down Geary Street, carrying with it the dampness of thick fog that coated the city of San Francisco and penetrated his bones. It pimpled his arms beneath the double-breasted pea coat he had bought the year before. It brushed briskly against his neck and swept up his tapered corduroy pant cuffs, snapping at his ankles as he strode down Geary, made a right onto St. Josephs, and headed toward Terra Vista Avenue. He flipped up his coat collar and crammed his fists into his pockets. His father's leather watchband he had adjusted to better fit him was tighter against his bony wrist in the chill. Forty-eight degrees. But he enjoyed this weather, the fact of its differentness. It felt like freedom.

Approaching Terra Vista, he leaned forward against the slope of the hill, his book bag seemingly heavier as he ascended. The slanted stoops of the row of Victorian homes in his periphery to the left and parked cars to the right went unnoticed as he trudged against the wind and gravity toward the warm apartment that awaited him. His thoughts were consumed by the comfort of bed: those soft flannel sheets, oblivion the moment his head touched the feather-filled pillow. Even the mattress, springy as it was, sounded appealing now, because although the work was satisfying, night shifts in pathology were exhausting, requiring a concentrated focus that left him drained by the end.

He did not have any specific aspirations toward becoming a pathologist, and was entirely unqualified when he went in for the interview two years before. It was still extraordinary to him that he had gotten the job, although the head pathologist, Dr. Levi, later told him that a good judge of character could always recognize a capable man the instant he walked through the door.

"Referred by Dr. Rosenthal, I see," Dr. Levi had murmured when Darshan first introduced himself. Then, his voice suddenly crisp, he said more loudly, eyes magnified behind thick glasses, "I like him…Rosenthal…a brilliant teacher. Very regrettable when he retired from Kaiser. In any case, to the point. My man is leaving on short notice. I need someone right away to fill his spot. When can you start?"

His mouth very dry, Darshan replied, "Now, if you need."

"Now?"

"Yes."

Considering this, after a moment Dr. Levi said, "That's good. Very good. So you say you drove ambulances?"

"Last year."

"So you've got some familiarity with anatomy?"

"I am not exactly sure what you mean," Darshan replied, suddenly uncomfortable.

"You had to help sometimes, yes?" the doctor asked, the large orbs of his eyes widening expectantly. "With the patients in the ambulance?"

"Not much, but I took a CPR class."

"So you do then? Have some familiarity with anatomy?"

Darshan slowly bobbed his head up and down. "Yes, I suppose I do."

"Do you know anything about pathology?"

Sweat had begun to bead on Darshan's lip. "Yes," he lied with feigned confidence, feeling as though he was being too timid. Pathology, pathology, he thought desperately, rapidly flipping through his brain in search of some memory in which he might have heard of it before. Perhaps in class. Maybe his father's medical journals. Or did he know it by a different name? He wiped his palms on the front of his pants, dreading being turned away to face a lifetime of washing dishes and serving food in restaurants, fated never to apply his knowledge and love of science.

"You have good hands," Dr. Levi said approvingly.

Darshan looked down at them.

"Surgeon's hands," the doctor told him. "And a very good temperament." He removed his glasses to polish them on his white coat. "Well, all right then. The job is yours." His eyes were strangely beady when naked. They blinked cheerfully.

"Mine?"

"I like Dr. Rosenthal," Dr. Levi said, sliding his glasses back on, the innocent pleasure on his middle-aged face once again intensified behind the lenses. "And as far as I can tell, you know enough about bodies to satisfy me."

"Bodies?"

"Anatomy."

"Dr. Levi, I…I have classes."

"Yes, yes, Rosenthal mentioned part-time. I understand. Now, let's begin."

When, on that very day, Dr. Levi had wheeled out a dead body on a steel table and explained that his new employee would need to eviscerate the organs, then cut them open to examine them, Darshan had nodded somberly. He concentrated every effort on appearing professional, like he had known all along that pathology was the slicing open of a dead body and the removing of its organs. He was given only two days of training—which included how to replace the organs after they had been examined; how to suture the body, wrap it in plastic, and roll it into the cold box; as well as how to section the tissue samples doctors had taken from live patient organs so the lab could check for cancer or inflammation. After those two days, Dr. Levi had abandoned him in the morgue. Though it should have terrified Darshan to be alone, holding the scalpel over the bluish, gray chest of his very first dead body, he had been invigorated. That first one had made clear his capabilities, the extent of his talent for defeating the unknown, and doing it well.

And the unknowns in those days had been numerous. From the moment he landed at San Francisco International Airport, nothing about the city resembled his fantasy of it while flying thousands of miles across the Pacific to America's West Coast. Though aware it had modernized since 1912, he had still imagined San Francisco to be the place he read about in one of his father's history books, as Ranjit Singh Toor might have experienced it: his great uncle striding through the hilly dirt roads past trolley cars and horses toward 5 Wood Street, the Ghadarite headquarters. Two generations back and just a short bus ride from Kaiser Hospital, Ranjit had been one of the Punjabis voicing his intention to eradicate global racism against their people.

Manmohan had told Darshan that the world was more

tolerant now, that the newer generations would benefit from Ranjit's efforts, that there was no more fear of being beaten in the streets, of being hounded and abused. And yet, the year Darshan washed dishes in the humid and steamy kitchens of popular restaurants, the clank and chink of silverware against china mingling with the happy chatter of light-skinned customers in the dining room, proved that there was still progress to be made. Sikhs were nominally numbered in San Francisco proper, and unlike Hindus, their striking appearance—long, full beards and turbans—was unsuitable for a society that favored clean-cut men.

Darshan had been so discomfited in the beginning, so hyper-conscious of his dissimilarity. After resigning from his ambulance-driving job—in which he was rarely seen and never heard—he had not been able to find proper work, and he knew it was because he was different. He endured a year of fruitless interviews and menial jobs before finally cutting his hair and trimming his beard. Perhaps he should have been more troubled by the sight of his long tresses on the barber's floor, more distressed by the betrayal to his culture, but when he looked in the mirror and saw before him a new person—hair long enough to resemble the cool hippies he saw loitering around campus, but short enough to be acceptable—he could not help but admire his own courage, the fortitude it took to make this concession, which was simply one of the many he had made in order to adapt here, just as with his plans for UC Berkeley.

Though he had been accepted and was due to report to the enrollment offices of the university in 1966, no one had warned him of the cost, and he did not have the money to attend. The tuition rates at San Francisco State were more reasonable, and disillusioned, he signed up for classes at what he initially deemed a far more inferior college. His disappointment, however, was quickly curbed by a number of challenging courses and the equally exhilarating events that were taking place on the State campus. He watched from the sidelines as students doggedly protested the Vietnam War. Police with batons and helmets patrolled the campus, their job to prevent students from scaling trucks where speakers had been set up for pro-War speeches. Darshan had seen it once. Samuel Hayakawa booed away, his voice drowned by the crash of a massive speaker hitting gravel, several small pebbles shooting out like shrapnel, stinging one man in the shin, and all the voices raised in outrage. Though remaining strictly on the fringe—not willing to risk deportation with only a student visa—the anti-Vietnam movement had roused Darshan's idealism, had made him feel as though he was in the middle of something significant, the world changing drastically at his feet.

For all his unfulfilled expectations, for all the rejection and adversity, for all the times he had gone to Ocean Beach to stare homesick at the sea, he had grown fond of San Francisco, the city awash in love, free spirit, youth, and bright colors. Everywhere he looked, a twenty-something baby boomer emphatically threw him the peace sign. Surfers-turned-skateboarders skirted the hilly streets, and Barbie dolls and G.I. Joe figurines decorated storefront windows. The city was a place to be young and adventurous.

Halfway up Terra Vista Avenue, Darshan turned toward one of the houses and climbed a short cement staircase. From the small square landing at the top, he knocked on the apartment door.

A young woman cracked it open. "Hey you," she said, eyes bright with affection.

San Francisco was the place where he had found Elizabeth

Quinn.

"Hey." Darshan smiled, pressing a palm against the cold paint of the door as she playfully tried not to let him in. Stepping inside her studio apartment, he set his bag down and pulled her close. "You look nice."

"You always say that." She kissed his cheek, then brushed the bangs out of her eyes. She had been a Catholic nun, in Oregon. When they met last year, she was only four months out of the convent where she had spent five sequestered years of her life. The first time he saw her, when he approached the Kaiser admitting desk with a clipboard of paperwork where she sat at her secretarial post, he could not understand how it was possible, how four months out of a convent she had no signs of it on her. No cross on a chain at her throat, no stiffness in her posture, only a shy self-consciousness normal for a girl of twenty-two fresh to the city from a small town in Oregon.

One of her dangly silver earrings caught the light, and he touched the end of it. Her appeal was not simply that she was beautiful, that she had a long body, that her face was comprised of sharp angles softened by round, kind eyes, or the way her pale back looked when he rested his brown hand upon it as she slept next to him, or even her ready willingness to laugh at everything he uttered because of his accent or the way he sometimes misunderstood the context of something she said. It was that Elizabeth's story paralleled his. The convent had been her island, San Francisco the place where they met to explore the infinite possibilities that lay beyond the surrounding waters.

"I made the bed for you," she told him, pointing to the gold-colored foldout couch centered beneath a window that looked out to a brick wall. Nowadays he rarely stayed at the boarding room he rented from an old Russian lady who refused to let him sufficiently heat it.

"Can you wake me at noon?" he asked her. "I have a one o'clock class."

"Sure. I'll ring from work."

"Would you and Stewart like to meet at the Fillmore when I'm done?"

"Sounds fun. Who's playing?"

"Jefferson Airplane." He smiled, running his hand through his thick, black hair.

"I promised my sister I'd have a late lunch with her after my shift, so save me a seat."

"Sure. Will you let Stewart know?"

"Yep. Now, get some sleep. Lie down and I'll see you later. I've gotta go or I'll be late."

He kissed her lips.

"Bye," she said. "Lock up after me."

He sat on the edge of the bed, untied and pulled off his brown suede shoes. The apartment was so quiet in Elizabeth's absence. Lining the opposite wall was a set of shelves, varnished planks of wood stretched across large decorative bricks, assembled layer by layer. It overflowed with knickknacks: purple and green glass-blown vases that sparkled in the light, a nail clipper, necklaces tangled with several pairs of earrings, a box of laundry detergent, a number of amethyst rocks that had collected too much dust to properly reflect light, a picture of Elizabeth's father who had passed away when she was twelve. A vine drooped lazily down one side of the shelf from its pot. Another plant hung from a hook in the ceiling. The kitchenette was cramped, the sink always full of dishes. In the corner on the floor there was a pile of large red, green, and blue pillows. A lamp with a fiberglass shade was centered on an end table.

Darshan leaned forward, took his wallet out of his back pocket, and placed it on the table. He could see his fish-eye reflection in the small television that rested on a flimsy stand. At night they sometimes watched Elizabeth's favorite show, *The Twilight Zone*, and Darshan's favorite, *Rowan and Martin's Laugh-In*. Vinyl records were neatly arranged like books on the shelf beneath. He thought about flicking on the television, but too tired to get up, decided against it. He wiggled tiredly out of his coat, tossed it on the floor instead of hanging it in Elizabeth's walk-in, swung his legs around and lay down against the corner-tasseled, orange throw pillows.

He groaned, remembering, and sat up. Last night, before his shift, he had picked up the mail from his landlady and shoved it in his bag. There was a letter from his father that he had not yet read.

His body heavy, he went to his bag to retrieve the letter. Sitting on the edge of the bed, he ripped open the envelope, expecting the usual correspondence: problems on the mill, a superficial account of the family's well-being, questions about San Francisco, his job, and school, to which he always replied with the same tedious response, questions about why he had not visited between semesters, which he always evaded, and news that they had found yet another lovely Indian girl from a nice family he should come home to meet before someone else married her.

As he unfolded this particular letter, however, he noticed that it was unusually short, which made him instantly uneasy. Quickly skimming the words, his stomach twisted in anxiety.

Darshan,

I have booked passage for the family on

The Oreana. We will be arriving to San Francisco 17 August with our visas. As you know, it has been difficult these past years to manage the mill on my own. Concrete is more and more in demand, and Mohan has nearly stolen away my few remaining customers. I have decided to terminate my lease. There is nothing left here in Fiji. Make arrangements, and we will see you in August.

Your bapuji

Darshan stood, pacing, searching for a pen and paper, then gave up.

A sudden flood of concerns struck him. They would need a place to live, furniture, a means of income, a car for Manmohan's doctor's appointments. He touched his cut hair, a bud of fear blooming in his chest, then said aloud, "Elizabeth." He had not told his family about her.

Setting the letter on the bed, he opened the envelope and ran a finger along the inside, but it was empty. His shoulders slumped as he balanced the envelope on his open palm in surrender. It had never once occurred to him that he would not return home to Fiji. A resurgence of homesickness he had believed long since conquered overwhelmed him. He missed the jungle, driving to Mahatma Gandhi in the Falcon, the scent of freshly-sawed wood, the feel of sawdust prickling the soles of his bare feet, the refuge of his shack, and the tuft of his favorite coconut tree. One last time he opened the envelope searching for something that would allay this abrupt onset of homesickness, an emotion that was in direct conflict with something else he was feeling: the distress of his parents alighting on his independent life and the desire to be left alone to explore the new things that were happening to him.

Guiltily, he felt the weight of Manmohan's old watch on his wrist. He had taken it to a repair shop on Valencia to shorten the leather band and get the face buffed. In the stillness of the apartment, Darshan could hear its faint mechanical tick. Placing the letter on the table next to his wallet, he lay down without undressing, pulling the covers over him. He remained like that for a long while, listening to the tick-ticking of the watch. When he finally fell asleep, he dreamt of blackness, of being blind. There was only a sensation of Fiji, the green smell of crushed taro leaves, the rain pelting the roof of his shack, and his coconut tree, which he wished he could still climb.

~ ~ ~

The Fillmore was crowded with concertgoers. Darshan waded and pushed through, searching for Stewart, spotting his six-foot-six-tall best friend waving a gangly arm over the crowd, beckoning to him. A lean black man with slightly bulging eyes and a long goatee that pointed in a V halfway down the length of his long neck, Stewart was not much older than Darshan, but his sunglasses, his black patent-leather, pointy shoes, his bellbottom pants, and the suaveness with which he carried himself made him seem far more mature. Only when he was sad—which was not often—or when he laughed, was it apparent that he was not older than twenty-two.

Darshan had first encountered Stewart over two years before, leaning against a lamppost just off San Francisco State's campus, looking downright melancholy. That first meeting was one of the few times Darshan had ever seen his friend so vulnerable and unhappy. Without uttering a word, he had reached over and offered his sandwich. He did not know what possessed him to do that, except that food always helped him and maybe a man so big and sad was hungry. Their friendship was instantly solidified when Stewart accepted the sandwich, eating half without first introducing himself, a grateful smile around his watery eyes. Swallowing his last bite, he sat with Darshan on the curb to share what had happened. He had not filed his admissions paperwork correctly and the school had asked him to come back the following semester.

"What in the hell will I do for a semester just farting around?" Stewart asked. "I don't have money and time for that. They want me to go back home to Philly where my mother would go ape if I walked in the house when I'm supposed to be in school. And I hate the snow. I can't go back there. It's nothing like San Francisco where everything is fresh and bitchin'. Doesn't this school care about anybody?"

Trying not to appear so impressed by the vernacular, Darshan suggested they try again because perhaps the rotund lady usually sitting at the admission's window had not yet had her lunch, which made Stewart chuckle. "You've got the funniest accent," he said, wiping his eyes with his newsboy hat.

Together they returned to the office, relieved to see a young, blonde woman beam at them as they approached, willing to let the error slide and push through the registration papers on account of Stewart's thick charm. After that, the two of them had met every day after classes in the library until the afternoon Stewart had decided his new friend would benefit from some healthy American socializing and they should get down at the Fillmore for Darshan's first concert.

The auditorium was hotter than usual as Darshan struggled to reach Stewart. He began to sweat under his coat as he pressed through the thick crowd of bodies, shimmying past excited teenagers and college students until he was standing right up against his friend.

"These were the best I could find," Stewart said, gesturing toward their seats that flanked a pillar.

"No problem," Darshan said. "At least our view isn't blocked." Taking off his coat, he asked, "Have you seen Elizabeth?"

"Told me she was having a late lunch with Colleen."

Darshan sighed with relief and sat. "I almost forgot."

"Everything all right?" Stewart asked. "You two fightin'?"

"No, nothing like that."

"You look like a cat being chased by a Rottweiler."

"I just found out that my parents are moving here," Darshan told him. "Everything will change."

"Can't be that bad," Stewart replied.

"They think it will be easier and better here, but they will be disappointed. They will be unhappy with me."

"You don't know that," Stewart said, sitting beside Darshan, his long, thin legs like two bent poles, his knees pressing up against the seat in front of him.

They sat not speaking for a while, Darshan thinking about the letter and his family, until Stewart suddenly snapped his piano-player-like fingers. Standing and removing his glasses, he scanned the chattering crowd, a hand over his brow, squinting as though staring into the sun. After a few minutes, he said, "I knew she'd be waiting. Wonder how long she's been standing there."

Cupping his hands around his mouth he shouted, his voice booming across the crowd, "Elizabeth! Over here! Hey, yeah you, man. Can you just make a little room for her? That's it. Thanks."

"Hi guys," Elizabeth said from the aisle, her cheeks pink.

"It's hot in here." She removed her long tweed coat and squeezed past Stewart, sitting next to Darshan. "Mind if I take your seat, Stewart?"

"Not at all." He grinned, moving to the other side of the pillar.

Just as Darshan pecked her cheek, Jefferson Airplane strode on stage and the crowd went wild. Elizabeth took Darshan's hand as everyone settled down for the opening song. He was certain that this was the last time he would ever do something fun with her. He watched the concert without enthusiasm, and when they played the final song, the last remnant of his freedom dissolved with the end of the performance. Jefferson Airplane signed off with *Share a Little Joke*, which was precisely how he felt.

On the bus ride to her apartment, gripping the metal bar that ran along the top of the seat in front of him, he stared out into the street at the dark shadows of apartment buildings, then refocused his eyes so that he saw his reflection in the window, Elizabeth beside him.

"What's wrong?" she asked.

He pulled his eyes away from the glass and turned to her. "My parents are moving here in August."

She thought about that for a moment. "That's really great, Darshan," she said. "You've said such nice things about your family."

Releasing the metal bar, he kneaded his fist into his palm. "I don't know how to tell them about my life here."

"I think you're doing really well."

"They won't like some things."

"Such as?"

"My hair.

"They'll get over that."

"It's not so simple. You don't understand what it means."

"They might not like it at first, but I'm sure they love you, and that's more important," she said. "What else is there?"

"Well, there's you. You aren't Indian."

"I believe that's fairly apparent."

"You know what I mean."

She gave him a sideways smile.

"It's like Colleen," he said. "Your sister does not like me much."

"That's because she thinks you're a playboy." Elizabeth laughed, like the idea was ridiculous. "She doesn't know you like I do."

"It might also be because I am different and the whole other reason is just an excuse."

"I don't know, Darshan. You'd have to ask her that."

"I just don't want to disappoint my father."

"Dating me is a disappointment?" She was not angry yet, but he could see the warmth toward him dimming.

"Indians don't date non-Indians."

Her face darkened. "So you have enough guts to suggest my sister is a racist, but you won't challenge that same kind of crap if it's coming from your family?"

"It isn't the same. This is cultural."

"I see," she said stiffly.

"You knew that. We talked about it."

The hardness in her face softened into hopelessness. "Well, my mom likes you," she said a little futilely.

He put his arm around her shoulder and she leaned in. Something about the way she sunk so willingly into him, the way her hair smelled like herbal tea, made him want to stop talking, to just enjoy her. He did not expect to like her so completely. Sometimes, because of her, he was more at home in San Francisco than he had ever been in Fiji. It was true that he often missed his high school classmates, the lazy afternoons at the beach doing his homework in the Falcon, or building things with Junker Singh. But life in Fiji had been full of unspoken and severe expectation, and the very real threat of being cast out if he did not obey. Here, with her, every second was without condition, and every part of it that differed from the islands—the big cars and wide lanes, the millions of people, concerts, and road trips—became home. And yet it was also dishonest and dishonorable.

"I remember a time in Fiji," he told Elizabeth. "I was maybe twelve. It was after school, and I was in Suva. I wanted a frozen juice stick so I bought one and went outside to wait for the bus to take me to my father's lumber mill. Just as I opened the wrapper, I saw him down the street walking toward me. He must have been in the city on business. As soon as I saw him I panicked. I thought that if he caught me with the juice stick I would get in trouble because I hadn't asked him if it was okay to have one. So I threw it under the bench. But he saw me. 'Why did you do that?' he asked and went inside and bought me another one."

"I don't understand," Elizabeth said.

"It always surprised me when he was nice to me, when he wasn't angry. I was waiting for his anger all the time. I still am. One day he will hate me for something." He sighed. "My father will not understand you. He cannot assess your value because he does not know what village you are from, who your relatives are, what kind of name you have in the community. You do not even *have* a community. He will not understand how I could have accepted this."

Elizabeth moved over, no longer snuggling next to him. The bus squeaked to a stop. Several passengers boarded. As the bus pulled away, he wished she would come closer again, but she did not. She was staring at the glass, her expression flat and lifeless. He was not sure if she was watching the buildings go by outside, or if she was observing his reflection as he endeavored hard not to appear ashamed and embarrassed, for himself and also for his father.

~ ~ ~

In the months before August, Darshan requested as many overtime shifts as he could manage between classes. Pathology had always been largely understaffed and Dr. Levi welcomed the additional support. "It's horrible," he said. "People keep dying and you and I are the only ones to pick up the pieces, quite literally."

It concerned Darshan that he had no clear sense of how much money Manmohan would bring. By Fiji standards the Toors had been relatively wealthy, but that wealth meant little in the Unites States. He had learned this after his first two months in San Francisco when the five-hundred dollars his father had given him had disappeared on the most basic of necessities.

Every dime Darshan earned after receiving the brief letter from Manmohan went directly into a savings account for his family's arrival, and every free second was spent in the morgue. Concerts at the Fillmore, strolls with Elizabeth through Golden Gate Park, learning how to play baseball with Stewart, or weekend trips to Yosemite: these were the activities that defined a San Francisco he had once visited but had since left, one that existed in a parallel dimension, where he could see an alternate him laughing and carefree, but in which this Darshan could no longer participate. Manmohan's letter had thrust him into a San Francisco that more resembled the lumber mill in Fiji, a place of responsibility and obligation.

In July he found an apartment on 24th Street in the Mission District big enough to accommodate his parents, his sisters, and himself. The rent was appealing, but the unit was littered with broken and abandoned furniture. It was covered in the previous tenant's moldy food and garbage, and dried, flattened mouse droppings were ground into the floorboards.

"This is disgusting, man," Stewart said, pinching his nose closed. "You sure you want to bring your parents here?" He was wearing old sweat pants that hung long and loose on his tall body.

"The landlord gave me twenty-five dollars off the rent if we clean it ourselves and keep the trash area at the side of the building tidy," Darshan said. "It won't be so bad once it's clean. And we can repair a lot of this furniture."

"If you say so. I'll get the tools," his friend said, descending the creaky stairs.

"We should let in some air," Elizabeth suggested, leaning into the frame of the bay window to shove open the windows in the living room, the brightest, most open area of the apartment. The shape of her body in the light was silhouetted through the hospital scrubs she was wearing. A gust of wind whistled through the screens.

He went down the hallway that stretched away from the street toward the two bedrooms, the kitchen, and the bathroom in the rear, opening all of the windows. When he returned to the living room, Elizabeth was gazing outside down to the street. She loved to people watch. He imagined it was quite different from up high, the people below smaller and more vulnerable. He thought that it might be possible to really truly see a person like that, without getting tangled in all the personal drama that always got in the way up close.

She gathered her hair at the back of her neck, twisted it, and pinned it up with a large clip. Turning toward him, she smiled, absently brushing away her bangs. He looked away because he knew the smile was forced. They had argued that morning.

"Do you want to come?" he had asked her over a cup of coffee. "I could use some help."

"Not really."

Swallowing a sip, he frowned, puzzled by her mood. "Did you make other plans?"

"No."

"Is something wrong?"

She opened a book. "I just don't want to go."

"Why not?"

"Because it's not important to me. We finally have a day off, and you want me to spend it cleaning rat shit for your parents who I'm not allowed to meet."

He dumped the rest of his coffee in the sink, shaking his head. "Can't you be a little patient with me?"

She looked at him, sighing in resignation and slamming her book shut. Standing, she wiggled out of her nightgown. Searching in her closet for an old pair of scrubs, she pulled them out and gave him a withering look as if to say, *Fine, I'll go.* Whipping the pants in the air with a snap to unfold them, she pointed at her portable stereo. "At least grab that," she had told him.

Now, as she stood by the window, looking at him expectantly, his mood lightened at the thought of the radio, and he ran down to get it from Stewart's truck, setting it in the hallway near an outlet and flipping it on before they began working.

Junker Singh's toolkit had been very useful over the last

three years, both for minor repairs at his boarding room and at Elizabeth's, but the job ahead of them required something more serious. So with tools Darshan had purchased at the corner hardware store, the three of them labored hard during the following weeks, repairing the heating unit, mending pipes, changing light switches, scrubbing the floors, and restoring whatever abandoned furniture they were able to salvage. Darshan's spirits were low while they worked. So absorbed with every detail of the apartment, terrified that nothing would be good enough, nothing perfect enough to balance out his father's fury, he had to force smiles whenever Elizabeth and Stewart sang stupidly to The Temptation's "I Can't Get Next to You," their paintbrushes sloshing white flecks onto the sheetrock and splattering the stereo as they mocked each other.

"Is that how they taught you to sing in the convent?" Stewart had asked her once, accusing her of being off-key.

"Listen to yourself," she retorted. "Maybe the nuns could teach you something."

"I wouldn't mind a bit, being surrounded by all those holy women."

"Why don't you ever sing?" Elizabeth asked Darshan. "I've never heard you sing before."

"There's a reason for that," he had told her, trying to sound playful despite his somber mood.

The evening before *The Oreana* was scheduled to dock, after they put away all the tools and locked up the apartment, Elizabeth and Stewart were also finally struck by the reality of what was coming next. Quiet now, they were no longer laughing, no longer cracking jokes. The three of them went to a Mexican restaurant for dinner, subdued and downcast.

"So we're probably not going to see much of you after this," Stewart said to his friend.

Darshan sipped his water. "Maybe just at first," he replied as the waiter set down their platters of carne asada.

"You really won't say a word about her to your folks?"

"Stewart," Elizabeth said, shaking her head and squeezing a lime over her meat.

Darshan pushed his plate aside, not hungry.

"All right, there's no need to get tense," Stewart said, reaching for some napkins. "I shouldn't have asked."

Elizabeth took a small bite of her food.

Darshan jabbed his fork into his carne asada. Ever since he could remember, he had always believed that family should be the utmost priority, that fathers deserved absolute devotion. Until now, that fundamental faith had never been challenged. He had never been faced with a choice between the Toors and someone else. He had not known such a choice was possible, and most times the notion of family was carved so deeply into him, it did not seem like a choice at all. Keeping his eyes on his food because he could not look at her, keenly aware that Elizabeth was doing the same, he already knew—if it really came down to it—who he would choose.

~ ~ ~

The Oreana loomed large on the waterfront. The massive steel ocean liner groaned against the dock, casting a shadow across the parking lot where a flurry of disembarked passengers embraced loved ones and lugged their baggage to their cars. Darshan regarded the ship with foreboding, also aware of the city behind him, that daunting stretch of homes and offices, of city streets and big cars, of highways and land that continued on eastward for over three-thousand miles, where life was lived so differently from the closed colonial community of Fiji.

Stewart clutched Darshan's shoulder in awe. "Check out the hairy size of that boat," he said.

"Do you see them?" Darshan asked.

"What am I looking for?"

"Turbans."

Stewart pointed over the many heads flooding off the gangplank, and the two friends slowly made their way through. The crowd thinned near the ship as the last of the passengers stepped down. Before leaving, several men in turbans waved at a man standing alone at the foot of the gangplank, and Darshan realized it was his father. Manmohan was surrounded by a number of suitcases and trunks. He gestured towards the men, then gazed toward the end of the docks at the horizon on the Pacific Ocean.

Darshan stopped, surprised and pained. He opened his mouth to speak, but he had no words for this man who was so hunched over, his head peeking out turtle-like from the shell of his body that was still big but no longer strong, leaning so heavily on a cane. At fifty-three years old, Manmohan's beard was now almost entirely white, the darker hairs scant, as though someone had taken a pencil and drawn them in to defiantly suggest there was still some youth remaining. He wore a warm flannel beneath his button-up coat, a thick scarf that exaggerated the strange forward thrust of his neck, and trousers that were too big for him. Slowly he turned, eyes alighting in recognition at the sight of his son.

Darshan rushed quickly over to hide the shock he knew was written on his face. He wrapped his arms awkwardly around his father's shoulders.

"Darshan!" Jai cried, struggling with a suitcase as she made her way down the gangplank. She dropped the bag to embrace him. She was a tinge grayer along her temples, and there were more lines around her mouth. She was familiarly dressed in her usual salwaar kameez, her chuni drawn around her neck, another thicker shawl for warmth wrapped about her shoulders.

She released him, pushing him arms-length away to assess him. "Your hair," she whispered, covering her mouth, scandalized.

Darshan self-consciously touched the top of his head, his face growing warm with shame. "It was necessary." He glanced at his father, fear choking his throat. The bags under Manmohan's eyes made him seem menacing and unforgiving. His father made no comment.

Through the portal, Navpreet and Livleen stepped onto the gangplank, each holding a piece of luggage. At nineteen and seventeen, they were so unlike the little girls Darshan remembered.

"The king himself," Navpreet said, walking down the plank. She had made an ardent attempt to look American, wearing a cardigan and custom-made fleece skirt, a wide headband in her hair like those modeled in the magazines Elizabeth sometimes flipped through on weekends. She glanced at Manmohan, then back at Darshan. "Nice haircut," she said.

"Enough," Jai said sharply.

Livleen gave Darshan a small smile.

Stewart cleared his throat. Realizing his friend could not understand what the rest of them had been saying in Punjabi, Darshan nodded uncomfortably. "This is my friend Stewart. He came to help."

Hearing his name, Stewart extended a hand to Manmohan. "Hello," he said.

Reaching out, Manmohan took the hand, slowly peering up at Stewart's full six feet, six inches with an up-wrinkled brow.

"Hello," he replied in English. "Thank you for coming."

Jai, who, even in Fiji where so many spoke English, had never learned, fondly smiled at Stewart and asked, "You tik, you fine?"

"Yes, thank you," he grinned at her. "I'm fine."

"Good, good."

Leaving Jai and the girls with the suitcases, Manmohan led the young men to the cargo compartment of the liner where the rest of the Toor belongings had been stored during the long trip at sea. Gesturing at which boxes were theirs, he then went back outside to wait as they loaded Stewart's Chevy. It was clear that Manmohan had left nothing behind that was not bolted down in the mill. Darshan read the labels and peeked inside boxes to discover tools (knives, wrenches, sockets and axes, pipe threading with the oil needed to use it, hand drills that Darshan remembered physically straining to twist into wood, rakes, machetes, shovels, and wood saws), kitchenware (boxes of brass and copper dishes that had originally come from India, an oval-based container with a narrow neck to store milk in the ground, a noodle maker, and the Steinfeld spice grinder), clothing (saris, turbans, suits, and frocks), gold jewelry sets, embroidered sheets and tablecloths, boxes of photographs, toy tractors, marbles, and slingshots made of discarded rubber tires and wood shaped like Ys.

After clearing out half the boxes, they had a better view to the dark corner of the cargo hold where something large was covered by a tarpaulin. Stewart pointed at it. "That yours, too?"

Darshan focused his eyes in the dimness, perceiving the shape of a car as he drew nearer. He bunched some of the tarpaulin in his fist, pulling it off to reveal his Falcon.

"Bitchin," Stewart nodded appreciatively.

"He brought it," Darshan murmured, walking around the

vehicle, pushing bags and trunks out of the way. Peering through the front window, he saw the chest and plywood box he had once discovered in the rafters of the main house but that he had been too afraid to open. Touching the Falcon's surface, he noticed the paint was not as smooth as it had once been. He thought of his shack in the jungle and his coconut tree at the top of the hill and how he would never see them again. This car was the only other piece of Fiji that was truly his. It did not matter the place, but if needed, it could take him anywhere.

~ ~ ~

"He won't always be angry," Stewart told Darshan after they had unloaded the truck that had been packed and bungee-corded with more than half the Toor family belongings. Manmohan had taken the key to the apartment and trudged upstairs without speaking to any of them, Jai and the girls trailing slowly after him.

"It's not at all what he thought it would be," Darshan said.

Stewart climbed into his truck. "He'll be all right."

"Maybe."

"Elizabeth's probably waiting," Stewart said, starting the engine. "You should call her, tell her everything." And then he pulled away.

Darshan leaned against the Falcon. He tapped his heel against the front tire, thinking how strange it was to have his car here. It was not as conspicuous as it had once been, in this country where everything was shiny and concrete. There had been nothing like it in Fiji, nothing as handsome, nothing as polished.

He stared up at the apartment on the second floor,

wondering if his family realized what he had given to them, what it had cost him. It was not perfect, the furniture old and used, the linoleum still peeling in the kitchen, the bathtub's clawed feet still rusty. At least the sink worked. He and Elizabeth had repaired it together. It previously had two separate faucets, one for scalding hot, one for ice cold. He had burned his finger in the hot water, and after Elizabeth had secured a bandage over his throbbing blister, they used plumbing tape and piping to connect the two taps together so the cold and hot water could mix. She would be watching *The Twilight Zone* now, after which she would turn on her paint-spackled stereo and wait for his call.

Gathering his courage, he rapped his knuckles on the side of the car then went up to the apartment. His parents were in the living room, Jai on the sofa, appearing so small in the sea of boxes around her, and Manmohan in a stiff wooden chair that was good for his back. His expression was severe.

"It is a nice place," Darshan told them. "You should have seen it before we cleaned. The landlord gave us a twenty-five dollar discount in exchange for keeping the trash area tidy. One-twenty is not a bad price for San Francisco."

"We have to clean other people's trash?" Jai asked, resignation in her voice. She had been uprooted, pulled from the hard-earned life she had established in Fiji to come here and clean other people's garbage.

"No, Bebe," he told her, sorry for mentioning it. "I will do it."

"Good," Navpreet said, entering the living room. "Because I am not cleaning garbage either. And neither is Livleen." She took her sister's hand, pulling her toward the couch. She demurely sat, kicked off her shoes, and propped her feet on the coffee table. Livleen sat beside her.

"Your hair," Manmohan said quietly, not looking at Darshan.

The room quieted, and no one said another word.

Darshan went to the bay window where he had set aside his new red toolbox that stored all his paintbrushes, screwdrivers, hammers, and nails, all of which he had to work overtime to pay for. Two tall plants flanked the window, leaning inward to catch the sun's rays. He had thought the green would be a nice, warming touch. He stared down to the street where the Falcon was parked, the trunk and back seat still full of boxes. Only a day and already he wanted to speed away, car and young man like outlaws, fleeing and laughing into the San Francisco hills.

~ ~ ~

The free spaces in Darshan's days narrowed and condensed over the following months. A mountain of responsibility had accumulated until there was nothing left of his time. The cross-town drive to Kaiser for Manmohan's frequent medical appointments. Overtime in pathology to pay for rent, food, clothing, and his tuition. Classes and preparation for exams. The weekly commute across the Bay to the Stockton gurdwara to see Junker Singh and his family who, following the growing migratory tide of colonial Indians to the United States, had come to the Bay Area shortly after the Toors. And at the end of every week, when he ached to lie down and close his eyes, he found himself in the dank apartment building alley sweeping up the putrid, rotting tenant garbage, wishing for a hot shower at Elizabeth's.

Fatigue caused him to be easily irked, and he often muttered dark, irritable complaints about his family while shoving his foot in the aluminum bins to compress everything down before taking it all out to the sidewalk. There was a general sense of surrender and loss in his parents' attitude, evidenced by the slow shuffle of Jai's feet when she walked and by the expression of bitterness chiseled permanently into Manmohan's face, making Darshan feel as though all his efforts were wasted. Livleen, who had taken a paper route, was the only one of them to offer help, and although he appreciated the gesture, her income did little to alleviate the pressure on him, which made him angrier with Navpreet, who had not made any attempts to search for a job at all. And despite the fact that their schedules were entirely at odds, Navpreet demanded that he drive her to San Francisco State where she was also taking classes, pick her up, bring her lunch, take her out to meet friends, never once offering to take public transportation.

One evening, sweaty and stinking of garbage, eyes burning with lack of sleep, he climbed the stairs to find Navpreet dozing in the living room. She was sitting on the floor against the couch, her legs stretched out under the coffee table, class notes scattered about her. Her mouth was slack, open in such a blissful state of rest that he resentfully stomped his foot hard on the wooden floor, startling her awake.

"Damn it, Darshan!" she said. "You scared me."

"Navpreet," he said, keeping his voice even. "You need to get a job."

She gathered her papers together. "I don't have time for a job."

"I have a friend in the lab at Kaiser."

"So," she replied, rubbing her temples, taking a sip from a glass of water on the coffee table.

"They need someone."

"I'm pre-med, Darshan." She closed her eyes in

exasperation, and when she opened them again she spoke to him as if explaining an obvious concept to a slow child. "I cannot work *and* study."

"I work forty, sometimes fifty hours every week now," he told her. "It is my last year of college. I have not slept in almost thirty hours. You need to get a job."

She clicked her tongue and rolled her eyes. "I am doing something important."

"I cannot continue to pay for your tuition."

A look of adolescent panic crossed her face. "But you pay for everyone else. You gave money to Livleen for her braces."

He exhaled forcefully, crossing his arms and balling his fists into his armpits. "Livleen is saving her own money for her braces." His voice grew louder. "Bapu and Bebe need our help. We are supposed to help them."

She gestured at her homework. "I am studying to become the future family physician. And it was not my choice to come here. I wanted something else, but they would not listen to me."

Releasing his arms, he gathered the hair at the front of his head and held it back. "At least a job in the hospital will get you school credits."

"Anything else?" she said, dismissing him with a wave of her pencil, preparing to study.

"Navpreet—"

"I'll do it if I have to," she said irritably. "But I am not taking the bus."

He had not wanted to teach her how to drive, to allow her access to his car, to let her abuse it and steal it away from him, but she insisted and he was too exhausted to refuse her. His only consolation was that she would be forced to assume some of the responsibilities that came with its use, and so, grudgingly, he took her to Serramonte Shopping Mall's parking lot, wishing fervently that she would fail.

The workings of a five-speed were beyond Navpreet, however, which became quickly evident during that first lesson. Holding his breath, he shut his eyes tight, fingers clutching frantically at the dashboard as she attempted to handle the gears and navigate the parking lot. She plugged the gas, set on a determinedly straight course that ended at several parked cars and the gigantic wall of Macy's beyond. The roar of the engine rang in his ears, echoing loudly against the pavement. The car began to grind in protest when she did not shift to second, and she made no attempt to turn.

"Neutral," Darshan said evenly, head down.

The car quieted somewhat, but did not slow. "Okay, it's in neutral," she said, her voice tight with terror. "Now what should I do?"

"Brake."

"But I can't," she shouted. "It jerks when I stop."

"That's why you're in neutral," he said in alarm.

The car slammed to a stop. Darshan gasped as braced himself against the dashboard. Opening his eyes, he was relieved to see there was still a reasonable distance between the Falcon and the parked cars. He turned to the backseat. "You okay, Livleen?"

"I'm fine," she said, slouched low.

"Won't anyone ask *me*?" Navpreet said, gripping her heart.

Darshan exhaled. "One more time. Now put it in first and slowly let go of the clutch at the same moment you press the gas."

The engine revved, and the Falcon lurched forward and died. He told her to restart the engine. "*Slowly* and *evenly*. Too much gas, not enough release of the clutch."

Again the car jerked forward and died. Navpreet pounded the wheel with her fist. "Damn it, Darshan! You are making me so nervous!"

"I am making *you* nervous?" He started to laugh.

"Fine!" she shouted and restarted the car. After an awful peeling of rubber and a horrible squeal, the car staggered forward and she drove a U before braking furiously. "There," she said triumphantly. "A turn!"

"Something is burning," Livleen said. She reached under Darshan's seat to retrieve one of her clogs that had fallen off.

"Navpreet," Darshan said in frustration, getting out to check for smoke. "You have to be slow and easy with her." There was no smoke, but fumes of burnt tire stung his throat. He bent to have a look under the car.

"Slow and easy was not working. And the car moved, didn't it? I turned, didn't I?"

"It's time to go pick up Bapu," he said. "Let me drive."

Fuming, Navpreet took her place on the passenger side. She glowered at him, but he ignored her, relieved to have his car back. He pulled out of the parking lot and onto the ramp leading to the 280 highway.

They drove in silence, the radio on low. Darshan could see that she was still upset, her arms crossed, her face stony.

"The bus isn't so bad," he finally said, feeling a little sorry for her. "You can study during the ride."

"I am not taking the bus."

"You have to do something," he told her. "I can't be in charge of everything. I can't drive you around everywhere."

"So you keep saying."

"We have to work together."

She rolled her eyes.

"I think we should pool our paychecks," he said. "I've been

thinking about it. We can save much faster, do something with the money to make sure Bapu and Bebe have nothing to worry about."

She laughed with scorn. "First you want me to get a job because you don't want to support me. Then you expect me to take the bus to get there so you don't have to share your precious car, and now you want me to give you all my money?"

"It isn't for me."

"I'll do it," Livleen said.

"Easy for you," Navpreet told her. "You have the least to give."

"Don't you care that this is hard for them?" Darshan asked.

"Don't talk to me about what is hard for them," she said angrily. "I know how hard things are for them, acting so miserable, all because of their own choices. You have had three years on your own when you did not once have to think about it. We never got a day without being reminded of what we owe them."

"It is not a contest, Navpreet," he said, trying to be gentle because he could see that she was genuinely upset.

She crossed her arms and kept her mouth tightly shut, staring straight ahead out the windshield with such aggravation in her pink cheeks and her turned-down eyebrows he thought she might actually cry.

~ ~ ~

"You're working too hard," Elizabeth said, rubbing Darshan's shoulders, straddling his back as he lay face down. She was wearing the ankle-length, halter dress he liked so much, her hair getting longer, brushing against his skin as she leaned into his body.

"I know," he said sleepily, his cheek pressed against the pillow. "But once we get everyone situated, it will be much better."

"You've been saying that for a while now. I hardly ever see you. It's Stewart and me all the time. It's not the same. We watched *Martin's Laugh-In* without you yesterday, and it wasn't that funny."

He missed sleeping with her, the warm reassuring presence of her body beneath the covers. This was the first time in months he had not gone to 24th Street for the night. He had just come off the day shift and had only a few hours before the night one began. It was easier to stay near the hospital.

She was silent for a moment, and he could hear her breath in the stillness of her studio as she massaged him. "I'd like to meet them," she said after a while. "Don't you think it's been enough time? It's already November. I thought it would be fun to make them a Thanksgiving dinner."

Her fingers were getting deep into his muscles. "I know," he murmured. "It's complicated. It's too much."

She bent, kissed his temple and continued massaging his shoulders, then worked her fingers down his spine. Closing his eyes, soon there was nothing at all, just a seamless, unnoticed shift from feeling her touch to a dreamless, weightless sleep.

~ ~ ~

"I think it's you," Elizabeth told Darshan, slopping mashed potatoes from a dish into a plastic container with a brisk, cold flick of her wrist. "Not them. I think they wouldn't mind so much."

He looked helplessly around at her studio, at the table and chairs she had borrowed from Stewart and crammed into the center of the room, the half-melted candles, the wine glasses, the cranberry sauce, and the untouched twenty-pound turkey centerpiece nestled in lettuce leaves. "I never told you they were coming," he said.

"No, you didn't. It's my fault." She locked a lid over the container and put the mashed potatoes in the fridge.

"I thought you had dinner at your mother's."

"Next year."

"But I never told you—"

"I know."

Trying to lighten the mood, he said, "There are too many of them anyway."

"What?"

"Too many Toors. They wouldn't have fit."

When she did not smile, he tried kissing her cheek. She stiffened. Sighing, he quietly gathered up all the plates and utensils and put them in the cupboard while she refrigerated the rest of the food. They watched some television, sitting next to each other but not touching. When he left, she was sleeping.

"You are late," Navpreet said when Darshan got home to 24th Street.

He breathed in deeply, the smell of the apartment reminding him of the main house at the lumber mill. It had been feeling more like home of late. Jai had fully settled the family in, covering the two beds in thick blankets, stocking the kitchen with plates, steel tumblers, and pots, and hanging photos and decorations. Everything smelled of washing and spices. The couch upholstery, the blankets, clothing, the walls themselves seemed to radiate the scent of Fiji.

"I am not late. You never asked me to take you anywhere."

"And now I am late."

Refusing to be baited, he smiled at her, then called to Jai

down the hall.

"In here, beta," his mother called from the kitchen.

"Sat sri akal, Bebe," he said, joining her. "Where is Bapu?"

"Lying down. And Livleen went for a walk. You want some chai?"

"Just a quick cup," he nodded as she pulled down a mug and strained the hot tea. "And one for Navpreet, too."

He took both mugs into the living room and placed one on the table by his sister's foot. He sat on his father's hard chair, the only place, aside from the bed, where Manmohan could rest without too much pain.

She reached for her tea. "You are making me late," she said again.

"It's Thanksgiving. Everything is closed." He blew into the steamy mug.

"I have plans."

"Tonight?"

"Yes."

"Just give me a minute to sit. I need to sit here and drink my tea."

She cautiously took a sip, grimacing as she burnt her tongue.

"I need you to take over my lab shift tomorrow," he told her. He had recently begun working in Kaiser's lab, learning the practical application of what he had been studying in school: hematology, microbiology, testing for glucose, cholesterol, drugs, and the condition of heart enzymes. Dr. Levi had been sad to see Darshan dropping shifts in pathology, but nonetheless wrote an impressive recommendation for a full-time job in the lab after graduation. "I could use one full night of sleep."

"No," she said. She had still not managed to make an

impression on her bosses in the several months that she had been employed in the lab and was more than a little affronted by Dr. Levi's high regard of her brother, as well as by Darshan's easy rapport with her direct manager, Dr. Gerard. She had even gone so far as to accuse Darshan of sabotaging her future career in medicine when she saw the recommendation letter on his dresser.

He set his tea on the table. "It will give you an opportunity to work more closely with Gerard."

She shrugged. "He likes me."

"He doesn't know you at all."

"I spoke with him the other day."

"How many more favors should I do for you before you help me once? What do any of us have to do for you to give even a little?"

"Did you know that I got accepted into Oxford?" she asked.

He shook his head.

She regarded him coolly. "I got accepted, but you were here so we *all* had to be here."

In the silence of that moment, he saw that she was not simply refusing, but that she was enraged by his request, that she hated him for it.

A sudden and loud noise caused her to jump and scream. Darshan turned sharply toward the window at the sound of a collision down on the street, at the cacophony of metal slamming into metal. They both vaulted out of their seats, running to look.

"What was that?" Jai shouted from down the hall.

"No, no, no, no, no!" Darshan cried and bolted down the stairs and outside. His Falcon was shredded against the curb, the engine pressed up into the front window, the vinyl seats twisted and bent in a contorted tangle of chrome and metal paneling.

The driver of the van who had lost control and veered against the line of parked cars along 24th Street moaned and called for help, a cut above his eye bleeding badly.

"Can you get out?" Darshan asked, rushing over to him. He pried the van's door open and took the man in his arms. "Let's call someone."

"How will I get anywhere now?" Navpreet shouted from the apartment above.

A crowd was gathering.

"Hey man," the driver said groggily, holding a hand to his face as Darshan helped him stand. "I'm really sorry. I don't know what happened."

"Don't worry," Darshan said, the man's arm draped around his shoulder. "No one has been seriously hurt. It is not a problem."

But it was. There, shattered glass and crushed metal pushed right up onto the sidewalk, was the last vestige, the last memory of Darshan's freedom, the last hope of flight.

Still Swallowed Whole
1970–1972

A massive open-jawed creature had come to Darshan in 1957, burrowing into his imagination, haunting him the whole of that year and far beyond, threatening to engulf him in its great cavernous gut. Death had manifested the creature, the death of a woman whom he had never met. She had known how dangerously close this monster loitered, tentacles extended ominously, brushing against the family, bringing enormous and calamitous consequences upon them all.

Sada Kaur's existence, the discovery that Baba Singh once had a woman in his life, was a disquieting revelation for Darshan at the age of ten. His grandfather seemed far too remote for such intimacies, so rigid and uncompanionably aloof, which was likely the reason he had locked her away in India, to be unseen and unknown so that none of them would understand him to be only a man.

There had been a kirtan at the main house to honor Sada Kaur's passing, and seventeen years later Darshan recalled that day as if there was no gap in time between then and now, the hairy shell of the coconut in his palm, the coldness of the mud under his bottom when he sat next to Baba Singh under the house, the slight give of earth as he placed the coconut between them. He could not say why he had believed a coconut would be an appropriate means to express his condolence. From up in the tree, when he saw his grandfather slip away from the kirtan and settle against a stilt under the house, a sudden rush of compassion forced upward from his chest to constrict his throat, making his eyes sting with gratitude. He had experienced it before, though not with any thematic consistency: Livleen's birth, the happiness of Diwali. And there had been episodes after: the afternoons he watched from his shack as Jai hung the clothing on the main house's balcony rail to dry, the days his father had been too weak after electroshock therapy to walk unaided to the car, and on the night Mohan was cast out of the house.

"Life will swallow you whole, Darshan," his grandfather had said that day, planting the first seed of apprehension. "That is what she knew; it is what she told all of us." Picking up the coconut, he held it out, gauging its weight.

He wandered off soon after, and Darshan had seen him only once more. On the evening before his grandfather's flight to India, Vikram visited the main house to summon Darshan, saying gently, "If you have a moment, your dada is waiting for you at the farm. He wants a word." The request, which sounded so capitulating, so unpatriarchal, also had the upsetting quality of a warning.

Baba Singh's home on the dairy farm was dark, humid like trapped tears. Bending low, his face close, his skin weak and weary, the old man asked his grandson, "You think I will see her again?"

Darshan's insides twisted with fear. "Should I know?"

"I thought you would."

"How?"

Baba Singh's eyes had lost focus, as though he were no longer there in that room. "Because I feel like we have met once before."

"Dada," Darshan whispered, his body stiff with terror.

Closing his eyes, Baba Singh smiled weakly, a thin, fatigued smile. "Everything is okay," he said then, turning away. "You can go."

Slim legs pumping hard the entire two miles home, Darshan had fled, bruising his right foot because he lost one of his sandals in his haste to get to the safety of his coconut tree, horrified because he understood more than he had been willing to admit.

The sensation of being devoured had always remained with Darshan, a residual impression on his mind like the incandescent outline of an overexposed photo. And now, after so many years, he dreamt of the beast once more. When he woke to the shrill ring of the rotary phone and went to the living room to find Manmohan dropping the receiver gently into its cradle, he was not surprised by what came next. "My father is dead," Manmohan told the family. "He was seventy-two. He was alone in that house. We should all be very sorry about it." He slowly rose from his chair and retreated to his bed where he remained for nearly two days, sick and growing older.

~ ~ ~

Manmohan's mood deteriorated following Baba Singh's death. His usually quiet severity escalated to impatient and irrational outbursts made worse by the tedium in which his body forced him to live. He snapped cantankerously about the intermittent hot and cold water for his baths, the taste of the city air in his food, the parks that were not green or lush enough, the hills he could not climb and which therefore limited his exploration, the contempt on people's faces as they stared at him on the streets. He demanded better doctors and medicines and more visits to the East Bay where the Indian population had begun to congeal. He hated the new Ford station wagon that Darshan had bought after graduating from San Francisco State, paid for with more overtime at the lab. When he dropped heavily into the front seat, lacquered wooden cane stretched between his legs, he complained that his body was cramped in the narrow seat and that the window crank was too stiff.

Darshan did his best to sympathize; however, his efforts so contemptuously disparaged, it was challenging to constantly deflect the criticisms, particularly when he had such industrious plans to manage the family's welfare. He had purchased an apartment complex south of Market on Howard Street in his parents' names with money he managed to save despite Livleen's meager contribution and the fact that Navpreet had steadfastly refused to share. Darshan intended to rent out the six units in order to provide a steady income for his parents who were in no physical condition to work, and yet Manmohan refused to accept it.

"No," his father said as Darshan drove the family to see the building. With a stiff forefinger he violently tapped the bank statement for the account his son had opened for his parents, then furiously held up the property deed. "You did not ask me. You put your mother's name on everything. I have never done that. I have always taken care of her."

Darshan glanced through the rearview mirror at Jai who

was sitting directly behind him, her expression inscrutable. "It is only a precaution," he told his father.

"Against what?"

"In the event something happens to you."

"What will happen?" Manmohan asked.

"You never listen," Navpreet said from the back, taking her sister's hand. In the center seat, Livleen stared through the windshield, apparently not paying attention.

"The laws are different here," Darshan said. "She will not have anyone to protect her if—"

"I will protect her," Manmohan said, jabbing his cane into the car's foot well.

Darshan took a breath and nodded. "I know you will, Bapu." Slowing the station wagon, he parked in front of a considerably derelict building. "I only want you both to be free of worry."

"This one?" Navpreet asked, looking at the building with angled bay windows and rotted hood moldings. The upper façade was a repulsive sea-foam green that contrasted horribly with the dark red hue of the entrance overhang. The paint was chipped and stained by car emissions, and chunks of molding were missing.

Circling around to the passenger side Darshan tried to help his father out of the car, but Manmohan drew his arm away, struggling with difficulty to get out by himself. When he was on his feet, he surveyed the street, the neglected condition of it, the shifty men on the street corners, the mini-marts run by Chinese and Mexican families, the shallow in the sidewalk leading to the building's one-car garage littered with stray newspapers, cigarette butts, paper-coated wire-twists, empty soda cans, beer bottles, and wads of black, flattened gum. He wordlessly approached the entrance, deed and bank statement gripped in his fist, waiting for Darshan to unlock the gate. Pushing through, the family trailing after him, he climbed the narrow stairwell coated densely in colorful graffiti.

Assessing the broken light fixture on the first-floor landing, Manmohan guardedly opened a door to one of the units. The worn and grooved hardwood floors inside had been painted the same dark red as the front overhang. A grayish, black strip of dirt was tracked down the long hallway past the two bedrooms and bathroom to the kitchen and living room. Jai opened the kitchen cupboards, releasing a flood of cockroaches that darted into crevices and corners. In the living room, she touched the yellow-orange tobacco residue on the walls with her forefinger, disgusted by its stickiness. The bathtub and toilet were crusted with body dirt and oils, and the linoleum in the kitchen and bathroom had large holes, the glue once used to hold it down now flaking off. Livleen curiously opened the rear door to a back staircase that led to a small yard below, but Darshan stopped her before she stepped outside. "The stairs aren't safe," he told her. "We will have to rebuild them."

"We do not belong here," Manmohan told Darshan, stopping in the front bedroom to look out onto the loud and heavy Howard Street traffic.

"It is not for us to live, Bapu. It is only for money."

Jai pulled her chuni up over her hair and gathered her heavier shawl more tightly about her shoulders. His mother appeared small to him now, but she had been so big in Darshan's memories. She had never shied away from hard work, aggressively attacking the projects set before her, systematically accomplishing everything asked of her without complaint, still energized when everyone else had collapsed with exhaustion. Darshan had always attributed the success of the mill and their family's prosperity in Fiji to Manmohan. Now, seeing an absence of the strength he had always taken for granted in his mother, he understood that it had not been his father. It had been her, beneath him, holding him up. As he glanced from his mother to his sick, bent father, he understood her fatigue. Manmohan, in this new country, was now a heavier burden.

"It is ours. It is everything we have," Darshan told his father, who would not pull his eyes from the street below.

Formerly the refined residence of intellectuals and professionals who dined and entertained in splendidly decorated rooms lit by gas lamps, over the decades the apartments had eventually been laid waste by alcoholics, chain smokers, and aging couples too feeble to care for them. The building's seventy-five-year-old Victorian spirit had been lost under layers of grime and thick piles of garbage. Upon inspection it was officially deemed hazardous, and the old and decayed apartments were hit hard with city code work, overwhelming the family with more labor than initially anticipated and requiring Darshan to continue working overtime to pay for more supplies and materials. The building, still outfitted with gas lighting, would need modern heaters, which would require complex and wall-invasive electrical work. They would need to re-floor, entirely replace weak walls as well as unsafe windows, reinforce the front stairwell, and erect scaffolding to repaint the exterior and change the window hoods and moldings that threatened to come loose and fall to the sidewalk.

Little by little, however, spending his free time renovating the units, Darshan began to develop an affection for the building as the family restored some of its old charm, reconstructing the back staircase, exterminating the cockroaches, scrubbing the insides with bleach and industrial kitchen soaps, repainting, and clearing away the years of accumulated trash. In his mind, Ranjit was somehow linked to this place. He had been here, had stood across the street in the fog, wistfully watching the warm, yellow-lighted windows as children were tucked safely into bed, their parents extinguishing candles before sinking into their own blissful dreams, hoping that one day he would be free enough in this world to call this place his own.

It was difficult work, in particular for Jai. With Darshan and Livleen's help, she handled her tasks—chiefly cleaning—with as much fortitude as she had done all things in her life, but now far more wearily, which made Darshan uneasy. On her knees, scrubbing claw-foot bathtubs, she appeared normal and as industrious as ever. But she was too quiet, no longer contentedly humming the Punjabi folk songs Darshan remembered her humming while working. And she was dangerously unsteady on her feet, often stumbling over one of the many stray nails lying around the units, staggering after landing too hard in a pavement dip on her way to the store, or lurching forward when one of her slip-on shoes came loose. Her surroundings seemed to have become irrelevant. As if there was no point any longer in paying attention to the world around her, she simply floundered through it.

"What can I do for her?" Darshan asked Elizabeth. He had not been able to sleep and had gone to see his girlfriend, to be reassured, to be told as she always told him that no problem was without its solution, without its measure of hope.

The smell of eggs in butter filled her apartment as she scrambled them in a pan with a spatula. "What was that?" she asked, sprinkling some salt over the eggs.

"My mother isn't well," he told her again.

Turning off the stove, she scraped the eggs onto a plate, shook some pepper over them, and sat on a floor cushion by the coffee table. "I'm sorry to hear that," she said, taking a bite. The eggs still too hot, she waved a hand in front of her open mouth.

He frowned. "Elizabeth, I don't know what to do."

She set her plate on the table and placed the fork next to it with a dull click of metal on wood. She laced her fingers together around one knee. "Was there something in particular you wanted me to say about it?"

"Why are you so angry with me?"

"You haven't even said hello."

"I did."

"No, you didn't. It's been over a week since I last heard from you, and you didn't even say hello." She picked up her fork and tried another bite.

Darshan sank to the floor beside her, pressing his forefingers into his eyelids. "I did not mean to ignore you. Or Stewart. If you knew what kind of person my mother was, you would understand."

"But I don't," Elizabeth said, regarding her eggs with disinterest.

~ ~ ~

The sun was warm on the pavement outside Howard Street, but the cool Bay air cut into Darshan's skin, intensifying his agitation. Elizabeth's hand was clammy in his as he helped her out of Stewart's Chevy. Tersely returning her smile, feeling pressured to bring her into the Toor fold, he gently pried her fingers loose to help his friend unload supplies from the bed of the truck. He lifted the tools mechanically, their weight straining his arms, stretching his tendons downward as he thought of his father waiting unaware upstairs, of the ruthless expectations that no son could ever hope to fulfill, of his own pitiful desire to fulfill them.

The three of them entered the lower left-hand unit that had become the Howard Street base of operations and set their tools down in the front bedroom. Darshan quickly stepped away, pretending not to notice as Elizabeth again tried to take his hand, and led them down the long, dim hall toward the living room where Jai and the girls were finishing their morning tea and his father was reading the *San Francisco Chronicle*.

Glancing up, Manmohan opened his mouth to speak, then slowly closed it when he saw Elizabeth, fixing her with a look of icy inquiry.

Darshan was acutely conscious of how close she was standing to him; of her warm shoulder touching his arm; her cold, nervous fingers brushing against his; of her delight when he had finally agreed to bring her here; of her hope for their future; of the sincerity in her voice when she had said she loved him; of everything good in her that his father would not see. She looked at him now, waiting, awkward and ill at ease, but full of optimism.

"Bapu," he said.

She smiled encouragingly at him.

"Bapu," he said again, then faltered when Manmohan shifted in his chair. An apology flickered across his face as he reached around her and affably patted Stewart on the shoulder. "This is Stewart's friend, Elizabeth. They have come to help for the day."

Elizabeth blushed.

"You good," Jai asked. "Tik?"

"Yes, thank you," she mumbled. "Nice to meet you." She

extended a hand, which Manmohan took with skepticism.

"You don't need me, then," Navpreet said, gathering up her coat and book bag. She nodded at Elizabeth. "Nice to meet you."

"Sit down," Manmohan told his daughter.

"Elizabeth," Darshan said, forcing a breezy tone, picking up a plastic spatula, and pointing to a container. "The plaster is there if you want to start with that."

"I know what to do," she replied, retreating to the corner with Stewart, who was clearly displeased.

Livleen collected the empty tea mugs and went to fill buckets with soap and water.

Navpreet put on her coat. "Bapu, you have enough help."

"Sit," he said flatly.

"This is ridiculous," she said, lifting her book bag onto her shoulder. "I have an exam."

"He told you to stay," Darshan said.

"It looks like she wants to go," Elizabeth told him, the bucket of plaster hanging at her side. She set it down, her face pink with anger. "You can't force her. She's not a slave."

Darshan shook his head. "That's not what we were saying."

"I may not be able to understand the words, but it's clear you are forcing her to stay."

Darshan appealed to Stewart. "She doesn't know the whole situation."

His friend lowered his eyes.

Navpreet raised her chin defiantly. "You see? It isn't fair."

"I never know the situation," Elizabeth told Darshan. "You never tell me." She dropped her spatula with a clatter on the wood floor, walking briskly away down the hallway. Stewart went after her.

"Wait," Darshan said, running outside to stop them.

"Leave me alone," Elizabeth said as Stewart opened the truck for her.

"I will explain," he told her, grabbing her by the arm, spinning her around. "I'll tell you everything."

"Why don't you ever put me on the same level as your family?" she asked, her face hot with misery. "Why do I always come second after everything? You aren't even happy with them." She pulled her arm away and climbed into the truck.

Darshan watched the Chevy drive away and make the turn onto the highway entrance, disappearing into the congested traffic. When he returned to the living room, Manmohan was alone. He could hear Navpreet blowing her nose in the bathroom, complaining about her exam. Livleen was with her, softly murmuring something.

"They are different," his father said. "They will never be like us."

"Her mother doesn't think like that," Darshan mumbled.

Manmohan reached for his cane and slowly rose from his chair. He removed his turban, revealing the shiny pate of his bald head. He shoved his son's chest with a hard buck of his fist now padded in the six yards of cloth. Holding the turban against Darshan, he glowered for several moments before covering his head, sitting, and again opening his newspaper.

~ ~ ~

Elizabeth's clothes were damp from the night drizzle. She stood with Jai, lost and afraid in the center of the 24th Street living room, shivering beneath her coat, thick strands of her hair pasted to her face. They did not see Darshan as he observed them from the hallway. Jai took the girl's hands and pressed them between hers for warmth, then reached up and touched Elizabeth's face to gently wipe away the cold and wet. He knew the feel of those weathered hands against his own cheeks, knew how much affection was contained within them.

Elizabeth noticed him first. Embarrassed, she stepped back.

"She came for you," Jai told her son. "She is wet and tired. She needs tea."

"Bapu—"

"Sleeping," she said, leaving the room.

Elizabeth removed her coat, gesturing around. "It's different than I remember."

"Did you come across town on the bus?" Darshan asked.

She nodded. "My mother told me I should see you."

"I was wrong yesterday," he said. "I should not have done that."

"It wasn't your fault. I pushed too hard."

He sighed. "My father is angry."

"I should go," she said. "I don't want to make it worse."

"Elizabeth," he stepped toward her. "You are important. They are important. All of it is important."

"I know. You're right."

"Is Stewart angry?"

"He never stays angry long."

"Maybe," Darshan said tiredly. He grabbed his keys. "I'll drive you."

"No, I'm not going far. Stewart and I are seeing a movie."

"Will I see you later?"

"My mother wants me to invite you for lunch. Colleen will be there."

"Okay," he said.

She slipped her coat back on. "They know now," she told him. "It wasn't easy, but we're fine now, I think."

"Yes," he murmured. But when she was gone, he dumped

the mug of her untouched tea and surveyed the room, clearing away any evidence that she had been there so there would be no questions, no hard stares when his father woke.

~ ~ ~

Manmohan ran his cane along the hallway wall, the fresh, white paint reflecting the light. He rapped his knuckles on the back of the new furnace, listening for the hiss of the pilot light. In the kitchen he tested the gas-lit stove, igniting the burners, then opened the refrigerator to sniff for any rancid odors, satisfied by the smell of antiseptic cleaner. Outside he squinted up at the building, now Easter-yellow with olive trim, pointing at the rental sign. "Change it," he told Darshan. "We can get more."

"We want good people, Bapu. Clean people. We want them to stay."

"Good people in America can afford it."

"We are asking market price. People are calling. We cannot ask for more."

"You used to be the only one who listened to me."

"I have only ever tried to help you, Bapu."

"This is not mine," Manmohan told Darshan. "It is yours. I do not want it."

Darshan pursed his lips in frustration, smoothing down his cropped beard, knowing what his father was thinking.

"Indirjit told me about a space in Berkeley," the old man said. "I want to see it."

"Bapu, the timing is bad. He did not even know what he was saying."

Indirjit Attwal spoke energetically about most subjects, drawing people into the vortex of his enthusiasm. But he became bored with his ideas as quickly as he uttered them. One afternoon, in his excitement after service in the Stockton gurdwara, he had convinced Manmohan to open an Indian restaurant in the East Bay where there was a demand but no one as yet to fill it. But the next day, when Manmohan had phoned him to discuss the matter in further detail, he had absolutely no memory of the proposal and a rather emphatic aversion to joining the venture. Manmohan, however, had resolved to move forward.

"I am still your father," the old man said.

Darshan nodded. "Yes, Bapu. I know."

~ ~ ~

Fiji had been a manageable place. A man could rule it in his way. If set upon such a course he could draw the whole of it under his thumb to mold and shape to his will. For Manmohan it had only taken a great storm—which had happened often enough—tenacity, friends for support and encouragement, perhaps a number of favors, and endurance to operate a profitable business. He had been lord and master over those islands, sovereign of lumber, of wife and children.

Berkeley—and in particular Telegraph Avenue just near the university—was like a Fiji of sorts, a confined island of Indians seeking and cooperating to rebuild the communities they had left behind in their native countries. To Manmohan, it must have seemed such a familiar endeavor to open his restaurant, to invest the little money he had brought with him on a project that would excel without fail within the societal parameters he believed to be enduring and reliable as long as there were enough Indians to uphold them. The name he gave the restaurant reflected this belief, made clear what it meant to be a

Sikh, and also what it meant to be the family monarch. The Lion of India he called it, and Darshan understood that his father meant them to know that this was precisely what he was.

Having reasserted himself, the old man set about issuing directives. Darshan was to make arrangements with a local Indian-run spice shop for discounts on large orders of rice, flour, turmeric, cumin, mustard seed, cardamom, cinnamon, cloves, and various other spices and sundries Jai would need for cooking, as she was now commanded to be the head chef. Livleen and Navpreet were to furnish the restaurant, to buy tables and chairs, dining ware, silverware, glassware, ladles, cloth napkins, tins for spice storage, an industrial-size gas-lit stove, huge pots and a step stool so that Jai could reach the pots to stir the contents that would soon bubble within them. Manmohan supervised, conducting his business with the tight rein of one who had no intention of being twice usurped of his authority.

It meant little to him that Darshan worked full time, managed the Howard Street apartments, and drove him to temple and hospital, or that Navpreet had exams. It was irrelevant that Livleen was too young and beautiful for such a dictatorship, that she was living in a country in which her peers went to school and met for ice cream and movies on the weekends. He put a stop to her paper route so she would be available to him, unconcerned that it was her only means to save for the braces she had been wanting since arriving in America. And he chose not to concern himself with the alarming condition of his wife, who was clearly unwell and in no state to cook for a torrent of customers.

Soldiers aligned and marching, it did not take Manmohan long to ready the restaurant, tyrannically directing the family to gather and organize all the supplies, polish the nine lacquered ship hatches Livleen had found to use as four-top tables, hang framed paintings of the ten gurus around the dining hall, scrub down the kitchen, paint and draw up signs that read *Coffee, 5 cents a cup with any order*, and craft a large chalkboard menu to hang next to the swinging kitchen door opposite the main entrance: chicken curry, rice, and vegetable *subzee* $2.00 a plate, *saag paneer* and roti $1.50 a plate, and rice pudding $0.50. Soon the scent of Jai's cooking—onions, garlic, spices, and turmeric—drifted down Telegraph Avenue, attracting a strong customer base of UC Berkeley professors, Indian exchange students, and hippies wandering in search of the unconventional, wishing to rid themselves of the usual deli sandwiches and pie. Unaccustomed to the seasonings, patrons welcomed the intensity of something different, and in only a few months the Lion of India built a steady clientele of regulars.

It was seven days a week of grueling toil. The kitchen was a hot pit, a cavity of steaming, oily residues rising from the huge metal pots on the stove, clinging to everything: the jars of pickles and ghee near the stove, the extra salt and pepper shakers on a shelf behind the sink, their clothes, their hands, and their faces. Jai ascended and descended her ladder in a frantic race to stir the curries, make dough for rotis, roll them out, and flip them on the hot plate. Often working twelve hours a day, she began to lose some of her color. Once, she became dangerously faint, and as she teetered on her stool toward the boiling food, Darshan snatched her salwaar, startling her so badly that, without thinking, she grasped the rim of a hot pot for support, slightly burning her hands before releasing it and falling into her son.

There was a constant backlog of dirty dishes by the dishwasher; clean dishes sat in the plastic rack because there was hardly enough time to put them away after running them through the machine. Livleen and Darshan managed to shelve them when they could, but more often they were running back and forth through the swinging kitchen door: out with orders and a water pitcher, in with busboy tubs of more dirty plates and glasses. Navpreet, her lips glossy, hair bouncy and styled, earrings dangling from her lobes, often stopped by in the middle of the dinner rush as Darshan, sweaty and exhausted, was on his way out for his night shift at Kaiser. Famished after work, she would grab a plate, spoon rice and ladle curry onto it and eat in the dining room, consuming her food slowly, taking her last bite just as the rush was over, and only then did she rise to halfheartedly assist with the clean-up.

From his chair in the dining room's rear corner by the kitchen, Manmohan watched as customers flooded into his domain. He thoughtfully assessed their empty plates and the over-stuffed satisfaction on their faces, until one evening, after closing and locking the doors for the night, he went into the kitchen and returned to the dining hall with a wet rag to wipe out the prices on the chalkboard menu. He scribbled in new, higher prices, then turned to Darshan and said, "We can go home now."

Darshan pulled the keys from his pocket. "I do not think that is a good idea, Bapu. People will be angry."

"Why should they be angry?"

"Because it is not what they expect. They trust you."

"How do you know what they expect?"

"They will stop coming," Darshan said. "I would."

Manmohan hung the wet rag over the back of a chair. He called to the kitchen. "Livleen, get your mother. We are leaving."

Darshan shook his head. "Bapu, we need our customers.

Bebe is not well. Without them we will never be able to afford to hire someone to help her."

Manmohan shut off the lights. "Your mother is fine."

"You do not even know where you are," Darshan mumbled. "You are still living on the island."

~ ~ ~

Elizabeth cautiously swung her apartment door open, her face puffy with sleep, her voice hoarse. Darshan pulled her toward him by the belt of her robe and put his arms around her, squeezing her into him, rubbing her back and smelling her hair. She allowed herself to be held, and he hugged her more tightly. "I'm tired," he whispered to her, looking longingly into the darkness of her flat.

She pushed him away then, suddenly angry. "You can't stay," she said.

"It's okay. I dropped my parents off. I called in sick."

"I don't want you to stay."

"What's wrong?" he asked.

"You only ever come when you need something. You never even came for lunch with my mother. You don't think about me. It's always you're tired, you're confused, you're struggling, your parents, your culture, your schedule. It's three in the morning."

He checked his watch. "I didn't realize."

"That's the only time that's ever good for you. But I was sleeping."

Taking a deep breath, he nodded. "I didn't mean to wake you."

"Yes, you did."

"I didn't realize," he repeated, numb now.

"But you did," she said, getting angrier.

He stepped back. "I won't come again."

Her eyes widened as he rushed down the stairs. "No, wait," she called out. "That isn't what I meant."

He began to run, turning onto Terra Vista, his momentum down the hill burning his feet as they slapped hard on the pavement, shooting him past his parked station wagon. Stopping, he turned around, panting. As he made his way back to the car, he heard her still calling to him, but he allowed the rushing of blood and the hammering of his heart to drown her out. Climbing into his car, he started the engine and drove home to his family.

~ ~ ~

Darshan quietly climbed the stairs of the 24th Street apartment, took off his shoes, and lay down on the couch without removing his coat, his legs curled over the armrest, his feet dangling. The room was dark except for the lights from an occasional car reflecting across the ceiling and far wall, glimmers of life beyond the Toor home. He could hear Manmohan snoring down the hallway.

He closed his eyes and remembered the night long ago in Fiji when no one had saved him while the flames of a fire had licked the other side of his bedroom wall. The heat woke him, and the smoke. Coughing, he ran to the washroom to scoop out a bucketful of leftover soapy water from the aluminum bathtub, darted to the kitchen, and pitched the water in, ran back to the bathroom for more water, and back again until the tub was empty. It had not occurred to him until he went outside and saw his whole family safe, that they had not accounted for him, that while he had tried to save them, they had already saved themselves.

The jaws of the invisible creature reshaped now in Darshan's mind. It solidified into something more real and tangible than it had ever been, a profound dark thing. It yawned over him, swallowing not just him, but all that surrounded him: the couch, the sound of his father's snoring, his mother and sisters in the other rooms, the apartment, his friends, the whole city of San Francisco and the Pacific Ocean beyond. It swallowed light itself, the whole world and universe, crushing even his shack in the jungle. Someone familiar and very far away whispered something unintelligible to him. He groped, his hands extended, reaching for an anchor in the darkness. It might not have seemed like much, but when his fingertips brushed against the rough bark of his tree, he reached further and clung to it.

The Hindu Pundit of Amritsar
1974–1975

Darshan checked his father's old watch. Breathing hard into his cupped hands, the white mist of his warm breath filtered through his fingers while he stood in Howard Street's front stairwell. He bounced on his knees, a little dance while he waited. Impatiently, he pushed the buzzer again, the black button leaving a slight indentation in the soft padding of his thumb. "Come on," he muttered, pressing his ear to the door. Raising his eyebrows and craning his neck forward in concentration, he tried to discern any sense of movement within, but there was only stillness.

Descending the stairs, jaws tight, he returned to his car. Larry, known to his neighbors as the guy who left cigarette butts all over the back staircase and played drums with his band at two in the morning, was one of Darshan's worst tenants. He had said he would be here at eight o'clock this morning, and the day before at two in the afternoon, but it was so rare that tenants were home—or awake—when they said they would be. Larry had been complaining about the heater for two days now, leaving irate phone messages, colorfully using the word "bleep" a number of times to emphasize his fury at being helplessly heatless. It seemed to amuse him to imply the word "fuck" rather than say it outright. He seemed to believe it set him apart intellectually and ethically. Slamming the car door and cranking up the heat, Darshan knew that tomorrow Larry would call again: "It's against the law to leave a person without bleeping heat. Where the bleep were you?"

Crossing the Bay Bridge on his way to the Lion of India, Darshan checked his watch again. Rubbing his eyes, he gave his head a vigorous waggle, attempting to shake off the sleepiness. Eyes dry, he turned the heat down and adjusted the vents away from his face.

Parking in the alley behind the restaurant, he shut off the station wagon and wearily got out, pulling a thick camping blanket and a pillow from the back to take with him to the storeroom. He laid the blanket over some stacked burlap sacks of rice and fluffed the pillow before stretching out on his makeshift bed. He tried to relax. Yesterday's bookkeeping records made clear that for the first time since the Lion of India's doors had opened two years ago, his father no longer needed to use Howard Street revenue to pay for the losses at the restaurant. His parents' bank statements now reflected a profit. He tried to remind himself that it had been worth the many quarrels with his father, the tantrums, the bleak and biting silence in the aftermath.

The loss of their original regulars had been a blow after Manmohan began to tamper with the prices. Disgruntled patrons spread their gripes like a disease along Telegraph Avenue, and it took a lengthy grassroots campaign, during which they offered free samples and special weekend deals to reinvigorate the business. Each suggestion to resolve the problem, each step that Manmohan finally agreed to take had only then been accomplished after a great exertion of protracted wheedling until they eventually cultivated a new customer base. Their renewed popularity had also won the restaurant a rather high rating from an anonymous *San Francisco Chronicle* food critic who heralded the Lion of India as one of the top restaurants serving exotic cuisine in the Bay Area.

As Darshan closed his eyes and wriggled his body to shape the rice sack to his hip, he fell asleep thinking of his mother, of the silvery black circles beneath her eyes and the strain on her increasingly wrinkled face. It was possible now to hire a chef, to free her from the kitchen. But he would once again need to address the matter with his father, who continued to hold steadfastly to the archaic notion of a family-run establishment that would have been greatly successful in Fiji, but here constrained its growth and kept his uncomplaining mother haggard and depressed.

The light woke him. He peeled his lids open to face the glare from the storeroom's bulb suspended on a thick wire. "So soon?" he mumbled. He heard pots clanging in the kitchen, and through the storeroom door he discerned the faint warmth of the stove that had been recently fired up.

Jai lightly patted his cheek.

"What time is it?" he asked, unable to move.

"Nine-thirty," she said, retreating to the kitchen.

He struggled to sit up, rubbing his eyes with the heels of his palms.

Livleen kneeled next to him with a large plastic tub. "Sorry, Darshan. I need some rice."

Rolling off the rice and onto his feet, his voice thick, he asked, "You need help?"

She ripped open one of the sacks. "Go wash up first," she

said as a waterfall of grains drained into the tub.

"Would you both like tea?" Jai asked from the doorway.

He nodded, making his way to the dining area where Manmohan was reading a Punjabi newspaper distributed by the new gurdwara a Sikh coalition had recently built nearby. Navpreet was with him, a cup of chai on the table between her hands.

"Sat sri akal, Bapu" Darshan said. He nodded at Navpreet and sat next to her, massaging his sore shoulders.

"You were not there to get us this morning," his father said.

"I got your note. I tried calling. I came by after work."

"Junkerji's niece drove us. She came all the way from Fremont."

Livleen brought in two steaming cups of chai, set them on the table and returned to the kitchen.

"The heaters at Howard are out again," Darshan told them.

With disinterest, Navpreet poured sugar in her tea, her spoon clinking against the mug as she stirred it in. Manmohan continued to read his paper.

"Larry has been calling," Darshan said. "And 3B is moving out."

Manmohan peered over the rim of his paper.

Darshan twisted the cap of the sugar dispenser. Granules fell to the table. "I need to withdraw money from your account for repairs and renovations."

Navpreet leaned back in her chair, pulling her mug into her chest, blowing to cool the tea, looking at Manmohan.

Manmohan folded his paper, eyes contracting. "I want receipts."

Darshan pushed his chair back. "As always, Bapu." He collected the spilled sugar in his palm and went to the kitchen to help prepare for the day, his tea untouched and cooling on the table.

~ ~ ~

Leaning into the full-length mirror that hung behind the door of Navpreet and Livleen's bedroom, Darshan lifted his right eyelid to scrutinize his eyeball, the red lines jutting across the wet surface, the light brown iris, the dilated pupil. The echo of his hammer throughout unit 3B still rang in his ears, and the noxious smell of paint clung stubbornly to his nostrils. Releasing his eyelid, he blinked, licked his finger to smooth down his eyebrows.

Turning to the dresser, he gathered all the receipts for building materials and additional tools he had to purchase for the last month of renovations at Howard Street, sealed them in an envelope, and wrote *Bapu and Bebe* in pencil on the outside. In another envelope he inserted two-hundred dollars cash and scribbled Livleen's name on it. He adjusted his tie, swept a lint brush down the length of his brown and white plaid suit, and combed his hair, parted as usual on the side. Tucking the envelopes in his inside coat pocket, he left early for the long detour to the restaurant to wish Livleen a happy twenty-second birthday before his night shift at Kaiser.

It was late when he arrived, the restaurant closed for the evening. Livleen was in the bathroom. Manmohan and Jai waited for her, their jackets on and buttoned. Navpreet also waited, irritably checking the time on the wall clock. She had finally passed her driving test and had purchased a new car. Manmohan now expected her to drive them home whenever Darshan was unavailable, and she sat, drumming her fingers impatiently on the table. When she saw her brother, she brightened hopefully.

He put up his hand. "Night shift at the lab. I just came to wish Livleen a happy birthday."

Disappointed, Navpreet gestured lazily toward the women's restroom. "She's changing."

"I have something for her," he told them, smiling, showing them the envelope of money. "For her braces."

Manmohan turned to Jai. "You see?" he said.

His good mood soured, he put the money back in his pocket. "I worked for it. I set it aside. It is a gift."

Jai put her hand on her husband's bent shoulder. "Your father is concerned," she said. "We know you work very hard, but it is a lot of money." She massaged her forehead, wavering unsteadily on her feet.

Manmohan murmured something softly in her ear. She nodded and went to the kitchen.

"It is not nearly enough for a new car," Darshan said, glancing meaningfully at Navpreet.

Playing with one of her earrings, his sister said, "You just want everyone to think you are some kind of saint."

"You have said that before," he replied irritably. "Why does no one question *you*?"

"Darshan," Livleen said, coming into the dining hall, her dirty clothes folded under her arm. "What are you—?" she began, then flinched violently, turning abruptly toward the dissonant crash of aluminum mixing bowls hitting the tile floor.

"Bebe!" Darshan cried out, sprinting into the kitchen.

Jai was crumpled on the floor beside her stool, buried under a bulk of metal pots and bowls. Shoving them aside, he carefully examined a bloody gash along her left temple where she seemed to have hit her head on the counter before falling to the floor. She was unconscious.

"Navpreet. Start my car." He threw her his keys.

They hit her in the chest, clattering to the tile, as she stood gaping and mute.

"Livleen," he said. "You do it. Quickly."

"No," Navpreet mumbled, retrieving the keys. "I know what to do." She went outside.

Darshan lifted the tiny, almost weightless figure of his mother while Livleen propped open the storeroom and alleyway doors. In the alley, Navpreet revved the station wagon's engine.

"Is it bad?" Manmohan asked feebly.

Darshan pushed past his father, unable to answer.

"I'm coming with you," Livleen said.

"Someone has to stay with Bapu."

"Navpreet, where are your keys? We will be right behind you."

"They're inside, in my purse," she said in a voice shaky with fear. Fumes trailed faintly from the station wagon's exhaust pipe.

Setting his mother carefully down in the back seat, Darshan turned to Navpreet. "I'll drive. Keep her head steady. You know what to do, what to watch for. You know it better than I do."

She steadied herself, trying to regain her confidence at the reminder that she was a medical student. Sitting beside her mother, she pulled the door shut.

They checked Jai in through Kaiser emergency. She had already been wheeled away on a gurney to be evaluated for head trauma when Manmohan and Livleen arrived. Striding back and forth through the aisles of plastic chairs, furious and frightened, Darshan stopped when he saw his father slowly shuffle through the double doors into the waiting room.

"I wanted you to hire someone," he told his father, making no attempt to mitigate his anger. "Is money so important to you?"

"It was never about money," Manmohan replied quietly.

Darshan grimly pulled the envelopes from his coat and shoved the receipts at his father. Manmohan hooked his cane over his wrist and took them.

Turning to Livleen, Darshan gave her the other envelope. "It's not enough for your braces, I know. But I will give you more when I can."

His sister received the envelope with uncertainty. It had been a long while since anyone had given her anything of value.

"Happy birthday," he said, stretching out his hand to touch her shoulder. On impulse she shied away. He lowered his arm. "You don't need braces," he told her. "You are already very pretty. And I don't mean anything by it. The money is yours. You earned it, and you don't have to pay it back."

~ ~ ~

The springs of Elizabeth's couch were just as Darshan remembered them, disagreeably jutting into his hamstrings as he shifted right to left until he found that amenable dip that had once been his. It did not feel the same, however, the indentation deeper, a bit wider. He gazed around the studio, at the seemingly unchanged surface of it, but like the couch, subtle modifications over the last two years made it feel unfamiliar to him now—the new records beneath the television, earrings he had not seen before hanging from a metal accessory tree, the scent of a different laundry detergent.

"Would you like some water?" Elizabeth asked him, standing in the middle of the room, helplessly looking about at the mess. "I'm sorry. After you called, I didn't have time to tidy up."

"It's not a problem," he replied. "I can't stay long. I only wanted to say hi."

She filled a glass with water from the sink in the kitchenette, put it on the table in front of him, and sat on the other end of the couch.

He lifted the glass to his lips and tilted it until his mouth filled with cold liquid. Swallowing, he asked, "How are you?"

"I'm fine."

"Work okay?"

She nodded. "Same. You?"

"Still nights, and every weekend."

"No day shifts?"

"Sometimes."

"I never see you."

He again sipped his water.

She laced her fingers together in her lap. "Your family?" she asked. "They doing okay?"

Hesitating, he once more surveyed her apartment. "I'm sorry," he said, slapping his knees, smiling. "I should get going."

"So soon?"

"Busy day. But it was good to see you again."

"Whatever it is, you can tell me."

His bottom felt peculiar in the sofa dip. He remembered why he had chosen not to be with her. "Thank you for the water. Maybe I'll see you at work."

"Maybe," she nodded.

At the door they awkwardly hugged, and she patted him stiffly on the shoulder. Regretting this very much, he pressed his hand into the small of her back and pulled her more tightly into him, breathing into her neck. "I'm sorry," he said again.

She struggled to free herself. "Darshan, please."

"I was wrong," he told her.

She pulled away and clasped her arms about her waist, hurt in her eyes. "We both were."

He tried to touch her face, but she turned her head. "It's been two years. You were never serious. You couldn't have been. You never called. Stewart and I—" She stopped short when she saw his face.

He stared at her for a moment, taken aback, then tearfully hung his head, his arms loose and empty.

She gave him a chance to collect himself and then asked him to leave, weakly smiling as he crossed the threshold to the cement landing outside where it was brisk and windy, and then she shut the door.

~   ~   ~

Sometimes Darshan thought that his mother was not really his mother, that this woman named Jai did not exist. She lacked substance of her own, her spirit driven not by self-rule but by compliance, in every respect belonging to her husband. But it had not always been so. She had been a girl once, a person before marriage and children. Darshan wished there was something of that young girl remaining, a fiery voice of rebellion and reason.

Her color still sallow, her mood somber, Jai brushed her hair, the soft bristles seeming to soothe her. She hummed. Careful around her stitches, she continued brushing, twenty, thirty, fifty strokes. She put the brush aside, coiled her hair into a bun at the nape of her neck. She slipped her shawl over her shoulders.

"There will be no one there to watch you this morning," Darshan told her. "I cannot always watch over you."

"It is not your job," she replied, refusing to be dissuaded. She tucked her small feet into her slip-ons.

"It is okay to rest a while," he said. "The kitchen will be there when you are ready."

She glanced at Manmohan. "It has been too long as it is. Your father needs me."

"Tell her to go back to bed, Bapu," Darshan said, desperate. "Tell her it is not time."

Manmohan took hold of a long-handled shoehorn and forced his heel into his sneaker. "The cook you hired makes everything taste like metal."

"She is your wife," Darshan said bitterly.

Jai settled her patent leather handbag in the crook of her arm. "Yes, I am," she said. "Now get your car keys. We are waiting."

"No," he said. "I will not take you back there."

Jai gently rested her hand on Darshan's chest. "There is a way of things," she told him.

"It is not the right time. Please go back to bed."

She pursed her lips with displeasure at her son's choice. She allowed her husband to take her hand. Manmohan glowered spitefully at Darshan as he led her out of the apartment and down to the street.

When the door clicked shut, Darshan stood there for many minutes, the silence of the apartment oppressive until the refrigerator's motor kicked in. Roused, he bleakly went to his sisters' room. He pulled a ring of keys from his pocket and unhooked the set for Howard Street. Circling around the bed, he placed them on Navpreet's pillow. Ripping a piece of ruled paper from a pad on the dresser, he scribbled down a list of his responsibilities at the apartments. *If you do this*, he wrote to his sister, *no one will thank you or help you. But if you do not, they will hate you for it*. He signed his name. Folding the note, he tucked it under the keys, then pulled out his savings from an irregular crease behind the dresser. He left half on Livleen's pillow. The rest he took with him. He did not see his parents again that day, not even when he left the apartment with a duffle bag packed full of his things. He knew his father's pride, knew that Manmohan had circled the block to avoid him, waiting for Navpreet to come home.

He hailed a cab and went to the hospital where Dr. Gerard was expecting him.

"I was sorry to get your call," the doctor said when Darshan closed the door to his office.

"I know it's sudden. I'm very sorry I wasn't able to give you more notice."

"Dr. Levi says you belong here in the lab, drawing blood, interacting with the live patients," Dr. Gerard said smiling. "Such a waste on the dead, he says. I think he's right."

"He once told me the same thing," Darshan replied, also smiling. "I will write to him."

Dr. Gerard nodded. "Does your sister know?"

"I left her a note. Please tell her that my parents are waiting for her at home."

"How long will you be gone?" the doctor asked.

"I don't know."

"Call me when you come back. You are always welcome here."

"I appreciate that."

"I mean it."

"It's good to know," Darshan said, shaking the doctor's hand on his way out.

There was a travel agency down on Geary Street. Darshan had seen the storefront every day since starting work at Kaiser, never really noticing it until now, those faded posters of faraway places, of palaces and mountain pinnacles. The bell sounded as he entered. He sat down with a travel agent, absently noting the smiling family photos on the desk, the glass paperweight containing a fossilized insect, the blue-haired troll doll. The agent offered him several brochures, which Darshan refused, asking for an open-ended plane ticket from San Francisco International to New Delhi where he would catch a train to the Punjab.

~ ~ ~

Darshan made his way through Amritsar in the back of a rickshaw, through Hindustani motorcar traffic jams and past bicyclists weaving precariously in the spaces between cars, tinging their bells. The air perhaps drier, Amritsar was a macrocosm of Suva, the closest he had come to home since he had left Fiji nearly nine years ago: the smell of food stalls; the vivaciously musical chatter; the rich, bright hues of cloth and food; the spice in the air.

"Twelve rupees," the rickshaw wallah called back over his shoulder, narrowly avoiding a bicyclist. "No trickery," he added heatedly.

"Of course," Darshan agreed mildly.

It was a sunny day. Nothing stirred. No wind, no clouds. Only lucidity, a precision of angles and corners. The Golden Temple rose up before them, a brilliant auriferous yellow, its dome sharply lined against the cerulean sky. The rickshaw wallah deposited Darshan near the banks of the surrounding manmade lake where the temple reflected crisply in the mirror-like water. The tiles shone radiantly and with so much reassuring warmth that Darshan's toes tensed in anticipation of walking barefoot along them, the skin of his soles ready to receive the soothing heat before stepping into the coolness of the lake.

"Twelve rupees," he counted, handing them to the driver, adjusting his duffle on his shoulder. The man held his palm out, insistent on a few extra coins. When he received none, he grunted and melted back into traffic.

The sun only one hour above the horizon, the temple was relatively quiet. Darshan sat cross-legged on the tiles observing the small number of people bathing in the water, pressing their hands together in prayer. Strange to think that Ranjit had died here in a torrent of bullets. It was impossible to imagine now, the chaotic flight of men along these banks, the splatters of blood and heaps of bodies. It had taken great courage to challenge such a tyrannical system of governance, but Darshan suspected that his great uncle had also meant to escape the family, to both lose and find himself in a purpose greater than the Toors, with whom life was often a futile grappling and sputtering for air.

He lingered for several hours, taking his lunch of garbanzo bean curry and chapatis on a bench, watching as the crowds began to thicken around the temple, pilgrims exiting from the morning service. A Hindu priest with long hair sectioned into braids and dressed only in an orange loincloth sat beside him. "Spirit reading?" he asked, smiling serenely, pushing the braids back behind his shoulders. His bare chest was stained with red powder.

Darshan placed his palms together to respectfully decline. "Not now, ji."

"You are most certainly in need of spiritual advising," the

pundit insisted, holding out his small tray of turmeric paste.

"It is a strange place for a Hindu priest," Darshan told him.

The man nodded with the same serene smile. "I suppose that is true. But it is nonetheless God's place."

Knowing the priest would not leave without a few rupees, Darshan set his food aside. The pundit dipped the tip of his middle finger into the yellow paste and smeared a small circle between Darshan's eyebrows. He placed the tray on the bench and took Darshan's hand.

"You are very discontent," the pundit observed, then said with a sly twist of his head, "But I admit this is nothing new. In any case, there are always second chances. You have been here before. There is an opportunity for you."

Something vaguely familiar alighted deep within Darshan's mind, reawakening that same chronic dread he had battled to repress since he was ten years old and Baba Singh's bleary eyes peered intently into his.

The pundit took a moment to study Darshan's palm, then cleared his throat. "You had a brother."

Darshan shook his head. "I have one."

"Perhaps there is no difference," the man said. "*When* is not important."

"I do not understand," Darshan said. His fingertips were cold.

"He will make you understand."

"He does not know anything."

"He knows everything," the pundit replied. He bowed and stretched out his hand.

"Is that all?" Darshan asked, pulling ten rupees from his wallet.

"There is nothing more," the pundit replied, taking the money. He gathered his tray, the veins in his arms thick beneath the muscle, and walked toward the lake, his bare feet painted with turmeric, his pace deliberate, supple heel to toe, heel to toe, vanishing into the crowd of Sikh men and women, humming folk songs and accosting no others.

~ ~ ~

Listening to the train's wheels screeching along the tracks, Darshan perceived Amarpur on the horizon. Behind his head, the warm wind whipped a yellow-aged window curtain against his hair, and the smell of earth and dust brushed against his nose. A charge of anxiety—a sense of wrongdoing, of trespassing—gripped his chest as he thought of his father, who had not spoken of Amarpur or Barapind since before Baba Singh had returned there. Darshan had the impression that something horrible had happened in this place, that family secrets had been buried but not forgotten, that he himself had played a part in it.

The train slowed as it approached the town, settling to a stop next to a short platform, the engine hissing like doused fire. Amarpur looked much like the deserted gold-mining settlements of California, a single strip of dusty road lined with wood- and tin-roofed buildings. There were few people outside. They glanced dolefully at the train before retreating from the midday sun. Many shops were boarded shut.

Duffle on his shoulder, Darshan descended the staircase at the end of the platform, appraising the town, disappointed by its lack of vitality. Wiping dirt from his face with a spare shirt, he entered the telegraph office, greeted by the curious and wary stare of a middle-aged Hindu man.

"Yes?" the man asked, revealing a mouthful of rotten teeth, his gums stained by paan.

Darshan courteously inclined his head. "I sent a message. My grandfather once lived in this town. I would like to find his home."

The young man's eyes narrowed. "Yes, I received your message. It has been almost five years since his death. No one came."

"Did you know him?"

"Not well, but I know it was not proper."

"I believe he wanted to be alone," Darshan told the operator. "He did not explain himself, but he had his reasons."

"His brother's family lives there, in the blacksmith shop," the operator said, pointing down the street. "I told them you would be coming."

"Thank you ji," Darshan replied.

There was no name on the shop front, but through the hazy window Darshan identified shelves of farming and gardening implements, tools, hammers, boxes of nails, buckets, and cooking utensils. He knocked gently, slowly opening the door. An older woman sitting behind a desk turned to look at him. Her forehead glistened with perspiration in the warm room. Her skin was very brown and far more leathered than Jai's. She wore a blue salwaar kameez, her chuni lined with pink trim. She pulled the shawl over her hair, rising, confusion in her furrowed brow.

"Was that today?" she asked. "I thought it was next week's train."

"Sat sri akal, Neena Auntiji," Darshan said. "I am sorry. I do not want to impose."

She smiled kindly, approaching him. "The time slips from me." Squinting, she touched his face, a tiredness in her skin, in the tense muscles of her shoulders. "We were very glad to hear from you."

441

"I was not sure anyone would be here."

She turned toward the stairs. "Gharwala!" she called to her husband. She took Darshan's bag. "Your grandfather spoke about you. He said you would come. I had almost forgotten. I thought he had just hoped for it."

A man descended the stairs. "Sat sri akal," he said, looking as if he had been slumbering, his turban askew, his clothes wrinkled.

"Shamsher Uncleji," Darshan said, bowing his head.

"Was that this week?" his uncle asked.

Neena put Darshan's duffle on a cot at the back of the shop. "Come," she said then, drawing him toward her desk. She removed paraphernalia from a few spare chairs, dumping it on the floor. "Sit."

Shamsher filled a pot with water from a bucket. He set the pot on a small corner stove and shook some tea leaves into it.

"Where is your father?" Neena asked. "We thought he would have come."

"He cannot travel," he told her apologetically. "And he does not know that I am here."

"Is he angry?"

"I do not believe that is what kept him away."

"Yes," she murmured, sighing. "Your grandfather did not want Satnam or Vikram here either. He was infected by too much pride and darkness, like he was the only one who ever suffered, as though nothing good ever happened. My own father remembered it differently."

"This place was his?" Darshan asked, gesturing at the shop, noticing two crossed swords with intricately carved metal hilts hanging above a door at the rear. They were oddly out of character in this sea of tools. The door appeared to have been sealed shut with mortar.

"Until his death. It once belonged to a man named Yashbir Chand." She waited then, for some sign of recognition, then blinked sadly, sighing. "It is a shame your father never spoke of him. He was very important to this family."

"I am sorry, Auntiji."

"And what do you know of Desa, Ranjit, and my father?"

"I have heard some, but very little."

Neena's chuni dropped, revealing her high forehead and austere grey hair. "I was born later," she said, "but I know many stories."

"Will you tell them to me?" Darshan asked her, smelling cardamom and milk brewing on the stove.

She paused, seeming to wonder at his sincerity. "Perhaps," she replied. "We have some time. The train will not come again for a week."

That evening, Neena took him upstairs to a cramped one-room apartment. Three charpoys were lined along the far wall, a pipe stove in the corner, and next to it a shelf cluttered with bowls and pots. Neena's mother, wife of Khushwant Singh Toor, was lying on one of the charpoys, staring unblinkingly up at the ceiling, a cool, wet cloth on her forehead.

"Bebe," Neena said gently. "Someone has come to see you."

"Who is it?" the old woman asked hoarsely.

Darshan sat beside her. "Sat sri akal, Simran Auntiji," he said, speaking softly.

"Gharwala?" she whispered.

"No, Bebe," Neena said, her voice soothing.

Simran's eyes sharpened, a fog seeming to lift. "Darshan?" She stared at him a long while. "It is good to finally meet you."

"Did you know I would come?" he asked.

"Of course."

"How did you know?"

"Because he told me. He told all of us. He remembered you very well." She closed her eyes.

"She is always so tired," Neena told him. "She should sleep now."

Darshan murmured his agreement, but was unable to move. He stroked Simran's hair, course and silver with age, and she smiled as though enjoying his touch. She had seen him. She knew him. As he looked up at Neena, who waited patiently, he realized they all knew him.

But he did not know why.

~ ~ ~

Mornings were different in Barapind village, the quiet more pervasive than in town. It was a sacred silence, the silence of peace and pigment, found in blades of grass and clods of soil, in slumbering creatures not yet awake. The Toor house resided in this tranquility, a monument to an end of things, slowly crumbling in its return to the earth, sagging under its own weight like the skin of an old person hanging on bones.

Several villagers gathered around inquisitively, regarding Darshan with warmth. A young boy kicked a rock toward him, giggled and ran away. Taking their offered hands Darshan murmured, *sat sri akal, sat sri akal.*

"We knew your grandfather," one of them said. "My grandfather was Onkar Singh. They were very good friends. You must come to us for tea."

"Of course, ji," Darshan replied. "I would like that very much."

Pleased, the man sent a girl in search of her mother to make preparations.

Shamsher indicated the house. "It is not safe," he said when Darshan put his hand on the door. "You should not go inside. There is nothing left."

"I will not be long," Darshan told him.

Pieces of plaster crunched under his shoes as he entered the main hall. Above him, a cracked ceiling beam bent downwards. Upstairs, the roof had collapsed. He found an empty burlap sack in the pantry, the cement floor stained the color of brown, red, and gold spices. He paced the main hall for a time, searching, dragging his hand along the walls, touching crevices and jutting nails where pictures had once hung. Finally he squatted in the center of the room, his head in his hands, making one final effort to rouse some feelings of regret, of connection and loss. He thought perhaps he might remember why he had really come here.

Disappointed, he rose, shutting the door behind him as he went back outside.

Another villager, breathing hard as if from the exertion of running, wordlessly gave him a bundle bound in a piece of dirty cloth that contained several figurines carved in wood.

"I had these in my house," the man said, pity in his eyes. "They were his. I saw him sometimes, speaking to them."

Running his fingertips over the rough splintery curves and etched lines of each figurine, a horse and cow, a policeman and farmer, a bullock cart, Darshan suddenly saw the truth of his own life, the many sacrifices he had told himself were necessary, the willing victim he had allowed himself to become. He saw his own future, his decline into old age, the years passing in solitude so that one day he too would be pitied.

"Do you still believe in God?" he had once asked Elizabeth.

"Not that one," she told him. "I have perspective now. I'm smarter. It isn't possible to learn all that we need in this one life, to earn heaven or hell in only seventy some odd years. It's ridiculous. It's beneath us to think so."

"Then what do you believe in?"

"Nothing," she replied, perhaps too quickly. "Everything." Exasperated, she had shrugged. "It doesn't matter. I'm trying to figure it out."

Darshan turned to the villager. "Please keep these," he said, rewrapping the figurines. "They do not belong with me."

He sat for tea with Onkar's family, listening to what he already knew, that Baba Singh had long ago fled the village with promises to come back, and although he had returned in body, in spirit he had not. For some years he had wandered the lanes of Barapind with an expression of horror on his face, speaking to no one, mumbling only the name of his wife.

~ ~ ~

Elizabeth's ruffled, loose-fitting sundress pressed against her body in the hot wind as she glanced around the New Delhi tarmac, the long line of passengers ahead of her already crowding the entrance to the terminal. As if feeling Darshan's eyes, she looked up, shielding her face from the sun with a magazine, squinting at him. He waved through the window.

She entered the terminal, a medium-sized suitcase in her hand. She took her time, walking slowly, and as she stopped before him, she regarded him circumspectly. "I was surprised by your telegram," she said, releasing the bag and letting it drop heavily to the floor. She pulled a small piece of paper from her purse. "I never expected this."

"I didn't think you would come," he replied, sitting against the slim, metal edge of the windowsill.

"After the last time I saw you, Stewart and I weren't the

same. I thought maybe you would come back. I tried calling, but you disappeared."

"Everything fell apart."

"Do your parents know?"

He shook his head. "But it doesn't matter. They will be angry with me in any case."

"Were you serious about it?"

"I would not ask lightly."

She took a moment to consider this, creasing the telegram in half, folding it over again. "I thought so," she finally said. "That's why I came. But I was married once before, to God. We had rings, meditated on his image. It was very symbolic. As it turned out, He was full of shit."

"He never asked you," Darshan told her.

She smiled slightly, then told him resolutely, "Nothing religious. I don't want people watching. We don't have to prove anything. I want it to be real."

"I understand," he said. "Are you ready?"

"Now?"

He took her bag and held out his hand.

The New Delhi courthouse was muggy, its once colonial halls shabby and unkempt, crowded with plaintiffs and petty criminals, all sweating profusely, their shirts stained at the collars and armpits. An official called out Darshan's name. He rose from his plastic chair and took Elizabeth's hand. She pinched a piece of lint from his trimmed beard and smiled. Her hair was pulled back, making the sharp angles of her face appear more elegant, accentuated by the blush she had dabbed on her cheeks and the brown eye shadow she had painted on her eyelids. People stared at her as she passed through the waiting area, her arm in the crook of Darshan's elbow.

The official pointed toward two chairs at a large desk, then seated himself opposite. Dabbing his forehead with a handkerchief, he began busying himself with arranging papers. A floor-fan whirred. Darshan cleared his throat into his fist. The official suspiciously glanced up, then returned his attention to his work.

Elizabeth did not move. Her hands were cupped together, resting lightly in her lap. Her posture was immaculately straight, her chin slightly elevated, her ankles crossed as her grandmother had taught her. Darshan reached for her pinky finger and her sitting etiquette began to crumble as she pursed her lips to hold back a smile, then fully dissolved as she slouched and rolled her eyes. He looked at her in amusement.

The official finally set down his pen. He briskly clasped his palms together, then stacked several papers in front of them for their review. "It is good for you?" he asked.

"It's written in Hindi," Elizabeth said.

The official regarded her with annoyance. "You like him?" he asked, nodding at Darshan.

"Yes."

He tapped the bottom of one of the documents. "Then please, sign here."

She scribbled her signature, a faint smile on her lips, and passed the pen to Darshan.

The official appraised their signatures before violently stamping the certificate. "Congratulations," he said briskly, bowing as he presented it to them. Without wasting any time, he then walked out of the room.

Elizabeth began to laugh. Hot, she used the marriage license to fan her face.

Grinning, Darshan loosened his tie. "I want to take you somewhere," he said. "I want you to meet some people."

"Who?"

"Family," he replied. "They are waiting."

And as they dined with Shamsher, Neena, and the villagers of Barapind in a makeshift reception, feasting on fresh foods, chai, and sweets, absorbing the wonders of the earth and accepting the unguarded affection of the Toor family that still existed here, listening to their stories, Darshan was wholly prepared for the flight back home to San Francisco, where Manmohan sat in his hard wooden chair, an inimical expression darkening his face.

~ ~ ~

Victoria Quinn fondly embraced Darshan. After a moment she released him, holding him at arm's length, a hint of sorrow behind the horn-rimmed glasses she wore on a chain around her neck. Her white hair glowed in the light of the dining room's antique chandelier. "I am very happy you are here," she told her new son-in-law. She took Elizabeth's hand, patted it affectionately before retreating to the kitchen and returning with a decanter of tomato juice.

"Tell us about your trip," she said, putting the juice on the table and taking out some glasses from the china cabinet. Adjusting her polyester dress before sitting, she gestured that they join her.

Colleen frowned at Elizabeth. "You said there was nothing left to say to him."

"Colleen—"

"I have never been to India," Victoria interrupted, pouring the tomato juice. "I expect it was beautiful." She looked pointedly at Colleen. "I expect it was exactly what they needed."

"Yes," Darshan said, opening a pouch of recently

developed photos and setting them next to the tomato juice.

"I would like to meet your family, Darshan," Victoria said.

He nodded apologetically. "I will tell them you said so."

She crossed her nyloned, varicose-veined legs, drank her juice. "By the looks on your faces, you seem to have made a very good decision." She gathered up the pictures and began to slowly flip through them, taking her time with each one before passing them to Colleen, a sentimental and mysterious smile on her lips. "Are they your family in India?" she asked Darshan, pointing to a picture of Shamsher and Neena posing in front of the blacksmith shop.

"A distant aunt and uncle."

"You look so much like this woman."

"I thought the same thing," Elizabeth said, taking the photo.

"And this house?" Colleen asked.

"It was my family's."

"It seems that you both had such a lovely time," Victoria told them wistfully.

"Victoria," Darshan said, "I'm sorry—"

"Don't be. It wasn't about me."

Elizabeth began to collect the dirty glasses. "Mom, we don't mean to rush off, but we'd better go before it gets late."

Darshan nodded. "My parents will have a lot to say."

"Yes," Victoria said, pushing back her chair. "From what I understand, it has been a while. They should know that you are home and safe."

In the driveway, before getting in the car, Darshan removed the picture of the house, looking at the balcony split in half and toppled inward, at the front columns ravaged by the might of monsoon seasons. Victoria was watching from the house, waving to them through the window. He waved back, and then he slipped the print into his blazer, separate from all the others, before gathering his courage to go home.

The apartment on 24th Street was strangely without scent; Jai had not cooked, had not put on tea. The girls had just come home from buying groceries, and Manmohan sat in his chair, which had been moved to the window, eyes flat as he gazed outside.

Elizabeth greeted everyone warmly. "I met your relatives," she said, holding out the photos. "They were very nice people." No one took them. She put them on the coffee table.

Navpreet scowled at her. "My first semester of medical school was wasted on cleaning up the mess Darshan left us with at Howard and the restaurant. My professors don't take me seriously."

"I don't think that's what he intended," Elizabeth replied. She still had not sat, and no one asked her to.

Darshan kneeled beside his father, who would not look at him. "Bapu? Shouldn't we try to be happy?"

"We have never lived for happiness," Manmohan replied.

"What will people say?" Jai asked. "How can we tell them that our family and hers are now joined and they were not asked to be a part of it?"

Darshan sighed heavily. "I am certain people will understand the unusual circumstances."

"How can they understand when I do not?"

"Thank you for the braces," Livleen said, her front teeth lined with metal brackets.

With relief, Darshan smiled at her.

She did not return his smile. "I tried to find you."

"I was tired. I had to do something for myself."

"We all need that," his sister said. "But we never ran away."

Looking at their faces, the resentment in each of their

expressions, he understood that his choice would be with him always, that they would never recall the efforts he had made for them, how readily and sincerely he had always loved them, but this one thing they would never forget.

~ ~ ~

Darshan could not remember the pundit's face, only the red stains of some sort of powder on his hairless, muscular chest, the terrifying might of his arms as he had offered his tray of turmeric paste. *There is an opportunity for you*, the priest whispered in his mind, nudging him to speak to the fat stranger with dark sunglasses now sitting in the living room across from him. *He knows everything*, the voice said, and as Darshan regarded the man who was his only brother, flanked by a toothless woman and two meek and terrified children, he shrank away, certain that it was not possible.

"You did not tell me he was coming," Manmohan said grimly to Darshan.

"I did not know," Darshan replied.

Mohan stared at Elizabeth, a mocking twitch at the corners of his mouth. He sat loosely, his legs carelessly spread, stroking the end of his long beard, tugging at it, wrapping the tip of it around his finger. Darshan saw his wife force a courteous smile.

Shifting his gaze from Elizabeth to Mohan, Darshan asked his brother, "How did you know where to find us?"

"I inquired, here and there," Mohan replied, relaxing into his chair, releasing his beard. "You are doing very well here, I see." He regarded Manmohan and Jai, the reflected streaks of light in his sunglasses like admonitions.

"Yes," murmured Lehna.

Smiling now, Mohan opened his arms expansively. "It is good to see everyone after so much time apart."

Manmohan rose slowly and with great effort, and then he left the room. Jai stood to follow him, as did Livleen and Elizabeth.

"Wait," Mohan said weakly, the scorn in his expression faltering, but they were already gone. His eyes lingered on the hallway down which they had disappeared, becoming thoughtful. "A wife like that will only ever make you sandwiches," he told Darshan.

Navpreet snickered.

"Lehna will do whatever I ask," he said, placing a meaty hand over his wife's knee.

Lehna lowered her eyes, and Navpreet's smile faded.

"Why did you come?" Darshan asked. "You must have known that Bapu and Bebe would not want to see you?"

"I thought time might have erased some things."

"What did you do to make them hate you so much?"

"I was not what they expected me to be," Mohan said, taking off his glasses, flinching at the word *hate*, his eyes more tired than disdainful.

"I met a man in India," Darshan told him. "A pundit. I ran away. I was unhappy."

His brother's eyebrows lifted with interest, and he again glanced down the hallway. "Bapu is not easy to please."

Darshan hesitated, ashamed, then said, "The pundit told me that you could help me with something."

Mohan polished his glasses on the hem of his shirt. Tucking them in his front pocket, he took his wife by the elbow and forced her to stand. "You should not believe him," he replied, signaling to his children that he was ready to go. "He was a charlatan."

A Baptism & a Kirtan
1976–1978

An atlas was open on the kitchen table to a map of what was now India. Two northern divisions were shaded a darker brown, illustrating what had been lost. The detached segments. Pakistan and Bangladesh. A mug of tea with too much milk and not enough ginger was getting cold beside the map. Another pot was brewing on the stove, this time to get it right, to make it taste like Jai's.

"She will be back soon," Darshan told his father, grating more ginger.

The tea simmered. Manmohan hunched over the map, his reading glasses pinching the tip of his wide nose. He traced his finger along the border of Pakistan and India, stopping at Amritsar where Jai and the girls were now. "Your mother has never traveled without me," he said tersely.

"Only a few weeks more."

"Add a little pepper. I cannot smell enough pepper."

Darshan seasoned the water with more pepper, then returned the grinder to the cupboard where Jai kept her spices.

His mother had taken the girls to meet a young man named Sarabjit Dindral. Sarabjit was from a well-established family of North Indian politicians and lawyers on intimate terms with Manmohan and Jai's Berkeley acquaintances, the Attwals. By the tone and tenor of Sarabjit's letters it was clear that he was expressive, poetic, and courteous. Also well connected, of appropriate birth, and wealthy Manmohan had therefore begun negotiations with the Dindral family. Terms and conditions set, Sarabjit had then offered a proposal, and—based on such an abundance of considerably excellent criteria—Navpreet had consented to marry him.

"Why are you doing this?" Darshan had asked her, thinking it an odd and unsuitable choice for his sister, disposed to spend her life with a man she had never met, at the mercy of the unknown, prey to the conservative sentiments of Indian culture that so often held women inferior. "I know you have met others."

"Yes, they were fun," she admitted wistfully, forcing the zipper closed on her suitcase. "But all of them were American. That was your mistake. No one likes you anymore, Darshan. They speak unkindly about you."

"That is not a reason to get married."

Filling another suitcase with gifts for her betrothed's family—American cookies, sticks of deodorant, and packets of Big Red chewing gum—she had laughed at him. "Maybe Bebe taught Elizabeth how to prepare curries and roll out perfectly circular rotis. Maybe your American wife goes to temple dressed like us. But what you did will always be an insult."

Navpreet's words, even after a year of marriage, rang with a very unpleasant truth. Since their wedding, Elizabeth had made generous attempts to assimilate. She helped Jai in the Lion of India's kitchen where she could interact with family friends and relations. She drove Manmohan to his doctor's appointments. She initiated the paperwork for the family's United States citizenship, sharing her research on the complex bureaucratic process with others who needed assistance. In every way available to her, she had tried to learn and adopt the gradations of Sikh culture, but the caustic murmurs and contemptuous looks of disapproval were unrelenting.

"Too much pepper," his father said, sniffing the air.

Darshan inhaled the steam. "Taste it first."

"I do not have to."

Sighing, Darshan dumped the pot of tea into the sink and started again, adding fresh water and sprinkling in whole, shelled cardamom and ground clove.

Manmohan swung the large atlas cover shut. "It is a different world now." He removed his glasses, seeming to contemplate the simplicity of the notion. "No," he said, after a moment's reconsideration. "The world is the same. It is us who have changed in different directions."

The water slowly began to bubble. Darshan turned down the heat and added the milk.

"Your mother has never traveled without me," Manmohan said again, turning in his chair to watch the tea, and Darshan realized he was not worried for her. He was worried for himself. She had never once abandoned him. As the world changed, she had always gone with him. And that was everything.

~ ~ ~

A flood of color whispered and rustled throughout the ballroom of the Sir Francis Drake hotel as guests arrived in saris and turbans for the reception in honor of Navpreet and

Sarabjit's arrival to San Francisco as a newly married couple. A table at the entrance was stacked high with gifts: jewelry, kitchenware, small appliances, bedding. Navpreet was at the head table, hair coifed, makeup thick like her face had been chiseled from stone. Stiffly, she looked around the hall, unforgiving, eyes finally resting with revulsion upon her husband sitting beside her.

Sarabjit's eyebrows were rectangular masses of thick hair, erratic and wiry wisps cased around a set of beady eyes. His shoulders were thin and weak, as was his neck, which strained to hold up both head and turban. His two front teeth were overly large, angled in opposite directions, leaving a wide gap through which he absently poked his tongue. He was grinning now, his crooked and jagged teeth adding a measure of childish joy incongruous to his currently regrettable circumstances, which were clear to everyone in the ballroom.

People deliberately looked away, discomfited by the animosity between the couple, distracting themselves with a buffet of biryani, tandoori chicken, spiced yogurt, and naan. Soon the room was full of chatter, and the hired musicians began a set of Indian love songs. To forestall further embarrassment, Darshan followed his mother to the table with an expansive and congratulatory smile.

Before he could say anything, however, Navpreet asked indignantly, "Do you see him? Look at him."

"Navpreet!" Jai hissed quietly.

"He knows what he looks like, a hideous fresh-off-the-boat nobody."

Darshan blocked her from view. "Stop it," he said firmly.

"Stupid FOB."

Sarabjit smiled feebly. Darshan wished he would at least keep his lips closed to cover his teeth. It was a smile of humiliation, but it looked as if he were idiotically in agreement with her.

Sarabjit politely tapped Navpreet's shoulder. She spun around to face him. "What?"

"Why did you bring me here?" he asked quietly, no longer smiling. "I was happy in India."

"Because it was too late to walk away. Because it was so obvious you needed help, and I did something for you. I brought you to America, where maybe, if someone like me helped you, you could be somebody."

"I already am somebody," he replied.

She violently pushed back her chair, lifting the hem of her lavender sari to reveal two-inch heels and newly manicured feet. Jai shoved her back down into her seat. "You will stay here," she told her daughter resolutely. "You will finish this."

Darshan looked feebly at his brother-in-law.

"She has been like this since our wedding night," Sarabjit said. "I should not have come."

~ ~ ~

The city was a wet, gray drizzle. People huddled under bus awnings, gloom on their faces as moisture seeped under their clothes and shivered their skin. Darshan felt sorry for them all, for their lack of spirit. He smiled at them as he and Elizabeth hiked up Terra Vista toward the studio, cheerful, his thoughts full of his future, of the wonderful life that awaited him. Shifting his bag of groceries onto his hip, he took Elizabeth's hand and kissed her fingers.

"I can take it if it's too heavy," he offered, nodding at the jug of milk she carried.

"It's only milk," she said, smiling.

"You're a little pale."

"Just light-headed."

"Then I'll open up the bed—"

"Darshan," she said, looking at their stoop, at the luggage sprawled up and down the length of the stairs. Navpreet sat mournfully in the center of it. She trembled against the cold, toes pointed inward, elbows digging into her knees, chin in her palms.

She rose as they approached, carefully wiping her trousers with the tissue she had laid on the cement beneath her bottom. "I forgot my umbrella," she said.

Elizabeth warily assessed the number of bags piled on the landing. "Navpreet…"

Balling the tissue in her fist, Navpreet said, "I'm getting divorced. I moved out."

Darshan hesitated, absorbing the implications of this latest drama. Slowly, he waded past his sister up the stairs, stepping over the luggage.

"So soon?"

"Three months too late."

"You should have called first," he said, unlocking the door.

"I don't have to call first," she said, piqued. "I'm getting a divorce."

"You can't stay here."

"Of course I can—"

"There isn't room."

"I can't stay with Bapu and Bebe. They will hate me when they hear. I have nowhere else to go."

Elizabeth clutched the milk jug with both hands. "It isn't a good time."

"How can you say that? This is important."

Elizabeth glanced momentarily at Darshan, her lips pinched

inward. He nodded in resignation to tell her she might as well share the news. "I'm pregnant," she said.

Navpreet's mouth parted in astonishment, and then she groaned.

"This is a chance for you to start over," Darshan told her. "Focus on your medical studies. You're nearly done."

"Don't make me go to Bapu and Bebe," Navpreet mumbled. "They don't want me. They never wanted me."

"That isn't true."

"Please," she said, her head hung. "Please can I stay?"

"Just for tonight."

"It wasn't my idea," Navpreet admitted morosely. "Sarabjit kicked me out. They won't forgive that. They can't forgive divorce. It's much worse than what you did." She pushed her hair back away from her face with both hands. "Forget it." She grabbed two of her bags and heaved them down the steps.

When Elizabeth, concern creasing her brow, moved to follow her, Darshan pulled her back. "She is always carrying on. I'll call her a cab, but the rest is her problem. For once she should sort out her own mess."

~ ~ ~

There was a house on the coast, large and flawless, its edges tight and beautiful. Babies would be born there, an endless line of generations secured within its walls, warmed by the fire crackling in the hearth, the auburn light reflecting the curvature of tiny sleeping bodies. A mother and father would pass time in cushioned chairs, legs tucked snuggly under throws, watching these babies grow, laughter in their eyes as the little ones danced and messed about with their games and whims. The bathtubs would be playgrounds where creatures of rubber would float as the children spun stories, splashing and puddling the tiled floor. Forts made of sofa cushions would be erected in the great expanse of bedrooms and living rooms, and would then crumble under a new game, a new discovery of imagination. The smell of savories would rise from the kitchen stove, pots glowing with the warmth of nourishment. There would be gifts and parties in this house, celebrations of first teeth and first steps, graduations and farewells.

Outside, from the west, a summer fog rolled in off the Pacific in a massive, low-lying spool. It unfurled down the hills to the east, inching nearer to the house, absorbing sound and claiming sight. In the driveway a station wagon huddled underneath the oppressive, hanging mist, its rusted metal shape blurred as the fog crept nearer, thickening. Condensation seeped into the wood at the edge of the driveway, but the house was insulated against such chills, protected by the skilled hands that had built it.

This was their house.

It was slightly visible in the distance from where they stood on the beach, the fog finally dissipating for the day. Darshan regarded it, this labor of his, his back to the ocean, the setting sun warming his neck as the soft but bitter winds chilled his body. The sensations of hot and cold gave him life and made him proud. In his arms he held a baby, wrapped against the elements. His baby. He called her Sonya and kissed her wrinkled head as her face contorted in tears because the world outside the womb was harsh.

She had been baptized in the Irish Catholic tradition, anointed with the sacred oils of Christ, assurances of heaven crossed upon her forehead. Her Indian grandparents had been sobered by the experience, skeptical of Christ's oils, of biblical prayer and blessing. Nonetheless they had risen to stand beside their Irish relatives, called upon to recognize this infant as one of their own, the progeny of their progeny to be saved in the eyes of the Lord.

"My mother is grateful," Elizabeth told Darshan.

"That's important," he replied.

"It's not easy to believe that way. Such unconditional conviction."

"And a kirtan?" he asked. "For my parents?"

Tenderly massaging her sore and full breasts, Elizabeth sighed. "Sonya belongs to all of us. You can't argue with faith. It is a waste of breath."

They continued to wander the beach, exploring the new territory around the house that Darshan had built, noting subtle changes in the air, the resonance of peace, the distance in miles from the city and from their families that would keep them sane in the future, whenever more of such compromises were necessary.

The days thereafter pulsed rhythmically, the rise and fall of each like the tide they could see from their living room window caressing the gray and jagged stones. In Kaiser's laboratory, blood samples needed analyzing, their cell counts and hemoglobin levels to be assessed and noted. Tenants at Howard Street left their units in disarray, a tumult of cigarettes and rotten foods. A frenzy of repair and then new tenants took their place, and the cycle continued. Fights ensued at the Lion of India. It fell from its briefly held peak of popularity, and Darshan strained to keep it from sinking under his mother's fragility and his father's arrogance. His father uttered threats. Darshan then offered appeasing capitulations. The old man's rage so often fostered defeat, and the burden was unrelenting. Sonya was walking. Darshan had missed her first steps. Still, he had seen her second ones. This balance was always a game, an exigent race.

San Francisco had finally grown wearisome, too, for Manmohan and Jai. The apartment on 24th Street had been a place of transition, of adjustment and too many concessions. They found a new home in Berkeley where they moved with Livleen. The soil in the backyard was fertile, freshly churned, flowers and dust thick in the air, as it had once been in Fiji. Back bent, Manmohan looked downward toward the earth, and from it, he drew life, patches of strawberries and tomatoes, trees bearing apples, lemons, almonds, and pomegranates. Watering his infant garden, the hose tight with pressure as turbid streams of water flowed down the side of the house, he said, "It is no use anymore. I am done with it." He was speaking of his restaurant. He was speaking of selling. "Your mother will grow plums."

"It is a very good thing," Darshan said.

"But we have lost money. We will need to solve this first."

"That will not be possible."

"Make it possible."

Squatting beside the mud, jamming his finger into the soft surface, Darshan replied, "I will do my best, Bapu."

A new decree, a new set of problems and worries, and the landscape of the family continued to shift.

Navpreet married again, impulsively and without warning to a man named Pravinder whom none of them had met, whose family was still in India. He insinuated himself into her life, his handsome, brown face insincere, his smile disingenuous, hers so smugly satisfied by his good looks. For a time, she wore him proudly and defiantly on her arm, giving the whole of her community the opportunity to look upon her with desire, admiration, and envy, ignoring the shame so evident in her parents' expressions. She and Pravinder made many friends together, Navpreet's impending career as a doctor holding the couple in high esteem. Wealth and beauty. It elevated them greatly.

But soon they retreated. Many months would go by before they would fleetingly emerge from the house they had bought far to the southeast. Navpreet would smile haughtily at her family during those brief encounters, eyes dark and dangerous, until again she and Pravinder would slink away to their den of conceit.

And as Navpreet disappeared, Mohan returned, paying the Toors another unannounced visit. "I have sold everything in Fiji," he told his parents, even as they refused to acknowledge him. "I am staying here in America," he called after them as they again walked away, taking Livleen with them. "I would like you all to know it."

"When will this end?" Darshan asked his brother.

"Perhaps when they finally see me."

It was all he said.

Mohan adapted quickly, governing minimarts and gas stations on the outskirts of Sacramento, his new domain. He often made an appearance at the gurdwara, Lehna and his two children scampering closely behind him as he shook hands and kissed babies, charming mothers with compliments and priests with donations.

"Won't you say hello to them?" Darshan once asked his father.

"I will not encourage him," Manmohan replied.

"Not even to Amandev and Dal? They are your grandchildren."

Manmohan stared firmly across the prayer hall to where Jai and Livleen were sitting. "We do not know them," he said. "*You* do not know them. They are not a part of this family."

And so Darshan sat back and listened to the prayer, as he did every Saturday with his father, riding the wave of days that seemed to escape him, powerless against such deeply rooted grudges. He glanced at Elizabeth sitting close behind Jai and Livleen, stoically resigned to the cultural obligations required of her even if she was not acknowledged for them. He breathed in deeply. The tabla drums beat metrically. Soon they would be home again, down on the coast, protected within the curtain of fog where their own changes were taking place, Sonya petting her mother's nascent belly, whispering encouragement to the new life within, saying his name: Anand. A brother. A son.

~ ~ ~

Darshan had never been invited to the home where Navpreet had been living with Pravinder for nearly two years. He imagined it to be a dishonest place where socialites and intellectuals of European descent gathered to discuss politics and previous tours to Paris, a place where Navpreet could be exotic and lovely in her Indian-ness—with her handsome husband who had learned to minimize his accent and laugh jauntily at empty jokes—yet still be American. But it was not at all like that, at least not today, not anymore. It had become much worse, and Darshan went there now with trepidation. The drive through the East Bay was long, the highways stretching for eternity, and his heart pumped wildly with fear.

She had been weeping when she called. "He won't stop," she sobbed into the telephone.

"Where are you?" he replied without thinking, already reaching for his car keys.

"In the closet. I pushed something under the knob and he can't get in."

He hesitated then, realizing he did not have her address.

"Darshan," she whispered, her voice steadier. "Pravinder is very angry. Please hurry."

He heard banging of some sort, hollow and indistinct, then a rustling of material through the receiver. "Tell me where to find you," he said, rummaging around for a scrap of paper.

"Go," Elizabeth had told him, seeing the panic on his face as he hung up the phone. "Don't think. Don't waste time."

The directions were on his dashboard now. He checked them again, then watched intently for the exit, his sweaty palms wrapped around the steering wheel.

But Pravinder had already left when he arrived. Navpreet was positioned stiffly on an expensive-looking suede couch in her living room. Pricy neo-renaissance-like paintings decorated the walls. Knickknacks were arranged throughout—a varnished, wooden camel with a rhinestone on its hump, a jewelry box, an oversized set of dice next to a vase stuffed with artificial silk flowers. A large mirror hung over the fireplace mantel, and a framed picture of Pravinder and Navpreet was on the coffee table.

"You're too late," she said, her mouth set in a sharp line. Her blouse was slightly ruffled, open at the neck, exposing her choke bruises. Her left eye was swollen. "He's gone."

"The drive was long," he replied, focusing his eyes on the sharp, ironed line down the front of her trousers. It made her seem otherwise untouched. Her feet were bare, her toenails red.

"Tea?" she asked with a hint of sarcasm.

"We should go," he told her.

She laughed harshly. "To your place?" Her eyes narrowed knowingly. "To Bapu and Bebe's?"

"You cannot stay here. Pravinder will come back."

She looked as if she was about to refuse, but seeming to think better of it, stood. "Let me get some things."

"How often does he do this?" Darshan asked, shifting his weight from one foot to the other, not wanting to sit.

"Sometimes."

"You never said anything."

"No. I didn't."

She disappeared down a hallway, leaving him to wander about the living room. He found only the one photo of Navpreet and Pravinder. He thought of the family portraits he had hung on the walls in his own home, of Elizabeth's aunts and uncles still in Oregon, of Colleen, Victoria Quinn, Manmohan and Jai, and Sonya. He lifted the picture from the coffee table. Navpreet and Pravinder were outside somewhere, a mountain in the distance. They smiled and held one another, posed. He put the photo down and saw Navpreet's medical school degree reflected in the mirror, hanging near the hallway next to a tall plant.

She returned with a suitcase.

"You finished this year," he said, indicating the degree.

She ignored him and pointed at the bag. "Help me with this."

He shoved the suitcase in the back of the station wagon, then held the door for her before getting in. He started the engine.

"You sure you have everything? We won't come back."

She nodded.

"All right," he replied, heading down the street, turning left toward the highway.

After a moment she pulled the sun visor down. "Pravinder shit on me," she said. "He just wanted a green card, and after that he wanted money."

"Shat," Darshan told her. "Past tense of 'shit.'"

She looked at him, eyes contracted and tight with anger.

He glanced at her apologetically. "Elizabeth told me that. I never knew."

She was suddenly glum. "Livleen is getting married." She prodded the bruises on her neck and winced.

"I know."

"I told her not to do it, not to throw away her beauty and goodness to someone who will never really know her."

"Do you talk to her often?"

"She tells me things."

They were silent for a time. The radio was off. Wind whistled through the edges of the windows.

As they neared Manmohan and Jai's, dusk a heavy purple-orange above them, Navpreet said, "I don't remember his name, the man she will marry."

"Taran," Darshan told her.

She nodded toward the house as they pulled into the driveway. "Bapu picked him for her. How does he know Taran is the right one?"

"Livleen agreed. Maybe she knows it."

Navpreet unbuckled her seatbelt. "She has never said no in her whole life."

Manmohan was reading in the kitchen when they entered the house. He removed his spectacles, eyes widening slightly at the sight of Navpreet's swollen face. Jai was rinsing dishes. A soapy bowl slid from her hands when she saw them.

Livleen looked up from the raw chicken she was massaging with tandoori paste. She released the meat, her hands stained red. "What happened?"

Navpreet pulled out a chair and sat opposite Manmohan. "It has been a very long day."

Jai wiped her hands on a towel. She collected herself, her expression flattening. "Did you leave him?"

Pointing at her face, Navpreet said, "Should I have stayed?"

"He is your husband. If he has ugly teeth, you make yours ugly. If he beats you, you let him."

Her words silenced the room. Manmohan stared at his wife in shock.

"Bebe," Darshan said softly. "She is your daughter."

Livleen paled. She clung to the edge of the counter.

Darshan reached for her.

She put up a hand, refusing his help. "It's nothing."

He regarded her carefully for a moment, conceding this next loss. Exhaling slowly, he went to the wall phone by the refrigerator and dialed home.

"I have to stay for a while," he told Elizabeth.

"I thought you might."

"How are you?"

"The baby kicked. Sonya felt it."

"I missed it."

"He'll kick again, just for you. He knows your voice."

"Does he?"

"Of course he does," she said. "It's okay."

"You'll wait up?"

"I'll be here."

He hung up the receiver and turned to his family. They were looking expectantly at him, his mother offended by the lack of respect so rampant in the lives of younger generations, Manmohan's expression an odd mix of disdain and sorrow, Navpreet's neck bruise darkening, the print of fingers now visible, and Livleen, pallid and frail.

Slowly, he returned to the table and pulled out a chair, the legs chafing along the linoleum. Sitting, he braced himself.

Sacramento's Greyhound Bus Depot
1985

Long fluorescent tubes running overhead on tracks lighted the bus terminal in Sacramento proper, washing out all shades and hues of color, leaving only a pallid surface spotted by shadow. Exposed steel beams supported the rectangular waiting area. In the corner a lone traveler cursed and kicked the vending machine that sold prepackaged snacks, candies, soda pop, and juice boxes. A ticket clerk chewed gum behind his glass-encased booth, snapping small bubbles through his teeth that echoed faintly through the loudspeaker. Manmohan tried his best to ignore the clerk, who had allowed them to use his phone several hours before. He could sense the young man looking at them, watching the old and abandoned Indian couple sitting stiffly in the plastic, cup-bottomed chairs, alone in the night.

Manmohan glanced around, the cold industriousness of the building depressing him. It is no wonder, he thought, how hard we must fight to be Indian here, how critical to uphold our customs: the clothing, the temple and prayers, marriages, the laws of patriarchy. The backdrop of this country is so ugly and barren, erected out of cardboard. It leeches us of our culture. It dilutes us.

Next to him Jai sniffled, a tissue squeezed in her fist, her purse clutched in her lap. He sympathized, but could not offer comfort. They deserved this. They deserved much worse, but she was having trouble accepting it.

In Taran's car, before being left at the depot, she had discerned the raw, barely restrained fury in the atmosphere. "Are we not going home?" she asked over the infant seat where Livleen's baby boy was sleeping, trepidation in her voice. The streets were not familiar, the route back to Berkeley markedly different than the one they had taken to the Sacramento temple.

Livleen said nothing, directing Taran left at the next corner with the flick of her hand.

"Are you sure about this?" Taran murmured to his wife, pulling into the empty parking lot of the Greyhound station. The daylight was thinning, the sky a phosphorescent rose.

"They are not children," she muttered tersely. "Together they have traveled the seas and settled on new continents. It's only a bus depot."

Panic flitted across Jai's face. "What are you d—"

Manmohan reached over the baby for her hand, and with a subtle shake of his head stopped her from protesting further. He looked regretfully at Livleen's handsome profile. Wedding her to Taran had undoubtedly saved her from scrutiny, from the flood of inevitable questions that would have surely descended upon them all if he had allowed such an attractive, eligible daughter to remain unwed. But she had never wanted this life. Since she was eight years old, she had never wanted any life.

They had climbed out of the car in front of the depot with no money, not even change enough for the pay phone inside the bat-beaten, graffiti-tagged booth. They never needed to carry any. Since arriving in America, their children always managed such details, always shuffled them from place to place on command, brought them groceries, settled their medical bills. It seemed, as Manmohan watched Taran drive off, that from the beginning, even as he fought to maintain his authority, he had relinquished much more of himself than he realized. Arm around Jai, back bent, he had led her inside to wait.

Several hours passed before the glass doors to the depot's waiting area finally flung open. Darshan rushed through them, noisily banging them against the inside wall. "Bapu, Bebe," he said, kneeling before them, wiping his mother's cheeks with the sleeve of his shirt. "How did this happen?"

"She left us," Jai said, weeping.

"She made appointments for tea," Manmohan said quietly. "She had friends to visit."

"Why didn't you stop her?"

Manmohan squeezed his cane in both hands, confused by the question. The idea had not occurred to him, but he knew by the surprised and puzzled look on his son's face that this was wrong, entirely out of character. He bowed his head, unable to muster anger, not even to pretend. Instead he was grateful that in Livleen's silent and passive fury, she had finally held him accountable for the thing that ruined and withered her when she was only a little girl. Manmohan again looked up, following the shifts in Darshan's expression, traveling along the filament of emotions from concern to curiosity, followed by protective anger, and finally surrender.

Such a good boy.

~ ~ ~

A man needed a son. Taran had made that intractably clear over two years before that unfortunate night in Sacramento. He sat with Darshan over tea, brother to brother, expounding on the great traditions of India, of men's role in those traditions, making the continuation of their line significant, imperative. "Now that Livleen and I are wed," he said, "my chief priority is to produce at least one descendent who bears my name."

He nodded soberly when, in response, Darshan reiterated the doctor's warnings, the great risks pregnancy would pose to Livleen's life, the childhood trauma of fever that had scarred her heart valves, making her system too weak to subsist under such conditions.

Still, a man needed a son.

"None of you ever told me she might not be able to give me one," Taran replied. "I should be angry about it, but it is too late. I am not a bad man, only a practical one."

Indeed, he had procured from her what was his right by marriage. Darshan thought that this must have been the point at which circumstances had shifted for her, that as her baby grew in her womb, the first seed of revenge also began to blossom. She told him once that even if she were required to suffer marriage, she would prefer to avoid the rest of it. "We all tread the same ground," she had told him. "A cyclical repetition: first marriage, then babies, then grandchildren. None of us ever asks why. Not all of us are meant for it."

Although she was fine in the end, the violence of giving birth—particular to her distressed body—had steeled and discontented her further. Perhaps that experience proved how

473

alone she was, how isolated, that people would do and take what they wanted, that she must learn to do the same. That was the only rational explanation for her behavior, for the streak of spite that came to define her.

On the day of her delivery she had lain in a hospital bed in a disinfected, white-tiled room, machines beeping, her legs swollen and wrapped thickly in gauze, her color gray under the sterile lights, the skin around her eyes and cheeks taut. Taran did not come to her, would not watch. Instead, Darshan sat with her, peering helplessly over the impossible swell of her grossly distended belly. She was sleeping, her face clammy with sweat. The contractions had abated for the moment. Using a wet towel he wiped the beaded moisture from her forehead.

She stirred, her breathing heavy and irregular. Opening her eyes with effort, she lifted a lethargic hand to wipe her mouth and push the damp hair from her forehead. "Where's Taran?" she asked, her tongue thick with thirst.

He searched for a water pitcher, but found none. "On his way," he replied.

"And Navpreet?"

"She's with a patient now but said she will be back soon to check on you. Bapu and Bebe are here. Elizabeth and the kids, too."

She closed her eyes again. "Don't you get enough of this hospital?"

"I don't mind."

He took her hand, but she pulled it away. "What about the restaurant?" she asked, a chill in her voice.

"Closed for the day. I would rather be here."

She looked directly at him then, the fog lifting from her eyes, replaced by a sharp mistrust. "I did not think Bapu would ever give it to you. We all know him. He would not have done it willingly."

Darshan exhaled. "Don't say that. He has never accepted help willingly. But we were both tired of fighting."

She turned away. "Just like that?"

"Not at first, but in the end, 'yes, just like that."

"Navpreet thinks if you persist enough, you can take anything from anyone, if that's how you choose to deal with people." A contraction tensed her body, and she gasped.

"Deep breaths," he murmured, not sure if he should try and touch her again.

I know," she said tetchily, breathing in through her nose and releasing from her mouth.

"Are you all right?"

She held her breath, then nodded and quietly moaned. "Tell Taran not to come in here. I don't need his help."

There was a sharp rap on the door, and it immediately swung inward. Displeased, Navpreet scowled. She held a medical chart and a plastic cup of ice chips. "Darshan, she didn't want anyone in here."

"She was alone."

"Knowing the hospital staff doesn't make it right to ignore Livleen's wishes, or to abuse the rules," she said, setting the chart on the foot of the bed and pulling a stethoscope from around her neck.

As he left, he saw Livleen's face contort in pain and fear, but her contraction was over and another was not due for several more minutes. Navpreet bent over her, stroking her head, murmuring.

Out in the maternity ward waiting room, Elizabeth was dozing in a chair, Anand between her and Jai, head lolling as he fought sleep. He clung to his mother's forearm with one of his meaty five-year-old hands and his grandmother's salwaar with the other. One of Elizabeth's coworkers from radiology had brought cake, and a half-eaten piece of it was on a paper plate in his lap. Sonya, frowning in concentration, sat on the floor where she had ripped up a page of a magazine and was trying to piece it back together. Taran was also there, several seats away, looking apprehensive.

"She is fine," Darshan told him.

Taran nodded, hands clasped in his lap, nervous.

Anand rubbed the sleep from his eyes. Squirming out of his seat, dropping the cake to the floor, he looked up at his father. "Did the baby come?"

"No, son, not yet."

"How much longer?"

"I hope very soon."

Sonya abandoned her puzzle. "Everyone keeps saying that."

Elizabeth threw some napkins on the floor and scooped Anand's mess onto the plate. "Let's go to my office for markers and paper," she suggested, tossing the cake in the trash. "We'll make something for the baby."

She took their hands and led them away as Darshan slumped down into one of the chairs, letting his forearms rest loosely on the plastic armrests. The waiting room was quiet, nearly empty aside from the Toors, with only a young girl in the back row, an older couple one row up from her, and a pregnant woman in a wheelchair waiting to be admitted, her husband beside her. The pregnant woman took deep breaths. The old couple whispered to each other. The girl flipped the pages of a magazine.

A nurse poked her head through the check-in window and called out a name. The girl in the back row stood and followed the nurse. Soft music trailed down from overhead speakers in the ceiling.

476

"I heard it is nearly time," a man said from the doorway, and Darshan turned to see Mohan.

Manmohan rose from his chair. "You cannot be here now. She would not like it."

"I will not leave," Mohan replied, resolutely selecting a seat and lowering his fat body into it. "You cannot banish me from the hospital." He removed his sunglasses and tucked them into his shirt pocket, his tenebrous gaze fixed firmly in front of him.

Darshan gently took his father's elbow, and Manmohan allowed himself to be led to the other side of the room where he remained with Jai, glaring implacably and hatefully at his oldest son.

None of them spoke.

Well into the night, Navpreet finally came out, wearily pulling a surgical cap from her head. She hesitated briefly at seeing Mohan, then said, "A boy. His name is Dhillon Attwal."

Mohan took a sudden and deep breath, coughed once, then cleared his throat, pausing to collect himself. "Thank you," he finally said to no one in particular. He slid his glasses back onto his face and crossed the room. Taking Taran's hand, he murmured his congratulations. And then he left.

When he was gone, Darshan stared thoughtfully at the exit, then shifted his gaze to the maternity ward, remembering a time when he and Livleen were children. One day a swarm of bees had gotten caught in his shorts, a deep, terrifying buzz that stung and tortured his body and droned in his ears. She had laughed at him, at his flailing arms, his dance of desperation as he tried to shake them off.

It had begun with a race.

"It is a fair challenge," he told her, assessing the winding path down the hill. It was one of those rare days when she came outside, when the residual aches in her bones from the fever that had almost taken her life abated enough to let her play.

"You know I cannot run very fast." She smiled, as though she had already agreed to give it a try, as though she already knew she would win.

"Of course you can. I have seen you."

Her smile widened, and she nodded. "Okay."

"Okay," he replied eagerly, rubbing his palms together. "No prisoners!"

Grabbing the folds of her sundress, Livleen kicked off her sandals. "I'm ready."

"To the river!"

"To the river!"

"One…two…three…go!"

Taking off down the path, Darshan could see the corrugated iron roof of the main house below and his father's garden of taro and onion in neat, planted rows, his memory now alive with detail; glimpses of the sparkling water through the foliage; the shadows of coconut trees; the fresh, dark mud squeezing between his toes. She had been in the lead, her two braids streaming like black, glossy ribbons behind her, tails like whips. She turned her head to look back at him.

Laughing, he ducked into the thick ferns and wild greenery to cut straight down. "That's cheating!" he heard her shout. He leapt over fallen tree limbs and trampled through the underbrush. And then he felt something soft tear under his feet. A sudden angry vibration erupted from the ground, something like smoke circling him in dark tornado-like flashes.

He recalled his desperate swatting, his pumping legs, sprinting no longer to win the race, but to outrun the hive of bees he had disturbed. Trapped at the bank of the river, he began to jump like a feverish monkey, but still the bees swirled about with their discordant, incensed hum. In the distance, Livleen turned the corner around a bend in the path to find him whooping in the air and thrashing about.

She cupped her hands over her mouth to call to him, but he was not able to hear her, his ears filled with a rush of adrenaline. As she came nearer, he realized that she was laughing hysterically. She clutched her stomach and sank to the ground, unable to control herself, to contain that tumultuous outpouring of mirth.

"Help me!" he shouted.

"Take off your shorts!" she called out again, wiping her eyes, unwilling to come too close. "Jump in the river!"

As he threw off his clothes, she laughed harder at his naked bum covered in red fire-burning welts. Jumping, still swatting the air, he crashed into the water, the chaos finally silenced.

"Cheater," she had said with a grin when he surfaced, his topknot undone and his long hair matted around his face.

No, he thought now. That day of the race, of the bees, *that* was the start of her withdrawal, the day she had begun to amass and harbor animosity. He suddenly knew this because he realized it was the last time she played, the last time he saw her laugh. She had been eight years old. There was a fire in the main house that night, and after, something had changed, for all of them.

~ ~ ~

The question remained unasked. It drifted above them, in what they would not say, caught behind boundaries of privacy and secrecy. Manmohan had seen the question, poised on Darshan's lips before being swallowed back down. He regarded his son. So haggard with apprehension for his parents. He wondered how much the boy knew, about the night of the fire, about Penitentiary Hill, about the reason why Livleen had left them here, so many hours from home.

Looking over again at the vending machine in the corner of the bus depot, he felt a rumble in his stomach, suddenly ravenous for one of those over-salted snacks, a bag of peanuts, perhaps a cracker sandwich filled with chemical cheese spread. Closing his eyes, he felt shame for this craving.

He longed for a meal prepared by Livleen. She possessed a clever skill with food, flavors strumming new points along his tongue. He would never admit this, not even to her. He had only to say the words, to tell her this one true and beautiful thing, but he could not. He would break, would choke upon his own greatly confused emotions for her.

When they spoke, he never said much and was always grim.

~ ~ ~

Elizabeth had been more aware of Livleen's growing unhappiness than Darshan. "She doesn't want to see us," his wife told him a few months after Dhillon's birth, assessing her reflection in the mirror. She held a brooch up to her salwaar, flicking her fingers through her short bangs, trying to give them life. Dissatisfied, she dropped the brooch in her jewelry box on the bureau and bit the inside of her cheek, thinking.

"Of course she does," Darshan replied, selecting a tie from a rack behind the bathroom door. "She's making us lunch."

"They had a little party last month, for Dhillon. Your parents and Navpreet. His six-month party. That's how long it's been."

"I spoke with my mom," Darshan murmured, his brow pinched as he knotted his tie. "It wasn't exactly a party."

"They had balloons. A cake." She selected a pair of earrings, cocking her head to the side, slipping one on.

He ran a comb through his hair. "She's making lunch. She hasn't canceled."

"No, not today. A person can only cancel so many times."

He handed Elizabeth her coat, then called out to the kids.

There was the sound of a scuffle down the hall, a game hurriedly being finished.

"She isn't the same," Elizabeth told him. "She's a mother now. She's angry."

"It's a lot to handle for some," Darshan replied, heading upstairs, checking his pocket for his car keys.

Forty-five minutes later they rounded the corner onto Livleen and Taran's street. Ahead, a car pulled out of his sister's driveway and came towards them. As it passed, Darshan saw Navpreet through the lightly tinted windows, her sunglasses on, rummaging for something in the middle console. She lifted her head, gripping the steering wheel with both hands, but did not look their way. The sun glinted off her lipstick. Irritated, he watched her through his rearview mirror as she disappeared around the corner. She had seen them, he knew.

Taran opened the door. His smile was wide, exaggerated. He shook Darshan's hand, awkwardly patting Elizabeth on the shoulder, inviting them in. Darshan turned his head toward the scent of garlic and chili coming from the kitchen. The children ran off to the nursery where Dhillon was playing in a pen.

Livleen poked her head through the kitchen entrance, forced a smile, then untied the knot of her apron and greeted them in the living room. She allowed both Darshan and Elizabeth to embrace her, but her back was stiff, unresponsive. "Would you like something to drink?" she asked, tossing the apron on the loveseat. "A pot of tea is ready."

"Thank you," Darshan nodded.

"I'll help," Elizabeth said, following Livleen toward the kitchen.

"No, I'll only be a minute."

She returned with a tray of mugs, a bowl of sugar cubes at the center. She put the tray on the coffee table but did not pass the mugs around.

"We saw Navpreet leaving," Darshan said, dunking two cubes into a cup and handing it to Elizabeth.

"Yes," Livleen murmured.

"I'm sorry she wasn't able to stay for lunch."

"She had to work."

Taran reached for a mug. "Speaking of, I hear Kaiser has promoted you," he said to Darshan. "Navpreet says you head the lab now."

Darshan nodded. "I suppose it was inevitable."

"I am surprised you have time to run the lab," Livleen said.

He smiled ruefully. "I had to make time." He winked at Elizabeth, playful. "The kids and the wife are expensive, difficult to keep satisfied."

Livleen reclined into the sofa cushions, her lips twisted in a slightly mocking smile. "How can that be? There has never been a long-term vacancy at Howard, and Navpreet tells me the restaurant has been full. Perhaps you should consider lightening your burdens."

Darshan looked at her in astonishment, taken aback by the implication. Her eyes flicked toward Taran who wordlessly stirred his tea.

"Now wait a minute," Elizabeth said.

Darshan gently touched his wife's forearm to quiet her.

The room was momentarily silent. They could hear the kids

laughing through the baby monitor.

"Is that what you think?" Darshan asked. "That I take Howard money, that the restaurant is suddenly profitable after Bapu signed it over?"

She did not answer him.

"Howard does not belong to me," he told her, straining to speak softly, conscious of the children. "And you saw what Bapu did to the restaurant. It will never be what it could have been. We're just trying to pull it out of the mess he buried it under."

"It could have been something," she said in a flat, monotone voice. "I could have made it something."

Taken aback, he did not understand her meaning.

"My food is better than Bebe's," she said.

His heart ached with sudden remorse. Helplessly, he looked at her. In this house, under this suburban roof only a mile from Manmohan and Jai, shared with a husband who could not see her and a son she did not wish for, held up by walls that would never display diplomas or doctorate degrees in her name, her pulse had slowed and no one noticed.

A timer bell dinged in the kitchen, and she stood. They waited for her, not speaking, listening to the chink of a metal pot lid as it was placed on the ceramic-tiled counter. The smell of bean curry grew stronger—a savory aroma of onion, cloves, coriander, a hint of ginger—the air now spiced and buttery.

A chef. Better than Jai.

~ ~ ~

Golden streamers crisscrossed overhead, from lamppost to lamppost. They swayed and glittered brilliantly over the masses of Sikhs parading the street toward the Sacramento temple.

Flanking the crowd were two unbroken lines of stalls in which families labored to prepare and sell food. Women sweated within them while rolling out dough for roti, flour caked up to their elbows. Their daughters tossed vegetables about in pans, stirring up clouds of humidity containing oil and masala mix. Their husbands stood out front, soliciting customers, holding aloft paper plates of Indian delicacies. Farther down the line, farmers shoved long green sticks of raw sugarcane through a large, industrial press, squeezing out sweet, green water for sale. Children clambered, reaching for cups, begging their fathers for money.

In the center of the street, the crowd parted in awe for a group of men issuing sonorous battle cries. The men whirled stealthily, spinning their swords, circling each other warily. Each appeared so much like the Hindu god Shiva dancing to the tune of destruction and creation within his ring of steel weaponry. People cheered, mouths full of samosas and pakoras. After a time the men slowed their pace, finally halting. They turned to face their admirers, bowed. Merely an act, a memory of India, a memory of war and self-preservation, of grace. A spring festival to mark the heritage of Sikh fighting prowess. The martial art, gatka, was not needed, not anymore, not here.

Closer to the temple, the priest could be heard over the speakers, kirtans now modernized, the holy scripture of the gurus extending beyond the prayer hall to the thousands on the street. Inside, the temple was slowly beginning to fill. Junker Singh listened to the priest, dreamily, Sonya on one hip, Anand on the other. "You do not need to understand the words," he told them when they asked what the priest was saying. "Just listen to the music of it. Goodness can often be encouraged by a beautiful rhythm." They stroked his beard.

"You'll hurt yourself," Elizabeth told the mechanic.

"They've sprung up like trees," he replied as he released the children, smiling. He pulled some bills from his pocket, sending them off into the crowd. "Stay together. Bring back sweets for your mother."

"You be back in five minutes," Darshan shouted after them.

Elizabeth lowered her eyes as several women walked past toward the prayer hall. They contemptuously stared at her, observing her salwaar kameez.

"A meaningless, self-important game of theirs," Junker Singh said, looking at Elizabeth. "It cannot be easy."

"Will it ever change?" she asked.

"I think not," the mechanic replied with regret. "Indians on the whole prefer not to evolve, prefer that in your own country you not be here to offend the purity of the customs we imported."

"We'll go soon," Darshan told her. "Eat something, then go."

Junker Singh peered into the prayer hall. "I am off now, to find my wife." He shook his head regretfully as he stepped away. "She feeds me so well I can no longer sit on the floor. I have to sit in a chair and avoid meeting eyes with older men in much better shape than I whose wives unjustly deprive them of good food."

Darshan grinned as the old man stepped away, his smile weakening when he saw Livleen and Taran at the hall's entrance. Elizabeth looked sadly at Dhillon clinging to Livleen's leg. "So big," she said softly.

"We should say hi," Darshan told her.

"We don't have to."

"She's my sister." He moved through the crowd toward the

hall.

Taran's face brightened in a superficially warm welcome. "Darshan," he said cheerfully.

Livleen glanced away, shifting her weight from one leg to the other.

"Thank you for bringing Bapu and Bebe," Darshan told her.

"I don't need to be thanked," she replied.

"I suppose not," he murmured. "Are they inside?"

She nodded.

Sonya and Anand returned with their sweets. Anand was upset.

"Hey," Sonya protested as the boy shoved her.

"Kids," Elizabeth said sharply.

Livleen turned her stolid gaze directly to Darshan. "You did not tell us you were selling the restaurant."

"It was time."

"Does Bapu know?"

"Of course."

Sonya was crying. "Mommy. Tell Anand to stop hitting me."

Elizabeth bent to face the children. "Both of you," she said. "Behave."

"And the money?" Taran asked.

Darshan shook his head. "Money?"

"From the sale."

"We were in debt. I paid it all off. There is no money."

"Taran," Livleen said, lifting Dhillon up onto her hip. "I am hungry." She indicated the langar hall where lunch was being served.

"Mommy," Sonya said, still crying. "I *was* being *hayve*."

Elizabeth sighed and kneeled to wipe the girl's face.

Livleen pushed through the crowd, her body rigid with fury, Taran close behind. And then Darshan spotted Navpreet standing at the mouth of the langar hall, waiting, craning her neck as she searched the crowd. She relaxed when she saw Livleen nearing. Her eyes then met Darshan's. She smiled at him, gave a slight patronizing wave before disappearing with Livleen into the hall.

He did not see either of them again that day. In the evening, after the three-hour-long drive home from Sacramento, he received a call from a clerk at the Greyhound bus depot.

~ ~ ~

Manmohan again looked away from Darshan. The man who had kicked the vending machine now sat, grudgingly eating a bag of nuts. Manmohan slowly surveyed the waiting area, stopping at the ticket clerk who openly stared at them, curious, his mouth frozen mid chew, a nugget of gum pinched between his front teeth. "It is late," the old man said. "We should go. It is a long way home."

Darshan nodded, reaching for his mother's hand. Jai allowed herself to be helped out of her chair, momentarily leaning into his chest, murmuring repeatedly, "She left us, she left us."

Manmohan stiffened, offended by her sniveling, his earlier sympathy spent. "Stop it," he said tersely. "Stop it."

She froze, then straightened, resolutely wiping her face with the back of her hand.

He rose on his own, refusing assistance. A small piece of weatherworn paper fluttered to the floor from his lap. Darshan bent to retrieve it. Manmohan took it from him, catching his son's surprise at seeing what was on it, the faded scratch of handwriting, the scribble of Darshan's phone number.

Face blank, eyes hooded, Manmohan tucked it away into the front of his flannel coat before leading the way outside to the car.

Manmohan's Garden
1993–1994

Vehicles were like children, Junker Singh had once told Darshan, fondly regarding one of his motorcycles, just restored. He ignited the engine and pulled on the throttle. It revved, eager to move. They required constant, devoted care, the mechanic said, a stroke of the gears for encouragement, a whisper of reassurance for better performance and faster speed, to excel beyond their capacity. They were fed oil and petrol, nutrient rich, like vegetables for the body. They gleamed with metallic skin that soon became scraped and bruised with play. They were a salvation. They freed the heart.

He had propped Darshan on the saddle of that bike, clapping the boy on the back with a rough hand before lovingly sending him down the unpaved Fijian road. But bikes did not engender the same sentimentality for Darshan, who in his fear steered, despite his best efforts, directly into a trench, bending one of the handles as he crashed through the underbrush of the jungle, snapping off the mirror and tearing a gash in the seat.

Laughing his way down the trench slope, Junker Singh had cried out as if to the trees themselves, "I wish I could still ride! I wish I could take you myself, boy!" Yanking Darshan up, he slapped the dust off the young man's trousers, checking for broken bones, examining a wound along a cheek downy soft with the first signs of a beard. Looking at the damaged bike with tremendous satisfaction, he had nodded. "Now it has new life in it."

So long ago. Darshan regarded his hands, discerning a trace of wrinkles forming on the back, so many lifetimes removed from his childhood, from that day of his first and only ride. He raised his head and gazed before him at the sickroom in which Junker Singh now lay, patiently waiting for death.

Beside him Manmohan stood, afflicted by an animal fear. The mechanic's wife had lit incense from a local Turkish shop. The smell infused the hallway. Downstairs, a loop of a kirtan played on the tape deck, the volume low, the priest's chanting voice somber.

"He was not always fat," Manmohan muttered tightly, hunched over, eyes cowled. "He was thin and flat, rode his bike like a dancer." He retreated from the door, giving ground to his dread.

Jai slipped her hand into her husband's, murmuring softly to him. Manmohan listened to her, but his face sagged with remorse and still he did not move.

"He asked for you, Bapu," Darshan said gently, taking his father's arm, feeling the seventy-seven-year-old bones beneath the flannel coat.

"He thinks he knows what is coming," Manmohan replied irritably, looking helplessly at the bedroom door. "He always thinks he knows everything."

Darshan turned the knob, and Manmohan exhaled,

readying himself.

There were no shades or curtains on the windows, only several holes in the sheetrock where a set of blinds had once been screwed in. The room was bright with direct sunlight, casting Junker Singh's body, slightly thinner now, in a pastel hue of yellow-white. The mechanic gazed contentedly outside at the thick cotton clouds, at the lime green of the tree leaves. The room had been recently aired and smelled fresh. Several pill bottles were lined tidily next to a glass of water on the nightstand. The old man smiled when the Toors entered, squinting against the sun.

Manmohan's demeanor changed. Gathering courage, he bent to kiss his friend's forehead.

Junker Singh lightly traced the tips of his fingers over his brow where Manmohan's lips had brushed the skin. "You are becoming too indulgent," the mechanic said, his voice no longer booming, but still powerful in its undercurrent.

"Nothing is ever serious," Manmohan said. A crack of a smile broke through his stonily pursed lips.

"That is precisely it," Junker Singh replied, also smiling. He then looked beyond his friend at Jai.

"We will come again next week," she told him.

"Yes, I would like that."

She nodded, refusing to cry, taking Manmohan's arm and leading him out of the room.

Junker Singh lifted his age-spotted hand to point at some coins on his bedside table. "Give those to Sonya and Anand," he told Darshan.

"They will say they are too old for coins," Darshan replied in amusement.

Unruffled, the mechanic lowered his hand onto the duvet. "We both know they are not."

Darshan laughed softly, then covered his mouth in apology.

Junker Singh grinned, a bit drowsily. "Do not worry so much, boy. You should always laugh. If it were you down here, I would be laughing."

Smiling, Darshan gathered the coins. "Do you remember that bike?" he asked. "The one I rode?"

The mechanic chuckled, eyelids drooping. "I remember everything."

It was all he said. Tired, he fell asleep, the rise and fall of his chest calm and steady, like an idling engine waiting for the kick of the throttle that would hurl it down the jungle road. Later that evening Junker Singh died in his sleep, his face toward the sliver of moonlight that cut through the glass of his un-curtained window.

~ ~ ~

The garden moved. Worms shifted through the soil, burrowing small holes. Creaks and rustles came from the trees. An apple fell, thudding to the earth. Birds broke from the branches, a flurry of wings, a crash of leaves. The Saturday morning air in Berkeley was bitter, but fresh and calm as the sun peered over the hill beyond the house, promising a day of warmth. Sitting in the shade on a wooden bench along the stucco wall of his parents' house, Darshan shivered as the line of sun inched across the cement patio.

The sliding screen door scraped along its tracks as Manmohan shoved it aside with his cane. He glanced sidelong at his son as he came outside, securing the screen shut against flies. "You are here early today," he said, unraveling the watering hose.

"Fence needs mending," Darshan replied.

"And the others?"

"Elizabeth took Sonya and Anand to see Victoria."

Manmohan twisted the knob on the faucet and swung the hose around, using his thumb to partially stopper the water, generating a spray that he waved over the strawberries. "Sonya tells me she wants to write a book." He seemed to find the notion deeply gratifying.

Unsettled, Darshan flipped a metal bucket upside down and propped his feet on it. "She is sixteen," he replied, as if her age justified his displeasure with the idea.

Manmohan dropped the hose, which continued to run in the mud. He did not respond. Using his cane, he shook a branch of his almond tree. A number of pods fell, splattering in the saturated soil.

"The world requires something different of her," Darshan continued, trying to explain. "Something more sensible."

Manmohan gestured toward the almonds. "Not a good crop this year."

Removing his feet from the bucket, Darshan brought the pale to the edge of the patio to gather the nuts. He settled them carefully at the bottom.

"In Fiji I grew cucumbers," Manmohan said, turning away from the tree. He shuffled slowly toward the bench, sitting with tired relief, his eyes closing momentarily as his muscles settled into position. "At the old house."

Darshan wiped his muddy fingers on his trousers, waiting for his father to continue.

The old man scratched a mosquito bite on his wrist. He was quiet for a time, then reached out a hand. Darshan placed several almonds on his palm.

"You remind me so much of someone," Manmohan said quietly. He peeled open a pod and removed a soft, white almond. He gazed at it for a moment, then placed it on his tongue, chewed slowly.

"Bapu," Darshan said, sitting beside his father, believing that he understood. "We all miss Junker Uncle."

Manmohan flinched slightly as if he had been wrenched out of a dream. The sun inched its way over the toes of their sneakered feet. The birds continued to chatter, to flit from branch to branch. "Let that girl of yours be," he said, his voice now gruff, cantankerous. "Whatever intellect you have came from books. It has to start somewhere. Let it begin with her."

~ ~ ~

Darshan loosened his tie to let the sweaty skin of his neck breathe. The emergency room lights were an angry, white glare. A stack of unfinished paperwork lay on his desk in his office down in the lab. He had rushed away after receiving the panicked call from his mother. He checked his watch. He had found it not long ago, forgotten in a box where he had put it some years before. Manmohan's watch. Although it no longer worked he pressed it to his ear, listening, waiting.

A gurney finally pushed through from outside, his father so small on the wheeled stretcher, surrounded by the bustling emergency crew, mouth and nose swallowed by an oxygen mask. Jai scurried after, her eyes wide and bloodshot, her chuni dragging on the ground. She had discovered Manmohan facedown on the floor next to his bed, staring paralyzed and helpless at the cream-colored fibers of their carpet, guttural noises coming from the back of his throat as he tried to call for help.

A stroke.

~ ~ ~

It had happened on a Wednesday, or so Darshan thought. He was not entirely certain. Isolating the day gave him a sense of order, calmed his groping, rattled mind. "What would you like to do?" the doctors had asked him, friends of his from the hospital. "There will come a time—soon—when his body will stop and the machines will do all the work for him," they said. "When that time comes, what would you like us to do?"

"Keep him alive," Navpreet said when Darshan reported the news to the family. They had gathered in Manmohan and Jai's living room. It was hot, the day unseasonably warm. A desert-like air smelling of rotting pomegranate filtered through the sliding screen door. "I am a doctor," she insisted. "There are options. I know the data."

Livleen stayed silent, focusing her attention outside where the garden sweltered under the sun, where the tree leaves curled inward, desperate for shade.

"Yes, keep him alive," Mohan agreed. Someone had called him to that meeting, had invited him to participate. He paced, tyrannically shuffling his fat paunch about the room in a show of renewed clout, the eldest able-bodied male. "Bapu would want to stay alive."

Darshan listened to them mull over the predicament, his attention weakening as he followed Livleen's gaze toward the garden. *What would you like us to do?* The doctors would not ask Livleen or Mohan, who had no authority to make such a decision. They had already approached Jai, who had indicated she was incapable of determining the fate of the person who had always directed hers. They would not even ask Navpreet, because although they worked with her, they did not know her well enough despite—or because of—her many spurious attempts to endear herself to them, not taking well to her brusque manner with patients, her inhospitable superiority in matters of medicine. There was only him.

"Sit. Please," Darshan asked his brother, fatigued, needled by the pacing, by the attempt to assert himself as family head after years of being the deplorable son who had roused so much hostility.

Mohan had gone to the hospital just after the stroke, had entered the room, disturbing the reverent quiet during Darshan's watch.

Pallid and gray, folding his sunglasses away in his shirt pocket, Mohan tentatively approached the bed. Unable to speak or move, Manmohan was forced to stare up at the ceiling. The room smelled thickly of antiseptic cleaner. Machines hummed and beeped.

"He is weak," Darshan told his brother. "Do not upset him."

"Bapu," Mohan breathed. "Bapu, it is Mohan."

Manmohan averted his eyes.

"What can I do, Bapu? Please, let me do something."

The old man whispered faintly. Mohan bent, listening hard, a fragile hope softening his face.

"No," Manmohan said more audibly. Voice cracked and parched, he again repeated himself. "No."

Agitated, the old man closed his eyes, moisture brimming at his lash line. Without thinking Darshan placed his warm palm on the crown of his father's turban-less head to protect the soft, cold skin, feeling somehow responsible.

Mohan had begun to quietly weep, murmuring over and over, "I will do anything. I will do anything," until Darshan led him out of the room, forcing him to leave.

Looking at his siblings now—at Navpreet fanning herself in

the hot room, at Livleen sitting stiffly, sweat at her brow, at Mohan who had stopped pacing to grudgingly lean against the open sliding glass door—Darshan locked eyes with each of them, full of angst.

"I do not want him to suffer pain, or shame," Jai finally said, standing, closing the discussion. She approached Darshan, placed an affectionate arm around his waist. So short next to him, he found himself pulling her head close to his chest like he often did with Sonya.

From where she sat on the sofa, Navpreet glared at him with outrage.

~ ~ ~

"It's time," the physician said across the line as Darshan held the receiver to his ear.

The bedroom was dark. The clock read 2:57. Heart beating, he switched on his night-table lamp.

"We need a decision."

Reaching out across the mattress for Elizabeth, Darshan placed a hand on her back, glad the ringing had not startled her awake. She stirred slightly, then stilled.

"Nothing," he said into the phone. "Just let him go."

~ ~ ~

He strummed his fingers on the ship-hatch table, a relic from the Lion of India now repurposed in his parents' kitchen, its heavy iron legs settled into indentations in the linoleum. The lacquered surface was scratched, beginning to yellow at the edges where cracks had formed. A bowl of plums sat in the center, the fruit overripe. He palmed one, the skin delicate, the meat beneath tender. Pressing his thumb into the fruit, the skin caved, and a trickle of juice ran down the side of his hand, dripping off his wrist and onto the table. His family wordlessly watched him. Across from him Navpreet frowned, and Taran, next to Livleen, shook his head in disgust.

Elizabeth reached behind her for a spool of paper towels on the counter. She tore off a perforated section, folded it in half and wiped away the juice from both the table and Darshan's hand. She took the plum from him, used her fingers to tear it in half and pry out the pit. She folded a clean paper towel and put the halves on it, then slid it over to Jai. Absently, Jai lifted a half to her mouth and sucked some of the juice. She wearily dropped the plum back onto the napkin and turned her stony gaze upon Mohan, who was leaning against the refrigerator.

"There is no point to this," Navpreet said, backing out her chair, threatening to stalk off.

"We will fly his ashes back to Barapind," Mohan said decisively. "Open a school in his name."

At this sudden proposal, Navpreet remained seated. Slowly she pulled her chair closer to the table.

Seemingly taken with the idea, Taran deferentially nodded his approval. Livleen, face drawn and sunken from lack of sleep, passively laced her fingers together in her lap.

Jai looked down at the mutilated plum in front of her. "Why?" she asked quietly, her voice flat.

"Because education was important to him," Mohan replied with a hint of censure.

She tensed, turning to him.

Chastened, he scowled with embarrassment. "He was my father. It is my duty to make this decision."

With a bleak, unblinking stare, she said evenly, "Darshan

will get the ashes. He will make the arrangements."

Navpreet stood abruptly, her wooden chair falling backward, hitting the linoleum with a dull, heavy blow. She glanced around the table, affronted, the grey hairs at the roots close to her temples more visible under the kitchen light. She took a breath, put her hands to her abdomen as if trying to bridle her rage. "I am a doctor," she said. "I could have saved him. We," she pointed to Livleen and Mohan, "wanted to save him. We should now at least be allowed to properly voice how best to put him to rest."

Elizabeth, who understood very little Punjabi, raised her eyebrows at the aggression in Navpreet's tone.

Darshan sighed, reached for another plum.

Jai clenched her teeth, jaw muscles flexing. She ignored her daughter, who stood for several impatient moments waiting for a response. "Take some apples before you leave," she told them all, gazing outside the bay window behind the kitchen sink. Fruit from the garden was scattered thickly beneath the trees in the mud, beginning to decay.

~ ~ ~

Dry grit caked the wooden handle of his father's old trowel. It grated against Darshan's palm as he tightened his grip, allowing the splinters and grains to dig into his skin. He swung it feebly in front of him, like a sword, then jabbed it into the ground at the base of the almond tree, loosening the soil that was drying without water. Striking the earth eased the beating of his heart, the oppressive quiet of his mind. He jabbed it down again, and again, leaving a number of half moons in the dirt.

The murmured noises of mourners inside the house

sounded so remote to him from out here. He turned to peer through the sliding glass door, trying to discern if his brother was still inside, hoping Mohan had gone home already. With a mix of frustration and revulsion, he again stabbed the earth with the trowel, picturing his brother repeatedly accosting the posed form of their dead father with a spritz bottle of perfume. Every few minutes Mohan would rise from the front row to spray the body, interrupting the line of mourners paying their respects before the scheduled cremation. After tucking away the bottle, his brother would then snap his handkerchief in the air before wiping his nose, whispering, "Waheguru, waheguru."

Darshan shut his eyes, haunted by the alien look of the embalmed body, the combed and net-tucked beard, the dark blue turban, the stretched skin of his father's cheeks and hands. It disturbed him now to think that he had once cut open bodies, had sutured their organs, had searched within them for diseases and causes of death. Looking into the casket, he had found himself wondering who had examined Manmohan's organs and what they had discovered. Perhaps the unnatural bend of the old man's spine had revealed something deeper, something in the ligaments and joints, like the patriarchal pressure he had always applied to his children, the uncertainty and discomfort he had caused them all. Perhaps the unsaid approval that Darshan had always hoped to hear from his father after bearing that pressure were stored away and hidden in the folds of tissue and organs and in the marrow of his bones.

A small ivory comb had rested on his father's chest, the one Manmohan used to comb his hair before growing bald. In Fiji he had run it through his tangles in the mornings as a matter of routine, flipping his head forward to get to the back strands, biting the comb in his teeth while briskly twisting his hair into a tight bun, finishing by shoving the prongs into his topknot before wrapping his turban. Darshan had watched him, had learned. Mohan, frantic for one small victory, had insisted it be cremated with the body. Grieving, aggravated with the incessant pestering, Jai had permitted it.

Darshan let the trowel fall to the ground and clapped his palms clean. He loosened his arms, allowing them to dangle at his sides. The pull on his shoulders felt good, a reminder of gravity, of the laws of nature. He surveyed the setting sun. The hills beyond the backyard were golden fire.

"Dad?" Sonya said from behind him.

Relieved to see her, he smiled. "Come."

She stood beside him, their arms touching as the sun deepened in color to an ochreous orange. After a time she gave him a piece of paper.

He unfolded it, read the brief note. "UCLA," he said without enthusiasm.

"I got it today. A bit of good news."

"What about Berkeley?"

She sighed, discouraged. "That's Anand's dream."

"It's a very good school."

"I need to see more of the world."

"LA is not the world, Sonya. It's just LA."

She took the acceptance letter from him, refolded it.

"Who will help me with Howard Street when you're gone?" he asked.

She did not answer.

"Maybe Anand," he murmured.

She glanced at him briefly, mildly surprised. Then her expression changed. She suddenly seemed drawn and older than seventeen.

He touched her face, nodding toward the house. "Your

grandmother needs help putting away the food. I'll be in soon."

She wordlessly turned and strode back to the house, kicking an old apple core on the patio before disappearing inside.

The sun vanished behind the hill, leaving behind a gaseous trail of color. Elizabeth called to him through the open kitchen window. "Darshan, can you please bring some foil in from the garage?"

He waved, nodding, going around the side of the house.

A chill rose from the concrete floor as he entered the garage. Weaving his way through years of accumulated boxes, two-liter soda crates, and canned goods, he found an industrial-sized roll of foil on a workman's table toward the back. There were several rusted garden tools spread out on its surface, as well as a roll of twine and several glass jars of seeds at the back edge by the wall. He ran his hand over the tools, like smoothing out dunes of sand, the tools shifting and clanking, giving way under his palm, melting into the table, everything undulating.

He blinked.

"Do you need help?" Mohan asked. His brother had come in through the kitchen, had propped open the door.

Darshan pulled his eyes from the tools. "No, I can manage."

"Hand it to me," Mohan insisted. "I will take it."

Gripping the roll under his arm, Darshan shook his head.

Brow creased, his brother said more forcefully, "Let me help."

"There is no point now."

Mohan winced, then shook his fist with rage. Voice loud and furious, he said, "You owe me your respect."

Jai rushed to the doorway. "What is this?" she said, pushing past Mohan. "What are you doing?"

"Bebe," Mohan said, "I want to help."

She glanced from him to the roll under Darshan's arm. "It is only foil," she replied.

He regarded her momentarily, and for one second, as he leaned over, seemed about to kneel before her. Instead he called to his family, to Lehna, to Dal, and to the recently married Amandev and her husband. Pushing the button to open the sectional garage door, which grated upward on its gears, he said, "I will not ever come back."

It was a simple statement of fact, and it was clear that he hoped she would contradict him. But she did not. When he was outside next to his car, shuffling the family into their seats, she pressed the button, waiting until the sectional door touched the ground, then asked Darshan for the foil.

~ ~ ~

Darshan flipped the latch to unlock the sliding glass door to the patio. The leftover food was packed away, some of it sent home with guests, and the house had been tidied. The day was gone and inside was lit with the soft glow of lamps, making his reflection in the glass mirror-like against the darkness outside. He momentarily stared at himself, at his sunken eyes and graying, neatly trimmed beard. He pushed his hair back, noticing for the first time that his hairline was receding. Sliding the door to the left with a faint grinding in the track, he then pushed aside the screen and stepped into the cold night. The moon cast a dim glow on the leaves of Manmohan's many trees. He took a deep, slow breath.

The priest who had presided over the service knocked politely behind him.

"Bhaiji," Darshan said, nodding at the priest. "I thought you had left with the others."

The priest shrugged as if to say *not yet*. "The smell is wonderful, isn't it? It is not quite the same as in India, but still, the scent of earth is familiar and comforting."

There was a dullness in Darshan's mind, a lack of emotion. "He provided a great deal of care and attention to this garden."

"Do you regret that?"

Darshan mutely shook his head, finding the question odd.

The priest made a general, broad gesture toward the garden and the house. "He told me how hard you worked, what you did."

"Did he?"

The priest nodded.

Darshan lowered his chin to his chest, his throat suddenly tight and painfully contracted. Directly beneath him, by the light inside, he could see several small wet circular marks darkening the cement patio, like light, fresh rain.

The Return of the Moneylender
2000

The house in Berkeley had settled into a pervasive quiet, broken only by the breath and hum of the old lady who dwelled there. During her youth in India, generations had cohabited under mud hut roofs, the elderly soothed by the bustle of family, by tradition and community. But not here. Not in America, where the Toors had been scattered across a vast network of modern cities by their accumulated wealth, believing themselves risen from and superior to the days of austerity and simplicity that had ruled their lives in the village.

Anomalous activity sprouted from the silence of that house, the senses muddled, Jai's seventy-nine-year-old mind confused. Knitting sticks in the laundry hamper, tucked into a pair of her dead husband's tube socks. A one-pound bag of flour on the shelf behind the television. Sofa cushions restuffed with folded blankets and bed pillows. Dirty mixing spoons in the utensil drawer. Fruit from Manmohan's garden found rotting in the farthest reaches of the bathroom cupboard. All forgotten. This was how it began. When her children came to visit, she would on occasion surprise them by inadvertently happening upon these items during moments of lucidity, gaping at the objects with apologetic tears when they questioned her about them, then suddenly chuckling in amusement, waving a dismissive hand.

But then there were other things, valuables surreptitiously secreted away, as if from fear. Family photos. Jewelry. A set of house keys. Bundles of Howard Street rent money. "I want only cash," Jai had told Darshan after Manmohan's death. "Because where will you be if I need it?" And he could not argue because she had once been left with nothing at a Greyhound bus depot. She meticulously wrapped everything in cellophane, then foil, then bathroom hand towels before expertly concealing them around the house. And soon these too were forgotten, erased from her memory.

The loss of her possessions stirred Jai's rage, provoking a powerful suspicion against others, a narrowing of the eyes. "Someone has stolen from me," she told Darshan in a low growl. She had then glanced about, eyes suddenly clearing, expression now worried. "I have lost my keys."

For a time none of them did anything, believing Jai's developing eccentricities were the natural result of old age. She was otherwise in exceedingly good health, mobile and relatively agile for her years. They left her alone during the day while at work, calling frequently but not often stopping by except on Saturdays for a weekly trip to the gurdwara, or when Darshan needed to mend something. Distances were too great across the Bay Area, traffic maddening. This was before any of them appreciated the significance of Jai's peculiarities. They did not know—not even Darshan, who was the first, though too late, to finally understand—that six years of loneliness had entirely unraveled her, had forced her to invent a new world of circumstances in which she was no longer the invisible, assiduous backbone of her family, but weak and frail and in need of rescue, of everyday bustle, of constant company.

~   ~   ~

The yoga mat was well padded, a defense against the cold of Manmohan and Jai's concrete garage floor where Darshan had managed to clear some space. He sat upon the mat as if on a pontoon, a vessel to safety as the sea of archived possessions—stacked high and in all directions—threatened to capsize on him. Many were in unopened boxes as if just purchased: a camping tent, an LED-lit vanity mirror bought in the early eighties, a handheld vibrating back massager, a VHS machine, a mini tape recorder. On the lower shelves he had found an entire set of dumbbells, cloth for tailoring suits, spare sets of silverware and dishware. High above were power tools never used, new bed sheets, lightbulbs, quite a number of spare house slippers in his parents' sizes, flannel coats, sneakers. Everywhere he looked, he had discovered excess, things stored in reserve. It was a bunker, a safe haven for an eternity of life in which one would always have the essentials.

The door to the kitchen was propped open. He could hear his mother affably chatting with the nurse they had all hired to live with her, the chink of a spoon on a ceramic plate, several moments of light, friendly laughter.

He organized much of the paraphernalia, for donation, while in search of the cash his mother had lost. None of it had been unearthed inside the house, several thousand missing—although Navpreet and Livleen had retrieved most of the jewelry and photos, storing them in a combination safe in the master bedroom. For her protection, he had begun, once again, to deposit rent money into his mother's account. Still, he rummaged through the garage hoping to find the hidden cash, to allay the family's worries, because it was his fault, his ignorance about Jai's condition, a habitual oversight when he had pressed the money into her hand every month.

He stood, hefting a wooden crate from the corner. Prying it open, he discovered some hand tools from the lumber mill. Refitting the lid over the top, he pushed the crate out of the way, the wood scraping unpleasantly across the cement. He shoved aside another crate of tools, working his way through the boxes toward the wall. He reached for a broom to brush away the cobwebs that had grown thickly in that corner, sidling between two boxes to access the recess. Looking down, through the shadows he detected the shape of a familiar old chest and small plywood box.

Resting the broom against a shelf, he made room, grunting as he pushed the crates farther out of the way. He knelt, the cold of the concrete biting his knees through the thin fabric of his trousers. Intimidated, he faltered, furtively glancing about, even now feeling it a betrayal to open these two remnants from Manmohan's past. He remembered that night up in the lumber mill's main house rafters, defiant and uncaring, willfully invading that private space, moving things about, attempting to uncover some secret, some personal element that would humanize his father. But in the end, when he had come across the box and chest, he was too afraid to pry them open, too afraid of what he might find, of what he could know.

Taking a breath, he finally unfastened the rusted latch of the plywood box and raised the lid. Pulling out an object wrapped in old and yellowing paper, he carefully peeled away the layers to discover a black and white photo of a little boy smiling into the camera. He pulled out his reading glasses, peered at the image, a memory of the main house's living room roused. But he had been very young and could not be certain.

Emptying the remainder of the box, he surveyed everything now on the concrete floor: an infant-size grey blanket, two halves of a coconut shell, and a cotton sling sack filled with plastic toy tools. Absently fitting the coconut halves together, he had the strange sense that all of this had once belonged to him. His body grew warm with a sensation of experiences not his own. The garage seemed to expand outward. He looked down at his knees, still firmly settled on the cement, and suddenly the feeling was gone. Touching the contents of the box, he willed himself to remember, but his mind went instantly blank, felt heavy as if with sand, and he gave up.

With regret he replaced the items and turned to the chest. He lifted the lid, giving rise to a concentrated bubble of stale air. A painted wooden elephant lay on top of a neatly folded red turban. He turned the elephant over in his hands, admiring the clear artistic skill despite the faded color, then placed it next to the chest. Holding the turban, moth-eaten and threadbare, he felt an incredible compulsion to bring it to his nose, to gather through his senses the history he believed was contained within it, inhaling the scent of something much like rusted metal. He found a set of sharp metal chisels, a broken-toothed wooden comb, a green vial, a smoking pipe, a woman's sari and salwaar kameez, an ivory bangle, a ledger of some sort, and a square tin of letters written in Gurumukhi, the sender's name he made as Khushwant Singh Toor.

Resettling the tin at the bottom of the chest, as an afterthought, he took off his father's watch and set it beside the letters, covering both with the red turban.

Opening the frayed leather cover of the ledger, he flipped through the pages, recognizing enough of the script to determine that the columns indicated names, debt owed and amount paid. A lender's book.

Guilt gnawed at him as he looked at the ledger, at the meticulous records, at the enduring and tireless order, reminding him of his great failure of the last few years. He had been careless after Manmohan's death, swathed in his own pain, blind to his mother's, to the rest of the family's. His role had always been caretaker of the Toors, a duty willingly shouldered despite the difficulties, the irascibility. But years of his steadfast diligence had crumbled, money lost, valuables missing, a family rightfully distressed. And his own shame.

~ ~ ~

The prejudice against him was growing. Darshan could feel it, the acrid, fermenting animosity. They no longer talked with him, no longer argued, his children, his brother and sisters. Instead they had stored and stored their bad feelings, allowing them always to grow. He looked back over the years, surveying his actions, his motives, the sacrifices he made for their greater good. He hated being forced to analyze and take stock of his own well-intentioned deeds, to question everything now. It had already all been done. But his siblings and his own children had no more faith, and he was beginning to lose his.

Sonya writing, poor and struggling in New York where artists were trampled by stampedes of Wall Street brokers and real estate moguls, so often needing financial support despite his best arguments for a more respectable job. Anand, much more pragmatic, working in finance for an international corporation, had stayed home to amass a savings, yet was so grudging with his free time, so unwilling to help his father with affairs of the family, with Howard Street, with Jai. And his brother and sisters, who had once given him the latitude—however resentfully—to manage their parents' care because they knew he was willing to shoulder the work, now endured his presence with a chilly, silent martyrdom, shunning him, making him lonely.

Sunday afternoon. He poured a capful of soap into a pale full of warm water. Immersing his arm to the elbow, he stirred in broad circles, the mixture bleeding through and between his open fingers. He clutched at the warmth, the soft suds dripping like talons from his fingers as he removed his hand. Opening the hose, spraying the loose grime off of his car, he watched the water cascade from the roof down the windows. Closing the spout, he dipped a large sponge into the bucket and began to scrub the trunk, working his way toward the front.

The phone rang, a muted peal from inside the house. He paused his washing, ears perked, concern for his mother sending a trill of dread through his limbs. He visited every day now, but it was not always enough. She sometimes forgot who the nurse was, incessantly calling his name, wielding vases and lamps, threatening to smash them until he showed his face and proved that there was still something recognizable remaining in her shrinking, tiny world.

"Your sister," Elizabeth called through the living room window screen. "Navpreet."

Wiping his hands on a rag, he went to the line in the garage, picked up. "Navpreet?"

"Darshan," she said without emotion. "Livleen and I would like you to come to Bebe's to discuss the future of her care."

"What's happened?" he asked. "Did something happen?"

"We have found a replacement for the nurse," Navpreet told him. "A woman Bapu and Bebe knew in Fiji, a familiar face." There was a pause over the line, and then his sister's voice went flat. "We brought her to see Bebe, but she would like to meet you as well. She will not take our offer until you've agreed."

"All right," he replied. "When?"

"She is here now."

"It will take me about an hour."

"Hurry up," she said. "I've made other plans."

He tucked the receiver onto the cradle, for several seconds staring outside at his wet, soapy car, feeling slightly encouraged by the call. He went to the kitchen, told Elizabeth, who nodded and kissed his cheek before pouring herself a glass of orange liquor and opening her cookbook. "Don't be too late," she said. "I'm trying something new today."

He went to change, slipping into a clean pair of trousers. Tying the laces of his sneakers, he smiled, recalling a time in Fiji when he and Navpreet had snuck off under the house with a loaf of Jai's bread. They had eaten the soft middle, returning the shell of crust to the pantry. Jai later sliced into it, crying out in surprise and anger. "Let's do it again tomorrow," Navpreet said as they laughed from the other room. It was a game they had played, together, for nearly a week before Jai caught them.

Arriving at his mother's house a little over an hour later, Darshan opened the front door without knocking, calling out as he entered. There was no answer, but they were there, waiting for him in the living room. He slowly shut the door.

A nervous energy sparked the air. Navpreet, Livleen, Taran, Mohan, and Lehna were all seated on the sofa, uncomfortably compressed together. The chairs had all been removed except a single empty one positioned opposite the sofa, a long, wooden coffee table between them.

Navpreet gestured toward the lone chair. "Come in, Darshan."

"Where's Bebe?" he asked.

"In the kitchen. Please, have a seat."

He did not move. "Where is the nurse?"

Navpreet smiled, her manner easy. "With Bebe. They are preparing tea. Please," she said again. "Sit."

Slowly lowering himself into the chair, Darshan glanced toward the kitchen where from his vantage he could see only his mother's house-slippered feet beneath the ship-hatch table. In front of him on the coffee table were many of the pictures Jai had hidden, now removed from the safe and arranged so that only he could see them. Several were portraits of Manmohan. Most were group photos of the whole family.

"What is this?" he asked.

"Shall we begin with a prayer?" Navpreet said, placidly glancing around. "From Guru Arjun Dev Ji's *Psalm of Peace.*" She closed her eyes and began, carefully enunciating. "'If a man meditates on the Name, he will not go the round of births. / He will be immune from the torture of Death, / and will shed off all mortality. / His enemies will keep away from him, / And he will be safe from all harm. / His mind will always be on the alert, / And will not be affected by fear, / Or troubled by pain. / This meditation is learnt in the company of the holy. / All riches in abundance for him who is God-intoxicated!'" She opened her eyes and smiled dreamily. "Waheguru ji ka khalsa, waheguru ji ki fateh."

"Beautiful," Mohan murmured.

Her gaze lingered on Darshan, who regarded her with impatience.

Reaching over the armrest of the sofa, she retrieved a manila folder. "To the point," she said, opening the file, suddenly business-like.

Livleen shifted uncomfortably, and Taran put his hand

firmly on her leg.

"We have all suspected it for many years now," Navpreet continued. "I have been watching you. I have been making meticulous records, which I have here compiled in an effort to bring to light what we have all known to be true since the beginning."

She paused for effect and waited for some reaction.

He frowned slightly, and she appeared pleased with this.

"We have concrete evidence now. Facts and figures." She raised her chin, anticipating a challenge, then proceeded, stressing each word. "Irrefutable proof that you have been stealing."

His frown deepened, and he regarded the photos. They were intended to inspire remorse, this once great family now shattered because of him. Yet none of the faces were smiling, expressions all sober. It was unnatural. He looked dispassionately across the table at his accusers.

"We are not stupid," Mohan said as Navpreet held up the file of documents.

Darshan flattened his palms against the tops of his legs. "Let me see that."

She tucked the folder onto her lap, crossing her hands over it. "I will not allow you to twist everything around. We are here today so you can admit what we already know."

"I do not know what you know," he replied, an empty space opening in his chest, a cavity of pressure, a growing ache.

Her composure crumbling in the face of his denial, she scooted to the edge of her seat. "You tried to get your name on the Howard Street deed. We all remember how upset Bapu was. And all the cash you gave Bebe the last few years just gone, disappeared." Her face reddened in anger. "You left for India, made us work at Howard without ever paying us properly, almost destroying my medical career. We had to slave away serving tables at the restaurant and dealing with tenants while you got married and traveled the world. And then you took the restaurant from them, profited off their loss. You always got everything you wanted, and we paid for it. We refuse to sit back any longer and let this continue."

While Navpreet spoke, Livleen eyed him stonily, saying nothing.

"I have asked you repeatedly for Howard income and expense statements for the years 1994 to the present," Navpreet said.

"I have always sent them," Darshan told her. "Every time you requested."

"That is a lie," she said, turning to face Mohan and Livleen. "He is lying. This," she again brandished the file and tapped it forcefully, "concludes that he stole in excess of sixty thousand dollars. That plus interest—"

"Interest?" Darshan asked, glancing around at everyone.

None of them replied. Navpreet breathed hard with furious self-righteousness.

He rose.

"If you pay it back, we will forgive you," Navpreet said, nearly shouting now. "It would be generous considering what you have done."

She quickly stood as he walked away, about to block his path, stopping when she realized that he was headed for the kitchen. "We'll be waiting for you here," she called. "We are not finished."

Jai smiled cheerfully at Darshan as he sat beside her. There was no nurse from Fiji. Only the one he had hired, portioning out a bowl of dhal to feed his mother. Jai raised a hand to place it on his head, and as he bent to receive her blessing he was surprised by his shock at his family's subterfuge, and the ache in his chest grew larger.

"She is having a good day," the nurse told him, setting the bowl in front of Jai. "She does not remember much of the present, but the past seems to make her happy."

"Good," he murmured.

The nurse blew on a spoonful of the lentils and raised it to Jai's mouth.

Taking his mother's hand, Darshan cupped it against his cheek. "Bebe, I am leaving now, but I will be back tomorrow."

She began to hum, chewing her food.

Navpreet moved swiftly when Darshan reentered the living room, sprinting to obstruct the front door as he strode purposefully toward it. "You cannot run away," she said.

"I have nothing to say."

Emotion made her voice thick. "I wanted to go to Oxford. But because of you, I had to come here where I could only be half as good as I wanted. Bapu never knew how good I could have been. He misplaced his trust in you. You took everything from us."

"I did not kill him," Darshan said quietly.

Stunned, her eyes grew wide, tightening. "I am a doctor," she choked, appealing to the others, who watched frozen in their seats.

"You did not know his favorite book. He could not let you decide his fate."

"He read everything," she said, her voice cracking. "He loved all books."

"Maps," Darshan told her, "of stars, of the earth, of where we were, of where we might be going. Not the ones with words, not the ones he could read, only those he could study."

She shook her head, refusing to believe him. Softly clasping his hand on her shoulder, she recoiled, but only slightly, still trying to hold her ground. He stared at her for a moment, his feelings of affection and suffering unguarded, hurled at her like weapons of defense. And then he tenderly shoved her aside.

~ ~ ~

"Who is it there?" Jai asked, squinting, shielding her eyes against the daylight that drowned the front porch. "Do we know each other?"

She seemed shrunken and surly, the unfocused medley of her thoughts interrupted as she was forced to invoke some measure of lucidity now that company had arrived.

"It is only me, Bebe," Darshan said. He carried with him a mini tape recorder from the garage archive, as well as the tin of Khushwant's letters and the debt ledger he had found in his father's chest, planning to spend the afternoon deciphering them. He stacked everything on his knees as he sat in a plastic chair next to his mother.

She considered his face for a moment. "Yes," she said less churlishly, turning away, gazing at the flowered front yard.

The sun arched over the house to the front, dappling the driveway with light that filtered through the small, scattered lemon trees. He placed the tape recorder on the railing in front of them.

She guardedly scrutinized it.

"It was Bapu's," Darshan told her.

"Is it important?"

"No, not very. I am not sure it even works."

"He would have tested it," she told him, "when he was ready for it."

"Yes," Darshan nodded, "he would have." He inserted a

blank tape from the packet he had also found in the garage, pressed the record button.

A car hurtled past, too fast, momentarily slicing through the afternoon peace. Darshan relaxed into his chair, his hands over the ledger and tin. Tapping her sandaled foot on the cement, Jai began to hum. He recognized the tune as one she had hummed often in Fiji while cooking or milking the cows. Absently, he began to hum along with her. She laughed, delighted.

"Good boy," she said contentedly. "There is always music to hear, to catch in the waves around us." She then lowered her voice. "My other children cannot hear this music." Her lip quivered. "But I love them, all of them. I know your bapu will never forgive me for saying it." She turned to look confusedly through the window into the house, trying to recall something important. Her face twisted slightly with sorrow as she remembered.

"There is nothing to forgive," he told her, thinking of his own children, of Sonya's last phone call, when they had spoken but said little, of Anand's bitter refusal to make eye contact when something was asked of him, angry sentiments seething just under the surface.

Jai resumed her humming.

Darshan thought that his mother had no business in this new century, in this year 2000. She was a woman of another era, who fed chickens; who balanced a clay pot of water on her head, carrying it from the village well to her mud hut; who baked fresh bread and rolled dough for rotis; who knew the secrets of clarified butter; who bathed herself and her children in the river. She knew this earth, had lived in it and with it, the seasons guiding the course of her life as she hummed the folk songs of her village.

He listened, and as she began to form words he used the melody of her voice to tether him to his childhood. "*Dhan bhag mera,*' peepal ache, '*kurian ne pingan paaian.*'—'How blessed am I,' says the peepal tree, 'that the girls have hung rope swings on me.' *Sawan vich kurian ne Pinghan asman Charhian.*'—'In the month of Sawan, girls have swung their swings sky high.'"

She again laughed, pointing at a mole on her chin. "A tattoo. Before I married your father. It was my secret. He never knew." And again, as suddenly as before, her face fell, horror spreading across her wrinkled brow, and then she started to weep.

"No, Bebe," Darshan said, taking her weathered hand, pity tightening his chest. "There is no need to cry."

"I am empty," she told him. "Everything is gone."

He dabbed her face with his handkerchief. "It is not true."

"Navpreet gave me a pen. I signed a paper."

"What paper?"

"From the bank."

He tried his best not to let the heat of anger creep into his face, remaining calm as he caressed his mother's cheeks. He forced a smile.

Reassured, she stopped crying, so he folded his handkerchief and tucked it back into his pocket. Another car tore down the street in a dangerous hurry, like they all were on this stretch of road. He switched off the recorder.

"Such a sweet girl and so sad," his mother said. "She brushed my hair." She sniffed, adjusted her chuni over her white hair. Smoothing her salwaar, she again began to hum, soothingly, like the breeze touching his face.

The melody drifted on the wind. He looked down at the tin of letters and debt ledger in his lap. Settling the tin on the ground next to his chair, he then opened the leather cover of the book. He ran his index finger along the columns, flipping the pages, one after the other, happening upon a notation for a Toor, a man named Lal Singh. There was a scribble next to the name he could not read, a line through the numbers canceling out the remainder of dues, perhaps a reevaluation, a setting of matters straight and right.

He raised his head, gazing out beyond the flowers and lemon trees to the street.

It had to be. They could not all be subject to the travesty of greed, swindled and made to look like fools.

The Apartments on Howard Street
2004–2005

South of Market, the building on Howard Street knew Darshan's touch. For over three decades it had survived under the care of only one man, and as a result had sometimes faltered on its one-hundred-and-ten-year-old limbs, stained by fuel emissions, pissed on by vagrants, tagged by young thugs. But Darshan had always managed to give it fresh life, revive it with coats of paint, with new and gleaming plumbing fixtures, wiring, heating, polished flooring, and caulking sealant to fight the chills that shuddered through its arthritic joints. He had carried the grit of this building's maintenance on his back, wood slivers under his nails. Only he possessed the instinct needed to care for its corridors, its walls and supporting beams, to maintain its vitality after being afflicted by the wear and tear of tenants, of wailing babies, of hysterical children, of drunkards and drug addicts, of rock musicians and old hoarders.

But there was something new in his body now, a grain of fatigue of a different sort, the kind that spoke of age and limitation. It promised to intensify as he got older, to deplete him. He wanted his children to be sensitive to this, for Sonya and Anand to develop their own bond with the roots he had bled so much to establish. He wanted them to love this building, to come and preserve it with him until they could carry it forward on their own.

And Sonya did come, returned from New York to live again with her parents. Twenty-seven years old, she had finally parted from those unconventional dreams that had stirred such rebellion within her, that caused her to go so far from him, to waste so much time, drastically reducing her chances of survival in a world that did not understand or respect her artistic impulses. He could not help but measure her lack of success against Anand's great and pragmatic achievements. That future tycoon, that business mogul, so silent and calculating in his maneuvers upward, money flooding his accounts, the best form of safety and independence.

Still, where was Anand now? Where had he ever been?

Darshan's brow contracted inward, eyes tight. He entered the front room of a recently vacated Howard Street unit, stepping around Sonya as she worked on the task he had delegated to her. Rankled, he crossed his arms, scrutinizing her efforts, her method, the sloppy disregard for detail as she plastered over the many nail depressions in a piece of sheetrock he had just hung.

She paused in his presence, her spatula lingering over an exposed nail. "You don't need to supervise."

"A little less," he told her. "It should be subtle."

She stepped back, unenthusiastically examining the sheetrock.

"You see?" he asked, pointing. "Too much. Too thick."

She nodded, scrapping her spatula over a few nail dimples

to clear away the excess paste.

He frowned, running a light finger over the areas where the plaster had already dried like tiny, horizontal stalactites. "You can find sandpaper down in the garage."

He retreated to the hallway where he had left his electrical kit. Loosening the buzzer from the wall, he began to strip the wires, muscles stiff, mind steeled against a vague sense of insult.

"It is a very subjective thing," Elizabeth had told him not long after Sonya returned home.

"She didn't publish her book," he said, affronted. It was all that had mattered, that mattered still.

"You can't be angry about it. I've read her book. You should read it."

"It has an awful tone, so emotional and self-indulgent."

"It isn't frivolous," his wife had said. "She worked very hard on it."

"Only for herself."

"That's unfair," Elizabeth replied crossly. But he had not been sorry.

He worked in the unit for hours. The delicate fingers that had once sutured bodies, that had once caressed the skin of his newborn children, gripped and twisted the handles of his tools with a surgeon's grace. But there was no more satisfaction in it. A leavened unease mounted within him as the day progressed, intensified by a sudden and consuming hunger that finally made him throw down his tools and flex his tired fingers.

Sonya was still in the front room, her task unfinished. She stood close to the wall, squinting at her work to consider the result, a piece of sandpaper in her fist. He again ran his hand over the wall, over its now rather impressively smooth surface. She waited, but as he looked at her, at the eagerness to please, to do right, he could only wonder why it had taken her so long to learn.

His stomach grumbled insistently. "Lunch?" he asked, already turning from the room.

Dropping the sandpaper, the worn sheet of it fluttering heavily to the floor, she followed.

They placed their orders at the counter of a Mexican restaurant on the street corner. Grabbing her cup of sweetened rice water, Sonya selected a booth seat by the window. She stared outside at the light flow of traffic down Howard Street, gnawed at her straw, picked at some dried plaster on her forearm.

"How is it?" Darshan asked, sitting across from her.

She looked down at her drink. "This? Good."

He popped open his can of Coke, poured some into the paper cup of ice the cashier had given him. "How's Anand?" he asked.

"Good."

"Big day approaching."

"Yeah."

"He and Roshna pick a wedding cake yet?"

"Not yet, I don't think."

"I told him last week, nothing too pricey. It's all the same in the end, and we've got a lot of people to feed."

"He knows."

"I'm waiting for his final guest list."

Sonya pushed aside her drink as the food arrived. "He told me he was waiting for yours."

Darshan sucked on his straw, Coke rinsing through his mouth. He watched his daughter slice open her burrito with a plastic knife. When did this happen? he wondered, glancing over at the swinging lip of the trash can, at the stack of trays above it. All this rubbish, all these low-maintenance accoutrements that dried out any sense of culture. He looked at his food, not sure it was really Mexican.

"Dev and Indirjit's families are coming," he told her.

"Does Anand know Dev and Indirjit?" she asked.

"*I* know them."

"He and Rosh wanted something intimate."

"He never told me that."

"I think he did."

He did not answer, but leveled his gaze with hers, reminding her who she was speaking to.

Unperturbed, she said, "This must be why you eloped."

"Different time," he replied. "A very different set of circumstances, something I earned."

"They almost did it," she told him. "Anand and Roshna. Almost went to Cabo."

Darshan squeezed a lime over his meat, the spray of acidic juice coating his plate. He set the lime aside and said, "But they didn't. They didn't earn it."

~ ~ ~

A cord of brake lights stretched boundlessly across the Bay Bridge, beyond to Berkeley, down Highway 80, likely all the way to Tahoe, slicing straight through the entirety of America. Darshan scanned the traffic, the stop-and-go flash of red torturing his insides, making him restless and peevish.

He sensed the strained calm of Sonya beside him, and his eyebrows sunk low with indignation. Her presence on this freeway, trapped by traffic, was a statement of reposed and self-assured martyrdom. He was certain of that by the way she focused her gaze just somewhat to the right, chin raised a little with the same defiance that had taken her to Los Angeles and then to New York. He knew that chin, that bunch of jaw muscle flexed against the downward pressure of her teeth.

"You don't have to go," he had told her in the morning on his way out to see Jai.

"No," she replied, tugging her eyes from her computer screen, a flicker of annoyance flashing across her face. "I *want* to go."

"You seem unsure. She's your grandmother. You shouldn't be unsure."

Snapping her laptop shut, she had said, "I'm not unsure."

The oncoming traffic on the opposite side of the freeway divider flowed like river water. Darshan ignored it, forcing his eyes to look directly forward. "Another story?" he asked her now.

"Hmm?"

"Your computer. Earlier."

"Nothing special," she replied, still not shifting her gaze.

"Job hunting?"

Her jaw muscle rippled. "A little." Pressing her lips together for a moment, she then asked, as if she had been pondering it for a very long time, "Why don't Anand and I speak Punjabi?"

A tsunami of memories smacked across Darshan's mind, all the lost time, the supplication to make his family happy, to satisfy their whims, to settle them all here with more than just the slew of useless things they had brought with them from Fiji, the compromises, the tightwire he had walked between them and his wife and children, the ache in the soles of his feet from so much balancing.

"Is that what you wanted?" he asked as she finally turned to look at him.

"It just would have been nice, not feeling on the outside.

Dadiji is my grandmother, but she doesn't know me. We don't know each other."

The traffic gave a little as they approached Oakland, brake lights easing, their speed increasing. "If you had spoken Punjabi, would you have stayed?"

She did not respond, but he could sense her mulling it over. "Anand tried to teach himself once," she said after a minute.

For some reason he found this flattering. "Did he? Why did he stop?"

She shrugged. "It made him angry to teach himself."

As swiftly as he had been impressed, her words punctured and deflated him. They said no more during the drive.

The familiar smell of spice and clean linens embraced them as they entered Jai's house a short time later. Darshan removed his shoes and went to his mother, that old and crinkled woman, grayed and toothless from age, memory ravaged by disease, but still the only one who had held him at birth, humming tunes in his ear. Seated on the edge of the sofa with the nurse, she smiled dreamily.

"I am here, Bebe," he told her.

"Darshan?" his mother asked, pointing at Sonya, face darkening with sudden suspicion. "Who is that?"

"Sonya, Bebe. This is Sonya."

She laughed then. "Sonya and Anand. Elizabeth and Darshan." She clapped her hands to the music playing in her head, then raised her voice in sudden song.

"*Sada chirian da chamba ve, babal assan ud jana. Sadi lammi udari ve, babal kehre des jana. Tere mehlan de vich vich ve, babal dola nahin langda. Ik it puta devan, dhiye ghar ja apne. Tera baghan de vich vich ve, babal charkha kaun katte? Merian kattan potrian, dhiye ghar ja apne. Mera chhuta kasida ve, babal das kaun kade? Merian kadhan potrian, dhiye ghar ja apne. Mera chhuta kasida ve, badal das kaun kade?*

Merian kadhan potrian, dhiye ghar ja apne."

"What is it?" Sonya asked, clearly ill at ease. "What does it mean?"

Darshan listened.

> Ours is a flock of sparrows, dear father.
> We'll fly away
> on a long, long flight,
> we know not to which land we shall go.
> Through your mansion's door, dear father,
> the doli won't pass.
> I'll have a tali tree uprooted.
>
> Go, for that is your home, O daughter.
>
> In your mansion, dear father,
> Who will do the spinning?
>
> My granddaughters will spin.
> You go to your home, O daughter.
>
> There is my leftover embroidery;
> Who will finish it, father?
>
> My granddaughters will do it, O daughter,
> You must depart, for that is your home.

"A song about birds, and their flight to God," Darshan told Sonya.

He sat on the floor, clapping with Jai, not aware if his daughter joined him, or if she retreated to the other room with the nurse. He clapped until his mother stopped singing, his palms throbbing with gratitude.

Jai passed away soon after that day, at the age of eighty-seven. Reflecting on her life, it bothered Darshan tremendously that he had been the one to visit her regularly and consistently, to cup her face in his palms when she grew afraid, to wipe her mouth after she ate, to hear the stories and burdens of her life. And still, he had not been there when she died, had been too late, the drive too long. She had spent her final moments in the hospital with Navpreet, Livleen, and Mohan positioned around her hospital bed.

During nights Darshan now shuddered in his bed as he foresaw a future in which there would be no one to caress *his* head, no one to cut his food and feed him, to wrap his neck with a shawl when the evenings were chilly, at the end left to die alone or with those who only meant to undo him.

His only consolation was that Jai had lost her memory, that she did not know he had not been there, that for her there was music and her voice raised in song.

~ ~ ~

For Sale, the sign read, its post dug into Jai's flowerbed, a wreckage of torn petals and snapped stems withering in the sun against the splinted wood. Her house had been emptied. Hastily, it appeared, by the scuffmarks along the walls, the debris of packing tape and the minutiae of life scattered about the carpet—stray buttons, safety pins, scraps of paper with long-forgotten reminders. The stench of Darshan's siblings still lingered in all the things that were not there: his mother's fine fabrics from India, the family photos, the paintings of gurus, her gold sets of jewelry, her furniture and linens, her spice jars and flour-coated rolling pins.

Sonya's mouth hung slack with shock, her hands held open. She had come to help him retrieve Manmohan's plywood box and chest, but those, too, were gone, as were all the tools and paraphernalia from Fiji, the whole of the garage archive swept away into trash bins. There had been letters, too, Khushwant's letters, most still unread, their Gurumukhi script difficult and slow to decipher, records of their history now lost.

Darshan circled the barren landscape of the garage, his thin, cotton-socked feet unprotected from the cement cold, certain that nothing stored in this room had been preserved, that it had all been discarded, that somewhere in a field of garbage, the Toor heritage had been flung atop a heap, was now loosened and fluttering in the Bay breezes.

Curling his lip with disgust, he stood in the center of that frigid space, overcome by the profundities of this loss, stiff and hollowed out.

"Dad." Sonya's voice gently tugged at him.

He waved his hand, shooing her back.

"Dad, it's okay. We don't have to stay here."

He shook his head. "No."

Shivering, she reached to press the button to the sectional door, to let in some sun.

"Don't touch that," he said grimly.

She froze. "Dad—"

"Don't touch anything. Get out of your dream world. Pay attention."

"I was only cold."

"This is not about you."

She stood there, hand lowering slowly to her side. The look of baffled hurt on her face cinched between her eyebrows fueled his own stinging misery. "I gave you all so much," he said, his voice like pebbles pelted at her. He gestured about the house. "*Them*. You and Anand. You all gave me so little in return."

Her brow softened, as if more certain with her position, not shocked, like she had known something like this would come, like she was sorry for him. "We give, Dad. Me and Anand. A lot. You just never notice because you always want more, because you expect something different. We're us. We aren't you."

~ ~ ~

Navpreet's heels clacked on the pavement sidewalk in a foreboding rhythmic beat, the sound growing louder. Darshan surrendered to it, to the swing of her skirt, the haughty flair of her lashes thick with mascara, her dyed and wind-blown hair, to the grim hatred surging through her blood, which told him she hated herself much more.

"Hey," she said, brisk, ready for business.

"So?" he asked her as Mohan and Livleen approached, not far behind.

"It's on the market. We are waiting for a buyer."

Darshan averted his eyes from the building. "Okay," he replied.

Mohan tucked in the hem of his shirt, which insufficiently covered the expanse of his gut. He looked at the apartment complex with distaste. "You are the only one who wants to keep it."

Navpreet flicked her finger against a tag of graffiti on the wall. "You can buy it, minus your share of the probate." She removed a wet wipe from her purse and cleaned her finger. "We'll give you a good price."

Reaching into his pocket, Darshan took out a spare set of

keys to the building and handed them to his sister for the real estate agent. "We've been through this already. I don't know yet."

"We won't wait forever," Navpreet told him.

Livleen stood off to the side against a parking meter, hands stuffed deeply into her coat pockets, her graying hair tossed up untidily. She would not look at Darshan.

They all turned to go. Darshan reached for Navpreet, touching her forearm. "Wait."

She halted, the contact startling but not angering her. Passing her keys to Livleen and Mohan, she gestured down the block at the car. "I'll meet you in a second," she told them.

When they were gone, Darshan shoved his hands in his trouser pockets, his left folding around an old tape recorder he had long ago found in his father's archive. "You threw away a box and a chest, from the garage," he told her. "They were Bapu's."

"It was all junk."

"It wasn't junk."

She tossed her wet wipe on the sidewalk and ground it into the cement with the ball of her foot. "Anything else?"

His hand squeezed more tightly around the recorder, his fingers caressing the buttons. "Why did you steal Bebe's money?"

She smiled rigidly, scoffing. "I didn't."

"She told me once. She told me that she loved you."

Navpreet's face flushed. She turned to go, but instead spun around on one of her heels. "Bapu and Bebe would never have chosen me over you. I had to depend on myself. You would have gotten everything." She stiffly clutched her purse, terror beyond the façade of her rage.

As he looked at her, he was struck by a swift and heated

exhaustion. He released his grip on the recorder. "Maybe," he finally said. "I don't know."

~ ~ ~

Moonlight inched across the living room carpet in Pacifica, penetrating through wisps of fog, creating eerie shadows in the dark. Downstairs, Elizabeth slept. "Don't go," she had sleepily beckoned when he first tried to slip away. Fitting his head in the crook of her arm, he had rested for a time, eyes pressed into the soft flesh of her bicep until her breathing again became regular. But he had not been able to stay, his mind aching with too much thought.

He tucked his bare feet up onto the sofa now, wrapped a throw blanket around his legs and gazed at the moonlit floor, his father's tape recorder on the armrest. He listened to his mother's voice, to the beat and measure of her words, her hum, her song. *I am empty*, she had said before forgetting again, before returning to her music.

With a click, he stopped the tape.

Turning on the end table lamp, the room was ignited with color, shadows dispelled. Untangling himself from the blanket, he rose, went to the kitchen, searching for snacks, for something to fill him. He rummaged through the pantry, dismissing the row of cereals, Elizabeth's stash of chocolates, the dried fruit and nut mixes, the box of Indian sweets he had recently purchased in Berkeley.

He crossed the kitchen to the fridge, reached out and grabbed the hilt of the door. His eye snagged a corner of familiar handwriting behind a mess of menus, photos, and souvenirs held up by magnets. Gingerly, he shimmied the paper out from beneath the others and held it up under the halogen track lighting. He had forgotten about this, last year's father's day gift. Sonya's gift, after she had returned from New York. A yearly calendar condensed onto one page, *Dad* written in blue felt on every weekend from June to December.

He had not given it more than a perfunctory glance when she gave it to him, this gift of time, of devotion, of nothing lacking.

Dad, Dad, Dad.

~ ~ ~

He slept. Flinching, he reached out to feel rough bark at his fingertips. Relaxing now, he then looked up at the deep blue Pacific sky from the base of his coconut tree. Tactically he assessed the bark for the best positioning of his feet. After blowing into his palms, he heaved himself up. Quickly and agilely he scampered to the top, grabbing hold of a palm branch, wriggling his way into the tuft. The tropical air filled his lungs as he settled into a comfortable position. Jungle plant life carpeted the island, spanning from the ocean to the inland volcanic ranges. The sparkling corrugated iron homes lay squat within the verdant foliage. In the distance the tops of Suva's five-story buildings poked through the trees. Beyond the city the blue waters of the Pacific nestled against the coast.

Shading his face from the bright sun, squinting, he searched for landmarks: his school, Colonial War Memorial hospital, Penitentiary Hill, the roads he had traveled in his Falcon, the river where he had so often played, the tractor on which Navpreet had once tried to teach herself how to drive, his one-room shack in the jungle, the main house where he had once been left to die.

Smoke now rose from the cracks and seams of that house,

the building's walls aflame.

His entire family, miniature creatures, scurried outside shouting warnings. The smoke buffeted upward, a plumage of black rising toward his tree tuft, filling his nostrils with stinging ash. Navpreet was panicking, alone in her room, waiting for someone to save her. But no one came. She grabbed her dolls and fled. Jai carried Livleen, who was a rigid rod of arms and legs, unbending and unyielding to her mother's protective touch. Jai shouted at her, but her cries could not penetrate the glassy stiffness of her daughter's eyes. In the chaos Mohan absconded on a motorcycle, nearly colliding with Manmohan, who from a safe distance stared in horror at his house as it melted down into the soil. Mohan rode farther away down the road, the engine spitting angry fumes. He drove past Navpreet, who had climbed up onto the tractor, spinning it around in an endless circle, frozen in fear. Finally skidding to a stop, Mohan glanced behind him at the house with helpless and powerless love.

A man stood on the road nearby, face stern. Leaning forward, struggling to focus his eyes in the thickening smoke, Darshan recognized him.

Baba Singh held out his hand in a gesture of greeting.

Darshan began to cough, waving the acrid smoke from his face. The fire swelled, expanding. It ate up Manmohan's books, consuming with greedy swiftness. It burned all the secrets in the rafters, moving beyond the house to the stacked lumber in the clearing. Jai ran furiously back inside to save her husband's books, to rescue his secrets, and then Darshan could no longer see her. The fire liquefied the corrugated iron rooftop. It spread up the hill, incinerating Manmohan's garden of breadfruit trees and chilies, yucca and taro. The flames ravaged the entire jungle, gathering at the base of the coconut tree, slowly working their way up, licking the soles of Darshan's dangling bare feet.

Shouting incoherently into the roar of the inferno, trying to make his voice heard above the deafening noise, face lit by flaring reds and oranges and moistened by heat, Darshan plucked a coconut from the palm tuft. Staring into the flames that now engulfed the whole island, with all the might of his skinny boyhood frame, he heaved the coconut into the fire where he knew it was needed.

~   ~   ~

Darshan's palm burned as he held his mug of coffee. The morning was brisk, the heat only just kicked on. He stood at the window, gazing at the large hill swelling behind the house, at the triangle of ocean view to his left. Sonya would be awake soon and this made him nervous. In the kitchen, Elizabeth added a sizzle of onions to a pan of heated butter, preparing eggs. The aroma thawed his hurt.

"Dad," his children had long ago asked at Howard Street, pulling at Darshan's trousers with little hands. "Did you build this place?"

"No, kids. It was here when I bought it."

Disappointed, both of them mulled over the truth of those words, then frowned, conflicted. Anand had spoken first. "But you replaced pieces of it."

Darshan considered this. "Yes, I suppose so."

"Then those parts are yours. You built them," Sonya told him. "And one day you will build the whole thing."

They had always been such clever children.

A ringing interrupted his thoughts. Setting his coffee down on the windowsill, he went in search of his phone. Passing the stairwell, he heard Sonya moving about downstairs, the bathroom door closed, the shower spout opened, water through the pipes. She would be upstairs and ready soon. He wondered if he should say something to her.

He found his phone in the living room between the sofa cushions, held it up, squinting without his glasses. After such prolonged and hushed strain, centuries of withheld sentiments, Darshan regarded Anand's name lighting up the screen. His whole life and future before him, tangled with his children's, he raised the phone to his ear, murmuring the same words, over and over.

Do not speak.

Listen.

Epilogue

Darshan rubbed the soft skin of his head in the bald center where even wisps no longer grew. The light seemed like morning light, pale yet warm. He glanced around his bedroom, searching for something. Betrayed by his memory, however, he could not recall what. The curtains for the sliding glass door had been pulled aside. He smiled contentedly at the sunlight streaming through the double panes. The light settled onto the deck beyond the glass in a morning shimmer. The mattress beneath him embraced the contours of his body as he spread his arms wide, reaching for this light.

His hand fell against the other side of the bed. A surge of confusion made him sit upright. Elizabeth was not beside him. Her pillow had been fluffed, her side of the comforter smoothed. Her nightstand was in its usual disarray, objects on it filmy with dusty residue. He listened carefully for the sound of her in the house, the creak of a floorboard, the smell of coffee. Nothing.

Sighing, he swung his thin legs out from under the covers to go and find her. He slid his pallid and icy feet into his house slippers, reached for his cane, and shakily rose. "Honey," he called out.

In the hallway, at the foot of the staircase, he paused, waiting for her response. "Elizabeth," he called again.

He had forgotten to put on his robe. A chill sparked a flash of goose pimples across his skin.

"Anand! Sonya!"

He cocked his head. From upstairs he heard a flock of birds walking across the rooftop's wooden shingles.

The heels of his feet were exposed at the back of his slippers, his pajama bottoms hiked too high, a draft skulking up the cuffs. He returned to his warm blankets.

In bed, he again contemplated the light on the deck, how it rested in and around the grooves of the wooden slats, the caramel brown color it produced, so different from the color in shade: a desolate, drab gray.

Allowing his eyes to soften, the unfocused sunlight expanded in his vision, becoming more and more brilliant. His eyelids weakened, and he let them fall shut.

Sweat soaked the sheets under his body. He shivered, taking great pains to breathe.

"I am happy to see you awake again," Baba Singh said, holding a coconut in his open palm. He regarded it for a time without saying more, consuming the details of it, the hairy shell, the warped ovular shape. Finally, he spoke: "A very good friend of mine once told me that this is life. It is everything any one man needs to survive."

Nodding gravely, Darshan said, "Yes."

"It seemed to me that you should know this." Baba Singh noted the sack of toy tools hugged close to Darshan's side as he placed the coconut under his grandson's free arm.

"Were you ever able to open it?"

Baba Singh sighed, turning away. After a time, he asked, "Where is Manmohan?"

"With Mohan. I suppose they need to discuss matters."

"I loved them. My sons and grandsons," the old man said with remorse. "But it was too hard. I needed to be forgiven for something. A very bad thing."

Darshan squeezed Baba Singh's hand and shivered again, tightening his jaw against the combination of cold and hot fevering his body.

"I built a two-story house in my village," his grandfather continued. "I thought it would make things easier."

"I built something, too," Darshan told him. "It was like yours, a place for me to go for a while, to be by myself."

"Yes," the old man replied in sudden awe. "I remember. I saw it. I was there."

"You helped me to build it."

Baba Singh shook his head. "I never helped anyone in my life."

Darshan curled his arm around the coconut. "There were others who also helped. I had to let them."

Baba Singh released his grandson's hand and leaned back in his chair.

"Dadaji?" Darshan asked, now holding his cotton sack over the side of the mattress, letting it hang on the edge of his fingertips, allowing it to slowly slip until it fell from his hand.

"Hmm?"

"Why the same name? Did the name matter so much?"

"It was yours." The old man shrugged. "It was always your name."

Appendix
Chima Family Photos

Village in Northern India

My paternal grandmother & grandfather

The Chima Family Lumber Mill in Veisari, Fiji

My father around age 16

Ravine truck accident

My grandfather in Fiji

My father studying for exams

My mother before she left the convent

My parents as a young couple

My father crashing in my mother's SF studio apartment

Howard Street in the 70s

Lion of India: The Chima Family Restaurant

My grandmother working in the Lion of India's kitchen

My father traveling in India

Clockwise from the top: my father, mother, brother, me

My grandfather (far left) with a toddler me in the dining room of the Lion of India

My grandparents home in El Sobrante near Berkeley

Acknowledgements

My mother Margaret Mary (Peggy) Barr Chima for knowing who I was before I did, yet nonetheless allowed me to sort it out on my own.

My father Harjindar Singh Chima for being my muse.

My husband Daniel Horvath who readily accepted that I would always follow my own path, and that perhaps this might sometimes mean he would be the sole provider of our little family unit.

Maria Sicola for the rare and invaluable gift of time.

Diane DeCorso and Pat Mandel for their unrelenting and zealous support of this book.

Rob Rogers and Josie Garcia for their insights, critiques, and numerous questions.

Ann Lam and Titanilla Fiáth for their positivity and encouragement during the last draft.

21727179R00328

Made in the USA
Charleston, SC
28 August 2013